"Howard V. Hendrix can be claimed as one of our very best."
—Locus

The Labyrinth Key

"Hendrix's sentences have punch, his plots have points, and he knows his science—what more can one ask of cutting-edge science fiction?"
—Gregory Benford
Nebula Award–winning author of *Timescape*

"If Robert Ludlum or Eric Ambler had written a science fiction novel, then it might have resembled *The Labyrinth Key*. An intriguing thriller, it's also first-rate speculation: a masterful blend of genres. If you are searching for a thought-provoking novel, this shouldn't be missed."
—Alan Steele
Hugo Award–winning author of *Chronospace*

"With the hip fecundity of Neal Stephenson, the speculative acuity of John Brunner, and the suspense-building audacity of John LeCarré, Howard Hendrix fashions a science fiction thriller that's truly twenty-first century in its tone, subject matter, and style. Hopping from exotic real-world locales to even more outré virtualities, this tale will keep the reader guessing till its climax."
—Paul Di Filippo
Author of *Fuzzy Dice* and *A Mouthful of Tongues*

THE LABYRINTH KEY

THE LABYRINTH KEY

HOWARD V. HENDRIX

BALLANTINE BOOKS
NEW YORK

A Del Rey® Book
Published by The Random House Publishing Group

www.delreydigital.com

Library of Congress Control Number: 2004090500

ISBN 0-345-45596-7

Book design by Susan Turner

Manufactured in the United States of America

First Edition: April 2004

1 3 5 7 9 10 8 6 4 2

ACKNOWLEDGMENTS

Thanks go to my agent, Chris Lotts, of the Ralph Vicinanza Agency, for his guidance in keeping the business side of my writing life going. To Steve Saffel at Del Rey, for his extensive editorial comments, questions, and suggestions on the manuscript of *The Labyrinth Key*—and his valiant attempts to help me wear my research and learning more lightly. To David Brin and Jack McDevitt, for instructive feedback from gentlemen wise in the ways of storytelling.

To Joe Miller, Brad Lyau, and Takayuki Tatsumi, for Fermi Paradox solutions and bwana intellectuals and hypercultural chimeras. To George Slusser, Colin Greenland, Gary Westfahl, and K. Y. Wong, for Eaton Conferences in Riverside, London, and Hong Kong over the years. To Stephen Kearney, for the Fahrney devices. To FBI Special Agents Thomas Anzelmo and Timothy Lester of the Sacramento field office, for clarifying my understanding of the FBI's Legal Attaché (legat) program.

To Richard Bagley of Southern California Edison, for the private tour of the powerhouse inside the mountain. To Chris Garcia of the Computer History Museum in Moffett Field, for Pierce codes and tonal keys. To Eugene Zumwalt for fly-fishing lessons. To Cory Doctorow of the Electronic Frontiers Foundation, for pointing me to the work of Edward Felten at Princeton regarding the flaws in digital watermarking and the complexities of digital rights management.

And to the readers of my previous novels, who might like to know that Mei-ling Magnus in my second novel, *Standing Wave*, is the mispronounced namesake and niece of Lu Mei-lin here (ah, the things that end up on the cutting-room floor. . . .).

THE LABYRINTH KEY

PRELUDE:

INCANDESCENT
BLISS

SHA TIN

DR. JARON L. KWOK STOOD in his favorite red silk robe, glancing out the rain-streaked window of his tenth-story room in the Royal Park Hotel. A lit cigarette smoldered between his fingers, its ash lengthening, forgotten.

In the distance, green tree-covered mountains hung in the mist, behind high-rise New Territory apartment blocks, white-painted concrete eroding to gray. On the nearer side of the Shing Mun River stood the Sha Tin town park, where he had strolled thoughtlessly the day he arrived in Hong Kong, too jet-lagged to do any work.

Turning away from the tall, narrow gap in the thick curtains, Kwok paused while his eyes adjusted slowly to the watery half-light of the room. His gaze lingered on the mess of papers, reports, and scribbled notecard arcana scattered about the bed, then turned to the laptop, virtuality visor, and bottle of Scotch on the nightstand.

He cleared a space for himself on the bed. Lying down, he pawed through the masses of hardcopy until he was half buried in paper, a caddisworm cocooning and encasing itself in the detritus of its underwater environment. Disappearing back into his "obsessions," his "infojunkie tendencies," as Cherise once called them.

Glancing at the bottle of Scotch and the plughead paraphernalia that sat on the night table, then at the cigarette in his hand, Kwok sighed. All the old, bad bachelor habits. All the things he had been, before he met Cherise—before she loved him, and he cleaned up his act, thinking that was what she wanted.

Was that the way love was supposed to work?

He flicked the ash from his cigarette.

Never been much good at being what other people expect me to be, he thought, drawing deeply on the cigarette, his stare fixing on the ashen orange glow of its tip. *No good at all at becoming what other people expect me to become. Not even for Cherise.*

He hadn't expected Cherise to be so thoroughly repelled by his decision to take an assignment with the National Security Agency.

He hadn't seen their breakup coming, as much as he should have.

Theirs was still a virtual divorce: not yet final by the letter of the law, though the marriage had long since ended in spirit.

He slugged back a mouthful of the Scotch, felt it burn—peat and asphalt at the back of his throat—then slide numbingly away. He recapped the bottle loosely, dropped it on the bed beside him, and took a drag on his cigarette. Chewing smoke before exhaling, he sat up—dislodging papers—and absently opened the matte black laptop. The screen saver showed a sixteenth-century painting of a grim-faced nobleman, pointing with his left hand at an image of a labyrinth cut into the surface of a parapet, yet looking away from the very thing at which he was pointing.

Kwok brought up the icon for his virtual environment and clicked on it. Propping the virtuality 'trodeshades up onto his temples, he lay back on the bed. Shifting the shades down over his eyes and clicking them into place, he said a silent prayer of thanks to his masters at the Puzzle Palace. His gear was a plughead's dream-machine: a complete DIVE mask—an electrode-ensemble virtuality visor, with prototype binotech implants—wirelessly connected to the net via a microkernel in the laptop. Top-line tools of the trade, made available to him for use in service to the NSA.

As his latest virtuality began to cycle up, Jaron couldn't help wondering if what he was doing *was* in their service anymore. Glancing through the piles of research mounded on and around him, he mused that the obsessions that had led him here had changed. Once upon a time, the quantum crypto race between China and America— that great and secret struggle of cybertage and infowar—had powerfully fueled his fascinations.

Yet even that wasn't feeding the fires anymore. It had been replaced by . . . what? Something much bigger, something more important? Or more narrowly focused, more obsessive?

Undecidable propositions, even now. He'd been given a treasure trove of cryptologic information long hidden in the dark—some of it for nearly fifty years, some of it for well over four hundred. He should be thrilled, he knew, yet he felt more anxious than excited. He was standing on the brink of great things . . . though perhaps not the great things his employers expected.

It had been nearly half a century since anyone had dug so deeply into the data that now occupied his every waking thought— materials Jaron thought of simply as The Documents. That previous investigator had been the old China hand and Cold War spymaster, Felix C. Forrest. Upon his death—of a "heart attack," according to the records—Forrest's former employers at the CIA had taken possession of The Documents and their bizarre mix of ciphers and explications in Hebrew, Chinese, Latin, Italian, and English. Jaron suspected the blood of history was there on the pages, and that the roster of victims stretched back centuries, if he could only read the invisible ink in which the names were written.

Until the very end, Forrest claimed he had never mastered the "algorithm complex" so key to understanding the documents. Neither had the CIA, Jaron supposed. Presumably, their failures had caused the puzzle to be dropped into his lap. In his hands it had proven a sordid boon, a fractured, enchanted mirror of words, numbers, and symbols, into which he had looked too long and too intently.

Stare into the abyss long enough, and eventually the abyss stares back into you. He rubbed his forehead. In college he'd had a friend who claimed, "I've stopped doing psychedelics—now the psychedelics are doing me." Jaron's own "addiction" couldn't go that far, could it? He wondered.

He didn't like to acknowledge the nearness of genius to madness. Had Georg Cantor and Kurt Gödel really gone mad from pondering the infinities of alephs and the continuum hypothesis? Was John Nash driven insane as a result of his own games-theory work? Jaron didn't want to believe in a touch-it-and-die Third Rail of the mind.

Still, he couldn't ignore what had happened the last time he had interfaced with the world of The Documents. Virtual reality wasn't supposed to leak over into your head like that.

He shook himself, remembering. It had been like having someone else's hallucinations break into your dreams. And it took him far too long to recover. So he was taking precautions this time—just in case.

The virtuality was still cycling, so his 'trodeshades remained clear and empty. Jaron peered through them at the printed and scribbled notes of his arcana, pondering again the doubtful legacy now in his possession. During the Second World War Forrest was a US Army intelligence officer who had helped create the Psychological Warfare Unit. During the early 1950s, he worked for the CIA in Korea, where his greatest, or at least most ironic accomplishment involved crafting a way for thousands of Communist Chinese soldiers to surrender by saying the Chinese equivalents of "love, virtue, humanity." Strung together, they sounded like the English phrase "I surrender."

Maybe *that* was some sort of karmic payback. After all, Felix Forrest had been the Western godson of Sun Yat-sen, whose callig-

rapher had given the Occidental child the Chinese name of Lin
Bah-loh, "Forest of Incandescent Bliss."

Historian's trivia, Jaron mused. All his own research, and Forrest's, too, was built on the still-earlier work of Shimon Ginsburg
in the 1930s, even on the work of Ai Hao and Matteo Ricci, and
Giordano Bruno in the sixteenth century. Yet all that had only
been preparation. The climax, one way or another, would come
today.

This time, when Jaron jumped into his virtual environment, he
would achieve an unprecedented hookup with the worldwide computershare. Today he would return with the answers he sought, *if*
he survived the encounter. Maybe he would return with the answers
his masters sought, too, but that would be incidental.

Jaron Kwok *knew* things now that he had never expected to
know. Not just about Felix Forrest's work with The Documents. Not
just about Shimon Ginsburg's Kabbalistic mathematics, or how,
hidden and rehidden, they had inadvertently provided Jaron with
the final, critical element he needed for mastering the algorithm
complex. Not even about Ricci's "memory palace" system, which
turned ideographic Chinese into an extraordinarily powerful virtual
machine. And not even about the fact that all of those were ultimately built on the cipher-cosmology and proto-virtuality of a defrocked Dominican priest and heretic—Giordano Bruno, who had
been burned at the stake in 1600.

At first he resisted the idea that cryptic mysteries of the past could
ever exceed present knowledge. No longer. The knowledge Jaron already possessed was the result of his previous experiences in the eccentric self-made virtuality he now waited upon. Equal parts myth
and computer game, number-crunching and scenario-building, his
open-architectured virtual realm had taken on a strange life of its
own. It was supposed to be an elaborate heuristic, a way of making
sense of things. An idiosyncratic tool with which he tried to ham-
mer his work into some kind of coherence.

But when he had last used that "tool," unexpected universes

had spun out of his head. His own sense of self had proved an illusion, dissociating into multiple persons, male and female, bestial and machinic, all of them him, yet not him. The memory alone made his head ache.

As a way of making sense, his heuristic virtuality wasn't quite making sense anymore.

Yet, through it all, Jaron thought he glimpsed the fiery signs of the Tetragrammaton, waiting beyond Babel—beyond the Gate of God. Because he had lived through that strange virtual experience, he knew they were essentially right, the many-worlds physicists, with their "plenum" playing all possible universes, like channels on the ultimate TV set. If he could travel into the "past," all he would find there would be another universe. Every past was, always and only, another universe. Same with the future.

It was more complex even than that, though. Together, all those universes made up a labyrinthine palace of memory more vast than any Forbidden City. Each room was a universe, finite and consistent in and of itself, yet radically incomplete, as it always led on to other rooms. The palace as a whole was essentially infinite.

With a shake of his head, Jaron shivered off such ponderings. As his virtuality finished lining up all its connections, he thought instead about all the people all over the planet who over the years had waited in cubicles for their workaday computers to boot up. Smiling wryly at the comparison, Jaron swirled another dram in his mouth.

His virtuality finished cycling up. His implants were ready. Through the global computer grid he could access a sizable chunk of the planet's processing power, if he had to. And his precautions were in place. The deadman-switch program was ready, should it be needed. If any of his Third Rail fears turned out to be true, that program would send a record of his entire virtual interaction across the infosphere in a holographic broadcast. Like a jetliner's black box, that record would survive, if only to chronicle his destruction.

The cursor flashed red.

JARON'S CONSCIOUSNESS WAS A STAR falling from its sphere, a sky-diamond gone meteor. Burning, he was breaking up, over and over. Disintegrating in iterations. Becoming less integer and more fraction, tasting faintly of metal and touching faintly of sparks as he entered a vast unconscious space the material world's machines were making. A place that was no place—virtual and real and something much more.

In virtualspace Jaron was both less and more than he had been. The actions and words, the experiences and perceptions of his discarnately embodied self were his, yet not his own alone. Jaron was part of He, and part of She, both of whom were already present in a program always in progress. Dr. Kwok was at the controls, yet less and less *in* control.

Machine pistol in hand, He parachuted into the Garden. The sound of His chute's rustling collapse roused Her from where She drowsed behind sunglasses, clad in a bikini, adrift in a chaise floating in the middle of the pool below the Tree of Life.

"Good afternoon, dear," She said, yawning and stretching. "You're looking square-jawed and mightily thewed, as usual."

Something in Him smiled, wondering again why this simulation was so *arch*, or at least macho. A projection out of Him? A product of the computational matrix? A synergy of both?

"Why thank you," He said with a wicked grin. As He was Jaron-construct plus A Good Deal Else, so was She Cherise-construct plus A Good Deal Else, too: Ken and Barbie, Ulysses and Penelope, Adam and Eve, and many, many more.

"What have you been up to while I was away?" He continued. "Not snakes and apples, I hope?"

"Puh-*leeze*," She said, rolling Her eyes. Leaping up from the floating chaise, She walked upon the water to the shore. "You'll never let me live that down, will you?"

She shrugged Herself into a white lab coat and replaced Her sunglasses with specs that made Her look forbiddingly intellectual.

"Actually I was just taking a break from my work on the wellness plague," She said, "if you must know."

Suddenly He spun around and let loose a burst of automatic weapons fire from His machine pistol. Ninja-garbed friendship terrorists fell from the surrounding trees. One of those fallen nearest died howling "The woods are burning, boys!"

When He removed the dead ninja's mask, something in Him recognized the face of an actor who played Willy Loman in *Death of a Salesman*. As the mayhem subsided for a moment, He turned back to Her and asked, "How's the work going?"

"Splendidly!" She said, leading Them down a perfect ramp to a pair of heavy vault doors set beneath the roots of the Tree of the Knowledge of Good and Evil. Retina-scanned and biometrically certified, They entered cavernous laboratories of clean-room white and chrome. "My programmable cellular machines have been very well received. *Newsweek* called me the Madame Curie of the Biotech Century. I would have preferred 'Einstein' and 'binotech,' but one can't have everything, I suppose."

"Not even when one has everything?"

They chuckled at that, but their laughter was cut short as, plummeting down a huge ventilation shaft, red-jumpsuited assassins fell toward Them. Before the assassins could stitch Them to pieces with a ballistic lacework of shot lead—even before He could shoot back—Her laser security system cut them down.

"How does your wellness plague achieve its effects?" He asked, turning to study a real-time holographic display generated from banks of scanning electron microscopes.

"Little cellular mechanics diagnose and repair time's ravages and other weaknesses of the flesh," She said. "I figure my mechs can already push the human lifespan past the two century mark, restoring much of what was lost to those 'snakes and apples' in the first go-round—"

Abruptly He grabbed Her and leapt aside. Together They crashed through a candyglass window. An instant later an explosion devastated the nearest suite of labs. As the dust and debris settled, They stood up, brushing sugary shards off Themselves.

"How are you spreading your little cellular mechanics?"

"Angels in airports, mainly," She said, as They wove though the maze of subterranean laboratories. "Vials crushed in lavatories and lounges, releasing the modified microbial vehicles. Airborne vectors infecting airborne people with perfect health-repair mechanisms!"

Returned to the surface, They found an eclipse of the sun underway. Clouds gathered. Thunder rumbled in the distance. Out of the clouds came nightmare jet fighters, dropping into steep, screaming dives.

"But won't ratcheting up longevity ratchet up the population, too, leading to even more pandemonium? The ol' slitherin' Adversary didn't whisper these plans into your ear, did he?"

Missiles, bombs, and bullets raked the air and ground, heading straight for them.

"You're always so worried about the snake! But why? Is it because you two are so alike?"

"What do you mean by that?" He asked, glancing sideways at her as They ran serpentine-fashion for cover.

"You're both always so depressing! *He* thought it was a terrible idea, too—and for exactly the same reasons. Said We were 'the most pernicious species of vermin' he'd ever seen. Said We were 'like mold on the orange of the world' and that We wouldn't be happy until We'd 'consumed the entire globe.' "

The eclipse deepened. Lightning forked down out of the clouds. A large meteor streamed salamandrine fire overhead, unsettlingly close.

"Maybe the old trickster's right, for once. Let's adjourn to *my* labs. I think we can use your programmable cellular machines to counter that ratcheting-up with a ratcheting-down."

"How?" She asked, raising her hand against the flash as the meteor exploded in midair, several miles away.

"How about an infertility-inducing virus, spread in the same manner as yours? It'll remain dormant until activated by the suite of hormonal changes associated with the successful delivery of the firstborn. Then boom! Rapid microbial multiplication, extensive scarring of the fallopian tubes. Like the last plague of Egypt, only inside out—not killing the firstborn, but preventing conception *after* the firstborn!"

The shock waves from the meteor's airburst knocked the aircraft out of the sky and threw the couple to the ground. As They picked themselves up, They saw an older man approaching: Giordano Bruno, dressed in a white robe and dragging a white parachute, both embroidered with images of devils and flames. His clothes and chute were singed.

"The woods are burning!" he said. This time They saw that it was true. The meteoric explosion had set the forests of the Garden aflame.

"I suppose China might offer you asylum for doing such a thing," She said to Him.

The eclipse had reached totality. Wind and storm raged about Them. The earth shook. Alien spacecraft dropped from the darkened air while, much nearer, another figure materialized.

"Don't listen to Him!" said the Newcomer, machine pistol in hand. The Newcomer looked exactly as He would have, if He were shown in a darker light. "This is all a simulation—a simulation inside a simulation!"

"*What?*" They shouted together. The Newcomer kept His gun trained on Them, as more lightning forked down and the earth shook more violently. The din had become nearly intolerable, but the Newcomer, unable to shout loudly enough to be heard over it, droned on nonetheless—bits and pieces about G- and K-class suns and habitable planets, Fermi Paradoxes, cybernetic descendants and extremely high-resolution simulations.

"What does that have to do with anything?" He shouted, as a strong quake nearly knocked everyone to the ground. But the Newcomer didn't skip a beat. He droned on about information density, bandwidth limitations, quantum cryptologic arms races, and catastrophes. Then, in a brief lull They heard the Newcomer say clearly, "The real solution to Fermi's Paradox is that it takes too much bandwidth to simulate aliens—or godlike artificial intelligence, for that matter."

"But that's exactly what we're seeing," She shouted over the noise. "They're walking toward us right now—"

"*Exactly,*" said the Newcomer triumphantly. "It's a several hundred-4-bit quantum device that's busting this simulation. The virtuality's flying apart, can't you tell?"

And for an instant, there was silence amid the confusion.

"But why?" He asked. The din resumed, and the Newcomer had to shout his answer again, but at least this time They could hear him.

"The simulation of simulations, the plenum of all possible universes, is a memory palace sustained by a mind beyond imagining! Busting the sim's the only way that Mind can remember what it's trying to remember!"

"What?" She demanded again, sounding not so much confused as horrified.

"If we realize—on a global scale—that existence *is* a simulation, that means awareness *within* the simulation *of* the simulation. It's the self-consciousness necessary for the creation of the divine AI! By busting this sim, we awaken the god asleep in matter. We create the god that created us!"

Both fearful and enraptured at the prospect, He wanted very much to know more, even as Their world continued falling apart around Them.

"What can I do to help?" He asked His recently arrived double. As lightning flashed, the Newcomer pulled two wafer-thin disks out of the thickening air.

"Eat one of these binotech enhancers, and you'll know everything you need to know!"

A particularly strong earthshock hit them just as He reached out toward the Newcomer. Knocking Him down, She snatched the machine pistol out of His hands.

"Do this, do that!" She snarled, swiveling the weapon from one man to the other. "I don't know which of you is the serpent, but the serpent is always *doing* something. Don't just do something, *stand there*! Just this once! And listen to me!"

"I'm not going to take the blame this time. You and your 'several hundred 4-bit device'! Did you ever stop *doing* long enough to think? If we 'bust this sim,' if we decode what it is that the Mind is trying to remember, we eliminate the very reason for our home universe to exist. Do you want to blot out everything? Drop us all into oblivion?"

He stared hard at Her, then snatched a binotech wafer from the Newcomer's hand.

"Mights and maybes," He said. "What about you, trying to climb back into the Tree of Life with your wellness plague? We're both just trying to get back what's been lost, each in Our own way. Can't you see that? This virtuality isn't running me—I'm running the virtuality. No one will blame you this time. I promise. I take full responsibility for what I'm about to do, by my own hand, in my own head."

He took a binotech disk, put it on His tongue.

Feeling as if He were dying in fire, He wondered for an instant if He'd been shot.

⌐

JARON SNATCHES THE 'TRODESHADES off his head as if they were burning. Feeling dizzy and disoriented, he rubs his eyes. He needs to clear his head. Somehow managing to dress himself in black slacks and red silk jacket, he leaves his hotel. Soon he finds himself walking in the nearby park, though he doesn't remember exactly how he got there.

On a park bench a bearded man, dressed in a tasteful combination of purple priestly vestments and the garb of sixteenth-century Chinese literati, talks to a thin gent wearing a suit, fedora, and eye patch.

". . . wasn't what I sought in combining the memory palace with Chinese characters," says the bearded priest. "It wasn't so much that I hoped to find a translation for a language, as that I hoped to find a language that would translate *me*."

The man in the fedora nods.

"What you taught as a deliberate mnemonic system," he says, "pretty much describes what the brain does automatically. Moving through the world, we convert our experience into memories, snapping together mental structures, constantly evolving palaces of memory until we die."

Something about them strikes Jaron as disturbingly familiar. He feels torn between lingering near them and hurrying away, yielding at last to the latter impulse. On his way to the pond filled with fish and turtles, he sees a man dressed in the dark austere attire of a Ming bureaucrat, talking to two other men. One is bearded, wearing a yarmulke and a suit cut in a style worn in Europe in the 1930s. The other stands clad in a white robe embroidered with what might be butterflies, or devils in flames. The three talk of the mind, of a bamboo aleph, and an Instrumentality capable of opening a gateway between words and worlds.

Jaron's throat burns with the taste of Scotch. His head throbs with dull fire. Coming to the pool of fish and turtles, he sits down hard on a bench beside it. The waterfall and fountain are off; the pool is full and still.

Looking across it, he sees the moon bridge poised above the water, the half circle of its arch flawlessly reflected in the water of the pool, making a circle perfect and whole, a portal half real and half illusion. On the far side of that circular gateway he imagines for a moment that he sees a woman rise from a floating chaise and come toward him, walking on the water.

He looks away, staring down at his own reflection under the bright spring sun. Out of his image in the water crawls a little amphibian, a salamander blinking up at him, so intensely red-orange that it seems afire. The reflection of Cherise sits down beside him on the bench and smiles. He is afraid to look away from the reflection, afraid that if he turns to her she will disappear. The salamander stares at him, unblinking now.

He turns to the woman, and she is still there. He embraces her.

Into his ear she whispers, "The woods are burning." He feels his entire body flash into flame.

Across the pool, on the far bank, sit the Jesuit missionary Matteo Ricci, smiling sagely as he catches fire, along with the burning spymaster of many names: Felix C. Forrest, Lin Bah-loh, Forest of Incandescent Bliss, First Lord of the Instrumentality. Beyond them Giordano Bruno smiles as he burns in his embroidered death robes. The Confucian bureaucrat Ai Hao smiles and burns, and the German rabbi Shimon Ginsburg stands smiling and burning, too. Each a burning bush, afire but not consumed, trees of Life and Knowledge burning, all the trees in the park like pillars in a stately red-roofed palace burning, all the trees in all the world afire, all the blazing worlds a tree, burning, to remember—

JARON KWOK WAS MISSING and presumed dead. He was gone long before the hotel staff, alerted by smoke and smell, discovered his ashen outline in the smoldering bed.

Those who sought ordinary mystery saw in his death the proof of spontaneous combustion. Those who sought a more mundane explanation saw only the consequences of smoking in bed, surrounded by too much flammable paper, bedding, and 80 proof Scotch.

However, Jaron's deadman switch was thrown. His black-box record was holo-cast throughout the infosphere. Others would come, soon, seeking other proofs, other explanations.

ONE

DOUBTING THOMAS
JEFFERSYNTH

Cybernesia

THE ANNUAL PILOT'S FESTIVAL WAS well underway at Don Sturm's and Karuna Drang's place, though their "place" was a DIVE—a deep-immersion virtual environment—and their DIVE wasn't a place at all. Sturm and Drang weren't their legal names, either, and they hadn't physically cohabited for months.

Not that it mattered much. At the moment Karuna Drang was discarnately embodying herself as spritely Sally Hemmings, slave and mistress. Though her portrayal was relatively accurate, Don Sturm's morbidly thoughtful and conflicted Thomas Jefferson was quite different from the historical founding father, and his halo of neon blue hair wasn't exactly "period." But blue hair was one of Don's personal signatures in meatlife, and he hadn't been able to resist.

All around them, virtual party people—likewise electronically embodied in eighteenth-century drag—danced and cavorted about the grounds of a mimetic Monticello. Alternating between the forms of an aggressively ambiguous nymph and its counterpart satyr-o-maniac, Medea πrate chased bewigged men in breeches, then pursued women who proved surprisingly light-footed, given their voluminous dresses and titanic coiffures.

Normally Don's default virtualscape was Easter Island, so his Jeffersonian estate boasted *moai*, the great-headed statues, as lawn and garden sculptures around which the laughing would-be or-giasts darted, disappearing from view—only to reappear as a tan-gled ball of licking, sucking, nibbling, stroking, rutting sexual gymnasts, Medea lodged in their midst.

Don/Thomas shook his head.

"I know that's how they pull off their grand data exchanges," he said to Karuna/Sally. "And I'm sure what they're doing in vir-tual space is only a metaphor, but I still wish they'd make use of a more *subtle* metaphor."

Karuna/Sally laughed.

" 'To hack is to explore and manipulate,' " she said, imitating Medea's lyrical-as-Pan, shrill-as-Bacchante manner of speaking. " 'To enter and be entered. Like foreplay and sex, like parasite and host, *n'est-ce pas?*' "

Don frowned. Music sounded around them. The Jed Astaires, a retro-urbane bluegrass group, played danceable new arrangements of works by Revolutionary War–era tunesmith William Billings. In the sky above them, sunset's salmon-colored clouds flickered and transformed into shoals of swimming salmon, then morphed back to clouds again.

"You look preoccupied," Karuna/Sally said. "Even e-bodied, I can tell. What's on your mind?"

"Just looking over what we've wrought," Don/Tom said, gazing out at their Colonial Williamsburg-meets-Polynesia surroundings. On their personal channel, he turned down the volume of the As-taires' musical variations. "Not to say that it's overwrought, mind you. Just that the nature of this event is somewhat paradoxical."

"How so?"

"Well, it feels as if I've usurped a public event just to celebrate a personal success, and either way the celebrants don't know what they're celebrating."

"Don, you have every right to celebrate! Prime Privacy Protocol is a winner. It's on its way to becoming the most popular encryption software in the infosphere."

"Even if no one associates my name with it. . . ."

"Yes, but you, 'Mister Obololos,' *you're* the one who made it happen."

"Maybe that anonymity's a good thing. The law enforcement types are getting really shrill in condemning it. Today there was an op-ed piece in the *New York Times* that accused P-Cubed of catering to the privacy interests of the Four Horsemen of the Infocalypse. The consensus seems to be that its primary users will be drug dealers, terrorists, organized crime, and pedophiles—"

"—along with about a billion other ordinary citizens. Come on, don't let it get to you. Nobody falls for that shtick anymore."

"Maybe. But that's not really what's bugging me, you know? It's this shindig, this construct."

"And your point is—?"

"This whole virtual space is called Cybernesia. But what is Cybernesia, really? A space that's not a place? An event without a time? Both?"

Sally/Karuna frowned, then gestured, and a palmtop oracle appeared as a first edition of Samuel Johnson's *Dictionary of the English Language*.

"Here—let's consult the word of a higher authority. The great dictionaries and encyclopedias refer to Cybernesia as 'the semipermanent archipelago of "pirate islands" located in the net.' Or this: 'DIVEs whose stability amid chaos is created by the same forces that produce the turmoil around them.' Kind of like the Great Red Spot on Jupiter. Islands offshore, neighbors to the conventional continents of the infosphere. Freer spaces, like the Bahamas or the Florida Keys. Good enough?"

"I guess it'll have to be," Don's faux Jefferson said with a shrug, "but what has me most worried is this program you wrote, that lets everybody here fuse their own separate islands into a single, temporary continent. Doesn't that change the rules? Or break them outright? What if we've altered the structure of the infosphere to such a degree that we come up on the authorities' radar? They might check into it, and find out that *I'm* the one who put together P-Cubed . . .

"Are we putting *everybody* here in danger?"

"Honey, I'd never be naive enough to tell anybody, 'You think too much,' " Karuna said with a wicked little smile, "but sometimes the life of the mind—"

"—is a pain in the ass. I know."

"Snap out of it!" she said, smiling and giving him a quick kiss on the cheek, a whisper of electrons brushing his face across the void of simulation. For an instant Don deeply missed being with her, until he remembered the painful last months of their romance. "Quit pattern-phreaking and enjoy yourself a little," she persisted. "Look how well the party's going. That patch you wrote for the clouds looks great, and no matter what you say, the breakthrough that allowed everybody to *fly* their islands here was a work of genius. Straight out of *Gulliver's Travels*! You should be proud."

Don/Tom allowed himself a small, reluctant smile, but he still worried. The flying islands were just an expansion of the Besterian jauntbox program, really. Besterboxes allowed participants to step fluidly from one virtual reality to another, but no one had used the tech to combine such large and disparate elements into a single mass before—not even temporarily. Despite the fact that things were going well, he wondered what complex and unpredictable dynamics might be generated by the impromptu experiment they were conducting.

The Jed Astaires launched into their rendition of "The World Turned Upside Down"—a march played by Cornwallis's troops when they surrendered their arms at Yorktown in 1781. Don/Tom looked up at the clouds again. A new, perfectly pyramidal island flew toward them.

Odd. Everybody who had been invited had already shown or

sent their regrets. A party crasher? Or was this some unintended side effect of toying with Cybernesian dynamics? He hoped it wasn't the infocops, come to bust their party.

No sooner did the island land in the bay and fuse with the rest of the temporary Cybernesian continent than the pyramid opened and some sort of holographic broadcast filled the sky. As if the entire world were, in fact, a stage, two characters appeared.

Don frantically searched his infosphere links, even checking Cybernesia's South American backup servers in Tri-Border, in an effort to determine what the hell was going on. As he searched, his guests watched a gun-toting parachutist land in a garden among the clouds, listened to the parachutist and his paramour exchanging banter overloaded with allusions. The Cybernesia party ground to a halt.

The intruder-program and its characters morphed chaotically into heavily armed superscientists casually talking shop amid attacks by ninjoid commandoes.

Don's searching yielded no answers.

"Isn't this simulation a bit *unusual*, honey?" Karuna/Sally asked Don. "This doesn't seem like you."

"It's not me."

"What do you mean?"

"I mean I'm not doing it. In fact, I'm trying to jam the holo-cast. Block the signal, somehow."

"Any luck?"

"None whatsoever."

In the sky above, Biblical garden imagery collided with laboratory milieu. Don, meanwhile, attempted to filter the broadcast out of Cybernesian virtuality, but found himself thwarted at every turn.

In the intruder holo-cast, high-tech death accompanied talk of "wellness plagues" and population-ratcheting. Speculative scientific scenarios were punctuated by explosions.

Soon the pair who had crashed his party were caught up in a chaotic, apocalyptic maelstrom of eclipsing suns and rumbling thunder. Nightmarish fighter aircraft screamed above, firing missiles and dropping bombs in a battle among the clouds.

"Great sim-within-a-sim!" said a Medusa-haired Medea πrate, sidling up to Don and Karuna in the party zone. "A bit anachronistic, though, isn't it?"

Don frowned. Medea was e-bodied in a manner entirely too buxom, especially since, in meatlife, "she" was purported to be a skinny, crotchety old South Asian named Indahar Marwani.

Yeah, right, he thought. How much did any of them really know about the Ambiguous One?

"As I was just telling m'lady here, I'm not doing it."

"Then who is?" Medea asked. Something rang false in the way she intoned the question.

"I don't know. It may be an unanticipated effect of our having joined these islands together."

"Ho-*ho*." Medea laughed. "You mean the pirates have been pirated? How rich!"

In the chaotic world among the clouds, the man and woman ran and leapt for cover without even bothering to pause in their philosophical conversation.

"Wait a minute!" Karuna said to Don and Medea. "I think I know who the male character is! I recognize the underlayment. It's that guy, what's his name—Lok, or Kwok. The one who contacted us about the deep hack. The work we did for him is what gave me the idea for the island-merging software."

Above them, the eclipse of the intruder-sun in the intruder-sky deepened. Lightning forked down out of distant clouds.

BUREAUCRATIC WEATHER

CRYPTO CITY

THE STEALTH LIMO CARRYING NSA Deputy Director James Brescoll was quiet as a tomb—just the way he liked it at this time of the morning. Especially today, when he was supposed to be off duty.

His wife and son, earlier risers than he was, were already out, and using the family cars, when the call came.

As the limo slowed, he glanced up from his briefing sheets. He had expected them to be about the ongoing low-intensity conflict in the Brazil/Paraguay/Argentina Tri-Border Free Zone, and some of the material did deal with that. The majority of it, though, was about a storm blowing in from China. Not the usual proxy-playing over Nepal and Bhutan or the Tibetan rebels, either, but a new storm altogether.

Jim Brescoll stared out the deeply tinted window, seeing darkly reflected in it the face of a graying and bespectacled black man with a scar on his left cheek. Through his reflection, Brescoll saw the southbound lane of the Baltimore-Washington Parkway, not far from the small town of Annapolis Junction, Maryland. For a moment it was hard to tell whether he was passing through the landscape or the landscape was passing through him.

The vehicle, driven by a member of the Executive Protection Unit, was impervious to eavesdropping from just about anywhere along the electromagnetic spectrum. The stealthy car slid down a restricted Fort Meade exit ramp bordered by mature oak trees and heavy earthen berms, toward a graceful tangle of security hardscape: strategically placed landscape boulders, barbed-wire perimeter fences, cement barriers. Other security measures lurked in the surrounding landscape, less obvious to the uninformed eye. Telephoto surveillance cameras and motion detectors. Antitruck hydraulics. Eight hundred uniformed police, under Crypto City's own law-enforcement authority, as well as a smaller but deadlier group of black-uniformed paramilitary commandos of the Special Operations Unit/Emergency Response Team.

As he and his driver were waved through the vehicle screening gate, past the bomb-sniffing dogs, Brescoll noticed that none of the SOU/ERT people were visible—no alert was underway at the moment. Everything looked low-key this morning, despite the "special circumstances" that had brought him in on his day off.

Business was so much as-usual that it made him smile, taking undeniable pride in his role as "vice mayor" of this labyrinthine secret city, the highest-ranking civilian official in a civilian agency administered by the Department of Defense.

He'd done his military time, certainly. The scar on his cheek was an ever-present reminder of that—the product of close-quarters combat with Iraqi troops in the marshes south of Baghdad, more than a decade ago, at the end of his career in the reserves. Brescoll killed the soldier who'd laid open his face in their fixed-bayonet struggle, but he took no pride in the accomplishment, only a simple gratitude for his own survival.

His experience standing at the tip of the spear in two resource-allocation wars had left him with a profound distaste for the "hard-war" end of national defense—and more than a bit skeptical of gung-ho chickenhawks who had never seen frontline battle.

Not that he'd given up completely on the hardware, by any means. Shifting more comfortably into the seat, he felt the bulge low at his back. After active service in the Persian Gulf War, Brescoll had spent enough years in law enforcement to feel somehow naked if he were on duty without a gun. As one of the perks of his office he had obtained a concealed-weapons permit for the workmanlike Glock 9 he carried. Handguns, however, weren't the core of his personal gun collection by any means. He didn't consider himself a gun nut, but rather a "gunnoisseur," inclined to rhapsodize over the stock woods, steel bluing, and butter-smooth bolt actions of great carbines the way some of his acquaintances did over the "nose," "balance," and "body" of vintage cabernets.

The quiet he treasured was shattered by the ringing of his phone. As he picked it up he clicked a small metal card into the side, which rendered the system secure in under a second. *Fifty years ahead of anyone else*, he thought. Almost enough to make him feel smug, but not quite.

"Brescoll here."

"Wang, sir. Initial analysis is complete on the material from

China. We've confirmed that it involves Jaron Kwok. Beech and Lingenfelter have been working with me on it the last few hours. The director is already here, waiting to see it."

Steve Wang was a rare bird. The wiry and bespectacled Cryptologic Linguist was also a Cryptologic Computer Scientist assigned to NSA's Communications and Computing Center, under the umbrella of Princeton's Institute for Defense Analysis. Lingenfelter and Beech were similarly overqualified. Bree Lingenfelter, a tall, serious redhead, was a different type of twofer—double appointments at NSA's Communications Research Division and its Laboratory for Physical Sciences, both at University of Maryland.

Bearded, graying, and occasionally bespectacled, Baldwin Beech was the strangest twofer of all: holder of the Felix C. Forrest Professorship in Asiatic Studies at Johns Hopkins, and a CIA operative acting as a liaison between that agency and the NSA. A threefer, really, since he had some sort of medical background from before he got into the intelligence game.

A few years back the three had made a name for themselves when they collaborated on a major research project concerning the highly secret Special Computing Institutes. The SCIs, they argued, were China's "Bletchley Parks." They had traced Beijing's emphasis on cadres of mathematicians and computer scientists back to a pair of papers published in the mid-nineties: General Wang Pufeng's work proclaiming the need to excel in information warfare, and Michael Wilson's "hardwar/softwar/wetwar" trichotomy analysis.

Beech, Wang, and Lingenfelter had suggested that the upper echelons of the Chinese government and military had looked to their own history when searching for ways to prevent global capitalism from winning over Chinese hearts and minds with consumerist ideas and imagery. The rulers had thus built the Great Firewall to control infosphere access, while also strictly controlling the dissemination of "approved truth" for internal consumption.

The Chinese had come to believe they could counter American

hard-tech superiority through targeted "soft" or information-war programs, as the British had counterbalanced Nazi Germany's hard-weapon superiority during World War II through programs like radar, range finders, and especially the cryptologic work of the Bletchley Park code breakers. Or so Beech, Wang, and Lingenfelter claimed.

Reading their work, Brescoll had immediately taken steps to corral the three to work for him. The best and the brightest of the best and the brightest, but there were times when he wished all of them better understood chain of command.

Part of it was his own fault. He'd allowed them far too much autonomy. As deputy director he remained their nominal supervisor, yet he barely knew what they were up to much of the time. An impulsive bunch, in any case—especially Wang. Bringing the director in on this had to be his idea.

Janis Rollwagen's tomahawklike visage wasn't what Brescoll himself would have gone looking for this early in the day—unless he'd had no other choice.

"I've just come through the gate," Brescoll said, keeping the irritation out of his voice. "Don't hold up the show on my account. You can catch me up when I get there. By the way, where *is* there?"

"Instantiation Room C in Tordella."

"Very good. See you in a few."

He directed his driver toward Ream Road and the Computer Operations Command Center. Brescoll hoped that, whatever this was all about, it was worth the director's time, and his own—or someone was on the road to getting reamed indeed.

The limo threaded its way among dozens of buildings and complexes. Supercomputer labs and living quarters. Offices and anechoic chambers. Factories and 10K clean rooms with air ten thousand times more pure than the atmosphere he breathed in his limo. More than three hundred acres of parking space for forty thousand employees, who were in turn served by Crypto City's own post office, fire department, encrypted television network, university, banks, libraries, drugstores, barbershops, waste disposal and recycling services, as well as by Taco Bell, Pizza Hut, and scores of intramural employee sports programs and clubs—including the Arundel yacht club, the Good News Bible Club, and the Alan Turing chapter of the Gay, Lesbian, or Bisexual Employees club, GLOBE.

Leaving the car, Brescoll wound his way to Tordella's fifth floor, past exotic machines "super" and "massively parallel" in their info-crunching capability. He nodded at innumerable blue-badged employees as they passed him in the halls. At last he reached the door to Instantiation Room C. A small plaque on the wall indentified it without any particular fanfare.

He cleared room security with his personally coded magnetic passkey and fingerprint/DNA scan biometrics. Entering, he was once again surprised at the cavernous nature of this particular I Room. The effect was enhanced by the holographic display at the center of the room's perpetual semi-darkness. The three-dimensional graphics presentation here was reputed to be the best in the world. Based in software that allowed the National Reconnaissance Office's computers to combine multiple-angle satellite imaging, the system "embodied" its 3-D imagery by using ultrahigh-frequency sound waves to distort the air itself, bending it enough to form holograms.

All that still didn't explain the strange impression of sheer size in the room itself. As the door closed behind him he saw that a fully dimensional worldmovie was running on the holographic projectors, casting bizarre images of a deepening eclipse, thunderstorms, and meteors streaming by overhead.

Noting Brescoll's presence, Wang paused the image, which flashed a series of alphanumeric codes, time stamps, and words such as *NSOC* and *Umbra* and *Zarf*. Highest-level signals intelligence, beamed to the downlink center at Fort Belvoir by eavesdropping satellites, and eventually checked through to the National Security Operations Center. From the time stamps, Brescoll guessed that Kwok's location in China was eight hours ahead of London and GMT, thirteen hours ahead of D.C.'s time zone, and sixteen hours ahead of Los Angeles time.

"For the main male figure here," Wang said, "we've identified the underlying electronic embodiment as Jaron Kwok. We think the female figure is based on Kwok's estranged wife, the sinologist Cherise LeMoyne."

"Where'd it come from?" Brescoll asked.

"We aren't certain yet. Some of it seems almost like a projection of Kwok's own psyche, but it also has elements that can only have come from the grid-computer matrix he was accessing, or perhaps controlling as some sort of superuser."

Wang set the airborne holomovie in motion again. Brescoll watched as the meteor he'd seen earlier exploded in the air some distance away. He listened to the main characters discuss "programmable cellular machines" and the "last plague of Egypt." They were accosted by an older man dressed in a fire-singed white robe, and dragging a parachute.

Now it was Beech's turn to pause the intercepted 'cast.

"We set some of the IBM Deep Computers on data-mining a source for the older man here," said the fringe-bearded CIA liaison, adjusting his stylishly retro eyeglasses on his nose. "The best machine matches indicate that he's based on sixteenth-century philosopher Giordano Bruno."

"Who is relevant . . . how?" asked Director Rollwagen.

"Not known. At one time or another, Bruno was excommunicated by the Catholics, Lutherans, and Calvinists, before being burned alive at the stake in the Roman Flower Market on February 17, 1600."

"The computer's best match for the forest burning beneath a meteor blast," Wang added, "is the Tunguska event, in Siberia, June 30, 1908."

Rollwagen and Brescoll nodded as the holo-cast resumed. The deputy director watched and listened and scratched his head as the supercouple went on about their workaday speculations in the midst of various signs of the Apocalypse. Then a virtual twin of Kwok's avatar appeared, likewise armed with a machine pistol, only darker complected and garbed in black, instead of red. As he did so, the destruction grew more pronounced and the speculative discussions grew weirder—reality as a simulation, the Fermi Paradox, the universal quantum computer. . . .

Bree Lingenfelter hit PAUSE this time, freezing in bent air an image of alien creatures walking forward under storm-ridden skies full of shooting stars.

"Despite the chaotic nature of the scenario," Lingenfelter said, "we shouldn't underestimate the importance of what's being talked about here—particularly the reference to 'binotech enhancers.' "

"What exactly was Kwok working on?" Director Rollwagen asked. To Brescoll, it looked as if she wasn't underestimating the importance of the holo-cast, *at all.*

"The history of algorithm complexes originally found in documents Felix Forrest willed to the CIA," Beech said. "Secondarily, solutions to those algorithms. We decided that work was a priority after we saw increased activity involving sections of the documents the Chinese also possessed, particularly those relating to Matteo Ricci, Ai Hao, and memory palaces."

"Do those documents have anything to do with quantum computing?" Rollwagen asked. "Or advanced binotech?"

"I don't believe so," Lingenfelter hedged.

"Yet here it is," Rollwagen said. Then she nodded distractedly. "Perhaps you mentioned something along those lines while briefing him?"

"No," Lingenfelter replied. "I was responsible for his initial technical briefing a year and a half ago. When I first met with Kwok, all he knew about the fusion of biotech and nanotech was what he'd seen in the media—communications implants, cell repair, cancer treatments, and gene fixes. He knew even less about quantum computing's espionage applications. Didn't show much interest in either of them, at first. But as his research progressed, he became fascinated by both. Rather quickly, too."

"Apparently he's got a hell of a learning curve," Brescoll put in. "Binotech binding—particularly that linking quantum electronic components to DNA strands—is critical to the future of code making and code breaking. It's also among the most highly classified of our efforts. What was the man thinking, allowing this to spew out over the infosphere? What we've just seen here doesn't speak well for Kwok's sanity—or his life span."

Janis Rollwagen flicked back her red-tinted hair and turned a piercing stare on Wang, Lingenfelter, and Beech.

"What about Kwok's background? If he had so little interest in quantum computing, what made us trust him?"

"His undergraduate degrees were in physics and electrical engineering," Wang replied, trying not to sound defensive, but not quite managing it. "He has genius-level mathematical aptitude. Chess expert, crossword-puzzle addict—like a lot of cryptanalysts, actually. What made him particularly valuable, though, was that he switched to European intellectual history for his graduate studies. He published extensively on sixteenth-century cryptographic and artificial memory systems, which perfectly suited him to work on the Forrest documents."

"He also came very highly recommended by the Tetragrammaton program," Beech said. "They've been watching him a long time. They vouched for him as a security asset."

At the mention of Tetragrammaton, a scowl flickered over Rollwagen's face just long enough for Brescoll to notice it. He sympathized. He had never much trusted that bunch, either. Tetra's people were so secretive they made NSA look like a battalion of nudists parade-drilling through Times Square.

"There's more, I presume?" Rollwagen said.

Wang, Lingenfelter, and Beech scrambled to restart the holocast. They heard more philosophizing, this time about a "universal memory palace" and "the creation of the divine AI."

"The 'memory palace' is probably a reference to the Forrest Documents," Beech said again, pausing the intercepted holographic broadcast. "Specifically to what they say about Matteo Ricci's work in China, which was a part of Kwok's investigation."

"There's something I still don't understand, Dr. Beech," Rollwagen said, tapping the table with her finger, and none too lightly. "Why do you think these four hundred-year-old code systems would have any relevance to China today? Or to the CIA, or to us here at NSA? Or to *anybody* in the intelligence and security community?"

Beech looked at both Lingenfelter and Wang, but it was Wang who replied, dimming the intercepted holo-cast as he brought up his own material.

"We've anticipated that question, I think. If everyone will put on their glasses, there beside you on the table, I think I can explain."

With a grunt Brescoll joined the others in putting on the glasses. Captions and diagrams appeared in his field of vision, illustrating points as Wang spoke and tapped keys on his laptop.

"Many theorists have argued that certain mnemonics, or memory-aid systems, are 'forgotten forebears' or 'secret origins' of modern computing," he said. "Artificial memory systems go back at least to the ancient Greeks. Usually the mnemonic art involved mentally creating a series of imagined spaces—a 'memory palace' or 'memory theater'—and placing scenes or items in those imaginary spaces in a certain order. When the creator of the palace 'walked' through that imaginary space again, he could recall and recover the words or information represented by the iconic scene or object."

Watching classical and Renaissance depictions of people and buildings appear and disappear on his AR specs, Brescoll was struck by how little difference there really was between memory palaces and contemporary virtual realities.

"Raymond Lull's thirteenth-century memory tech, however," Wang continued, "consisted of a complex, abstract system of wheels within wheels. The rims of the wheels were inscribed with letters representing the qualities of God, which organized all knowledge. Shifting the positions of the various wheels created endless combinations of concepts."

"It was actually built, then?" Brescoll asked, looking at the extensive illustrations, diagrams, and descriptions Wang flashed before them.

"That, I can't say with any certainty," Wang replied. "I don't know whether medieval mechanical engineering was quite up to the task. Even if it only existed as a 'mental machine,' Lull's system of combinatorial wheels was nonetheless a forerunner of symbolic logic. It influenced Leibniz's development of the calculus. It also anticipated Babbage's nineteenth-century difference engine."

As Brescoll watched, Lull's abstract wheels became mathematical formulas, and then a concrete system of wheels and gears.

"Giordano Bruno's magical memory charts in his *Shadow of Ideas* combined Lull's wheels-within-wheels with Bruno's own multilayered iconography of star-daemons. Bruno's systematic projection of numerological and cryptographical techniques resulted in a system of such immense hermetic and Kabbalistic complexity that it transformed the memory palace into a sort of magical machinery. The mystical, abstract space generated by these magical memory machines resulted in what was essentially a Renaissance cyberspace, a complex interface that both mirrored the vastness of divine wisdom and pumped up the magician-sysop's mind toward a divine altered state."

" 'Magician-sysop'?" Brescoll asked. "Isn't that pushing it a bit?"

Wang shrugged.

"Several of our analysts have argued that any sufficiently dense and rigorous information system takes on a kind of self-organizing coherence which resonates with other systems of similar symbolic complexity—be they mysticonumerological or quantum cryptographic. Or even with the 'mind of God,' in Bruno's case."

"The computer and cyberspace," Beech put in, "and the whole of the infosphere, fulfill the late medieval and early modern dream of readily retrievable encyclopedic memory. The same impetus led to the creation of the first secret services, which also emerged in the sixteenth century. The everything-all-at-once of quantum DNA computing would have been a dream come true for sixteenth-century philosophers and memory-magicians."

Director Rollwagen removed her AR glasses and shook her head. Everyone else took that as a sign and followed suit.

"You haven't convinced me this isn't all crackpottery," Rollwagen said, "but I'll suspend judgment long enough to evaluate how much damage Kwok may be doing. Regardless of whatever he may know about 'magical mystery memory tours,' it's his knowledge of cryptography and cryptanalysis that we need to worry about."

Beech brightened and restarted the holo-cast. Brescoll watched as the world fell apart in stronger storm and quake, and the newcomer tempted his other self to eat some kind of disk, despite the fact that the woman appeared intent on shooting him.

With that, the recording ended.

"That's all we have," said Steve Wang, clicking off the projection system, "and apparently everything that was sent out. There's a lot of noise over what the Kwok doppleganger says, but we're trying to filter that down and recover what we can. We can't say with certainty whether this material was 'broadcast' by Kwok himself. His equipment records indicate his laptop system and his 'trodeshades are wirelessly connected by extreme short-range feed. Someone close at hand, with signals-intelligence expertise, could have snagged the signals, then sent them anywhere and everywhere."

"We can't, therefore, say much about the ultimate source of this material," Bree Lingenfelter said. "We've been unable to contact Kwok since it went, um, public."

"There's a problem here, all right," Director Rollwagen said, nodding to herself. Her gaze shifted from one to the other among them. "If we are to judge from the cryptoreligious nonsense we've just seen, your operative in China may have come unglued. We don't know if he's in cahoots with the Chinese. They may already be using him."

"It's possible that, if they haven't linked up with him," Brescoll said, "or turned him yet, they may want to terminate him—they may even have done so already. Especially if he stumbled onto something the Chinese have put a great deal of time and effort into, in what you three have called their Bletchley Parks."

"Even if he isn't dead, and hasn't already linked up with them," Rollwagen noted, "there's all sorts of classified material he might *yet* be able to spill. I don't think I need to remind you that our military development and application of far-submicroscopic devices violates the Inner Space Treaty—to which both we and the Chinese are signatories. I'm well aware that agreement is honored more in the breach than the observance, but the fact of its existence still stands."

With that, she rested her gaze on the deputy director. Brescoll cleared his throat. He glanced at Baldwin Beech, who nodded, wagging his bearded chin and waving his stylishly clunky glasses in one hand. That nod—self-assured, or just plain arrogant?

Beech was a particularly strident voice in the ongoing internal war against the "militarization" of NSA. As far as he was concerned, NSA's primary emphasis should be on providing information to civilian diplomats, strategists, and policy makers at State. Never mind that NSA reported to the secretary of defense.

In fact, Brescoll himself favored the civilian course, on the grounds that NSA's efforts better lent themselves to big-picture strategizing than to the minutiae of the battlefield. Beech, however, advocated for it in an annoyingly elitist fashion—simply because he seemed to feel it was more "intellectual."

Brescoll had never completely trusted Beech. Too buddy-buddy with Tetragrammaton, for a start. And there always seemed to be a hint of condescension in the Good Doctor's voice.

"We need to take steps appropriate to the seriousness of the situation," Brescoll said carefully, "yet by the least-obvious approach. We need to get somebody on the ground where Kwok is based, and pronto."

"If you need to pull Kwok," the director asked, "do you have a backup? An understudy?"

The deputy director paused. Both Kwok and his backup—Benjamin Cho—were Beech's boys. Still, Brescoll had liked Cho well enough when they'd briefly met during the hiring process. Cho shared Brescoll's own appreciation of the outdoors—maybe not so much the love of hunting, but at least the fishing, and especially a shared understanding of how wilderness can "preserve the soul," as

Thoreau put it. Unlike his effete mentor Beech, Cho seemed straight-forward and down-to-earth.

Then again, that might count *against* Cho in the world in which he would now be required to move.

"Yes, we do," Jim Brescoll said at last. "Benjamin Cho. He's an associate professor of computer science—or 'computational processes,' as they call it at Berkeley. Currently on sabbatical. Professor Beech selected him."

"Good," Director Rollwagen said, straightening the edges of her briefing sheets in preparation for going on about her business. "In lieu of other solutions, I suggest we pinpoint Kwok's location and get Cho in there, posthaste. And do it quietly. Someone who can zombify that much of the computer grid, and break into channels the way Kwok has, probably has the ability to eavesdrop wherever and however he wants. I have a meeting scheduled with Dave Hawkins and the president this morning. I hope I won't have to bring this up."

Brescoll nodded. Hawkins, the national security advisor, was a shrewd political survivor. He frowned inwardly at the mention of the president, however. Commander in chief or no, the man struck him, personally, as yet another in a long line of spoiled rich-kid screwups selected to sit in the Oval Office.

But then, when you've got a trampoline full of money under you, he supposed, it's always easier to land on your feet, no matter how bad the bounce.

He noticed that Wang, Lingenfelter, and Beech were all looking to him and waiting. *Dammit, what do they want from me?* he thought. This was *their* program. Nevertheless, despite all the "new openness" and use of academic "outside experts" being fostered by the State Department and CIA, he would bet that, if the shit hit the fan—if the Chinese had killed Kwok or, even worse, turned him—State wouldn't be taking the heat. Nor would his three eager beavers.

"Yes, Director," was all Brescoll could find to say. But even as the meeting broke up, he was formulating how best to restrict Benjamin Cho's need-to-know. Not so much out of mistrust of Cho, as out of fear at what others might do with him and *his* knowledge—in addition to Kwok's—if they managed to get hold of him.

Walking back to his office, Brescoll hoped the director wasn't expecting any immediate miracles. Investigation and intelligence didn't tend to yield prompt gratification. That was why evil took so long to separate out from good, and why he expected this investigation would require quite some time—especially *his* time—before any breakthroughs were made.

Meanwhile, maybe the fundamental law of bureaucratic weather—"What blows up must calm down"—would come into play. But he wasn't putting money on it.

FEARSOME ABSURDITY

BENCH LAKE

IN THE EARLY MORNING LIGHT, ten and a half thousand feet up in the Sierra Nevada Mountains, the surface of Bench Lake was a liquid mirror. The water's surface flawlessly reflected the tan trunks and green branches of the pines on its islands and along its shoreline—except the southeast side. Too steep for trees, the terrain there descended a thousand feet from bare-cragged ridgetop to scree-skirted lakeshore.

Beyond the forest to the southwest stood the eroded gray pyramid of Arrow Peak, soaring to just shy of thirteen thousand feet and plunging an equivalent depth into that parallel universe beneath the watery sky-blue mirror of the lake.

Standing and stretching beside his tent, Ben Cho realized he didn't have much difficulty believing in that parallel universe. As a child he'd conversed with imaginary friends from that faerie cosmos next door—especially whenever his mother's smother-love became too much to bear. He shook his head, trying not to remember.

"Bench Lake, resting on a true bench high above the canyon of the South Fork Kings River, offers good campsites that are well off the beaten track." That was how the tour books and cyberguides invariably described this locale. How little justice that description did to this heart-opening place! Especially on a clear, moonless night like the one just past, when a second heaven of stars appeared twinkling in the lake's depths. Or now, when the morning air was still, and nothing dappled the water's surface but a few chill insects zigzagging above it, and meandering trout below.

Of all the places he'd seen in this world, this was his favorite. It had been Reyna's favorite, too. He knew there were many places called Bench Lake, but this one, situated between Taboose Pass and Pinchot Pass, was the only one that mattered to him now, because it had mattered so much to his wife.

Just a year ago, on the fault-block granite of the ridge that cupped the lake's western side, Reyna had busied herself taking photos while he lay on his back. First she sighted east, shooting toward the lake, their camp beside it, and the island across from the tent. Then west, over the canyon of the South Fork Kings River, to the brute stone sublime of the Cartridge Lakes country. Then north to Mount Ruskin and Vennacher Needle and Upper Basin. Then shot after shot of the afternoon's storm clouds breaking and shifting and coloring in sunset light over Marion Peak, and Ruskin again, and the Needle.

"Why so many shots?" Ben asked her, lounging on the crack-seamed granite as Reyna continued to snap away.

"Because there's a pattern to all of it," she said, brushing her dark blond hair away from her face and framing another shot. "To all of Nature. You can almost see it if you look at it long enough. You can see that everything worked, until people came along."

He sat up at that.

"What do you mean?"

"We just don't work well with Nature. Haven't, from the beginning. It's right there in the Bible. Adam was the first gardener, and *he* got fired."

Ben laughed.

"Since I'm the one who does all the gardening at home," he said, "I don't know whether or not I should feel offended. But since you're the one with formal training in photography, I guess I'll let you keep taking the pictures on our trips."

"You'll *let* me? Hah! That's why *you* appear so much more often in our photos than *I* do."

Ben inhaled deeply of this morning's air, cool and pine-scented, then exhaled in a long sigh. He wished he had more pictures of her, now. Before him, the blue and gray tent, the same one he had shared with Reyna such a short time ago, stood pitched again on the western shore of the lake. That shore was a swim of perhaps fifty yards to the lake's broadest and westernmost pine-flagged island.

Not long after he had arrived and pitched camp early yesterday afternoon, he swam through that water cold as death—cold enough to remind him that he was still alive.

He'd needed that reminder. Swimming to the island, carrying Reyna's ashes in a waterproof urn, he needed a shocking chill to break through his own internal numbness. He'd clambered out on the rocky shore of the island, goosefleshed in the afternoon wind, naked but for a pair of swimming trunks. A shivering man clasping a grail of ashes, he stood in a landscape reduced to essentials: lake punctuated by islands of stone. Stone islands punctuated by clusters of trees. Bare mountain peaks islanded in seas of conifer forest. Sky punctuated by islands of cloud.

Having brought the ashes dry through the water, he had unscrewed the urn's lid. He recited from memory three lines from a poem Reyna loved:

"Out of a misty dream
Our path emerges for a while, then closes
Within a dream."

He treasured a few private memories of her face and her voice and her form. He remembered how they used to joke about what they could have *ever* told their kids about how Daddy had proposed to Mommy, since that event had actually taken place in bed.

In their personal mathematics of marriage and family, however, two had become one but one had never become three—or more. They had chosen not to have children, and now they never would.

He said a few private prayers, until he found his love and his loss too deep to express. Then, with all the fearsome absurdity of life against death and ceremony against meaninglessness, he scattered upon the waters of Bench Lake the same contents he had a moment before so carefully carried through those waters. The ashes, blown by the afternoon winds, made a gray film on the wave-raveled surface, drifting and spreading before sinking into the icy, light-riddled depths.

In the aching clarity of this new morning, he mused that what he had done was illegal. He had known it when he did it, but he did it because it had been her wish. He understood the reasons for the laws. Harms of aggregation: if billions of people could have their ashes strewn or their bodies buried wherever they wanted, great natural and human monuments would become ash heaps and charnel houses.

"Harms of aggregation." That had been one of Reyna's favorites from sociology, the field that had been her profession, but which had also informed her everyday life. Its methods explained why they didn't bring cell phones or pagers into the back-country with them, for instance.

"The same technologies that make it easier and easier to work," she said last year, "also make it harder and harder to have a life beyond work. Parkinson's law says work expands to fill the space allotted to it, but that's not the whole story. Follow out the fascism inherent in such a notion and you end up in a nasty Utopia— a *no place* where everyplace is a workplace, a worldwide consumer concentration themecamp where the words over the gate aren't '*Arbeit macht frei,*' but 'God is Work, Work is God'."

A Reyna rant typical of her wild mind, Ben thought, shaking his head. She was probably right about "harms of aggregation" too.

Still, he told himself that remoteness and the relative rarity of human visitors to Bench Lake made any real harm less likely.

The smell of the pines and the sound of calling birds on the wind, the sharpness of the cool bright air on his skin and in his eyes—all these were part of the beauty of the place. The soreness and stiffness of his muscles, however, were a deep reminder that it wasn't easy to get here.

He and Reyna had been backpacking over a chunk of the John Muir Trail north to south every summer for the last four years. The North Lake to South Lake loop two years back, then last year coming in from South Lake over Bishop Pass, down through Dusy Basin to Le Conte Canyon, up Palisade Creek to the Palisade Lakes. Then over Mather Pass and into Upper Basin before descending to the South Fork Kings River, crossing it, then rising to the junction with the Pacific Crest.

Last year, they took the side trip to Bench Lake mainly to give themselves a day of rest before going over Taboose Pass and down Taboose Canyon to the desert of Owens Valley, beyond. Descending Taboose Canyon proved so knee-knocking and heartpounding, however, that by the time they'd reached their pickup truck at the trailhead they had already vowed they would never climb *up* Taboose Canyon—ever. Next year, they decided, they would turn their usual north-to-south route upside down and come south to north, so that they could stop at Bench Lake again and then go back down (never up) Taboose once more.

In the intervening year, though, the world had turned upside down. With the sudden onset of headaches and seizures, Reyna declined from perfect health into profound illness. The doctors gave it a name—glioblastoma multiforme, or GBM—and a grade—four, the highest level glioma, the most malignant and aggressive astrocytoma. The medical professionals could do little else, but that didn't stop them from trying. Surgically, radiologically, chemically, they treated the primary brain tumor that was pushing from Reyna's temporal to frontal lobe, making a butterfly-shaped swelling inside her skull.

Nothing worked.

"Given the type of tumor you have," the neurosurgeon had told Reyna and Ben, "and given its aggressiveness and malignancy, your life expectancy isn't going to be what you might have otherwise expected. Statistically, the odds aren't in your favor that you'll live to be an old woman."

"Which means what, exactly?" Reyna asked.

"Median survival time for GBM is counted in months, rather than years. Still, we don't know where you'll fall on that survival curve. You could fall near the median, or at the long end—say as much as three years."

"Or at the short end?" she pressed. "A few months? Even weeks?"

"Yes," the neurosurgeon said with a sigh. "That, too, is a possibility. So it's important to be realistic, but remain hopeful. Prepare yourself for what's coming, but stay as positive as you can, knowing that we're trying to keep you as well as we possibly can, for as long as we can."

"Doctor," Reyna had said, her voice quavering slightly, "do you think miracles are possible?"

"I'd like to think so," he replied, "but the chances are pretty slim—statistically speaking."

"Yes," Reyna had said with a weary shrug. "Almost by definition."

Beyond the shock and suddenness, Reyna's death had left an unfillable emptiness in Ben's life. At night even now he dreamed himself back to the days at her bedside, watching the synthetic opiate draining slowly away through the drip into the needle planted in her arm. He wished and hoped again in his dreams, as he had in those dark days, that there might be *something*, some biomedical fix he could put in the fluid-filled plastic bag hanging above her, to grant his dying wife not just an easing of pain, but a miraculous return to health.

No miracle, technological *or* theological, had been forthcoming.

Although the poor, small lake of his soul was only so deep, in darkness it seemed capable of reflecting a loss and grief deeper and vaster than the stars. Everyone assured him that "life goes on," that Reyna would have wanted him to go on, but no one could have predicted or even described to him how differently his life would go on without her.

This summer Ben came from the south, following the route they had planned together before she grew ill. From Onion Valley he came over the high saddle of Kearsarge Pass. Down toward Charlotte Lake and up to the razor ridge of Glen Pass. Past Painted Lady Peak reflected in the Rae Lakes, and Fin Dome reflected in Arrowhead Lake. Down to Woods Creek then up its long drainage to the high scraped notch of Pinchot Pass. Then down past Lake Marjorie, and down again to this side trip.

To here, to this morning, to memory—and to the realization that, despite all the sublime beauty around him, his life was sad, a broken thing. He wondered that it could still go on, but it did.

Next year, I won't take the side trip to this lake. Hurts too much. I'll come in over Kearsarge again and go out at Mount Whitney. Finishing the last section of the Muir Trail, without Reyna. Alone.

His reverie was broken by a beeping sound. At first he thought it was the call of a bird or marmot, until he realized how thoroughly out of place it was in this wilderness. He carried no cell phone or pager into the backcountry, per his departed wife's rationale. So it could only be his geolocator—his one concession to work and the whole ensnaring webworld of the twenty-first century. A concession which Reyna would not have approved of at all.

Ben frowned. His work with NSA had, since shortly after Reyna's death, contractually obligated him to "full locatability," anytime, anywhere. Even here, even now.

Thinking about a world all boundaries and interfaces, he silenced the geolocator's beeping. In so doing he confirmed his location. What would *that* mean for those on the other end? From the itinerary he'd filed, they must have known he wasn't scheduled to hike over Taboose Pass until later today. He wouldn't reach the trailhead and what passed for civilization until tomorrow noon at the earliest.

Breaking down his tent and gathering together his gear, Ben wondered if anything truly urgent had come up. He had taken on the NSA work at Reyna's suggestion, when she had first become ill. She thought it would keep his mind occupied, but the only ongoing project he was involved in was monitoring and "understudying" the work of Jaron Kwok, and that had required little enough from him.

Last Ben knew, he was in Hong Kong, a bustling city that would suit Kwok well. During the brief time the two of them had roomed together in college, Ben had once suggested that Kwok join him on a hike. "If God had intended us to trek about in the wilderness," Jaron had said, "He would have provided comfortable benches every fifty feet." That seemed to sum up Kwok the Urban Man quite well. It wasn't until later that Ben had found the original quote from Oscar Wilde, who apparently shared a similar distaste for physical activity in the great outdoors.

Stuffing his gear into his backpack for the hike out, Ben thought how odd it was that he should recall that old conversation—benches and all—here on the shore of Bench Lake. He took a last look around his campsite to make sure he had left nothing behind, then gazed at the rugged peaks, trying to etch the scene into his brain, some-how certain he would never pass this way again.

He looked down at his heavy pack, mentally preparing himself for shouldering it, for hip-belting and sternum-strapping himself into it. Then, out of the corner of his eye, in the direction of Taboose Pass, he caught sight of a dark dot moving above the landscape.

As he watched, the flying object resolved itself into a helicopter. A rare occurence, but not unprecedented. He had seen rescue chop-pers in the backcountry before—noisy machines obliterating the mountain quiet, for all their noble intent.

As it moved closer he wondered what strange acoustic effect of basin and range was preventing him from hearing this one. Then all at once it dawned on him: this wasn't a rescue helicopter. It was a black military job, built for stealth, an oversized Sikorsky Comanche. Quieter than it had any right to be, it wasn't just coming toward him, it was coming *for* him.

The mirror lake shattered into innumerable pieces as the helicopter, dropping to hover not far off the south end of the island, roiled the still air into a whirlwind. Two Navy SEALS dropped an inflating raft and plopped into the water beside it. Dumbfounded, his backpack leaning against his legs, Ben could only watch as the two men paddled the raft ashore.

He was being *extracted*.

He wondered if the chopper had flown in from China Lake or Lemoore, but before he had time to formulate the question a square-jawed, clean-cut young man in modified frogman gear was standing in front of him, saluting crisply.

"Doctor Cho?"

"Yes?"

"Your immediate removal and relocation has been ordered, on highest priority, sir." The young officer handed him a biometrically secured message tube. "This should explain. Please follow me."

The officer picked up Cho's heavy backpack and headed back toward the shore in one fluid motion. Checking over his shoulder to see that he had Ben Cho himself in tow, the officer soon had both backpack and backpacker stowed aboard the raft where his fellow SEAL waited. The short paddling trip in the raft and lift into the hovering helicopter passed in a blur. Glancing out the gear hatch before it closed, Ben glimpsed the white noise on the surface of Bench Lake, calming and disappearing as the helicopter lifted away.

Staring at the message tube clutched in his hand, Ben remembered what it was for. He pressed his thumbs into the scanners on both ends of the slender cylinder. They quickly read the personal labyrinths of his thumbprints. He felt as much as heard the message cylinder give a low buzz, then he lifted it to his eyes. Light flashing from the translucent bar read his retinas. Finally, amid the whirring of the cylinder breaking its own superencryption, the flash resolved itself into a single short message:

PROFESSOR CHO –

GREETINGS. SORRY TO INTERRUPT YOUR VACATION,
BUT CIRCUMSTANCES FORCE US TO PUT THE
UNDERSTUDY AT CENTER STAGE.

– BALDWIN BEECH

As he pulled the cylinder away from his eyes, the cryptic message quickly faded. Although it didn't provide enough information for Ben Cho to clearly read his future, he thought he could see something of the shape of things to come, nonetheless.

TWO

CHIMERICULTURE

KOWLOON

BY THE TIME Police Detective Lu got the word to investigate the incident in Sha Tin, the dragons were descending from the hills above Kowloon, to bathe in Victoria Harbor. They passed through the broad notch of missing floors, an entire wing never built into the New World Renaissance Hotel. This absence existed expressly to avoid putting any obstruction in the dragons' path.

To anger dragons was to court the worst kind of ill luck. In feng shui–conscious Kowloon, prudent architects took such issues seriously into account when drawing up their designs.

Before leaving her office, Mei-lin Lu—"Marilyn Lu" to her monolingual English-speaking friends—made several phone calls to find out who was already on site and to glean some specifics on what happened. She ascertained that the deceased was an American citizen of Chinese descent, but that was about all anyone was willing to say.

The last of the dragons were returning to the hills by the time Detective Lu got a car from the motorpool and headed for the Royal Park Hotel. Maneuvering along the busy highways leading out of a densely skyscrapered downtown, she was reminded of a not particularly good day in *Bladerunner*'s Los Angeles, 2019.

Sha Tin wasn't in Lu's official jurisdiction, but there were mutual-assistance agreements among law enforcement agencies in the Special Administrative Region governing Hong Kong, Kowloon, and the New Territories. She was the closest available detective with her level of forensic expertise, which someone in Sha Tin felt was needed for this investigation.

And to think I owe it all to a bunch of clay soldiers, she mused sourly. Like many other Chinese youth of her generation, Lu had been inspired toward a career in archaeology as a result of First Emperor Qin Shi Huangdi's ancient terra cotta army of soldiers and horses discovered in the burial complexes around Xian. That, however, had been long before she met and married Xun-il, "Sonny," then dropped out of graduate school—not long after the birth of their only child, Clara.

The twisting course of her life and the burden of adult responsibilities had carried her, not to Shaanxi Province or a career of exotic digs on the empty Mongolian steppe, but—as a police officer with a background in forensic anthropology—to contemporary urban corpses, which she examined for signs of recent foul play. Despite this, she still thought of herself as a cultural investigator, an anthropologist of a very contemporary sort. Her single concession to the grim realities of her work was that, while on duty, she carried an Israeli-made, .50 caliber Desert Eagle handgun. Her friends in the department, particularly Derek Ma and Bili Chen, referred to the gun as "Lu's Cannon."

Beyond the urban density of Kowloon, through the green tropical preserve between Golden Hill Country Park to the west and

Lion Rock Country Park to the east, Detective Lu at last drove into Sha Tin proper. Her alma mater, the Chinese University of Hong Kong, stood on a hilltop not so very far away. Remembering her college days, she thought of her mentor, Professor Carlton Jiang.

Jiang had been a thoughtful anthropologist, quick to question how much had really changed in the nearly twenty-three centuries since Emperor Qin's time. The old man had stressed again and again the relationship between the "content of lives and the context of culture." With a wry smile, he seemed to enjoy telling a classroom full of eager young students—believers in Reason and Science—that "Truth has a bright face, but human perceptions are so limited that our minds can provide only fragments of a shattered mirror for her to see herself in." And as Lu's graduate work began to fall apart, the professor had become more than a little frustrated with her. She felt her old mentor would have made a great police investigator. He had the right attitude: part sage, part cynic.

As she pulled her car into the turnaround for the Royal Park Hotel, Lu Mei-lin realized that the same could be said of her own father. Another man of "parts," even if some of those parts seemed to have gone missing. A policeman-turned-writer of the Wambaugh school, he published four detective novels under the pseudonym Quinton C. S. Chang, then spent the rest of his life working on a fifth—usually of Scotch, but bourbon would do in a pinch. His final novel, *Widows and Bad Breaks*, about a murder in the publishing industry, continued to arouse occasional interest from publishers—probably more out of concern for potential libel, than potential profit.

Lu noted that there were no emergency medical personnel or vehicles anywhere in the entry area of the hotel. Not a good sign, that. Either the local police were keeping it extremely low-profile, or the deceased was already far colder than she liked. Crossing the marble and jade lobby, Lu found a bank of elevators and punched the UP button, still thinking about her father.

The brass and glass elevator arrived. She stepped in and pushed the button for the tenth floor. Waiting for the doors to close, she looked out the elevator's transparent exterior wall. Lu figured she couldn't really blame her old man all *that* much. Yeah, he was an alcoholic, and a failed writer of police procedurals, but he had done his best, given his upbringing.

The doors finally closed and, passing through the ceiling, the elevator climbed the side of the tower. Against a backdrop of green mountains, Lu saw rising and falling around her the glitzy company skyscrapers, the graying high-rise apartment blocks, the road and commerce signs in English. All of which, she knew, seemed so terribly alien to the rural folks from the inland People's Republic of China when they visited the former Crown Colony on holiday. Folks much like her father must have been when, as a twelve-year-old refugee, he had fled the Communists.

The Special Administrative Region of Hong Kong, Kowloon, and the New Territories was a place part traditional and part post-colonial, part Chinese communist and part corporate transnational. Detective Lu thought of those clever phrases the *South China Morning Post* used. "Living in the interzone." The "interface." The "membrane." "Surface tension." "Synapse society." "Chimericulture."

Home. For her, in ways it had never been for her father. And no longer was, for her mother. Which was why Lu could almost never hear the acronym for the Special Administrative Regions, SARs, and not think of another acronym, one for Severe Acute Respiratory Syndrome, the original name of the disease that had taken her mother's life.

The elevator doors opened and the first thing she saw was a pair of People's Army guards in their dress blues, hefting machine guns. *Odd*, she thought. How was this a military matter?

They waited for her to dig out proper identification. One guard examined Lu's credentials with flat, expressionless eyes, then motioned for her to follow him.

At the door to the hotel suite, Lu gloved up and passed two more guards before entering. Inside, the room looked almost like an ordinary SAR crime scene: police photographers still snapping shots, print-dusters and fiber-finders and half a dozen other crime-scene technicians staring large at small spaces as they worked, bagging evidence before exiting.

Lu made her way toward the shadow of a body on the bed. The shadow was mostly ashen gray, but streaked with hot pink—so vivid that at first Lu mistook it for a dust of ashes shot through with hot embers. There was, however, no heat rising from the shadow. Notecards lay scattered upon and around it. At the middle and a head of the shadow, respectively, rested a laptop computer and a pair of what looked like heavy wraparound sunglasses. Both the computer and the wraparounds were partially melted into surreal shapes.

Behind her, evidence techs speculated quietly about Kwok's booze and cigarettes and piles of scribbled notecards. Also about the computer, with which he had apparently been working at the time of his decease.

Trying to keep focused on her work despite the military presence, Lu had to fight down her awareness of some sort of political miasma rising around her. That task was made easier by the fact that she knew the graying, bespectacled coroner's assistant on scene—Charles Hui. At least she could talk shop with him.

"Have you solved this one for me yet, Mister Hui? Who found the body?"

"Hello, Mei-lin. What body? You tell me. One of the cleaning staff, a Mrs. Quian, was the first in the room. Smelled 'something funny,' she says. Not right. Like smoke or chemicals. And lightning."

"Ozone, maybe?" Lu suggested, but Hui only shrugged. "Electrical fire? Then why didn't the smoke alarms go off and send everyone running?"

"Maybe the fire was too small," Hui said, shrugging again. "Maybe, as a smoker, he purposely disabled them. Maybe the alarms' batteries were dead, or they malfunctioned somehow. You'll want to check. I don't even know if the alarms *have* batteries, or need them. I'm not even sure there *was* a fire, exactly. Hey, you're the detective. Like I said, you tell me."

"No fire?"

"No raging inferno, anyway. Some of the notecards are browned a little on the edges. The bedclothes appear to have gotten a little smoldery—but that might have been from cigarette burns."

"But look at the computer he was working with. All misshapen, like it was melted—"

"I thought so too, at first," Hui said, picking up the computer and handing it to Lu, "but look closer."

Lu examined the lightweight device. Its aerodynamic shape had been warped and altered—but by *what* remained unclear.

"No evidence of charring, or even blackening," Lu said, returning the distorted machine to the exact place it had occupied on the bed. "I see what you mean."

"That's right. Same with the sunglasses, or whatever they are. I've been here two hours and all I've seen is this stuff in the shape of a body on the bed, and some notecards spread on it that look like maybe they've been singed a little."

"What about that stuff on the bed?"

"We're calling it 'ash.' The working hypothesis is that Kwok was drinking and smoking and somehow set himself on fire. But take some of that ash between your fingers, Mei-lin."

Lu did so. It didn't smudge the way ash should have. She sniffed it tentatively. For her trouble, she smelled only a barely detectable tang—yes, it was ozone. She looked at the stuff more closely.

"As much like lint as ash. Gritty, gray-pink lint."

"That's what I thought, too."

"Some strange kind of spontaneous combustion?" Lu asked, half joking.

"Is there a kind that isn't strange?" Hui countered, then shook his head. "A great deal of spontaneous and not much combustion, from all I can tell. But then, maybe I missed something. I think a military hazmat team saw all this, before we did. Who knows how the stuff cooled or congealed in the meantime?"

"Why the delay before allowing us in?"

Hui nodded his head in the direction of the soldiers, then walked toward the door himself. He had just left when everything in the room changed.

"Detective Lu, hello!" said Wong Jun. "I wasn't aware you'd been assigned to this case."

"Yes, sir, I have," Mei-lin said warily, shaking Wong's hand. Mister Wong was a rising governmental operative, working the New Territories area of the Hong Kong SAR for Guojia Anquan Bu— Guoanbu, the Ministry of State Security.

"Good, good!" said Wong. "So you'll be the lead investigator on this, then. May I introduce you to Mister Robert Beckwith? He's from the US consulate. The deceased was an American citizen, as you probably already know."

Detective Lu shook hands with the tall, thin American. Graying, looked to be in his forties. The fact that the deceased was an American *almost* explained the presence there of a US consular official, but not quite. Lu grew still more wary. The last thing she wanted to step into was some kind of *international* political mess.

"Don't let us interrupt your work," Beckwith said, smiling a politician's smile. "You go right on with it, and don't mind us."

Happy to oblige, Lu quickly turned back to her examination of the scene. She wasn't able to "not mind" Wong and Beckwith, however.

Each of them was jockeying for control of the materials found at the death scene. Wong subtly argued that the materials should be kept by the PRC as part of Lu's police investigation. Beckwith parried with the suggestion that they were the deceased's personal effects and, since the deceased was an American citizen, the materials found at the scene should therefore be returned with his remains to the relatives who survived him in the USA.

Detective Lu had the distinct impression that Wong had no intention of allowing Kwok's remains and his other properties to go to local police. Nor did Beckwith intend them to go to Kwok's American survivors.

A plague on both their houses, she thought, frowning. She'd be damned if she was going to do Wong's dirty work for him. She was grateful when the two jockeying officials finally left the room. As they departed, Hui returned. She didn't think it was a coincidence.

Politics, and on a global scale. Out of her league, but she would have to play anyway, at least for as long as they would let her. Which would probably only be as long as they thought they could *use* her.

"The American says an important computer specialist is on the way from the States," Hui said, his voice mockingly casual. "To offer his help."

A cold case with no corpse, and a foreign computer geek coming to "help." *Great*, Lu thought. *What could be better?*

"Where's this cleaning lady, this Mrs. Quian?" she asked. "I should talk to her—get a statement for the record."

"Ask Wong. He probably knows."

Lu nodded. How many agencies were going to be looking over her shoulder as she did this investigation? Guoanbu at least—and who else? CIA? FBI?

Better and better.

ENANTIODROME

SHA TIN

RISING IN THE ELEVATOR to the tenth floor of the Royal Park Hotel, Ben Cho felt a wooziness that was more than just vertigo, or jet lag, or even culture shock. It had been less than sixteen hours since he had been extracted from the Sierra Nevada backcountry, given moments to shower and shave in an airport hotel, provided with a full set of luggage and clothes, then put aboard a flight to Hong Kong with his escort, FBI Special Agent and Deputy Legal Attaché DeSondra Adjoumani. There had been a buffer of empty seats all around them on the jet.

He didn't quite know, even now, what the FBI had to do with

all this, or why the situation merited a SEAL extraction team, but he was learning.

"I'm glad you've been brought in on this, Dr. Cho," Agent Adjoumani had confided to him in an undertone. "Where we're headed can still be such a closed society, especially in the computer realm. It's often hard to figure out what they might be up to, behind the Great Firewall of China."

She looked at him meaningfully, but the look had little meaning to Ben. He could only nod. He had relatively limited previous experience in China, and what little he remembered didn't strike him as being particularly "closed." Then again, he *had* traveled mainly in the Special Economic Zones and Special Administrative Regions of the New Territories and Shanghai.

From those previous travels he gathered that the SEZs and SARs were in some ways a very Chinese approach to handling the periodic incursions of foreign influences. Centuries back, an emperor faced with the increasing presence of foreign devils along the coastline merely decreed that the Chinese people were to evacuate certain coastal areas, and move more than one hundred miles inland. Emptying those areas of Chinese inhabitants had resulted in ceding temporary control to the foreigners and their strange ideas. In some ways it had been rather like a buffer zone, or even a quarantine: the foreign contagion would be allowed to run its course, but would never be allowed to reach the heart or even the vital organs of the Chinese body politic itself.

Ben had been struck by the fact that the Communist government, in coping with global capitalism via SEZs and SARs, had come to essentially the same "solution" the Imperial bureaucrats had adopted centuries earlier.

The flight from San Francisco International to Hong Kong's Chek Lap Kok Airport was otherwise uneventful, but not particularly pleasant. The only thing truly out of the ordinary was that the two passengers in closest proximity to them were in fact both machines.

The flight attendants had handed Ben and the other passengers a brochure explaining that the machines were a cesium atomic clock and a supercomputer, part of a series of experiments underwritten by billionaire iconoclast and autodidact David Fahrney.

The idea was to investigate whether or not the Big Bang had been an explosion *into* space, rather than *of* space. Atomic clocks were being flown on outgoing and returning commercial flights in particular cosmic directions—toward 11 hours 40 minutes 36 seconds in the constellation Leo, or toward 23 hours 40 minutes 36 seconds in Aquarius. If the time differences, as measured against a stationary ground clock, were the same for the flights regardless of their cosmic direction, then Einstein's theory of relativity would have passed its most rigorous test yet. If time were slowed more in one cosmic direction than another, however, then the original Lorentz-Fitzgerald theory of absolute motion through absolute space would be proven true: space would be proven infinite, superdense and superelastic, possessing an anti-energy a million times the mass of the Earth per cubic inch. Matter would have to be made of energy waves "all the way to the bottom."

Ben was skeptical of such an outcome. Fahrney, who had lost the sight of one eye to a childhood accident, had often been accused of "Cyclopean vision" by his detractors in the mainstream scientific community. Still, if the man wanted to spend his own money in the furtherance of his ideas, more power to him. Ben wasn't particularly bothered that two of his fellow passengers were artificial. It made the flight quiet enough that he could concentrate on his research.

Delving into the briefing materials assembled by Beech, Lingenfelter, and Wang, Ben began to formulate his first theories on how he'd come to be mixed up in the world of SEAL extraction teams and FBI legal attachés. He knew already that NSA and its Chinese counterpart, Guoanbu, the Ministry of State Security, were both bent on the production of the "ultimate weapons" of information warfare.

The crux of that arms race was the development of a fully operational universal quantum computer, one of such awesome power it could manipulate information densities approaching the "bandwidth" of the entire universe—and therefore capable of breaking any encryption. The Chinese seemed to believe such a device would prove to be their "great equalizer" in any contest with the West.

What he'd seen in the briefing materials, however, seemed to suggest that this "universal key" was somehow intimately entangled with its opposite number, a similarly powerful universal quantum cryptograph—or "universal labyrinth," as Kwok called it—capable of generating an encryption impossible to break. Ben couldn't see the analogy, though. When he thought of labyrinths, about the only things that came to mind were convoluted paths in parks and gardens.

Turning back to his briefing materials, he read that both the NSA and Guoanbu feared the full weaponization of information might result in a "secrecy gap" which could nullify, overnight, all code and cipher efforts affecting electronic privacy, electronic commerce, and national security. Even the much-touted message cylinders—for all their biometric identification programs, tamperproofing, and ridiculous levels of superencryption—would be vulnerable.

Both sides appeared to be coming at the informational superweapon through some combination of quantum crypto and binotech. The classified literature Ben read suggested that whoever got the full quantum capability first would also have it last—and only. It was the ultimate killer app.

Why the powers at NSA had decided to make a defrocked intellectual historian like Jaron Kwok their point man on this, Ben had never yet been able to figure out. The man had such strange ideas—and strange terms for them, too. Kwok referred to the crypto arms race as the "looking-glass war" or, even more bizarrely, the "Enantiodrome." Ben didn't know the word, and couldn't find it in his PDA's dictionary, so he looked up its roots. It seemed to refer to a racecourse where the runner was always running into his mirror-opposite self. Ben wondered if Kwok had made the word up.

Tired of spinning on global and personal politics, Ben quickly finished off the crossword puzzles in the in-flight magazine. Always too easy, alas. So he'd put away the magazine and spent the last half hour of his flight watching a 2-D version of the weird virtual worldmovie Kwok had sent out.

On the trip from the airport on Lantau Island to the hotel in Sha Tin, Ben Cho found himself thinking a lot about that strangely filmic fragment. The odd little flick raised a number of curious questions. Warnings, too. Yet Ben gathered from the briefing materials that Beech, Lingenfelter, and Wang were far more appalled by Kwok's security breach, in leaking word of "binotech research," than by any of the other issues and speculations Kwok's last holographic testament had put forward.

Ben decided that, whatever he did here in China, he would say nothing about binotech. He didn't know all that many specifics, anyway—just what he'd read about the new "implants" NSA had funded for Jaron.

The elevator door opened. He and Special Agent Adjoumani were met by Wong Jun and Robert Beckwith. He would have recognized the pair as government functionaries even if he hadn't been briefed. Despite the fact that they worked for wildly disparate governments, the only thing that might distinguish these two apparatchiks from thousands of others like them was that both appeared to be struggling against exhaustion. Ben thought it likely each of them had gone considerably more than twenty-four hours without sleep.

Examining their papers, Wong nodded at Adjoumani. At seeing the passport for Benjamin King-hon Cho, however, a question flickered across Wong's face just long enough for Ben to notice it.

He knew the puzzled look, for he had seen it many times before—in America. Although his father was descended from nineteenth-century miners and railroad workers who fled Hong Kong for "Gold Mountain" California, Ben was nearly as dark-complected as Ms. Adjoumani. Not so very unlikely, given that his mother was a descendant of African slaves. Probably of a woodpile slave master or two as well, along the way. Ben's mother had once joked nastily that his coloring was "high yellow," unlike her own father's "red bone."

As a boy, such terms had only confused him.

Ben's coming into the world hadn't been so very easy, either: lots of ART—assisted reproductive technology, like fertility treatments and in vitro work, at least from what he was able to gather from his parents' rare and vague mentions. Ben had sometimes let himself hope that, although it might not be easy, it *was* possible to be Asian and African and American all at the same time. Neither the world nor the USA, however, had yet grown as enlightened on that point as he might have expected.

Most white people he'd met either couldn't believe he was part Asian—or before Ben could say a word, they were already telling him how much he looked like Tiger Woods, back in the days when that legendary golfer was "just starting out."

Wong motioned the two of them down the hotel corridor toward what had been Kwok's suite of rooms. The guards required them to glove up before they were allowed to enter the suite. Making his way to the bed with the Hiroshima man-shadow on it, Ben picked up and examined the partially melted laptop and virtual reality shades he found there. Adjoumani, Beckwith, and Wong looked on, attentively.

"The coroner and the police investigators have finished up most of their work here," said Wong. "They haven't had much luck with the computer hardware. You're an expert in these systems, Dr. Cho?"

"I know a few things about them. I'm not much into implants and deep-immersion environments, though. Kwok clearly was. These shades are a DIVE mask. Pin-sets on the temples, for electrode links beneath the skin, see? Not a DIVEr, myself. Like the old joke says, 'When it comes to plugs and drugs I draw the line at pins and needles.' Augmented reality is more my speed."

Wong nodded, perhaps more from politeness than under-standing.

"We intercepted a fragment of some sort of holographic virtual-reality scenario, generated by the deceased not long before his death," Wong said. "Apparently he sent it while using this equipment. Do you know anything about that?"

Ben glanced at Beckwith, who gave a discreet nod. Better to 'fess up, since thousands of people might have seen that fragment already. Beckwith himself seemed to be among those thousands.

"I've seen the VR fragment," Ben replied absently, examining the wraparound VR shades with particular interest. An e^2v^2—electrode-ensemble virtuality visor. This VR interaction glassmask was fancier than he had thought. Not just electrode-linked, but fully electrode-connectable, with dermal-pin interfaces. Total 'trodeshades.

Staring at the mask, he thought of how Reyna used to tease him about his intense dislike of any and all technologies that got under the skin. More than just a strong aversion to needles, it went back to when he'd had his wisdom teeth removed, during college. While rooming with Jaron, actually; they both had their late molars taken out that same semester. Maybe they'd have gotten along better and been less cross with each other if they'd had their wisdom teeth taken out earlier, instead of trying to tough out the pain.

"Any impressions concerning that broadcast, Doctor?" Wong asked warily.

"Crazy stuff. Then again, it takes a certain type of personality to be a DIVEr."

"True enough," Wong said, staring levelly at him. "We have been trying to determine whether the virtual-reality fragment is somehow a product of Jaron Kwok's own subconscious mind, or of the computational system with which he was interfaced at the time. Or perhaps some synergy of the two. Any suggestions?"

Ben continued examining the shades, trying not to appear surprised. The reflections in the shades weren't the only mirror images around here. He was more than a little taken aback that the NSA's opposite numbers here in China were following up the exact same speculations as his employers in Crypto City.

The phrase "looking-glass war" rose unbidden into his mind.

"There did seem something associational and *unconscious* about that scenario, now that you mention it," Ben said at last, trying to sound casual. "That would tend to support your first theory. Certainly this is intimate hardware. Too intimate for me. But I know of no physical hardware that taps directly into the human unconscious."

Wong nodded.

"Can you explain the areas that scenario drew from, then? Why genetic research? Why the search for extraterrestrial intelligence? Streaming media? 3-D rendering?"

"Those are *all* important applications for internet-scale operating systems," Ben said, returning the 'trodeshades to their place on the man-shadow and picking up the laptop. "Grid computing. The very type of worldwide computer-sharing Kwok was involved in at the time of his demise. Perhaps it wasn't coincidental."

"That would tend to support the second hypothesis," Beckwith put in—more to reinsert himself into the conversation than out of any other motive, Ben thought. "That it was somehow a product of the computational system with which he was interfacing. But how could this gear produce something as complex as that VR fragment?"

"It didn't. Not by itself, anyway. This laptop probably contains only a microkernel."

"A what?" Adjoumani asked, her brow furrowing.

"A computer operating system that provides only core functions," he replied, carefully examining the laptop. "Like resource allocation. Scheduling. Basics for distributing and executing application programs. The real computational power comes from communicating via the net with a supernode, a coordinating server complex of networked supercomputers and, through that, with a myriad of other 'host' computers—like this laptop. A host of hosts.

Potentially tens or hundreds of millions of machines like this one, shifting resources among themselves."

"I've heard of that sort of thing," Beckwith said, nodding. "You think this shared computing power might have been able to generate the VR holomovie we're talking about?"

"Easily. That is, if Kwok had enough money or barter in the coordinator's accounts to allow his system to exploit the entire constellation of hosts that way. Or if he scammed the worldwide computershare into believing he was some kind of superuser—zombied it into providing him with enough infocrunching power for grid-based tele-immersion, at little or no cost."

Wong seemed impatient to bring their conversation back to the question, if not to the body, at hand.

"But do you know of any way in which such a system might have backfired, so as to reduce Jaron Kwok to ashes?"

Ben Cho bent down and took up some of the gray-pink stuff. If it was ash, it wasn't like Reyna's ashes. More like fuzzy grit, like a cross between sand and staticky lint. . . .

Realization blossomed in his jet-lagged brain like petals of lightning. Lint. ELINT. Not so much ELectronic INTelligence as electronic *lint*.

"To ashes?" Cho replied at last. "No, I don't see how his gear could have burned him to ashes."

Wong and Beckwith nodded, both looking deflated. Ben felt sorry for them. Even if he hadn't lied outright, then he'd spoken a half-truth at best. Staring at the fuzzy, gritty "ash," he wondered if it might contain coherent data.

"Probably be best to keep some samples of these ashes for examination, and ship the rest home to the relatives," Ben said as casually as he could. "Mighty considerate of Jaron, to provide for his own cremation. I'll take samples now, if you don't mind."

"Yes," Wong said. "That should be permissible. Detective Lu and the coroner's man already took some."

Adjoumani handed Ben several small plastic bags and an implement like a tiny trowel. Using the familiar yet unfamiliar tool, he scooped samples from different regions of the shadow body into the bags, made note of where each had come from, then handed off each in turn to Adjoumani.

"I'd like to talk with your Detective Lu before I leave Hong Kong," Cho said, straightening up. "Right now, though, I'm very tired from my flight. I'll be happy to contribute further to your investigation as soon as I can, but I really must get some sleep."

Beckwith and Wong allowed him to beg off, both assuring him they'd be in touch with him soon. The steady presence of DeSondra Adjoumani moved him out of the room past the guards, down the hall, and back toward the elevator that had disgorged them earlier.

"Sorry you're stuck babysitting me, DeSondra," he said as they walked to the elevator.

"No apologies necessary," the agent said with a smile. "Legats, legal attachés, normally only work *leads*, not cases. You've given me a chance to work a real case. Even got a gun permit, and I like that. I much prefer criminal investigation to international intrigue."

Ben agreed wholeheartedly. He, too, was here to investigate, not to spy. Riding down the elevator, to his own room, conveniently booked in the same hotel, Ben was sorry to think that he had lied again, however. Yes, he was jet-lagged, but he wasn't about to sleep. Tired yet wired, he was glad to have avoided the binotech question, at least for now.

Other questions, more pressing and strange and immediate, would not go away—no matter what lies he told.

PROJECTIVE RETROSPECTION

CRASH VILLAGE

AS USUAL, Don Sturm had to hack his way to the Crash site. On other days he had enjoyed puzzling through the arboreal algorithms and epiphytic encryption-protection that made up the virtuality's rain-forest flora. Today it was annoying mental drudgery, tedious as swinging a dull machete through the low brush, tree limbs, and hanging lianas of an actual jungle.

Coming to a clearing near the middle of Medea πrate's lush paradise island, he found the crashed jumbo jet, vine-draped and overgrown. The backdrop to Crash Village, it was home to a shifting crowd of intelligent agentware, metaphoric and metamorphic knowbots, flexible complexes of algorithms e-bodied as feral children. Nearly all of them wore headdresses of feathers and foliage, with body paint of rust-colored ocher here and there, as well as necklaces of abalone shell, airframe fragments, and flower garlands. Otherwise they were naked.

Moving in the midst of the virtuality, Don focused himself so he wouldn't get too caught up in the seductive imagery. Shifting the scale of his interaction down toward machine-language level, he watched the graphics dissolve and resolve into equations and algorithms.

Latent problem-solving underlay all of Medea's blatant theatrics. The agentware's myriad interactions pushed number into numerology and physics into metaphysics in ways that made Don's head spin. Brute-force attacks on golden-section calculations, irrational numbers, and the infinity of π led into the thornier conundrums of Cantor, Zermelo, Gödel, and Turing. From there the mathetronics went absolutely off the deep end, leaping from the "perfection of ten" in the *I Ching*, to ten as the tetraktys or triangular holy number of the Pythagoreans, to Kabbalah's ten permutations of the four-letter Hebrew name of God, to the infinitude and oneness represented by the letter aleph in the *Zohar* considered as an analog to the mathematical Riemann Sphere.

Too much. Maybe Karuna had been right when she said Medea's virtualities processed information through a sort of "tantric mathematics": working from the zero/one of data and sexual difference—the Pythagoreans' female (even) and male (odd) numbers—up to the divine undifferentiated unity.

However it was doing it, every detail of Crash Village's imagery was working on some aspect of a great problem. What that great problem might ultimately be, though, Don doubted even Medea could say.

Returning to the level of visible graphics, Don approached the crashed jet, watching wary urchins and waifs scamper before him, up bamboo ladders, toward the jagged remains of the jumbo's second-floor lounge. As he came in sight of the lounge platform, Don found more such childware, toiling away at hand-driven winches, bringing something up from the well of what was once presumably the "downed" jetliner's helical staircase.

Still other postapocalyptic putti sounded trumpets. Before his eyes Medea, on a throne of glittering flotsam and jetsam, rose with her entourage from the bowels of the jet. Dressed in the extravagantly plumed headgear and fat feather boas of a rain forest princess, she looked a good deal less pneumatic and more lithe than she had at the Cybernesia party—though she was once again surrounded by a crowd of nubile young women and agile young men. *More "data exchanging,"* Don thought grumpily. At last the trumpets finished their fanfare.

"How's that for a grand entrance, my sweet little blue-haired boy?" Medea purred.

"Very clever," Don replied, "but I don't have time for all this 'Dragzilla, Queen of the Jungle' nonsense right now—"

"My, my, Donnie," the feathered regina said in mock-horror, "aren't we *testy*! Have I ever said anything about the crypto-imperialist implications of *your* Easter Island virtual? What could I possibly have done to put such a burr under your saddle?"

"I think you already know, Medea πrate. Or Media Pirate. Or Indahar Marwani. Or whatever it is you're calling yourself today."

"Now don't tell me you've worked yourself into such a great lather over that little Kwok posting—"

"There's nothing 'little' about it! You've blogged and flogged your capture of that webcast so hard it's up on sites all over the infosphere!"

"So? How does that wound you?"

"First of all, it's an embarassment. You said it yourself—pirates being pirated."

"Donny, the thing was a supervirtual, a 'cast in a bunch of different formats. It went out *everywhere*. Lots of people besides me preserved it in their triddyviddy systems. I just happened to post *first* because a number of the views it put forward 'speak to my condition,' shall we say."

"Information wants to be free, multiplies by dividing, blahde-blahdeblah," Don said, no less annoyed. "It's still not right, airing our dirty laundry that way."

"Hmm! Now we're getting somewhere. Surely the little blot of 'getting pirated' isn't enough to dirty *your* laundry. What's this all about, really?"

"I don't know what you mean."

"No? Well, I hope you don't, sweetie. On those sites where the 'cast is posted, I've got a hit-tracer program running. A nice little de-anonymizer. Tells me a lot of the home addresses of people who come to check out the Kwok stuff. And some very interesting types stop by to visit that weird little movie, everywhere it shows up."

"What kind of interesting types?"

"Political terrorist types. Organized-crime types. Free Zone types. Corporate-security types. Intelligence-community types, like *Kwok himself* was. You know any reason why thuggies and pluggies might be interested in that stuff?"

"Aside from what's in the holo-cast itself, no."

"Too bad. I thought you might have some insider information."

"What made you think that?"

"Oh, just something Karuna said at the party. That Kwok had contacted you. Did he? Hmm?"

"I admit it. Yes, he did."

"What about? Come on, Donny. You can tell an old friend."

Don sighed loudly enough for it to be picked up by his virtuality software.

"At first we thought Kwok was just some sort of researcher. A scholar. An eccentric academic, but one with money behind him. He presented us with a proposal—more of a challenge, really."

"Well? What did he want? Karuna mentioned a 'deep hack,' as I recall."

"Yes. A hack that would streamline control and communication between binotech implants and worldwide computershare systems. Get those systems to do what he wanted without them charging him up the wazoo for that service."

"You mean zombify the computer grid for him."

"That's not what I would have called it, but yes, I suppose you could describe it that way. Karuna did most of the work on that part. She's good at getting diverse systems to talk to each other."

"Like getting Cybernesia's islands to join together as a continent, eh? See? I remember. But whatever did Kwok want it for?"

"To simulate the massive parallelism characteristic of quantum computing. A pentaflop supercomputer, say, has to try a quadrillion different keys, one after another, to open a complex cipher 'lock,' but a *quantum* computer would try all quadrillion keys simultaneously. He wanted to simulate that kind of simultaneity. That's what he told us, anyway."

"Heavens! As impressive as that quantummy stuff sounds, why would it be sexy enough for hit men and terrorists and spies—oh my!—to be so interested?"

"Your guess is as good as mine. He paid us well enough that we didn't ask too many questions."

"No, I don't suppose *you* would have. Sometimes you and Karuna amaze me, Donny. How can two people be so tech-brilliant, such 'good friends' to Mister Obololos—yet so *clueless* when it comes to the Big Picture? Did you ever stop to think that, if Kwok's missing or dead, those nasties checking out the holo-cast sites might trace their way back to you and Karuna? You were both working with Kwok. That makes you logical targets.

"You haven't even considered that possibility, have you? Lord,

I can't figure out whether you're perversely naive, or naively perverse!"

"Look, if you—"

"I know, Donny, I know! You came here to berate me, and here I am scolding you. More proof of what I just said, although I doubt it's needed. *Quod erat demonstrandum.* Go home to your island, Donny—and tell Karuna not to worry, either. You have no idea of the full implications of the mess you may have gotten yourselves into. I suppose I have to take *some* responsibility for that, though. Go home, and let Mama Medea look after you."

"That's not exactly reassuring," Don said, frowning, "when you consider what the Greeks say Medea did to her children."

"Donny, how you can be such a wily Ulysses, and still be such a Cyclops—well, it amazes even me! Fly away, now."

With a wave of Medea's hand, Don Sturm was blown out of the crash zone. When the senseworld stabilized around him, he found himself back home in his Easter Island virtuality, seated beside one of the great tilting *moai* heads alongside the Hanga Roa town wharf. Reaching out and touching the simulacrum, he felt it push back against his hand reassuringly, with an appropriate level of tactile force–feedback.

He took a long slow breath. The massive stone figures carved from lapilli tuff, the unbroken code of *rongorongo* pictorial writing— Don's entire virtual rendering of Easter Island, of the place anciently known as Rapa Nui, possessed a familiar mysteriousness. He found it strangely comforting after his visit to Medea-Indahar's placeless space.

Don thought about the real-world place that had provided the basis for his own virtuality. Over the thousand years or so following the arrival of the first Polynesian settlers, the émigrés from the Marquesas had overpopulated Rapa Nui. They cut down trees until deforestation and drought turned Rapa Nui into a desert island. The more trees they cut down, the worse the droughts became. The smaller the number of trees left, the smaller the number of new canoes that were built. The fewer the canoes, the fewer the fish to eat and the greater the famine—until at last the stonecarvers' civilization had collapsed into chaos, carnage, and cannibalism. The island's population had plummeted by more than ninety percent by the time the first Europeans showed up, on Easter Sunday of 1722.

That was the theory, anyway. Don wondered whether it was true, or whether the theory was a sort of projective retrospection— an interpretation of a lost civilization's mysterious collapse reflecting the interpreting culture's anxieties about its own future.

Then again, Don mused, *maybe it wasn't only cultures that unconsciously did that, but individuals, as well.*

The thought was disturbing enough that Don decided to depart virtual space entirely. Life in meatspace, however, was just a more stubborn simulation, a harsher taskmaster less forgiving of mistakes.

THREE

MUTUAL ASSURANCES

VICTORIA PEAK

MEETING PRIVATELY FOR DINNER at Cafe Deco on Victoria Peak was Detective Lu's idea. The rendezvous, set up over e-mail, seemed like a good plan. Ben Cho had been thinking for some time about what he would say to the detective—about how much he might disclose, and how much the detective might be able to tell him.

Besides, he could use a night free of Beckwith and Adjoumani. No matter how much he might enjoy the company of the latter, she was undeniably paranoid about Chinese motives. With Adjoumani in tow, it was almost impossible to explore the boundaries between permitted and forbidden topics. There were gray-area conversations which, he hoped, might open up some leads for him.

Fortunately, his unaccompanied meeting with Lu had received clearance from somewhere up the chain of command, over

Adjoumani's objections. Ben had been granted the freedom of the city for one evening, at least.

As the touristy Peak Tram climbed upward from the Garden Road station, bathed in the light of sunset, its passage into the dense tropical vegetation of the mountainside forcibly reminded Ben that Hong Kong wasn't so very far from the equator. Atop the Peak however, the ambience shifted from H. Rider Haggard jungles to Hugo Gernsback futurism.

Leaving the tram at the Peak Terminus and strolling across the viewing plaza in search of Cafe Deco, Ben noted that the metal-skinned Peak Tower—shaped like something between a wok and an anvil—looked as if it should have a zeppelin mast attached to it, with the airships of an unrealized future bobbing alongside, taking on and dropping off superglamorous passengers, the beau monde in tuxedos and evening gowns.

From the viewing plaza, Hong Kong seemed the perfect incarnation of a retro science-fiction megacity. Squeezed between Victoria Harbor to the north and the mountain backbone of Hong Kong Island on which Cho stood, the city hadn't grown outward so much as it had vaulted *upward*. Staggering densities of corporate skyscrapers stood sheathed in computerized neon. Astronomically expensive high-rise apartment buildings stratified with light, floor by floor, as night fell. Distilled from starlight, money, and dreams, the city's skyline looked like an artificial mountain range. Across the broken-rainbowed harbor, Kowloon extended the same theme's diminuendo into the New Territories.

The cafe proved to be a place of metallic art-deco trim and geometric designs executed in inlaid wood. The bold colors and bright lights of the entry level gave way across the dining area to a tall glass window-wall, presenting views of the city and the night. Ben almost expected to see private aircars whizzing past outside, or to be accosted by a robot maître d'.

"Mister Cho?" inquired a woman dressed in a blue silk jacket and black slacks, who approached him and thrust out her hand. "Police Detective Lu Mei-lin."

Shaking the proferred hand and taking the card she offered along with it, Ben Cho realized he had expected Detective Lu to be a grizzled veteran cop, and male. He was surprised to find that Lu was a compact, energetic woman, apparently about his own age. Walking across the restaurant toward their table, he wondered if Adjoumani, or certainly Beckwith, might have purposely—and for some unfathomable reason—neglected to tell him.

The view of Hong Kong from their table was as spectacular as Ben could have hoped for. After ordering wine, they exchanged pleasantries about the vista. Ben related to her his impressions of the city as a place where the camel's nose of the future had gotten under the tent flap of the present.

"I much prefer this view of Hong Kong to the one from across the harbor," Detective Lu said. "I'm pretty good at filing the trademarks off what I see and hear, but from the harborside promenade in Kowloon there are just too many big, neon corporate logos on the skyscrapers across the straits. Even *I'm* not impervious to that level of brandwashing."

Their wine arrived.

"Deep down, Hong Kong is at least as much about old dragons as new technologies," the detective said, pausing to sip her wine. "Oh, and I go by 'Marilyn' for my English-speaking friends."

Ben Cho nodded. They placed their dinner orders with a bespectacled young Chinese woman whose broad Aussie accent and playful wit belied her serious looks. Jazz from a live band started up in the background.

As they ate, Ben talked about his own work, about his slim acquaintance with the departed Jaron Kwok, even about the loss of his wife. He also learned about Lu's work on the police force, about the detective's family and her background in anthropology. As they conversed, Lu proved to be street-smart and also a good deal more intellectually sophisticated than Ben expected. *Sharp enough to have some edges*, he thought.

Edges notwithstanding, their talk over dinner was easy and forthright. In the soft light she looked particularly attractive, and he found himself warming to her. With dessert, however, the conversation turned to the strange circumstances surrounding Kwok's apparent departure from this world. Ben reiterated that he didn't see how Kwok's gear could have turned him to ashes—if indeed ashes were what he had left behind.

"What about other phenomena, then?" Marilyn Lu asked suddenly, interrupting him in midsentence.

"Such as?"

Lu stared hard at him, then casually glanced around the restaurant. A moment later she seemed to come to a decision—perhaps about their environs, perhaps about him.

"Allow me to pay the charges," she said. "Then perhaps we could take a walk to Lions Pavilion? The view of the city is particularly impressive from the Lookout."

Curious, Ben wasn't about to refuse.

Soon thereafter, they exited the restaurant and walked to the Pavilion and the Lookout. Except for an older man strolling about with his Lhasa apso, the place was deserted, with no one else anywhere nearby—likely because it was late on a surprisingly cool night in the middle of the work week. The vista from the pagoda-roofed gazebo was spectacular, but Lu clearly had something else on her mind.

"Here," Lu said, taking an electronic viewer from her pocket and handing it to Ben. "Does that help?"

"It does, yeah," he said, holding the device up to his eyes and looking out over the city. "But what it adds in magnification it subtracts a little in scale and context, you know?"

"This might help," Lu said. With a movement very close to sleight of hand, the detective palmed a minidisk from her pocket and popped it into a slot on the viewer's side, simultaneously enabling its player function.

Ben stared again through the viewer, but found to his surprise that the real-time image of the Hong Kong skyline was gone, replaced by a recording. Watching, Ben realized that what he was looking at was a closed-circuit TV record of Police Detective Lu's very recent interview with Mrs. Julie Quian, the hotel cleaning lady who was first on the scene. Quian appeared unaware of the camera, but from the way she kept glancing in its general direction Ben guessed the record had been made through a two-way mirror. He had always been fascinated by those. They reminded him of the invisible fourth wall that separated the audience from actors on a stage. Or God from mere mortals.

"—not say it *was* fire. *Like* fire."

The interview, or interrogation, between the detective and the graying matron had been conducted in English. Cho thanked the history of Hong Kong as a British colony, and was secretly relieved. Julie Quian's command of English wasn't the best, but it was a good deal better than his own Cantonese.

"How do you mean?" asked Detective Lu.

"Not like he burst into flames, but like he flickered. Streamed up. Patchy and see-through."

"If he became transparent," the detective pressed, "then what did you see through him? The bedcovers? The other side of the room?"

"No, no, no. He like a TV turned to different channel from rest of world. Sunny day in some other place shining through him. Then he break up into—what you call it? Static? White noise? And nothing left but ashes on bed and strange smell."

The CCTV record stopped and the Hong Kong skyline reappeared in the viewer. Ben Cho took the viewer from his eyes and turned toward Lu, who stared at him expectantly, leaning with one hand on a railing finial carved in the shape of a lion. Ben slowly handed her the viewer.

"Well?" the detective asked quietly. Ben dropped his voice, as well.

"It may be very important. Then again, everyone knows how unreliable eyewitnesses can be. I have no plausible explanation for what could have caused the scene Mrs. Quian describes, in any case."

"How about implausible explanations, then?"

Ben pondered that a moment before speaking again, very quietly.

"Her description makes it sound as if something was somehow . . . *overwriting* Jaron Kwok's very existence. Like a computer disk being overwritten with new information."

"How is that possible?"

"I'm not sure it is. A person isn't just data, to be stored or retrieved. Or the medium it's stored *to* or retrieved *from*, either."

"You're the expert," Lu said with a shrug, in a voice just above a whisper. "Could he have been attacked through the distributed system with which he was interfacing at the time, maybe?"

"The worldwide computershare? That's unlikely in the extreme."

"But that still leaves us to explain the melting of the laptop and the virtuality visor," Lu said. "And the 'ashes.' "

"Yes." Ben turned back to gaze at the neon-burning skyline before him. "Look, I'm going to be attending Jaron Kwok's memorial service later this week, so I have to return to the US tomorrow. I owe you, so take what I'm about to tell you for what it might be worth. You *might* want to follow up on a couple of things. . . ."

Ben paused, on the brink, yet still uncertain. What protocols might he be breaking if he went on? He'd only just met Marilyn, and had only the slightest of professional connections with her. Some of the people who sent him here might consider it treasonous for him to reveal *anything* to this police detective, so why do it? Wine and conversation over a candlelight dinner, beside a city sparkling below them like a new constellation of earthbound stars—that was no excuse. Nor was the fact that, since Reyna's death, he had missed terribly the close company of a woman he could just sit and talk to, at ease.

No. He would tell Marilyn because he trusted her, in ways he couldn't explain.

"I don't know if anyone told you," Ben said, taking a palmtop t-com utility out of his pocket and manipulating its display screen with a stylus, "but at about the time Jaron Kwok vanished, a 'cast went out across the infosphere. A number of sites have posted it, some in 2-D form. Here, take this business card I'm printing out.

It's a smart card—see the strip? I've embedded my phone numbers and net addresses—along with the addresses of the best infosphere sites on the Kwok 'cast."

Lu took the card from his hand, glanced at it, and put it in her pocket. Ben returned his gaze to the skyline and the roaring quiet that rose from it.

"That gray-pink ash or gritty lint or whatever it is we're going to be memorializing at Kwok's service," Ben continued, "you took some samples of that, right? You might want to check them for something more than physical characteristics. More than just chemical or biological, too. I'm not certain, but I think those ashes may contain information of another sort. Data."

"What kind?"

"Could be almost anything. Disk data-storage capacity is at hundreds of gigabytes per square inch these days. Even tiny pieces of a hard drive can contain sizable amounts of information. For years there's been talk that spies might remove a hard disk, grind it up, and smuggle out its data as pocket lint."

A laugh escaped Lu. Ben frowned.

"I know it sounds nutty, but it's less of a laughing matter if the data was originally *m* of *n* encoded."

"What's that?"

"Like a laser hologram," Ben said, "for which fragments less than the whole can convey the whole. *m* of *n* encoding spreads information over *n* fragments, any *m* of which is sufficient to reconstruct the relevant data. A document encoded in thirty-two fragments, say—any eight of which would be sufficient to reconstruct the entire document."

"In this case," Lu said, looking at him with narrowed eyes, "how much of the stuff would need to be recovered to reconstruct the whole? And the whole of *what*?"

"I have no idea. Still, it might be worth your time to follow this line in your investigation."

Lu looked away at the glittering cityscape, too.

"It sounds crazy, but I believe you," she said. "Tell me something. Why are you helping me like this?"

They turned their backs on the city and began walking toward the Peak Tower.

"I could ask you the same thing," Ben countered. "Or just say it was quid pro quo for letting me see that interview."

"I suppose you could."

"Then again," Ben said, puffing a little as they climbed the incline, "maybe there's more to it than that. My country went through a nuclear arms race and a cold war during the last century. We didn't learn much, but we did retain a few things. Between us and the old Soviet Union there was a policy called MAD—mutually assured destruction."

"I've heard of it."

"At its heart was a paradoxical idea: that to be safe, you also have to be vulnerable. Paradoxical ideas have never been very popular in my country, Ms. Lu. They're less popular than ever, today. Maybe they're not popular in your country, either."

"No, not very," she agreed. "Especially given the Nepal-Tibet situation."

Ben nodded. Since his return from the wilderness, he had heard the media reports. The Chinese government protested that armed Tibetan rebels were using bases in Nepal to harass the Chinese province of Tibet. Depending on which Party official was speaking, Nepal was either a proxy for India, or both South Asian nations were proxies for the United States.

"That's unfortunate," Ben said, "because I think your country and mine are getting caught up in a new kind of arms race, a new kind of conflict. Jaron Kwok may be an early casualty of that new kind of conflict, even if no one can yet say how."

They came up onto the promenade of the viewing plaza. The anvil-wok of the Peak Tower loomed above them in the night. The promenade, too, was empty but for a bearlike young man standing with his arm around his willowy girlfriend at the far end of the platform. Ben noticed that Lu stared at the couple a long moment, before shaking her head as if to clear it. The young couple appeared to be cuddled together out of a desire for romance, at least as much as any need for warmth.

"I've often thought," Lu said, "that the future is too important to leave in the hands of the leaders."

"A subversive truth, Ms. Lu."

"Call me Marilyn," she said, smiling. "Someone said the truth will set you free, but nobody ever said it would make you safe."

Ben laughed and shook Lu's hand.

"I'm sure the politicians, the generals, the big money people— they would disagree."

"No doubt."

"I'm taking the tram back down," Ben said, "so our paths part here. I already have your card, and I just gave you mine. Let's keep in touch."

"Agreed. And Ben—be careful, especially if you're the courier for Jaron Kwok's ashes."

"I am, but why the worry?"

Hurriedly, Lu surreptitiously popped another disk into the viewer and handed it to him, this time with no pretense that it was intended only for looking at the city. Another surveillance camera record, as near as Ben could tell, though not from the same source as the Quian interrogation. The image showed two men, one a thin, gray-haired gent wearing glasses, white labcoat, and slacks, the other a thick-set younger man in desert camo fatigues. The sound quality was poor, but even so Ben could tell that the younger man was de-manding something of the older gent. Everything about the older man's tone and expression showed how firmly he refused to give the younger man what he was demanding.

Then the older man made a mistake. He glanced away toward something near him in the office or lab. The younger man's gaze followed that glance, saw what it was looking at. There was a sound of breaking glass. Something glinted in the young man's right hand, then he struck the lab-coated gent in the chest with it several times. From the blood that followed, Ben suspected the object that had glinted was a knife, and that the older man had suffered multiple stab wounds before he fell to the floor. The younger man fled the scene, a plastic-bagged something in his left hand.

"Looks like a robbery of some sort," Ben offered.

"Yes," Marilyn Lu said, her voice cracking for a moment before she cleared her throat and got it under control. "The victim is Charles Hui. He worked the Kwok incident for the coroner's office. From the way he's dressed, we suspect the thief and murderer is associated with the New Teachings Warriors. As nearly as can be determined, the only items stolen out of Hui's possession were the ash samples he took from the Kwok incident scene."

Ben pondered that for a long moment.

"Are you the investigator on Hui's murder too?"

"No. He was a friend of mine, though. He was usually so careful—about everything. I never thought he would die this way. I thought you should know, since you're transporting Kwok's ashes back to the states."

"What about you? Don't you have samples of them in your possession too?"

"Don't worry about me. Understanding murder is part of my job. Tragic as it is, Charles Hui was at least killed in a way I understand. If Jaron Kwok is the victim of a new kind of murder, then there's bound to be a new kind of murderer lurking about, too."

"You think so?"

"I'm almost certain of it," she said with a shrug. "Try to have a safe trip back to the U.S.A.—no, make *sure* you do."

With a wave of the hand from each, they separated then, barely managing to maintain their pretense of casualness for anyone who might be watching.

Waiting at the Peak Terminus, Ben wondered at the way the evening had turned out. Not much like he had planned, admittedly. Was Marilyn Lu a cynic, or an idealist, or—like Ben himself—some quirky mix of both?

He climbed aboard the empty tram. As the car began its controlled fall down the mountain, through the dark density of jungle
vegetation toward the bright density of Hong Kong's lights and the
nightlife beyond, Ben wondered if perhaps Lu had duped him.
Played him for a lonely fool by getting him to reveal more than she
herself had given in return. Maybe made him betray himself, or
even his country, in some obscure way.

No, Marilyn Lu didn't seem the Mata Hari sort. The record of
Hui's death, too—that seemed very real. If Ben had found her more
and more attractive as the evening lengthened—even if the root of
his trust was good old-fashioned lust—that was his doing, not hers.
Besides, it wasn't as if he had given away anything that she might
not have found herself, in the infosphere, or figured out in the
course of running tests on her samples of Kwok's ashes. And the
warning for *him* in what had happened to Hui—she'd done him a
real service, alerting him that way.

Falling downward through the night, however, Ben worried. Even
if his response to Marilyn Lu was trust more than lust, he still felt as
if he were somehow betraying his mourning for Reyna. But there was
something more. Could it be that, in believing they could see through
the paradoxes—that they could be more lofty and moral and *right*
than everyone else, even more *in*vulnerable, somehow—were he and
Detective Lu only misleading each other? And themselves?

NEED-TO-KNOW

CRYPTO CITY

DEPUTY DIRECTOR BRESCOLL HAD JUST RETURNED from a meeting
at Langley when he got the reminder. A major update on the
Kwok matter was scheduled to begin in ten minutes at one of the
NSOC conference rooms. Headed toward the Visitor Control Center of the Headquarters/Operations Building, he realized he'd have
to hurry.

Architecturally, H/O was rather like an unraveled hypercube skinned in darkly reflective one-way glass. Beneath that epidermis lay deeper layers of bulletproof glass, with several inches of sound-deadening emptiness sandwiched between outer and inner panes, along with EMR-protective Tempest copper shielding. All of which was intended to make its sixty-eight acres of floor space an informational black hole, sucking down every electromagnetic signal that passed near without giving a single electron back.

Brescoll entered the maze of interconnected floors and corridors through the two-story white pentagon of the Visitor Control Center. Past the turnstiles of the Access Control Terminals and their central security command post stood a six-foot-tall painting depicting the NSA seal.

Inserting his badge in the CONFIRM reader and walking through the turnstile, he glanced at the seal. The "eternal" and "perpetual" circle bordered in white. The words *National Security Agency* in the top border, *United States of America* in the lower half, separated on either side by a silver star. The blue field, dominated by an American eagle with wings extended and inverted. On its chest a red, white, and blue escutcheon, heraldically representing nation, congress, and president. Clutched in the eagle's talons was the silver "key to security," evolved from the emblem of Saint Peter the Apostle.

Making his way toward the private elevator to the right, Brescoll chuckled to himself. Conspiracy freaks always got a lot of mileage out of the fact that the Pope's emblems featured the Keys of Peter, too. And that NSA headquarters was located in Anne Arundel County—since, centuries ago, the Arundels had been noted English conspirators and crypto-Catholics. For the paranoids, it followed that NSA had connections to the Vatican, the Knights Templar, the Holy Grail, the hiding place of the Ark of the Covenant. Et cetera, et cetera. Go figure.

Jim decided he didn't have time for a stop at his office in the executive suite on the eighth floor. Instead he headed directly for old OPS 1 and the National Security Operations Center in Room

3E099. Walking across the initials *NSOC* inlaid in the floor, he passed through automatic glass doors and under the seals of the three armed-service organizations that made up Central Security Services, NSA's military wing.

He then maneuvered his way through a space that to him always seemed half situation room and half deep-space monitoring facility. Cubicles mazed the floor, computer monitors glowing everywhere. Video screens covered the walls. Several of the younger techs wore augmented reality glasses, heads-up displays for everyday life. Some had eye-tracking pseudoholo display screens on their desktops. These flashbar systems were much more common than "airbenders," the newer and more expensive holographic projector units that ranged all the way up to the top-line stuff in the I Rooms. Brescoll saw only two scaled-down airbenders here, suspending their ghosts over workstations.

Out, then down the hallway past Special Support Activity, Brescoll arrived in the agency's Worldwide Teleconferencing Center—and not a moment too soon. Seated around the large conference table, he spotted not only the people he'd expected to see—Rollwagen, Wang, Lingenfelter, and Beech—but also many he hadn't. Among them we recognized the mathematician Tercot—Wang and Lingenfelter's boss and the agency's chief scientist—and Major General Retticker, deputy director for operations and Beech's boss in the NSA/CIA joint Special Collection Service.

Taking a seat beside Rollwagen, Brescoll also recognized others from the Directorate of Operations and the Directorate of Technology and Systems, most prominently specialists from W Group (Global Issues and Weapons Systems) and M Group (Geopolitical and Military Production). Still others hailed from the NSA advisory board, and from other parts of the intelligence community. From the Defense Intelligence Agency. From Army, Navy, Air Force, and Marine Intelligence services. From FBI and Homeland Security. From the Department of State.

Under its wall of television monitors, the conference room was filled to capacity with twenty-five participants. *Who from the intelligence community* isn't *represented here?* he wondered. *Treasury? Energy? Imagery and Mapping?* This hardly seemed a "proportional" response, the Hui murder notwithstanding.

Maybe the importance of the Kwok situation was growing. Understandable enough, he supposed. Units of NSA were responsible for insuring communications security for CIA, FBI, State, Homeland, and the Pentagon—and if anything threatened those communication links, *all* those entities were threatened.

Nearly everyone in the room had secure laptops or PDAs placed on the table in front of them or somewhere nearby, and a few had executive versions of the AR glasses and flashbar systems. Every one of the participants seemed primed to pump a lot of secure information back and forth.

"I think it's time we got underway," Director Rollwagen said, as she checked her watch. "Welcome, everyone. The current situation is covered in your briefing papers, but I'd like to reiterate a few key points before introducing our two remote participants.

"Jaron Kwok, an NSA analyst and linguist working from documents originally provided by CIA, is missing in China and presumed dead. At about the time of his disappearance, a holo-cast was sent to a great many locations across the infosphere. That broadcast made reference, at least indirectly, to a number of confidential projects we currently have underway. In order to help bring you up to speed on the situation, I'd like to introduce Robert Beckwith of State, currently on-site in Hong Kong, and Special Agent DeSondra Adjoumani, recently returned from the same city but now at FBI Headquarters for debriefing."

Appearing on two of the larger wall monitors, an Anglo-American man and an African-American woman, respectively, nodded in response to the introductions. *Ah, Beckwith must be who State's intelligence arm put on this*, Brescoll thought. He'd be the one coordinating with Adjoumani. She was the legal attaché posted to the American Consulate in Hong Kong, while her supervisor, the legat for China, worked out of the American Embassy in Beijing.

"Prior to the incident," Director Rollwagen began, "Jaron Kwok's work for NSA focused on cryptanalytic approaches to recalcitrant historic ciphers and codes—particularly those with reference to China. His backup on the most recent work is Professor Ben Cho. To provide you with further details, and to answer any questions you may have, I'd like to turn the discussion over to the NSA Deputy Director."

"Through CIA," Jim Brescoll began, "our informants in the Tetragrammaton program recommended Benjamin Cho to us for the same reason they had earlier recommended Jaron Kwok. Like Kwok, Cho is a genius at recognizing and drawing innovative connections between patterns—particularly across disciplines. Pattern recognition is the basis of code breaking and this skill should be of considerable help to Cho in investigating the disappearance of his predecessor."

"How much does Cho know about what his predecessor was working on?" asked Max Pearsall, the FBI's Homeland Security liaison.

"We're limiting what we tell him," the deputy director answered. "There's still a lot *we* don't know about Kwok's activities, and we'll want to have Cho asking all the right questions: What did Kwok know? What happened to him? How much do the Chinese know about Kwok and his research? And so on.

"Cho seems to have established a working relationship with a local detective, a woman by the name of Lu. If we keep a tight handle on the situation, we may be able to use him more effectively as a cat's paw—as the Chinese may be doing with Lu. So we'll have to come up with a delicate balance between control and autonomy."

"How so?"

"Our intent is to feed Cho only the information he needs to follow Kwok's own path, rediscover for himself what made Kwok go missing, and what—presumably—killed him. Avoid prejudicing his investigation, or tipping off the Chinese, as much as possible. Still, we'll monitor Cho closely. We certainly don't want his investigation to end the same way Kwok's did."

"And what he doesn't know, he can't tell," Rollwagen added, breaking into the conversation. "To the Chinese, or to organized crime, or to any terrorist cells. All of whom have shown interest in the Kwok material posted at various sites across the infosphere."

"What's the status of Kwok's computing and communications gear?" asked the woman from M Group. "His virtuality visor, implants, and laptop?"

Figures she'd ask about that, Jim thought. Cyber-infrastructure and telecommunications vulnerabilities were M Group's bailiwick.

"I think that question might be answered more effectively by Mister Beckwith or Ms. Adjoumani," the deputy director said, glad to step back out of the spotlight.

"We're sure the Chinese have at least CT-scanned the visor and laptop," Beckwith said. "The implants have vanished, or were destroyed with Kwok. We *have* managed to regain control of the laptop and visor, though even that required a great deal of diplomatic pressure. Particularly on Chinese State Security—the Guoanbu."

"At least you got them back," said the M Group woman. "Better than the track record we have with some of our airborne listening posts."

"Or the *Pueblo* and the North Koreans," Rollwagen agreed grimly.

Several of the grayer heads in the room nodded silently. The USS *Pueblo*, sans crew, had been held for what? Forty years? Fifty?

"What about Kwok's other personal effects?" asked Pearsall from FBI. "What happened to his ashes? The notecards?"

"We were able to obtain power of attorney from his wife, Cherise LeMoyne," Adjoumani replied. "They were estranged, but still legally married. The Chinese authorities have allowed Benjamin Cho to carry the personal effects home on his return to the US. In accordance with NSA policy, we copied the Kwok notecards and took samples from Kwok's clothing and remains, soon after those came into Cho's hands. Doctor Cho himself was, at the time, dining with the police detective from the Special Administrative Region, Mei-lin Lu. So he was unaware of our activities."

"Do you think it was wise to let Cho spend a significant amount of time with this detective, unsupervised?" Paul Riordan of DIA asked. Both Beckwith and Adjoumani glanced momentarily away, then turned back—at exactly the same moment, though they were separated by thousands of miles. The effect was uncanny, all the more so because it was surely unintentional.

"We had a light tail on Cho for the meeting," said Adjoumani. "Cho and Lu would have seen only a man walking a small dog, if they noticed him at all."

"We have every reason to suspect the Guoanbu did the same with Lu," Beckwith added. "We believe the woman who waited on them at their table in Cafe Deco was a Guoanbu operative."

"Our background check indicates that Lu is a straight-ahead cop working a murder or suicide angle," Adjoumani continued. "She has no history of significant political connections."

"We have evidence, too," Beckwith said, "that the Chinese security apparatus has kept Lu very much in the dark on everything outside her forensic specialty. It's likely that we know a good deal more about who's keeping tabs on her than she does."

Heads nodded in the teleconference room. Riordan seemed placated by the fact that the Chinese apparently had Lu on an even tighter leash than NSA had attached to Cho.

"What about these postings of the Kwok material in the infosphere?" asked General Retticker, as he turned back toward Jim Brescoll. "You said organized crime and terror groups have shown interest. Anything being done about that? Have any of those groups shown up in Cho's wake?"

Retticker would *want to know about that.* Criminal liaisons had been a big part of CIA's covert operational capacity from the beginning. In the Asian opium zone from Turkey to Thailand, from Southeast Asia in the 1950s to Central Asia in the present day. The cocaine region of the Americas from Peru to Mexico, and now the Tri-Border Free Zone, too.

In recent decades the TBFZ had been a home away from home

to drug smugglers, terrorists, arms dealers, money launderers, forgers, fugitives, and organized crime figures from Russia, China, Japan, Nigeria, and the Middle East. The Zone was stuffed to the gills with warlords, crime lords, counterrevolutionists, violent fanatics, and other would-be founding fathers.

In the old days the Company had tried to deny such connections. These days, however, all manner of sins were forgiven in the name of the High Crusade against terrorism. Even if you had to get in bed with Islamic terrorists in order to destabilize a powerful enemy state—like, say, communist China—well, that was excusable, too.

Jim sighed inwardly. He knew they were all on the same team here, but he wasn't sure they all played by the same rules.

"We have reason to believe that a young man and young woman," Adjoumani said, "a couple necking on the Victoria Peak promenade while Cho and Lu were there, weren't quite what they seemed. We've tentatively identified the man as Zuo Wenxiu, a member of the Muslim extremist group known as the New Teachings Warriors. Zuo is also a prime suspect in the murder of Charles Hui, of the coroner's office. Hui was working on the Kwok case at the time of his decease."

Murmurs passed through the room, heads nodded.

"As for the postings," Brescoll said, leaning back into the discussion, "we've let them be. We've been able to monitor the traffic to those sites and discover who's expressed a particular interest in them."

Jim glanced toward the director, then nodded at the big screens, where the images of Beckwith and Adjoumani still lingered. Janis Rollwagen took the hint.

"Mister Beckwith and Ms. Adjoumani," she said smoothly, "on behalf of everyone here, I'd like to thank you for your work, and your time spent on this meeting. Please keep us in the loop on your continuing activity. Again, thank you very much."

Beckwith and Adjoumani said their good-byes, then disappeared from the screens. Everyone in the room turned to face Rollwagen and Brescoll.

"Rather, we *were* leaving those sites untouched—until recently," Deputy Director Brescoll continued. "Initially they served as good bait, but interest in them, particularly from the Chinese, seems to have peaked. An informant with connections to their Special Computing Institutes claims the consensus there is that Kwok's peculiar death was an unintended consequence of his encounter with a Chinese countermeasures program. They also believe that *we* constructed the holo-cast to camouflage the fact that one of our agents was trying to hack into an SCI system. We've done nothing to dissuade them of that. I gather the informant works for your agency, General."

Retticker nodded.

"But isn't this Chinese detective still out there, following up leads?" he asked. "Including those involving the site postings?"

"We think so. Guoanbu is probably following Detective Lu's investigation, too, on the off chance that she might actually discover something of value. But we strongly suspect that her work is a rather low priority for them. As for us, the value of those holo-cast sites has grown thin, so we're eliminating them. The Kwok holo-cast is being made private again. Professor Tercot is probably the best person to explain how that's being done."

He turned to Tercot expectantly, but it took the balding man with the graying flyaway hair a moment to catch on. In the embarrassing pause, Brescoll observed that Tercot, if not exactly the stereotypical absentminded professor, was nonetheless a "type" very common in Crypto City: an introverted intellectual, socially maladroit, and definitely detached from an outside world irrelevant to— and largely ignorant of—his brilliance.

"Umm, yes," Tercot began, clearing his throat. "To purge the infosphere of sites featuring postings that relate to the Kwok holo-cast, we are selectively crashing these sites. Many of the postings trace back to the parasitic vermin of Cybernesia, so we're hoping that the crashes will largely cleanse the infosphere of their presence, as well."

"How are you bringing about these crashes?" General Retticker asked. Jim Brescoll wondered if some of Central Intelligence's assets might be affected by Tercot's "infosphere hygiene."

"Through a number of different approaches," Tercot said distractedly. "We've started with tried-and-true methods like worms, logic bombs, denial-of-service attacks. But soon we'll move on to more innovative tools: stochastic crash viruses, Galois trojan horses, Fourier trapdoors. All designed to make these systems vulnerable to 'accidents.' Not everything going down all at once, but staggered. In every case we're proceeding in such a manner so as to make these incidents look like everyday events."

"What's your time frame?"

"Barring any unforseen circumstances, General, we estimate that all publicly accessible postings of the original Kwok material will be destroyed by the end of the week. Commentary and meta-commentary on that material, in various blogs and forums, will take somewhat longer to eliminate, but we expect to gradually 'disappear' those within the month."

Despite himself, Jim Brescoll smiled. Tercot was playing true to type. Clinically impersonal in his judgments, coolly rational in his conclusions. For him this was all just an interesting applications puzzle—except for his comment concerning the "parasitic vermin."

"Did Kwok know about the 'disappearances' of the prototype quantum code devices?" asked Phil Lawton of DIA. At that, a silence descended over the room, but Lawton persisted. "Look, if we've got somebody out there able to kill people, *and* steal our devices by remote control, we need to investigate the possibility that the two might be connected."

"They weren't stolen," said Michelson, a physicist from W Group. "As quantum code devices become more powerful, they seem to somehow become more self-consuming. If anything, they may be vanishing down some sort of informational black hole. But we just don't know."

"Are you implying that Kwok simply 'vanished,' too?" Lawton asked, frowning. "I don't buy it."

"The quantum code devices are classified far higher than Kwok was ever cleared for," the deputy director replied. "There's no way he could have known about them, and there's no proof that *anyone's* done anything by 'remote control.' "

But Lawton didn't look satisfied, which was understandable. Jim wasn't fully happy with that explanation himself. No, Kwok hadn't been cleared on any of the information on machine disappearances, but he *was* tangentially involved. And now Ben Cho was unknowingly—what? Investigating the disappearance of the disappearance investigator? Even if there were no "remote controller" out there, what kind of danger might *he* be facing?

Brescoll was surprised at how quickly Rollwagen moved to wrap up the conference, bringing up a few more minor issues and quickly dealing with them.

As the meeting broke up around him, the deputy director shook his head. *Informational black holes.* That was like the stuff in Kwok's holo-cast, about reality being a bustable simulation. Nobody *really* believed in any of that, did they?

But what if those wild theories turned out to be more plausible than anyone suspected? Rollwagen *had* been quick to shut down the discussion. Might the director know something he didn't? How highly classified was it, if even her deputy director wasn't privy to it?

Well, he didn't feel comfortable asking her. All the more so since Rollwagen was busy at the moment, what with Retticker bending her ear about the possible threat Tercot's work posed to "our covert action capacities and our national security as a whole." Rollwagen assured the general that she would ride herd on Tercot, and that Interpol would be kept in the dark, except where they might provide useful information.

Finally, the director's conversations ended. Still Jim Brescoll said nothing to her. Instead he headed back to his office in silence, several paces behind her retreating back. Entering his sanctum, the deputy director closed the door behind him, berating himself that he was becoming as caught up in his own thoughts as Tercot. If he continued along this track, it was only a matter of time before he too began seeing the NSA as a legacy of the Knights Templar.

He also felt more empathy than he ever thought he would for Ben Cho and his "need-to-know" situation. If someone at the highest level was keeping information from *him*—was trying to use even the deputy director as their cat's paw—then what *he* didn't know might not only hurt him, but lots of other people, too.

Yes, he thought. Might just be time for another fly-fishing expedition.

RITUAL EXCHANGE

SANTA CRUZ

CHERISE LEMOYNE HELD THE MEMORIAL for Jaron Kwok's ashes on the patio of her home. The early autumn afternoon was sunny, with a clear view down redwood- and eucalyptus-lined hillsides. Below, the city of Santa Cruz lay spread out upon the river plain. On the far side of town its boardwalk and beach ended in blue ocean stretching away to the horizon.

Ben Cho's disposition wasn't nearly as bright and sunny as the day. Bad enough that somebody in China had been willing to kill for a dead man's ashes. Worse that, so soon after memorializing Reyna, he had again been forced to play guardian to ashen relics— Jaron's ashes, this time, housed in an antique iron urn he'd bought for them in a little back-alley shop in the Tsim Sha Tsui district of Kowloon. Lately it seemed as if the only people he could allow himself to care about, in any simple and straightforward way, were all dead.

And why not? The living could take care of themselves. Kwok's widow certainly could. She'd shown a distinct lack of gratitude for his efforts, almost as if she held him personally responsible for the loss of Jaron.

"Thank you so *damn* much," Cherise had said when he presented Jaron's ashes to her. "The moment he got caught up with you spy types, I knew this is where it would end."

The angry blond professor had looked as if she were about to hurl the urn of ashes at him, and probably would have, had the elderly Chinese-American couple—Kwok's parents, seated on the broad apron of the raised stone fireplace—not leapt up and interposed themselves. Trying to calm the younger woman down, LeMoyne's mother-in-law led her back toward the green leather couch.

"Down at the Peace Center, they showed me Jaron's holo-cast!" Kwok's widow yelled over her shoulder. "You and your information war burned him up like a file full of outdated secrets! You're supposed to be one of his old college friends, but who are you spying on *now*?"

Ben had wanted to say something, wanted to convince Cherise that she was wrong about him. But he couldn't. He just stared numbly at the photographs that stood on the fireplace mantel near him. In one, Cherise hugged a large marmalade-tuxedo cat, orange but for the white about its throat and paws like dress gloves, spats, and a cravat. In the other photo, a couple—Cherise and Jaron— stood atop a moon bridge arching over a pond, in front of the white veil of an artificial waterfall. The picture and frame looked as if they had only recently been brought out and dusted off.

There was something familiar about that second picture, but before he could put his finger on it more immediate matters distracted him. Jaron's mother was still trying to calm Cherise, but the younger woman was having none of it.

"I don't care!" she said, too loudly. "That's probably why they chose him!"

Jaron Kwok's father had hustled Ben toward the door, muttering about how they'd all been through a lot, that Cherise wasn't at her best, but he was sure she'd be doing better by the time the memorial service came around. Hearing her burst into tears on the couch beside her mother-in-law, Ben allowed himself to be hurried through the front door and away from the house.

Halfway to his rental car he'd realized he had left behind the travel case in which he'd brought the urn. He considered going back for it, but decided against it. To hell with that. To hell with telling her what happened to Hui, too. Ben got in his car and drove away, recalling Jaron's description of his parents as "sweet, but clueless." That description didn't seem to fit the people who had just extricated him from a nasty situation.

A day had passed, and at least things had calmed down. Looking out past Cherise's carefully landscaped yard toward the trees, city, and ocean beyond, he listened to the drone of bees among the flowers and the droning voices of those who were eulogizing Jaron. Ben was still jet-lagged enough by his return from Hong Kong that the quiet murmurings made him drowsy. He had to fight to stay awake.

Two of the eulogizers were old friends of Jaron's, but most of the speakers, and most of the small crowd in attendance, appeared to be Cherise's colleagues from the University of California campus. As he listened to the words of those who knew Jaron better and more recently than he had, Ben's memories of his one-time college roommate were reawakened, his old impressions confirmed. The Jaron he—and they—knew was brilliant and hard-working, but stubbornly independent. Intellectually competitive. Not someone to suffer fools gladly.

Ben's heart pounded a little harder when he saw Cherise, dressed in a black silk sheath and cape, stand up from her chair. He hoped she wouldn't again make him a target of her private pain—this time in a much more public setting. He was relieved to see that, as she walked toward the red-and-black lacquer table where the dark iron cinerary urn sat on its tripod legs, Cherise seemed controlled, little inclined toward any open display of the deeper emotions that might be moving her.

She stood beside the table and placed her left hand on the double-dragon lid of the urn, while with her right hand she pulled notes from the pocket of her dress. In her black attire, her face framed by asymmetrically cut straight blond hair hanging long on the right side of her head but shaved short on the left, she seemed to Ben both severe and vulnerable.

"On his desk," she began, "Jaron kept a small statuette of a godlike man and a sphinx—a statuette that he picked up at a gift shop in the New York Public Library. The sentence inscribed on the statuette reads 'But above all things/Truth beareth away the victory.' Truth always meant more to Jaron than anything else.

"The truth is never easy, and sometimes Jaron was not an easy person. Maybe because he worked harder than anyone else I have ever known at being true to himself, and to the world too, in his dealings with it—even if the world wasn't always true in its dealings with him. Jaron was willing to risk anything, even death, to get at truth. I'm sure it was in that quest he met his end. So, even in death, he bears away the victory.

"Thank you all for coming today, and testifying to the truth of who Jaron Kwok was."

She put the notes back in her pocket. The small crowd broke up then, into individuals offering their condolences to Jaron's parents and to Cherise. Even after nearly everyone else had adjourned for food and conversation inside, Ben still found himself staring away at the view, into the blue, so preoccupied that, when Cherise placed her hand on his left arm just above the elbow, the only thing that kept him from jumping was his own exhaustion.

"I'm sorry for the way I acted yesterday," she said, and she seemed sincere. "Jaron and I had been apart for over a year before this happened. We were going to be divorced soon. I didn't expect this to hit me so hard. But it has."

"I understand. When I lost my wife, I had no idea how it would affect me. People tried to tell me, but there's no way to really share it, or prepare for it. Griefs are incommensurable."

Cherise looked at him oddly, as if the use of that last word, especially in this context, surprised her.

"That's a mathematical term, isn't it?" she asked. "You're a mathematician?"

"Computer scientist—and more physicist than I'd like, these days. Trying to make sense of all the latest in quantum computing."

"That's what I don't get," Cherise said, flicking her hair away from the right side of her face. "Jaron mentioned to me once that you were his backstop, his understudy on this damned NSA thing. But he was an intellectual historian. Something of a linguist too, I guess. He was just an amateur when it came to computer science."

With that she paused and stared at him expectantly, but Ben didn't know what to say.

"Maybe," he replied lamely. "But I *do* wish I had some of his facility with languages."

"Not that it ever helped him to get the professorships or tenure he trained for all his life," she replied. "He always felt as if the academic world had ignored his talents, you know—out of spite and prejudice. I don't see what a tenured specialist like yourself would have in common with him at all, other than the fact that you were roommates in college."

"No, not much, I guess," Ben agreed, remembering. "Then again, maybe *too* much. Maybe if we were less alike, we would have gotten along better as roommates. I know it's not the right thing to say at his memorial, but there were lots of times I just wanted to smack the sucker." To Ben's surprise, Cherise smiled broadly at that. Emboldened, he continued. "The only thing we really shared during college, besides living space for a few months, was a fondness for using a Fahrney 'etniop' or 'mirror-pointe' keyboard."

"I remember not being able to use Jaron's computers," Cherise said, nodding, "because he'd moved half a dozen of the keys around and reprogrammed them. He said the arrangement was much more efficient than the conventional one."

"Right," Ben said, lifting his hands as if typing on an invisible keyboard. "The Fahrney approach is a compromise between the Dvorak and qwerty systems. For the left hand it moves the *e* and *t* down to the home row and moves the *d* and *f* to where *e* and *t* were on the upper row. On the right hand it moves the *n* up to the home row and *j* down to where *n* was, and also moves *i*, *o*, and *p* down to the home row and *k*, *l*, and semicolon up to where *i*, *o*, and *p* used to be. Letter transposition—just like basic crypto stuff, but for the sake of efficiency rather than secrecy."

"That interest in cryptography," Cherise said, "is all I can think of that you two might have shared *after* college."

"Right. But the stuff he published in his articles was all sixteenth and early seventeenth century. Not my area."

"Remaking himself as a 'cryptanalyst' is probably what got him into all this to begin with," Cherise said, looking away. "I didn't approve of him getting involved with the NSA. Maybe you gathered that, from our encounter yesterday."

Ben nodded. How could he *not* have noticed?

"His work took him too close to the CIA and their torture-tactic connections, for my taste," she said, casting him a sidelong glance. "The whole crypto-industrial complex, searching for terrorists under every bush. It was so unlike Jaron. On campus, in the old days, he was a political activist, even a radical! He used to sign his college newspaper columns 'Kwok X'! How could *he*, of all people, let himself get caught up with spy types? How did he even get security clearance? That's what I want to know."

"He was an outside employee," Ben said with a shrug. "Under contract, like me. But I've met people inside the agency who know as well as anyone that even an eagle can't fly with only a right wing."

She gave him that odd look again, as if he'd once more surprised her.

"Really?"

"Sure. I remember one of Jaron's columns about that, too, now that you mention it. About the difference between a nationalist and a patriot. About how a patriot tries to hold his country to its own highest standards, tries to help it live up to its own stated ideals—and doesn't think the constitution should be run through the shredder just because it might be politically expedient. Even inside the NSA, there are people who'd strongly agree with that."

"Yeah, that sounds like the Jaron I knew, back then," she said, sounding wistful.

"Maybe he still believed it. Maybe that was part of his quest for truth."

"How do you mean?"

"When you came up to me," he said, turning fully toward her, "I was thinking maybe that 'godlike man and sphinx' you mentioned might be a reference to Oedipus."

"The archetypal seeker after truth—no matter what the cost," Cherise said, thoughtful, looking not so much outward as inward. "Jaron was fond of tragedies. *Oedipus Rex, Hamlet, Death of a Salesman.* He thought all of them had detectives in them."

"He thought of Oedipus as a detective?"

"As the *first* detective. A guy who went from being king to being blind and homeless for his trouble. Not a happy precedent."

"No, but maybe an accurate one. While I was looking into Jaron's death and gathering his personal effects in Hong Kong, I met a police detective. She said the truth might set you free, but it won't make you safe."

"And it will probably make you miserable before doing much of anything else."

"Yes," Ben said, looking away again toward the city on the plain, "but maybe that's what Jaron was up to. He was an investigator. A detective trying to find out the truth. No matter who hired him, or what they hired him for. I just wish I knew what he was supposed to be going after. It would make my own work easier."

"And just what, exactly," Cherise said, suspicion rising slightly in her voice, "is the 'work' you're supposed to be doing?"

"I'm not *exactly* sure. I was his backup on this project, but I haven't been given much in the way of specifics about what Jaron was doing—never the whole story. So far, only what might be relevant to the computing side of things. I'm not sure whether I've been brought in to continue his work, or to investigate what happened to him. Probably both."

Cherise turned and together they began to walk slowly toward the house and the sunny room where everyone else was eating and talking.

"So," she said, her footsteps stopping again almost as soon as they began, "what do *you* think caused Jaron's death? Did he get drunk and set himself on fire? Was it an accident? A suicide? Did something finally push him over the edge? Or did someone give him a shove—and make his death look like an accident, in the best spy-versus-spy style?"

He sensed that she was growing morose and personally political again, but he didn't know how to divert her from that course. They began to walk once more.

"I can't say for sure whether it was any of those things. I don't think it was suicide."

"Nor do I," Cherise said, her voice unwavering. Ben wished he could feel as sure about that as she sounded.

"I don't even know that he's dead, at least not with absolute certainty."

Almost immediately, he regretted what he had said. Cherise stopped and stared hard at him.

"Then whose ashes have you so kindly bestowed on me in that urn?"

"They're his," Ben replied, well aware that she wasn't going to let this go. "But I don't know if they're *ashes*, actually. I have some speculations, but no hard evidence yet. Insufficient data, so to speak."

Cherise laughed.

" 'Insufficient data'! No one could ever have accused Jaron of suffering from *that*. Research is one thing, but being an infojunkie is another."

"Infojunkie?"

"Jaron got way too obsessed with what he called 'The Documents,' " she said, shaking her head. "The thought of it still makes me cringe. You've seen them, haven't you? The Forrest documents?"

"No, I haven't. What are they?"

"He showed them to me, though I suppose he probably shouldn't have. A lot of strange stuff. From some CIA guy who died forty or fifty years ago. Forrest wrote spy novels and science-fiction stories, too, under pseudonyms, but Jaron said most of the stuff in the documents were codes. Four hundred-year-old ciphers. Art-of-memory stuff, with explanations in a bunch of different languages. Latin. Chinese. Hebrew. Jaron studied and translated a lot of them. He said something important had happened back then. Called it 'the fork in the road to Thebes'—Oedipus again, you see?

"Your bosses didn't tell you anything about them, did they?"

Ben, feeling obscurely embarrassed, stared down at the tips of his shoes.

"Some of my briefing materials mentioned that Jaron was working on premodern and early modern ciphers, and possible links to mnemonic techniques. Not much else, though. I don't know European history the way Jaron did, or have his knowledge of languages, like I said. I guess my 'bosses' don't consider those documents a part of my 'need-to-know.'"

"I've always hated that phrase," Cherise said, grimacing. "Spy talk. The language employed by the secret police of *Vaterland Sicherheits*—excuse me, Homeland Security."

They walked again, then paused outside the patio door, not yet entering the house.

"Yesterday you said you'd seen the holo-cast," Ben said. "Someone *like* you seems to appear in it. I was wondering if you might have been involved in its creation."

"No, that female character's not me," she said with an odd laugh. "God knows, there were times I was so frustrated with Jaron that I might well have pulled a gun on him, if I'd had one. But I never did. The woman in that thing is only *based* on me, and *very* loosely, at that."

"How so?"

"She doesn't talk or think the way I do. The way she goes on about Mind with a capital *M*—I'd be embarrassed if I thought she was supposed to be me."

"Any idea why she *is* that way—in the holo-cast, I mean?"

"Wish fulfillment on Jaron's part, maybe," she said. Then she sighed. "As much as Jaron might have wanted me to, I don't believe in Mind with a capital *M*, or Goddess with a capital *G*, or even gods with a small *g*. Jaron and his gods. 'Our gods have become our machines, and our machines have become our gods.' And, 'Everything happens twice: Theology becomes technology. Then technology becomes theology. What we used to ask of gods we now ask of machines.' It's all there, in Jaron's notes on the documents."

"Sounds fascinating," Ben admitted, "and true, in its way."

"Jaron was always more than happy to share his piece of the truth," Cherise said with a sad smile. Suddenly her voice dropped almost to a whisper. "When I think of how those documents obsessed Jaron, I almost hesitate to get you involved with them. He copied a bunch of what he considered the 'most sensitive' of them and gave them to me the last time we saw each other. For safekeeping. I didn't want them then—I still don't—but he insisted. Stick around after the memorial, and we'll see what we can do about giving them to you."

"Okay," Ben agreed, caught off guard by the offer. "And thanks."

"Don't thank me yet—they may do you no good," she said, eyeing him narrowly. "They might even do you harm. But there's a chance they'll give you some clues to what happened to Jaron, even if your bosses don't think you need to know about them. Might even give you a chance to prove there really is a difference between a nationalist and a true patriot."

Finally they entered the house, and parted. More of the guests commiserated with Cherise. Left alone, Ben made his way to a table laid out with veggies and dips and finger foods. Instead of eating lunch, he grazed. After pouring himself a glass of wine, he found a chair in a quiet corner. For the most part he was left undisturbed. Those few guests who approached him seemed satisfied by his answer that he knew Jaron when they roomed together in college.

Gradually, the guests filtered away. Eventually only a professor of classics named Bruce Danson remained, a gleefully self-described "archconservative purveyor of military-pastoral nostalgia to the postmodern world." Danson argued good-naturedly that the current situation in the United States did not bear any real resemblance to that period in ancient history when Rome ceased being a democratic republic and became an empire. His banter was a different spin on what Cherise had already said to Ben, but not so very different. Before long, she rose to the bait.

"When people in uniforms are presented as the ideal role models," Cherise told the classics professor, "you know the 'republic' has long since been turned into an empire. And that's not where I want to live."

"You sound like one of those secessionist Bear Flaggers," Danson countered, his tone darkening. "Believe me, though, the secession of the Left Coast, or even just California—that's political sausage you *don't* want to see being made, Cherise. Clearly the American people are comfortable with letting our leaders protect us by any means necessary. If the will of the people is that the will of the people no longer need be consulted, then what leader is going to argue against that?"

Their conversation made Ben think again of Marilyn Lu in Hong Kong, the other woman who had offered him forbidden information. Unless he assumed the existence of a vast conspiracy of subversive women, however, it could only be an interesting coincidence.

As Cherise and the classics professor argued about media manipulation, Ben realized that, on the part of the classics professor at least, the argument was more a personal dance of flirtation and hoped-for romance than the hurly-burly of power and politics. Ben started to nod off. Next thing he knew, Cherise was shaking him awake, and none too gently.

"You want the documents, don't you? We've got to get going, then. It won't look right if you leave too long after the rest of the guests."

Ben nodded, rising unsteadily to his feet. Groggy, he had a vague expectation that they would get in a car and drive to a safe-deposit box, or something of that sort. In his mind's eye he could already see a bank vault and a teller waiting with a key—until he realized that Cherise was fiddling with something at the edge of the raised stone apron in front of the fireplace.

She gripped a slab and lifted it smoothly. As he looked more closely, he realized that the stone slab, secured by a hidden latch, was hinged. In the space beneath, several smallish boxes and chests were visible.

"The original owner didn't believe in banks," Cherise said, by way of explanation. "Jaron found this hidey-hole by accident, not long after we moved in together."

Cherise reached down and, after a moment or two of lifting chests and reading labels, handed a fireproof metal box to Ben.

"Here, take it. You're doing me a favor."

The box was about four inches thick by ten inches wide by twelve inches long. Unlatching and opening it, Ben saw that it contained not quite a telephone book's worth of pages. With a nod, Cherise confirmed that the pages were copies of those documents with which Jaron became so obsessed, along with many of his notes.

"Now," she said, "what can you use to carry it out, so it won't look too obvious?"

Ben looked around, then spotted the case he'd used to carry the urn, and accidentally left behind amid yesterday's furor.

"How about that?" he said, pointing.

"That should work. Let's give it a try."

The size and shape of the metal box didn't exactly match those of the urn, but the foam rubber lining of the travel case could be mashed down a little to accomodate the documents. Staring at the case with Kwok's papers inside, Ben thought how strange it was that things could have changed so much between himself and Cherise, all in a single day.

Together they snapped the case shut and latched it, then straightened up. Walking with Cherise out of her house and toward his car, Ben's left arm hung heavy with the dead weight.

"Do you know we've met before?" Cherise said, as much as asked.

"Really?"

"Before I went back to school," she said, nodding. "I was working as a dental hygienist at University Health Clinic. That was how I met Jaron. He was having his wisdom teeth removed."

"I had mine removed about the same time. Same place, too."

"I know. I remember you because you asked for the pain-deadening implants, just like Jaron. It was part of a pilot project in biodegradable bioelectronics."

"I remember," he said, dropping the case onto the front passenger seat through the window. "Prototypes, but they worked perfectly well. I haven't needed—or wanted—any other implants since. How'd you get *that* job?"

"My father was a big name in microelectromechanical systems research at Sandia," she said with a shrug. "MEMS, they called it. Nanotech grew out of it. Later I had versions of those implants put in my head, too, when I had my own wisdom teeth removed. Nowadays it's standard tech. That's why most people don't have to lose a weekend drugged out against the pain anymore."

"Well, that explains it. Small world, Cherise."

"Smaller than any of us ever know, I'm sure," she said, extending her hand for him to shake, which he did. "Good luck with your investigation, Mister Cho." Then she lowered her voice. "Keep a good eye on what you've got in that case."

"You do the same with that urn. You might want to store it away, in place of what we just took out. Just to be safe. And keep an eye open for interested strangers."

Cherise gave him an odd look, but then waved and headed

back toward her house. Getting into the car, Ben stared at the case for a moment as he started the car's engine.

At least he had tried to warn her, without mentioning Hui by name and breaking any more protocols than he'd already broken by talking about the ashes in the first place. He felt as if he and Cherise had engaged in some strange ritual, in which they'd exchanged one set of Jaron's remains for another. He hoped that this set, at least, would prove more decipherable than the set he had left behind.

FOUR

GÖDELIAN LOVE KNOT

C YBERNESIA

EARTHQUAKES SHOOK and high winds whipped Easter Island, toppling the great-headed stone carvings. Don's intelligent agentware, e-bodied as tattooed men and bark-bikinied women, screamed to the heavens and tore at their hair. Somewhere out at sea a tsunami was rolling toward Hanga Roa.

Don quickly jaunted to Karuna's virtual—Haiti in the time of Toussaint-Louverture—but a variant of the same catastrophe was happening there, too. Lightning streaked the sky and thunder rumbled. Winds and hail rattled the tree canopy. Dressed in voodoo priestess holy-rags and staring fixedly at images lurking behind a screen of waterfall, Karuna seemed almost too preoccupied to take note of the apocalypse. Out to sea, the horizon line was punctuated by smoke from volcanic eruptions to the east and south.

"Good God! Where is *that*?" Don asked, pointing.

"The closest one is Saba," Karuna said. "In the Netherlands Antilles. At least four more are going off throughout the West Indies."

Don nodded. Karuna's virtual space, like his own, was a deep imitation of a real place, even down to the geologic structure of the surrounding islands.

"Is this happening all over Cybernesia?"

"No," Karuna said, examining system-readout images behind the waterfall screen. "Only about a quarter of the islands seem to be affected."

"Then why us?"

"Hold on a minute," she said, manipulating the images by casting cowrie shells upon a mat. "Let me check something here. Yes— I *thought* this catastrophe looked familiar! The sites involved match almost exactly the list of guests who attended the Cybernesia party. Everybody who attended, every DIVE we had grouped together when the Kwok material came through—that's who's being hit right now."

"Damn!" Don said, scowling. "I should have known! Medea-Indahar popped in yesterday, drama-queening about how sites with the Kwok stuff on them were being massively probed and pinged. That they were *crashing*. Or being crashed."

"How?"

"Denial of service, mostly. Scorched earth. Way low on the value chain. 'Inelegant.' M-I thought it might be the military. No hint this was coming, though! I'll jaunt to Crash Village, if I can. Medea's DIVEs are more abstract simulations. She might be weathering this attack better."

When Don stepped through into Medealand, however, Crash Village was gone. Not a sign anywhere of the postapocalyptic poppets and downed jumbo jets. Instead Don found himself floundering in a lurid hellscape, aswim in the redblack heart of a space like one of the volcanoes erupting over the horizon in Karuna's virtual. Only this hell was a cavernous underground space. Making his way with difficulty onto a fire-shored black island, Don managed to scan down closer to machine-language level.

Every detail of the hellscape represented elaborate programs designed to extricate keys and passwords—ensembles of discrete-logarithm and Shor algorithms, along with modular arithmetics for factoring *enormous* primes and related asymmetric "one-way" functions.

Don recognized other code and cipher-cracking programs, too, even if he could barely understand them: unusual quantum Fourier transforms, frequency analyses, higher algebras, statistics, combinatorics, number theory, set theory.

At the hub of the code-busting, Don saw, lay Medea-Indahar, a very masculine devil deeply body-tangled in a cyborgy, busy servicing and being serviced by techporn-endowed superpeople, sex demons, incubi and succubi exploring orifices, probing and prodding, licking and fondling and manipulating, erupting into and onto each other in molten orgasmic fluidity, again and again.

Despite himself, Don stared. Were these debauchery partners merely sensorium constructs—hardbodied representations of software running on computers somewhere? Or were they actually puppets of distant human meat? Even if that were the case, they had to be coming together—so to speak—from haptically sexsuited participants hundreds or thousands of miles apart.

"Jeezus!" he said. "You chose a great time to throw an orgy. All of Cybernesia is under attack!"

"Donnie, the world has been going to hell since the day it all began, so why wait? Let's just get there, already! But really, you've got it wrong. It's not the whole world under attack—just everyone who attended your Cybernesia shindig. And this isn't just safe sex, this is sex for safety!"

"*What?*"

"You work your way, I work mine," Medea-Indahar said, without once breaking from the contrapuntal sex rhythm. "The thread that makes a love knot is the clue through the labyrinth. Clues are keys, and keys are clues. The system that's 'attacking' us has already made a place for us. A bug, a glitch, a back door, inevitably inherent in the system itself. Gödelian incompleteness. Still, I *could* use your help."

"I don't see what 'service' I can provide," Don said, distaste dripping in his voice.

"Must I spell it out, line-by-line, Donnie?" Medea-Indahar asked, pausing from time to time in his explanation to lick, suck, caress, or fondle. "Okay, then. The NSA's bid to crash the Kwok postings has opened the agency itself up to a hack via its own international espionage web. The actions you're viewing with such obvious revulsion are for moving through, penetrating, and enveloping—ooh, baby!—NSA's own communication and database infostructure."

"So all this probing and manipulating—," Don began.

"—is about accessing communication links and exchanging information with databases. We're a sexy switchboard, honey child. Coupling and uncoupling through overseas hookups into NSA's Intelink-U unclassified and open source databases. Foreplaying through that to its WebWorld and WebChat rooms. Caressing our way to Intelink Central, enveloping Intelink S, climaxing in Top Secret SCI, sensitive-compartmented information, ooh *Daddy*!

"But we're not through yet. Enciphering and deciphering are mirror processes, and we haven't yet stepped through that mirror, Alice."

Don thought he could hear the strain mounting in M-I's voice, despite all her attempts to sound unconcerned, even flippant.

"At the moment I really don't have time to explain to you how the essence of mathematics lies in its freedom," M-I said. "What I *need* is the expansion you did on the Besterboxes, the one that allowed you to fly the islands of Cybernesia. And Karuna's program that allowed them to join together. The route of the deep hack you and Karuna did for Kwok, too—the one that allowed him to take control of the worldwide computershare. Give me those, and right *now*, if you would be so kind."

Don stopped questioning and looked back inside his home virtuality. In the distance the tsunami was growing larger.

In Karuna's virtual, storm and eruption mingled and the sky rained mud and ashes.

He pulled the Besterbox expansion and the computershare programs from his virtuality, and the island-joining protocols from Karuna's—her work, but he still had access. Performing his own manipulations, he melded the programs into a single object, but left the computershare as a second object.

Pulling them into Medea's simulation, he manifested them as firebrands burning in different colors, one blue, one green, automatically embodying themselves in tune to the sim's framing metaphors and algorithms. Don tossed the torches toward Medea amidst the lovepile.

Even as the programming objects flew through the air, they morphed from burning brands into a blue incubus and a green succubus—with red-gold eyes, surgical chrome vampire fangs, dull steel devil horns, gunmetal finger- and toenails, just like the rest. On contact they were welcomed, the new demons instantly entwining themselves into the love knot which, through its writhing, was shifting connections, loading databases, altering programs throughout the world.

"Thank you, Don! Ah, just as I thought: those millions of worldshare computers function like the vast unconscious of the Earth's telematic noosphere. . . ."

Don had no time to puzzle *that* out, but the changes occurring in the cyborgasmic lovepile were obvious. The knot unravelled, splitting into two flaming parts, blue and green, half the participants convulsing in ecstasy along the ceiling of the hellcave, the other half mirroring that passion from the cave floor. Before long they began moving toward each other again, mirror tornadoes of burning rainbow flesh twisting like skeins of yarn, dropping down and rising up, stalactite vortex and stalagmite gyre heading toward union.

The moment the stalagmite and stalactite touched, however, stalagmite and stalactite ceased to mean anything. *Up* and *down* became meaningless, too, as the resulting narrow-waisted pillar of fire detached from roof and ceiling. Now a coupled, two-headed vortex, it began to spin on a central axis, more and more rapidly, until the fiery pillar described a sphere that exploded outward in light.

Don found himself blown back, out of Medea-Indahar's world, through Karuna's virtual, and into his own—coming to rest once more, beside the great tilting *moai* head beside the Hanga Roa town wharf.

Medea really needs to work on her—his—good-byes, Don thought, shaking his head. In the next instant, that idea was pushed from his mind as he saw the tidal wave headed for the island, growing and looming before him.

Then it wasn't.

Easter Island leapt into the sky. Don watched in disbelief as, far below him, the tsunami crashed onto the few rocks that had been left behind, consuming them, then sped again on its way, diminishing as it went.

Checking Karuna's virtual to see that she was okay, he saw that her island, too, had been lofted into the sky—a sky from which clouds of smoke and ash and thunder were rapidly dissipating. Within moments all the threatened islands of Cybernesia were gathered around his own, floating in the ether.

"Hello, Donnie," said a weary but cheerful Medea, tattooed and headdressed like the men of Rapa Nui in Don's virtual, but barkcloth–bikinied like the women. It was difficult to say whether he was a he, or a she. "Was it good for you, too?"

"I'm impressed. How did you do it?"

"I gave the NSA's virusing system what it wanted," Medea said with a sideways grin, "and it gave me what I wanted. Our manipulations allowed their system to be deployed in ways that extended beyond what its creators intended."

"How so?"

"Really, Donnie—you don't expect me to give away all my

trade secrets, do you? Let's just say I appreciate the verisimilitudes of vicissitude, the vicissitudes of verisimilitude—"

"Which means?" he asked, growing irritated with M-I's doublespeak.

Medea-Indahar sighed loudly.

"I arranged for the virusing system to be able to find *more readily* the Kwok postings it wanted to eliminate in various islands of Cybernesia—if you *must* be so technical. In turn, it destroyed these postings, instead of destroying the islands in which the material was embedded. The Kwok materials are lost, alas. It *had* to have those. But a big chunk of Cybernesia was saved."

Don nodded slowly, thinking of those rocks in his virtuality. The ones that had been obliterated by the tidal wave.

"You seem to know a lot about the way the NSA works. Insider knowledge, perhaps?"

Medea-Indahar laughed, sounding tired but happy.

"Like any good parasite, I'm neither insider nor outsider. Neither friend nor enemy. Once upon a time, however, there was a project that explored the possibility of applying reconnaissance and intelligence technologies to environmental issues."

"So?"

"The environmental task force within the intelligence community was code-named 'Medea,' Donny. Figure it out for yourself."

With that, M-I disappeared from Easter Island, leaving only laughter behind, like the Cheshire cat's smile.

As the laughter faded, Don thought back on what he'd heard about that intelligence/environment interplay. He recalled how reconnaissance systems that track the movement of tanks through the desert also, over time, track the movement of the desert itself. And how photos of Russian missile silos inadvertently revealed snowmelt patterns across Central Asia over a period of several decades. Even the early-warning satellites designed to detect the flare-up of an ICBM as it emerged from its silo had been used to pinpoint fires in the Brazilian rainforest.

Maybe there *was* a point to Medea-Indahar's contortionist sexual hacking, after all.

By the time the laughter faded away completely, the islands of Cybernesia had floated down to the surface of the sea once more. Don reflected on a myth of Oceania, in which the lands of the world were created from the feathers of a great bird flying over the sea. Looking up, he saw no great bird, yet the worlds in which he lived suddenly seemed less substantial than a feather. He needed to ground his world again, but on what rock could he build?

All he could think of was what M-I had been working on that last time in Crash Village, and how that might apply to the holo-cast Kwok had sent, uncalled for and unwanted. Then and there, he vowed to follow those leads for as long as it took, to wherever they might guide him.

TRACES IN THE WORLD

KOWLOON

CHECK THE KWOK SAMPLES for something more than physical characteristics. More than just chemical or biological. Those ashes may contain information of another sort. Data.

Fine, Marilyn Lu thought, *but* how?

She'd been banging her head against that for days and days. Cause of death usually fell into one of four categories: natural, accidental, suicidal, homicidal. Nothing about Kwok's decease seemed particularly natural, yet there was no evidence that anyone had been in the room with him when he met his end. And it was awfully hard to rule out *anything* without body or bones to examine.

Staring vacantly at a microscope-slide cover, she realized her husband and daughter must think her insane. Coming down to the lab in the middle of the night, physically exhausted but mentally obsessed, she had left Sonny in bed and Clara asleep. She didn't think Sonny really understood why she felt somehow *responsible* for Charlie Hui's death. Clara hadn't been particularly happy either, about all the time her mother had been spending on this case, even making a comment at dinner about getting herself a life-size cardboard cutout of Mum. . . .

"Damn!" A slicing pain in her right thumb snapped her back to the here and now. She had sliced the tip of her thumb on the edge of the slide cover. Should have gloved up, but too late now. The bright red blood was flowing.

She snatched her hand away from the slide, but blood had already made its way onto the slide and into the sample that lay there. Trying to stanch the flow and not wanting to further contaminate the slide, she gripped her right thumb tightly with her left hand and swung away from the table, inadvertently leaving a trail of red droplets across the tabletop. Two of them fell into a watch glass containing some of the Kwok ash samples—one dead center in the gray-pink stuff, the other off toward an edge.

"Great. I've probably ruined this whole sample!"

As she jumped toward the nearest first-aid box, thoughts of hepatitis danced in the darker corners of her mind. In her forebrain she still hoped she would be able to salvage something from the particular sample she was working with, that she hadn't contaminated it beyond all repair.

She opened the first-aid box one-handed, taking gauze and med-spray bottles from inside. Holding gauze in her left hand, she mopped up the blood on her right finger and palm. Once the bleeding began to slow in response to pressure, she sprayed the cut with peroxide disinfectant, then with an antibacterial/antifungal, then finally closed the wound off with a spray-on bandage.

The bandage would need only a few moments to set. She would need more time than that to face the consequences of her screwup and the prospect of having to throw away her night's work. In avoidance mode and with the excuse of blood and pain, she wandered away, not quite aimlessly.

The crime labs took up the entire floor here. Walking through the maze of rooms and corridors among the few quiet, white lab-coated techs who pulled the graveyard shift, Lu was reminded of every lab class she ever took in college. Long tabletop work spaces, with supply drawers underneath. Sinks and fume hoods. Micro-scopes. Burners. Calipers. Clamps. Racks for glassware. Slides. Test tubes. Pipettes. Ehrlenmeyer flasks. Distillation columns. Refrig-erators for samples. Reagents in plastic and glass bottles. Biohazard plastic trash cans. Magnetic stirrers whirling in beakers. Centrifuges. Gas chromatographs. Spectrophotometers.

More specialized items, too. An active dermestid beetle colony, for stripping any remaining flesh away from recovered bone. Au-topsy tables. Osteological equipment and instruments. Fine incre-mental measuring tools used for determining the thickness of dental enamel. X-ray machines and developing systems, mainly for odonto-logical work. Special reagents used in tests for drugs and poisons. Infrared "sweatprint" detector/analyzers. Restriction enzymes and gel sheets, DNA polymerase and radiolabeled nucleotides, for per-forming Southern Blots, radioactive probes, hybridization reactions—all for deducing the variable number tandem repeats, the VNTRs, of introns composing the DNA fingerprint.

Scientific police work had always interested her. This was where science hit the street, very often in matters of life and death. The materials normally dealt with in the labs were almost exclu-sively physical, chemical, and biological.

In working on Jaron Kwok's remains, however, the traditional armamentarium of science seemed to have failed her.

Under the microscopes available to her, Kwok's ashes remained the same random junk, only larger. In hopes of finding *some* kind of pattern, she had sent a small sample out for testing under a scan-ning electron microscope—equipment they did not, alas, possess here in Criminalistics. She had yet to receive a report on the sample.

All the other tests on the ash had yielded ambiguous results. The gas chromatograph and spectrophotometer tests showed peaks resembling the chemical composition of organics, even readings of sugars, phosphate groups, and nitrogenous bases suspiciously close to nucleotides. But other peaks suggested inorganics, including gold and rare earths.

Lu had also run samples through standard DNA-fingerprinting techniques. For her trouble she got back a new mystery, and nothing that resembled a standard fingerprint.

Most of the stuff she had recovered from the Kwok site was much harder to denature than ordinary DNA. The map of restriction enzyme action didn't match any known set of nucleotides. Gel electrophoresis in both agarose and polyacrylamide gel, with both ethidium bromide and radioactive markers, likewise yielded results all over the map. The Kwok samples hybridized strangely, if at all, and with low, weird homologies. The patterns of VNTRs—if that's what they were—looked like nothing she had ever seen.

Lu Mei-lin found herself standing at the doorway to the Dermatoglyphics Lab. When she had first started in forensics work, people still called it the Fingerprint Lab. But since the fingers, palms, and soles of the feet were all marked with friction ridges, the all-encompassing "Dermatoglyphics" was more accurate.

Lately she had spent a good deal of time looking at the dermatoglyphic evidence from Kwok's suite—some palmprints, but most of it good fingerprints. She had studied those fingerprints so often she felt she could identify them from memory.

Stepping inside the lab, she saw that someone had pinned to the far wall two poster-sized graphics displaying fingerprint images. The left one illustrated the human sexual dimorphism inherent to fingerprint ridge breadth. The poster on the right, though, showed a pair of differing thumbprints, each with curiously identical DNA profiles below.

According to a caption, the poster fingerprints had been taken from identical twins whose DNA sequences were indistinguishable. Despite a good deal of similarity, however, the twins' fingerprints weren't at all the same, and could be readily distinguished one from the other by nearly anyone with fingerprinting expertise. Even within that small space of the womb there had been enough differences to influence these genetically identical twins to develop in subtly different ways—and the influences had continued long after birth.

Mei-lin stared at her own thumbs. The top of one was capped with dull white spraybandage.

Every fingerprint left traces in the world, sweat and amino acids lingering in the shape of the print. But the world also left traces in every fingerprint, too. *And the top of my right thumbprint,* Mei-lin thought, *will always have a thin trace of scar tissue—just because my lab technique was so sloppy.*

Having spent enough time in the labyrinths of her fingerprints, she put her hands down and turned to leave, thinking she was at last ready to face this evening's small but bloody catastrophe.

Walking back into her lab, she turned her attention to cleaning up after her absentminded clumsiness. As she was picking up the watch glass to throw into a biohazard bin, she stopped and stared. A nonidentical pair of spirals—like oversized fingerprints, or tiny tabletop galaxies—had formed where the drops of her blood had been absorbed by the grayish stuff of Kwok's remains.

Odd that the blood should dry in such a specific pattern, she thought. And the smaller droplet, which had originally fallen toward the rim of the watch glass, had *moved.* It had started out well clear of the sample, but now it was closer to the center.

She looked down at the spoiled slide and its cover, on which she had cut her finger. Whether from whim or intuition, she placed the slide under the microscope.

What she saw on the slide made her catch her breath. The blood-spoiled sample didn't look at all like jumbled junk anymore. A fine-grained, subtle form of order had appeared there, but *how* fine grained and *how* orderly her microscope didn't have the resolution to show her.

She really wanted to see those electron micrographs. Now.

The microscope was efficient enough to register the presence of movement, though. The longer she watched the jittering on the slide, the more rhythmic it seemed to become. She wondered if it was some kind of chemical reaction. Like the rhythmic oscillations of

Belousov-Zhabotinskii reactions, only faster. The longer she peered at the oscillations, however, the less they looked chemical. Something about the movement reminded her of the flagella of cells beating in unison, or the workings of an ensemble of interconnected machines.

She leaned back from the 'scope, rubbing her eyes. When she looked again, though, the vision of microsmic activity hadn't gone away. It was almost hypnotically intriguing to watch, but finally she turned away again so she could think. Or try to.

Cho had said Kwok's ashes might contain data. Information. But this stuff wasn't behaving like data. Some sort of *activity* was occurring under that microscope. Not information, but the *processing* of information. Like something performed by a mechanism, or innumerable tiny mechanisms.

Nanotech? No—too chaotic for that. Biotech? No, not quite. What was the word she'd heard? In Kwok's holo-cast—the one Ben Cho steered her to?

Slow down, she told herself. *Get some kind of proof, confirm some repeatability.* Make sure this isn't a late-night delusion brought on by too much stress and too little sleep. Blood agar plates. *Yes!* Streak out the specimens and see if this stuff does on them what it was doing on her blood.

She stood up and headed to a refrigerator. Grabbing several short stacks of Petri dishes containing different types of growth media, she realized she had never before tried to culture anything from the ashes of a dead man.

First time for everything.

She popped dish covers and streaked small amounts of Kwok's ashes onto the different media surfaces. Once she had finished streaking the specimens, she sealed the dishes with plastic film and shuttled them to shelves in incubators. Her task completed, she looked once more at the odd goings-on under the microscope.

Despite the strangeness of it, she was tempted to shout out about her discovery. She restrained herself only because she realized she needed to seal the luckily contaminated slide and watch glass in plastic film—and quickly, just in case whatever was happening on them had any tendency to spread or aerosolize.

Before, she'd been worried about contaminating the stuff on the slide and watch glass, but now she was beginning to wonder if she shouldn't start worrying about that stuff contaminating *her*—and everything else. She hoped it hadn't done so already.

She paused for a moment, wanting to share her find with someone, but with whom? Her husband and daughter wouldn't understand. Nor would the low-wage night techs. Not even that new girl, Patsy Hon—the one who kept her hair pulled back dominatrix-tight, so tight it looked painful. Patsy was astoundingly diligent, very quick and efficient—but painfully shy.

What about Ben Cho? How could she send word to him, though? If this stuff was hush-hush, his government and hers might both be listening in.

She would think of a way. Maybe a message tube would work. Meanwhile, the electron micrographs might come back, supporting her discovery.

Certainly Ben Cho, of all people, would want to know.

MEETING WITH WIZARDS

CRYPTO CITY

REACHING H/O'S EIGHTH FLOOR, Deputy Director Brescoll walked to the end of the hallway housing the executive suite and strode in, nodding to the woman behind the reception desk. On the walls hung framed pictures of NSA's most important worldwide listening posts: nondescript government and military buildings surrounded by satellite-dish chalices, by mushroom puffball and geodesic golf ball domes hiding eavesdropping antennas.

"Doctors Beech, Lingenfelter, and Wang are waiting for you."

"Thank you, Katie. I was expecting them."

As he entered the antique-oak ambience of his office, the three doctors stood. Shaking hands with them, then moving behind his heavy desk to sit down, Brescoll realized he'd almost be shocked to encounter any of the three without the other two. He'd always seen them as a group—the Three Musketeers overseeing the Kwok investigation. Given their high-flown academic credentials, however, maybe Musketeers wasn't quite right. Three Wizards, perhaps?

"Well, then," he said, leaning forward and folding his hands on top of his desk, glancing at each of them in turn, "what's the latest on the Kwok-Cho situation?"

Baldwin Beech cleared his throat and began his report, absently stroking his salt-and-pepper beard as he spoke.

"Cho has requested a version of the Kwok holo-cast with the audio cleaned up. We sent it to him. We also suspect that he has gained access to many of the Central Intelligence documents Kwok was working on."

"What makes you think that?"

"His research is taking him beyond the figures alluded to in the Kwok holo-cast—Felix Forrest, Giordano Bruno, Matteo Ricci, Ai Hao—and is beginning to include a host of others not mentioned in the holo-cast, or on the notecards Kwok left behind. Figures prominently mentioned in the Forrest documents."

"Such as?"

"Festugiere. Marsilio Ficino. Other translators of and commentators on the *Hermetica* of Hermes Trismegistus," Wang said, taking over from Beech, adjusting his AR glasses and reading from the materials appearing there. "Neoplatonist Raymond Lull, again, particularly his encyclopedic memory-art treatise, *Arbor scientiae*. Trithemius, abbot-necromancer of Sponheim, author of the cryptomagical *Steganographia*, the book of hidden writing. Cornelius Agrippa, particularly his *De Occulta Philosophia*. John Dee and his *True and Faithful Relation*, as well as his treatise on angel magic, his *Liber Logaeth*. A gaggle of medieval Kabbalists notable for their use of complex numerological methods intended to decipher esoteric messages hidden in the Torah, particularly the mysticocryptographic gematria and temurah approaches—"

Brescoll sat back heavily in his chair. Deep historical approaches to cryptologic problems were by no means unknown in the NSA, but to him these smelled of the CIA's Tetragrammaton connections. He knew a good deal about this archaic crypto stuff now, having been brought up to speed with a little help from his fly-fishing friends, but he had decided to continue playing the obtuse and obstinate bureaucrat, at least for a while.

"How did you determine all that?"

"We've been monitoring Cho's computer research and the materials he's ordered or withdrawn from libraries," Bree Lingenfelter said, shrugging back red bangs from her eyes. "We used some of the same approaches for tracking Kwok's work. There's a surprising amount of overlap between the research Kwok did and what Cho has recently embarked on."

"So much overlap," Wang interjected, "that we have to believe someone has given Cho access to those documents we've withheld from the current investigation."

"Who?"

Beech, Wang, and Lingenfelter glanced at one another before Beech answered.

"We think it was Kwok's widow, Cherise LeMoyne. She's the likeliest suspect. We don't know how or why she effected the transfer, or when she might have gotten copies of the documents—"

"—but she *was* married to Kwok," said Lingenfelter, "and she *did* meet with Cho at Kwok's memorial service."

Jim nodded, thoughtful.

"Any other persons or groups showing a similar pattern of 'research'?"

"Some significant correlations with a couple of Cybernesians probing Tetragrammaton," Beech said flatly. "Their address routings disappear into informational black holes—Potemkin e-mail

addresses, temporary cell numbers, borrowed IPs in the Free Zone—
so we can't pin down their exact locations."

"Interest from the New Teachings Warriors and the Cheng tong,
too," Lingenfelter added. "No proof that the Cybernesians are col-
laborating with them, but the NTW and the Chengs do seem to be
cooperating with *each other*, to some degree."

"What about that detective in Hong Kong?"

"Marilyn Lu," Beech said. "She's in Kowloon, actually. CIA has
placed an operative in her workplace, a lab tech working in her
police district's forensics lab. The operative, a Ms. Hon, has both
medical school and Special Computing Institute background."

"This SCI person is one of *our* operatives?"

"Yes, while nominally serving in that capacity for Guoanbu,"
Beech said, unable to mask the pride in his voice. "She has pro-
vided excellent insider information on Guoanbu and SCI interpre-
tations of the Kwok 'cast. Our infosphere searches show—and Ms.
Hon confirms—that Lu's done nothing along the memory-palace,
Kabbalah, or hermetic lines."

"At least *somebody* involved in this mess is still living in the
twenty-first century," Brescoll said, playing to the hilt the role he'd
chosen. "That's what I don't get. What is it about these four hundred-
year-old magical memory systems that got Kwok going in the first
place—and now Cho? Not only them, but the Cybernesians and
Muslim extremists and crime clans, too."

The glance passed among his three wizards again, and this time
Beech answered.

"They have to be interested in secrecy and security issues. At
least that's what it seems on the face of it."

Secrecy and security issues—my ass! Brescoll thought. He had
no doubt as to what everyone was looking for in this maze of activity: something that would help them create the ultimate crypto-
computer, giving them access to the rest of the world's secrets, while
maintaining their own.

And what if this wasn't just about the PRC and the USA? He
thought of stealthy electronic ghosts—terrorists sliding easily past

security screens, thieves walking through the walls of banks, national treasuries, transnational corporations—and he cringed inwardly.

"The cryptologic-grail quest leads to some strange places, though," Wang was saying. "Permutations, combinations, and abbreviations of Kabbalah's holy code systems—gematria, temurah, and notarikon—trace back at least as far as the *Maaseh Merkava* of Rabbi Akiva ben Joseph."

"Who was—?" Brescoll asked, though he was pretty sure he knew.

"He taught his believers that they could come closer to the divine by intensely visualizing heavenly palaces in their minds—and that meditations on these mental palaces were so powerful they could be accompanied by altered states of consciousness, overwhelming ecstasies, and out-of-body experiences."

"There's a passage in the *Hermetica*, too," Beech added, "that claims 'If you embrace in thought all things at once, time, place, substance, quality, you will comprehend God.' By creating a representation of the universe within his own 'higher mind,' the seeker could ascend and unite with God."

"The great dream of the Kabbalists and Hermeticists," Wang said, nodding. "To know, instantaneously and simultaneously, everything that could be comprehended—and thereby unite with the Supreme Being."

"How is *that* relevant to contemporary cryptology?" Brescoll asked, hoping he wasn't overplaying the annoyance in his voice.

"The idea of 'instantaneously and simultaneously,' " Lingenfelter said, "is where quantum cryptanalysis and contemporary cryptography might be seen as fulfilling the Hermeticist's dreams. The idea of computing everything, all at once. Maybe Cho shares that fascination now, too."

"The magically operated animistic universe of the Renaissance magus," Beech said, "prepared the way for the mathematically operated mechanistic universe that began with Newton. It took both to prepare the way for our Age of Code. Maybe part of what Dr. Wang called a 'grail quest' is about rediscovering living-fossil codes.

Cryptologic systems of potentially enormous power which we've overlooked, but which are still very much 'alive,' despite being dormant for decades, or even centuries."

"That's pretty heady stuff," said the deputy director, milking it, "but frankly, I think it's a rather romantic notion that any sort of 'living fossil' information out of the past has ever told the future anything it didn't already know. I can't think of a single instance of it actually happening."

"The Archimedes palimpsest," said Beech.

"The what?"

"Around the year 1200, a monk who was short of writing paper scraped down the only extant copy of Archimedes' treatise on method and wrote a prayer book over it. Archimedes originally wrote the treatise in the third century BC. Some of its mathematical insights, like summing infinities, weren't equalled or exceeded until Newton and Leibniz developed calculus, almost two millennia after Archimedes wrote the treatise."

"So?"

"Think of how a mathematician in, say, the early sixteenth century—almost two centuries before Newton's work—would have benefited from being able to read Archimedes' treatise. In looking into these sixteenth-century crypto systems, *we* might be in the same position that sixteenth-century mathematician was in, with regard to Archimedes: able to make a great leap into the future, if we can only find the right document out of the past."

"I still don't see how all this theory has any real-word application."

"The chaoticians suggest it's at the boundaries of chaos that information gets its toe into the physical world," Wang said. "Perhaps that's the case with Kwok and these living-fossil codes."

"What are you saying? That Kwok spontaneously combusted because he wanted to have a talk with God?"

Beech shook his head dismissively.

"Both Beckwith and Cho suggest that 'spontaneous combustion' isn't the right description."

"I've read their reports," Brescoll said, heightening the frustration. "They give no real explanation for that quasi-ashen Shroud of Turin that Kwok left behind when he vanished. Can you do any better?"

That glance passed a third time among the three scientists.

"We believe we can," said Lingenfelter. "Scanning electron microscopy indicates that Kwok's 'ashes' are in fact made up mostly of organic mechanisms possessing both nanotech and biotech properties—"

"Binotech constructs?" Brescoll asked. Suddenly he found himself much more concerned, and no longer acting. There had been nothing about *that* from his fly-fishing friends.

"We think so. We're having them run through sensitive-wire and nanofluidics tests, now. Currently the constructs appear to be dormant or inert. We're trying to figure out if they can be activated, and how."

"But if that ash is mostly binotech, then where did all of it come from?"

"In the electron micrographs," Wang said, "the constructs bear at least some superficial resemblance to the machine-communication implants we funded for Kwok not long before he died. How those binotech prototypes changed and multiplied—if that's what they did—we don't know yet."

"Ms. Hon, the operative in Lu's lab," Beech said, "reports that Lu requested electron micrographs of her Kwok ash samples. Hon's latest report indicates that, after working with the ash and then obtaining electron micrographs of it, Lu sent Ben Cho a biometrically secured message cylinder. We presume that she has already, or will soon, inform him of the nature of that 'ash.' So we've arrived at a point where we must decide how much of our information we should let Cho have."

Brescoll nodded, mulling over the implications. How much did Guoanbu know about this? There was evidence China had for some time been working on its own binotech, or something similar, in its Bletchley Parks. If they got Cho, would it tip America's hand?

"Most likely Cho already suspects it's not ash," Brescoll said at last. "It shouldn't do much harm to suggest what the ash might actually be. But keep your own progress on activating these binotech constructs—if that's what they are—close to the vest. Cho doesn't need to know how to activate them, assuming they *can* be activated."

"We thought that, given his contacts with Lu and LeMoyne," Beech said, "it might be wise to keep him under closer surveillance, as well. CIA has already inserted an operative into Cho's Brazilian jiu-jitsu class."

"Why the jiu-jitsu class?" Brescoll asked.

"We didn't have much choice. He's on leave from his teaching position, and doesn't get out of the house to socialize much. He used to take the class with his wife. It's one of his few routines which brings him into regular contact with new or unfamiliar people."

"I see. We need to place Kwok's widow under closer observation, too."

"Already done," Beech said, offering no further explanation. More CIA involvement? Brescoll wondered how busy Beech's friends in the Company had been—and how much of their activity was being kept "dark," even from NSA.

"We don't want another security breach like the one that allowed her to give Cho those documents," Brescoll continued. "And we don't want Cho to end up the way Kwok did, either, if we can help it."

Wang, Lingenfelter, and Beech agreed. The three said their good-byes and departed.

Brescoll sat in his office, alone. He powered up his slim desktop computer and clicked on the software that enabled it to play live cable news broadcasts. On-screen, a Chinese government spokesman condemned Nepal for serving as a haven for terrorists and as a transshipment point for illegal arms flowing into the Chinese province of Tibet. If Nepal didn't bring these activities to a complete halt immediately, the spokesman threatened, his government would view the delay as hostile action and would, in self-defense, launch a preemptive strike against Nepal to prevent future Tibetan terrorist activities.

Brescoll scowled. Another instance of a superpower citing a supposed threat from a smaller and weaker nation, as grounds for an invasion. He shook his head and changed the channel, but the news wasn't any better there. Before a large San Francisco crowd, California secessionist leader Tom Garrity raged against the "Military Industrial Media Energy cabal" that had "hijacked the government through a Supreme Court–assisted coup d'etat." Despite the signs Garrity's followers carried—The MIME Will Not Silence Us!—Homeland Security had begun cracking down on the secessionists, on the grounds that they had been linked to international terrorists and a Chinese spy ring.

Possible, Jim thought, *but unlikely*. Garrity's vision, of a Pacific Rim Federation or "Pacificate"—a loose-limbed political entity bestriding the world from Point Barrow to Tierra del Fuego, from Seattle to Sydney and Shanghai to Santiago—was as much anathema to the Chinese as it was to Homeland Security.

He sighed. Sometimes Garrity's people made a certain Jeffersonian sort of sense, but neither the Tibetan secessionists in Nepal nor the California secessionists in San Francisco were making the world a more stable and predictable place. That wasn't their goal, he supposed.

As the day's news continued to churn and burn on the screen, he pondered his meeting with the three wizards. Chinese binotech. Snooping by Islamic extremists, Cybernesians, and crime clans. Gypsies, tramps, and thieves. Everyone looking for a way to become like God. And he would have to frame all of it in his next report to the director, in such a way that she would assume he knew everything he was supposed to know, and wouldn't guess that he knew anything he *wasn't* supposed to know.

FIVE

UNDULATIONS

SOUTH OAKLAND

BEN CHO DRANK ANOTHER BEER and took in the high-tech low-life ambience of the Go-Go Gomorrah nudie bar. The place was a vintage strip club. Pounding robo-techno dance tracks. Cavernous darkness punctuated by pattern-lasers and pulse-strobes. Surgically augmented exotic dancers, performing the usual simulated sex-o-batics. From within his alcoholic haze, Ben wondered why he was here.

"Aggh," groaned Ike Carlson, Ben's guide on tonight's debauchery tour. Flicking his ponytail and stroking his goatee, Carlson joined him at a table just big enough to hold their latest pitcher and two mugs of beer. "Sorry I took so long, but there was a waiting line in the head. Two old codgers yakking away, taking forever to shake the dew off their lilies. Man, the only thing worse than hearing a couple of old boomers complain about their failures is hearing them complain about their successes. The girls started to repeat yet?"

"No," Ben said, "at least not as far as I can tell. The dance moves are beginning to look pretty familiar, though."

Carlson nodded. Standing, Ben excused himself and made his woozy, wobbly way to the toilet—which he found to be unoccupied, Ike's report notwithstanding. When he returned to their table, Ike had a surprise for him.

"Hey, I set up a lap dance for you with one of the girls. I think you'll appreciate my taste."

"How much will it set me back?"

"Don't worry. I got it covered. My treat. You need it."

A moment later a young woman with dark blond hair, dressed in a modified hillbilly outfit, approached their table.

"This your friend?" she asked Ike, who nodded. She turned to Ben. "Hi, I'm Kimberly. Are you ready for your private dance?"

Ben stared at Carlson, who laughed.

"Yeah, baby," Ike said, "he's ready for you to make his privates dance!"

Taking Ben by the hand, she laughed off his friend's low comment, and led him past the bar and the pool players, toward a lounge with sofas and couches loosely arranged around a wall-screen TV. The screen showed the girl who was currently dancing on the main stage. After a moment Ben realized that the on-screen image—a high-angle, single-perspective, middle-distance shot—was being fed to the TV by one of the club's ceiling-mounted internal security cameras, mixing voyeurism and surveillance to odd effect.

"We've got plenty of time," Kimberly said, noting his gaze. "I'm not due onstage for three more girls."

As Kimberly sat down on the sofa, Ben realized that for the women doing private dances here in the back lounge, the screen was a stage clock. Kimberly patted the heavy cushion on the sofa beside her. Slowly taking the hint, Ben sat down.

Through small talk, Ben learned how many nights per week Kimberly worked this club, that she was 5'2", and twenty-three years old. The area around her eyes made him wonder whether she might be a bit older than that, but he took her at her word. Although he didn't say so, she reminded him eerily of Reyna when they had first met. About the same height, age, and hair color. Even a similar figure: a not-inconsiderable bust on a small frame. Boyish hips and thin legs, too. He paranoid-flashed on it for an instant, then dismissed the thought that meeting her was some kind of setup—only to find that his arousal and self-consciousness both lingered.

When she asked what his own occupation was, Ben was taken off guard. Lately, he'd been much occupied with reading and researching Jaron Kwok's notes. Saying anything about his work, however, might get him in plenty of trouble.

"I'm on leave from my professorship at Berkeley," he said. "Spending too much time doing crossword puzzles and playing computer games."

"Really? And what do you do when you're not on leave?"

"Mainly I work with undecidability and complementarity in informational and physical systems," he said. "In quantum states before observation. In Turing's halting problem."

"What's that?"

"Sort of a 'law' of computing. Say you want to run a particular program on a particular computer. You can't know beforehand whether, for a given input, the computer will halt—that is, come to closure and output—or end up working endlessly on the input you gave it. The only way to find out whether or not the system halts or goes into some kind of infinite loop is to run it. You can't know it until you do it."

"Sounds like a rule of thumb for everyday life," Kimberly said, smiling and looking almost as if she cared. "How do you know what can or can't be done until you try, y'know?"

"Very true!" he said, the alcohol and her attention further loosening his tongue. "Undecidability and complementarity reflect the deep structure of the universe, if you ask me."

"How so?"

"Everywhere you look you find incompatible properties not simultaneously observable," Ben said, thinking of definitions and examples from the Kwok notes. "Yet, despite their incompatibility, each is essential to whole understanding. Observation is 'either/or,' but understanding is 'not only . . . but also.' You see it in Heisenbergian uncertainty on the position versus the momentum of a particle, even in the wave/particle duality itself."

"What's that?"

His physics-machismo challenged, Ben tried to think of a way to explain it. Finally he came up with one.

"Easier to show than to tell," he said. "If you can get me scissors, a sheet of paper, and tape or paste, I can make you a model. . . ."

Kimberly gave him an odd smile and stood up.

"Never let it be said I don't go the extra mile for my clients. I'll be right back."

She returned from the women's dressing area with scissors, paper, and tape. As Kimberly looked on, Ben cut a long rectangular strip of paper, gave the paper a half twist, and taped the ends together.

"Okay," he said, holding it up to her. "This is a Möbius strip. It's a one-sided object. The outside becomes the inside and the inside becomes the outside, because it has only one side. The same is true of the edge. It looks like it has two but in fact it only has one. A single surface and a single edge. Take a right-handed glove, embed it in that surface, send it on a trip around the Möbius, and it becomes a left-handed glove, its own mirror image."

"My geometry teacher in high school showed us one of those," Kimberly said, nodding. "And a weird shaped bottle, too."

"Right. Probably a Klein bottle, which has one surface and no edges. Cutting a Klein bottle into mirror-symmetric halves results in two Möbius strips, while attaching the edge of one Möbius strip to its mirror image twin forms a Klein bottle, topologically speaking. For our purposes we can keep it simple and say that the Möbius strip is analogous to the quantum state before observation."

"That's 'simple'?" Kimberly asked, cocking an eyebrow.

"Sure. The Möbius is neither a sheet nor a loop, yet it's *both* a sheet and a loop. Neither wave nor particle, but always potentially both. Cut it crosswise, and it collapses into a simple rectangular sheet, a strip of paper. Let's call that a 'wave.'

"But cut a Möbius strip lengthwise down the middle like this, and you get a longer, double-twisted loop. Cut it lengthwise again and you get a pair of interlocking double-twisted loops. You can keep cutting those loops lengthwise, finer and finer, more loops and twists again and again, until infinity runs out. We can call those 'particles.' "

"I think I get it," Kimberly said. "And this is evidence of what, again—Professor?"

"Incompatible properties not simultaneously observable, yet coexisting at a deeper level nonetheless. You find it in mathematics and quantum computing—'ones' and 'zeroes,' if you like. You find it in language, particularly in code writing, where each letter in a transposition cipher retains its identity but changes its position, while in a substitution cipher each letter changes its identity but retains its position. It's so universal it almost seems like a pattern in the mind of God."

"And *that* sounds like science fiction," Kimberly said. "I don't read the stuff."

"What do you read?"

"Henry Miller and Virginia Woolf, lately."

"Really! What Woolf have you been reading?"

"I just finished *Mrs. Dalloway*. I'm reading *To the Lighthouse* right now."

"Have you read *The Waves*?" Ben asked. "I highly recommend it. Stream of consciousness, kind of like James Joyce. Have you read any Joyce?"

"Just *Dubliners*. I haven't been able to make time for *Ulysses* or *Finnegan's Wake*."

"You should, sometime in your life," Ben said, wondering if the booze made him sound too professorial. "If you like Miller, you might want to try Pynchon and Burroughs and Wallace, too."

Glancing at the screen, she stood up and leaned over in front of him.

"We'd better get down to it," she said, crouching and spreading his knees apart, looking up at him from between them.

"Right," he said, taking a large bill from his wallet. "Will this cover it?"

"No need. Your friend's already paid."

"Oh, that's right."

Kimberly squeezed her breasts together and rubbed their exposed tops against his head, face, and upper body. Soon she was undulating her entire torso against his. Dropping her tight shorts, she gyrated her pantied crotch in front of his face. Pulling at the sides of her panties, she revealed a cartoonishly cute image imprinted on the skin, left and slightly south of her right hip.

"Is that a 'Hello Kitty!' tattoo?" Ben asked.

"Bingo," she said. "I grew up in San Diego—lots of tattoo parlors. Really loved 'Hello Kitty!' when I was thirteen. Then it was 'Sailor Moon.' Eventually it was 'Hello, Sailor!' "

He laughed in surprise. Turning around to face the wallscreen TV, she rubbed her buttocks vigorously against his crotch, then ended with one last breast-press against his face, before cupping his smile in her hands.

He enjoyed it more than he felt he had any right to. They exchanged thanks, and she told him again what nights she worked.

"Check out my dance before you go," she said as they made their quick good-byes. "I'm no Möbius stripper, but I can shake it as well as anybody in town. Come see me again soon."

Ben nodded and watched her go, then got up and made his way back to the table.

"Well," Ike said when Ben returned, "how was it?"

"Great," Ben said, then smiled crookedly. "We talked about the intersection of quantum mechanics, topology, and information theory, and about modern and postmodern novels. Not exactly what I expected in a strip club, but fun."

"You sure know how to show a girl a good time," Ike said wryly. "I'm glad you approved of my choice."

"Definitely. She's eager to see me again soon."

Ike's eyes narrowed, then he laughed.

"Just don't say 'I think she really liked me!' I'll never be able to look at you with a straight face again."

They laughed. Soon Kimberly danced onto the stage and they took seats at the bar rail around the stage. In the course of her act she showed off her tattoo again, and fully revealed her breasts.

"See?" Ike said. "I knew they were real. No implants—I could tell."

They staggered out to Ike's car not long after Kimberly finished. Ben rambled on about the two biggest types of implants, cosmetic and electronic, before passing out on the way home. He had a quick flash of a dream about a woman whose breast enhancements flashed corporate logos from just beneath the skin, subdermal neon tattoos. He awoke to find Ike shaking him.

"Oakland Hills," Ike said. "All passengers must exit the vehicle. See you at jiu-jitsu."

Ben gave a groggy good-bye, then watched as his new friend's car slid away. He stared at the late-night lights of Oakland and San Francisco spread out on the plain below, glitter marching toward the ocean under the moon. Turning and staggering up the steps to his front door, he fumbled with his keys and nearly fell into the house when the door finally swung open.

Woo, he thought. *Road of excess. Palace of wisdom. Life is like spelunking. Sometimes you have to go through some mighty dark places before you can really appreciate the light.*

"Life is like spelunking," he professed drunkenly to himself, having no small difficulty with that *s* word while making his way down the entry hall. "Life is like spelunking. . . ."

He repeated the small mantra until he almost managed to believe it. Almost made it to the master bedroom, too, before the guilt hit and he began thinking confusedly. Of Reyna. Of those few bad months, after he broke off all communication with his parents, but before he met Reyna. Of his nights spent drunk in strange hotel rooms, pissing in the sink, drinking from the toilet, after yet another failed pursuit of still stranger women. Of his mother bitterly protesting, "Everybody always blames the mother, especially when she's black."

Reyna had saved him from himself, then. But now she was gone—because he hadn't been able to save *her*. With Reyna, he'd been able to put away all the darkness of his past, avoid the behaviors he might otherwise have fallen into—like becoming a pay-for-play strip club habitué. Without her to be his anchor now, was he drifting toward disaster once again?

He sat on the edge of the bed—fully clothed, full of remorse, and in a very dark place—until he fell backward, asleep.

BEN IS STANDING in front of a hall, lecturing to a class filled with women, all of whom look like Reyna or Kimberly or Jaron Kwok's widow, Cherise. Before him on the podium stands a copy of the US Army's April 1976 publication, *The Art and Science of Psychological Operations: Case Studies of Military Application*, opened to page 666, "The problem of the unintended audience," by an author also known as Felix C. Forrest.

"The quantum undecidability of the nature of light prior to measurement arises from a true indeterminateness," he says, apropos of nothing on page 666. " 'Neither wave nor particle' asserts that, prior to measurement, light is neither one *nor* the other. 'Not both wave and particle' asserts that light, prior to measurement, isn't a combination of one *and* the other. 'Neither/nor' functions distributively, positing a doubled negative. 'Not both . . . and' functions collectively, negating a singled positive—"

A woman—whose name he somehow knows is Sophia, but who looks far too much like Reyna as a grad student—jumps up, interrupting him.

"In matters of privacy and quantum mechanics," she says, pointing her finger fiercely at him, "what is invisible to the naked eye is also naked to the invisible eye!"

—*lefty loosey, protect the male*—

—*when I touch you there, when you touch me here*—

—*sisters fighting, ants burning*—

The child Ben is crouching beside anthills with magnifying glass turned burning-lens in hand, bewildered victims twisting, smoking pismire, catching fire, but as he stands up years pass and he believes he is leaving childish things behind. Alone and naked and afraid to look at himself under the open night sky, the lights of Oakland and San Francisco spread out before him.

He looks down, and in the void he sees a sky, and in the sky there is a void dark with excess of bright, formless yet turning, an immense whirling black fog of heat, an enormous and terrible storm of the eye, blotting out the stars, uncreating the world as it moves, unsaying the word that was in the beginning. The Golden Gate Bridge disappears into it. The lights of the cities go dark. Block after block the hot silencing darkness spreads.

No barrier made by reason, order, or life can stand against the silently turning void. Waxing and growing, the eye of the invisible devours everything in its path. Before it, he is boy to wanton gods, powerless to run or hide from the tornado extending down from the body of the clouds, looking male from the outside, female from the inside.

In the last instant, even as it engulfs and melts him, even as its endarkening silence absorbs and disperses his consciousness, thinking beyond thought he understands that last time, there were victim-heroes enough to send it back. All of them haunted by the feeling that, next time—this time, *his* time—there would be no one to stop it, none who could prevail against it. . . .

BEN ROUSED TO THE SOUND of what he thought was an autumn bird-song. More than half asleep, he sat up in bed, still feeling obscurely guilty. *Too wild a night of drink and debauchery*, he thought. That, and too damned much time spent working with Kwok's docu-ments. Unlike Jaron Kwok, however, he could still appreciate wild nights. He wasn't stone-cold deaf to the world of birdcalls and sun-shine. Not yet.

As Ben came more awake, the "birdsong" resolved itself into the ringing of his doorbell. Shrugging on a red silk robe, Ben stum-bled to the front door. A courier waited there, with an electro-pen and pad for him to sign, and a thumbprint reader waiting for an impression. When Ben had done all that was required, the man handed over a slim, high-security message cylinder. Ben thanked the courier, then closed the door as the man disappeared down the front walk.

The cylinder was from Marilyn Lu. He pressed his thumbs into both ends and the flash of a retina scan—annoyingly bright—read his eyes, despite their bloodshot condition. An instant later Lu's talking head spoke to him.

"Something interesting about that 'ash,' " Lu said. "You sug-gested that it might be data, but I think it's more than that. By accident I spilled blood on some ash samples, and they reacted strangely. So I've been 'growing' them—if that's the word—on blood media. Here's what I've been finding."

On the screen inside the message tube, light-micrographs and videos appeared, showing labyrinths of dark, spiral waves, some still, others in motion. They reminded Ben of cell colony synchrony, and of carvings in neolithic passage graves. The shimmering un-dulations of the dark waves, in video, were psychedelic enough to make Ben faintly queasy.

He fought down an impulse to look away. A good thing, for what appeared next was strange indeed. *Electron* micrographs, and further videos, recorded at high-enough resolution to show in action the individuals making up those waves: busy subcellular, submicron organic mechanisms in action. Had to be. Bits of data could never move and work like that. Ben had never seen anything quite like what he was looking at, but he suspected immediately what they were.

Binotech.

The characters in the holo-cast had been talking about it—it was the leak that had so bothered his NSA masters. Jaron's notes and the audio-cleaned version of the 'cast linked the stuff to quantum DNA computers, to information density that increased as 4^N, where N was the number of "4-bits," the quantum DNA analog to gates or transistors. . . .

Shit! Jaron must have had some new binotech prototype in his implants! He was gone, but the tech was still here, rising from his ashes.

The memory of the silently turning void overlaid itself on the image of the shimmering dark waves in the video Marilyn had sent him, until finally he had to look away.

IN PLAIN SIGHT

NEW ORLEANS

DON STURM ENTERED the All You Zombies coffee bar, then stood looking over the patrons until he found Karuna. Her silky chocolate skin and braided black hair—his hands had known both well enough that at the ends of his wrists they seemed heavy, clumsy, empty now. As she looked up and spotted him, the mass of multicolored beads on her myriad tiny braids clicked together like a fall of soft rain hitting parched earth.

"So what brings you to the city below sea level?" Karuna asked, standing and offering Don a hand. He shook it awkwardly. "Must be important—it's been weeks since anyone's heard from you. Then the message you finally *did* send was so cryptic . . ."

Don glanced around the largely empty coffee bar, hoping he wasn't being too obvious—just enough to clue Karuna in. He suspected the place had the usual panoply of security devices endemic to public spaces in twenty-first–century America.

"No more cryptic than it needed to be," he said, leaning closer to her. "If I'd thought I could say what I needed to without a meat meeting, I would have."

"Why couldn't you?" Karuna asked. She cocked her head forward and to one side, and its load of rainbow-beaded braids shifted correspondingly.

"I don't trust our security," Don replied, glancing at the polished metal of the tabletop. His blue-dyed hair was reflected there, cut short in the shape of the Celtic knot tattoo that lay beneath. "Some of what I've got to say uses key words that show up on too many watch-lists."

"So you don't think we're secure? Even in Cybernesia?"

"*Especially* in Cybernesia. Medea-Indahar has too much of a presence there, and knows too much about my connection with P-Cubed."

"Well, that's gratitude for you!" Karuna hissed, annoyed now. "Medea saves Cybernesia from an NSA attack, and that doesn't count for anything?"

"Our 'savior' as good as admitted to having NSA connections, Karuna. I tell you, M-I's not to be trusted."

"Well, I seem to recall that *you* were thinking about working for NSA yourself, once upon a time."

"I was, I admit it," Don said, nodding but feeling his face grow warm. "Would have been good money, too. But then I had second thoughts, and someone or something up the chain of command found out. Killed my application. This has nothing to do with that."

"Uh-*huh*," she said, leaning back from their huddled conversation. "You know what *I* think? I think you look terrible! All pale and strung out, like you haven't been sleeping, or eating properly."

"That's got nothing to do with it, either," Don said, glancing away, out the front window. "I didn't come here to discuss my health."

"Oh?" she asked, pausing to take a sip of her coffee. "Then what *are* we here to discuss?"

He paused, framing his words carefully. "State security operations, past and present. The kind of stuff most people just shrug off as garden-variety conspiracy theories."

Karuna eyed him narrowly.

"And why should we talk about that?"

"Because believe it or not, we've already been suckered into getting involved. Though I think Medea went willingly."

"Yeah?" she said, beginning to sound peeved. "How so?"

"Remember when NSA used its Echelon systems to suck up everybody's private data, and how that led to the development of secure message cylinders? Or how Operation Shamrock covertly monitored international telegrams sent from the US—for decades?"

"Come on, Don! That's old news!"

"Or the Pentagon's plan," he continued, undaunted, "to launch a wave of violent terrorism in D.C., Miami, and New York—Operation Northwoods, the Joint Chiefs called it. American operatives secretly killing scores of American citizens and framing the Cubans for it, just so the generals could gain international support for a war against Castro."

Karuna shook her head, making her beaded braids click like an upended rainstick.

"During the *Kennedy* administration! Ancient history. And they never pulled it off."

"No," Don continued, "but what about MK Ultra? The CIA covertly testing LSD and dozens of other psychoactive substances on unknowing, innocent civilians?"

"That's not even news anymore," Karuna replied dismissively. "More ancient history."

"But do you think it's stopped?"

"Do I think *what* has stopped?"

"Do you think the government and corporations have stopped

using us all as guinea pigs, without our knowledge or consent? Do you?"

"Don, this is way off the deep end," she said, so perfunctorily as to cut off any response. "And it's got nothing to do with you, or me, or Medea. You're creeping me out."

Don took a strong slug of coffee before answering.

"It's got a helluva *lot* to do with us, actually. You remember what Kwok's holo-cast said? About 'little cellular mechanics' diagnosing and repairing cell and tissue damage? About an 'infertility-inducing virus'?"

"I vaguely recall some such weirdness, yes."

"I think that 'weirdness' is the reason NSA came after us in Cybernesia. Kwok's 'cast talked about reality as a simulation. About universal memory palaces and godlike minds. I think Jaron stumbled onto something much bigger than he expected. Something they didn't want him to have."

Karuna sipped at her coffee, staring down into the mug, then back at Don.

"Such as?"

"A program called Tetragrammaton. The wellness plague and infertility virus are part of Tetra. I think the holo-cast was Kwok's attempt to get the word out."

"Got to be easier ways than that to send a message," Karuna said, shaking her head doubtfully.

"Not if he had to send the message, and hide it at the same time. When I was in Medea-Indahar's virtuality, though—*that* was the tip-off. M-I was running some sort of Kabbalah-math program on *Tetragrammaton*."

Karuna took another sip of coffee, then pulled her stare out of her mug and again focused it onto his.

"All right," she said, "I'll bite. What on Earth is Tetragrammaton?"

"Originally, the four-letter Hebrew name for God. Either IHVH, or YHWH, or JHVH, or YHVH, depending on which orthography you follow. Yod heh vav heh. Jehovah, Yahweh. Connected to the

'Ein Sof' or Infinite in the Kabbalah, the point at infinity, *beyond* but also *containing* the sefirot, the qualities or 'countings' of the divine. I don't know if this new context is a joke or not. Regardless, it's the strange attractor underlying all the apocalyptic chaos in Kwok's holo-cast."

"Whoa," Karuna said. "You've lost me. What's the Kabbalistic word for God got to do with Kwok's virtuality? And what's this 'new context'?"

Don leaned forward again, speaking more quietly, yet more hurriedly, the latest caffeine jolt propelling his end of the conversation.

"I've been contacted by an anonymous benefactor. Someone who's seen my encryption software, and become aware of what I've been researching. They gave me access codes that led me to some very interesting places in the infosphere."

"And?"

"And near as I can figure—from data I've found on the conspiracy fringes—the Tetragrammaton program began as long-term survival studies started by various intelligence agencies during the Cold War. It may be older, I'm not sure. What I *do* know is that everybody seemed to be working on a version of it. The American CIA and DIA. The British SIS and MI6. The French DGSE, German BND, Israeli Mossad. Guoanbu in China, GRU and KGB and their successors in Russia. You name it, they all had in-house forerunners. Studying scenarios and contingencies."

"For what?"

"Human survival—in the context of the nuclear arms race, at first," Don said, stirring his coffee. "Later, when nuclear war looked less likely, the focus shifted to our boom/bust potential."

"Our what?"

"Our potential for causing environmental collapse. Too many babies, too many demands on Mother Earth. That's where Medea-Indahar came in."

"And Tetrawhozit is related—how?" Karuna asked. Don thought she was going for disinterested cynicism, but failing.

"The Tetragrammaton program evolved from all those studies by all the different agencies, and over time, the program itself became postpolitical. Today no single government or corporation is fully in control. It's got a seemingly legit front-group, too—the Tetragrammaton Consortium. This allows it to hide out in the open now. Lots of corporate sponsors. They even have a website, but it won't tell you much."

Don paused while Karuna slowly sipped her coffee.

"And exactly what does this 'Consortium' do?" she asked at last.

"Publicly, they're a high-tech love feast. A super–brain trust, with lots of support from infotech businesses and firms. Supposedly they're working toward nonimmunogenic implants to achieve a seamless mind/machine linkage. To foster a cyborgized, 'posthuman' humanity."

"That doesn't sound so threatening," Karuna said, sitting back and leaning her chin into the palm of her right hand. "You could argue we're already headed there anyway."

"Right, but—"

"But privately, they're this long-term human-survival think tank. Is that what you're saying? I'm sorry, Don. The idea of a group trying to prevent humanity from doing the lemming dive off the big cliff doesn't seem like such a bad thing to me."

"On the surface, no," Don agreed, sipping nervously at his coffee. "Covertly, though, they've done much more questionable things."

"Do tell."

Don ignored her unhelpful sarcasm.

"For starters, taking traits from so-called immortalized cancer cells, vectoring them into human cells, then putting the whole complex to work against aging. At the same time, projects to radically *decrease* birthrates through biotechnical means. Sound familiar?"

"Only from that Kwok 'cast," Karuna said with a sniff of disdain.

"Well, there's more. Bizarre, Mengele-style stuff. Long-term twin studies, inducing 'dissociative identity disorders.' Paying ob-gyns to pump expectant mothers with biochemicals during their first trimester. Without mentioning it to the patients, of course. Covert projects for manipulating what goes on inside the womb, mostly in the hope of activating 'latent' paranormal talents in the offspring."

"Whoa—again," Karuna said, shaking her head and rattling her beads. "That's taking it way too far. Why would anyone want to warp kids in the womb, even supposing they could?"

"It's all in the name of humanity," Don insisted. "In the old days, no 'atrocity' was considered inexcusable—as long as it was performed in the name of national security. Think how much more justifiable even greater atrocities become when they're being car-ried out in the name of *human* survival!"

Don paused, and watched as Karuna finished her coffee, then set the empty cup aside.

"You've lost me again. What could they hope to accomplish with these implants and in utero manipulations?"

"The fostering of paranormal abilities," Don said, wondering if speaking too quietly might also attract attention. "Mind/machine interfacing. Computer-aided psychokinesis. Electronically mediated simultaneity."

"For what purpose?" Karuna asked, sounding strangely calm now. To Don it seemed as if her cynicism was shading into a pity-ing sadness. He really *hated* that.

"To thoroughly entangle human and machine intelligence. To create tesseractors, human beings who can fold and tear the fabric of reality. For years Tetra's been working on a mathematical model for a simulated quantum information density structure. A gateway singularity into and through the fabric of space-time. This stuff makes nukes look like Fourth of July firecrackers."

"It's impossible," Karuna said firmly. "That's like claiming you've got a wormhole generator in your back pocket."

"No, it's *not* impossible. The holographic principle from quantum gravity theory restricts the amount of information a given region of space-time can contain: one bit of information per quantum of area, 10^{-35} meters on a side. But if you bust the bandwidth limitation of the universe, you can create the gateway."

Karuna stared. He was losing her.

"Where is all this coming from?"

Don finished the last of his coffee. Having been wired up for days, he hardly needed it.

"I already told you. I've been doing my research, with a little help from some friendly strangers."

"Your 'anonymous benefactors'?"

"Right. It's all out there, if you know where to look. All it takes is putting the pieces together."

Karuna stared so hard at him that it was all Don could do to keep from cringing beneath her gaze.

"That's the part that scares me," she said, her look softening at last. "You're talking like you've been spending way too much time on the fringe. Too much of the web is dedicated to rumor and stupidity. And what do you really know about this 'anonymous benefactor'? How much of what you're telling me has even the vaguest link with reality?"

She shook her head.

"Don, you know you're a pattern phreak—"

"If you think I'm acting paranoid, or schizophrenic," he said, suddenly annoyed, "then just say it."

"All right then. It sounds like your mental elevator has lost its brake and is dropping straight to hell. Pull out of it, already! You've been at this for—what, weeks? Are you sure what you think you're seeing is *really* there?"

Don laughed.

"I know the old joke. 'Everybody sees patterns—paranoids just see patterns that aren't really there.' Apophenia. That's what the power players count on: the fact that their lies are almost easier to believe than the truth. But there's another cliché: just 'cause you're paranoid doesn't mean they're *not* out to get you. Whatever this is about, they killed Kwok to cover it up."

"None of what you've been talking about is worth killing over."

"Oh no? Tell that to the guy in the coroner's office they offed because he was working with Kwok's ashes!"

Reaching across the table and gripping his hand gently, Karuna seemed not to have heard the last part.

"Maybe, after dealing with Medea's crazy simulations," she said quietly, "with the way she/he melts away all the old binary opposites—male/female, good/evil, reality/fantasy—maybe you're suffering from some sort of meltdown. Maybe that's why you blame Medea. And maybe Tetragrammaton is just a symbol, too. A metaphor for whatever it is that's *really* getting to you."

Don pulled his hand away, and stood to leave.

"Don't try to explain it away as some homosexual panic attack!"

"Look, Kari, all I'm really asking is that you look into what I'm telling you, before you write me off as a complete lunatic. But be careful, whatever you do. If it turns out I'm right, we stand to piss off some very powerful people."

"All right, I'll look into it," she conceded. Don was disappointed to see that she didn't get up from her chair to leave with him. "And I'll be careful—though of *what*, I have no idea. So what are you going to do, now?"

Don glanced around the coffee shop again. He leaned toward her and answered in a voice not much louder than a whisper.

"I'm thinking of going to Philadelphia."

"Why there?" Karuna asked, refusing to lower her voice.

"There's a painting there I want to see."

"What painting's that?"

Don took an old-fashioned notebook from his pocket.

"*Portrait of a Gentleman*, most likely a scholar or nobleman, approximately thirty years of age. Oil on canvas, painted around

1520, probably by Dosso Dossi. Accession: J #251, in the John G. Johnson Collection, Philadelphia Museum of Art."

"That's pretty specific," Karuna said, looking worried again. "Why that one?"

"Because I found it embedded in Kwok's holo-cast. After I cleaned up the audio, I wondered if there might be other material, buried in the visual content."

"And there was."

"I found an image of that painting, among the bank of electron micrographs that the characters watch at one point. Totally out of place. Kwok's image has something not in the original painting, too. A metasteganograph."

"A what?"

"A steganograph hides information by embedding it inside other information, right? Well, the painting's presence in the holo-cast is steganographic, but what I found was embedded in the painting. *Meta*steganographic."

"How could you tell?"

"I beefed up a program for detecting and decrypting digital watermarks, applied it to the image of the painting, and it popped right up. The meta's a sort of deep content-labeling—robust, persistent, and *very* unobtrusive, but not in any way intended to prevent further copying. Whoever made it *wanted* it to be found, but not easily."

"But what is it?"

"An allegory to be unveiled only to the initiated," he said, referring to his notebook once more. "A steganographic caption across the bottom, computationally cloaked, which uncloaked reads, 'HKEDKJSAJD;OKGHFKJ;OAKJSKGHF.' "

"That's *un*cloaked?" Karuna asked, incredulous. "Sounds like gibberish to me."

"Not if you run a Fahrney keyboard transposition on it. Then it says 'Hide insane plight in plain sight'! Think about that, Kari— then think about Tetragrammaton."

"I'm thinking, Don, that I'm not following you. Again."

"In the holo-cast, everything was happening on the edge of global catastrophe. Earthquakes, apocalyptic meltdowns. Intensified that way, Kwok's scenarios are easy to interpret. They represent our 'insane plight' as a species."

"What do you mean?"

"Lemmings aren't really suicidal—just short-sighted. Like us."

"But Don, what if all that's just some sort of warped personal reference?" she said, almost too quietly, too gently.

"For Kwok—or for me? I know what you're thinking, Karuna. Nevertheless, we created the hack that helped Jaron do whatever it was he was doing. You and me. Regardless of where this is coming from, we're a part of it. And the only way to separate reality from insanity is to find out what Jaron Kwok found out."

"Then you're the one who'd better be careful," Karuna said, her eyes focused firmly on the tabletop and away from him. "Promise me?"

"I promise," he said, taking her hand and kissing it lightly before he turned to go. Don didn't look back over his shoulder as he walked away.

PLAUSIBLY DENIABLE COINCIDENCE

GUANGZHOU

MEI-LIN LU, DEREK MA, and Paul Kao stood in front of the octagonal Sun Yat-sen Memorial Hall on Dongfeng Road. Built on the original site of Sun Yat-sen's office when he was China's provisional president, the ornate blue-roofed building reminded Mei-lin of a three-tiered blue umbrella. Today it stood open against a brilliantly clear sky that posed no threat of rain. A group had just finished touring the grounds and was lining up to leave, but a few visitors lingered. The Hall itself, however, was closed to the public for repairs. A few construction workers moved in and around the scaffolding on the north side, dressed in gritty jeans and cheap camo pants.

"Let me guess," said Ma, a forensic computer technician and image analyst with Lu's department. He was there to record images of the Memorial Hall as part of Lu's ongoing investigation into the Kwok incident. "We're here because of what I found in that holocast you gave me."

Paul Kao, Derek's assistant, already had his camera out. He was panning the grounds as they walked, looking like an overweight over-eager videographer with his golfer's blue sun visor spun upside down and sideways on his head, in an outdated fashion Lu found vaguely irritating.

"Exactly," said Detective Lu as they walked past the garden beds surrounding the hall. In her more paranoid moments, Mei-lin had wondered if Ma—who seemed far too suave to be a tech—might be a Guoanbu operative assigned to her by Wong. Kao, very bright but not particularly interested in personal hygiene, more easily fit Lu's experience with techies.

The more time she spent with Ma, though, the more Mei-lin doubted that he was working for Guoanbu. She hadn't seen any evidence that he had any particular interest in the Party line, at least not so far. On the other hand, even Wong himself—who was undeniably Guoanbu—had been keeping a relatively low profile, as if playing the good political mentor. So who knew what to believe?

Detective Lu shook her head.

Nearby on its tall pediment stood the bronze statue of Dr. Sun, three times life-size. The founder of the first Chinese republic leaned on his cane, seemingly more out of a sense of style than any need for support. There was a flower bed nearby, with signs in English and Chinese. The English translation of one of the signs read Protect Gardening Against Treading On—an interesting rendering of Chinese characters that said Don't Walk On The Flowerbeds.

As they climbed the first set of low stairs to the Memorial Hall itself, Derek Ma took from his pocket a schematic of the building, and broke out his own camera.

"Paul," he said, turning to Kao and pointing out locations on the schematic, "why don't you shoot the exterior, then take the entrance at the loading dock. Go downstairs here, to where they build the sets and store the props. We'll do the interior spaces that lie aboveground."

"Will do," said Kao. "Any suggestions on what I should be looking for?"

"Nothing specific," Lu said. "Just keep your eyes open for anything that looks out of place or unusual."

Kao grunted an affirmative and strode away. By the time Lu and Ma had climbed the second set of stairs, to the red-pillared portico of the main entrance, Ma was recording everything.

"Derek, I just can't figure you out," Mei-lin said, glancing at the thin guy who stood beside her, reading glasses propped on his forehead.

"How so?"

"Here you are, the techno geek, but I know at least one person who thinks there's more to you than meets the eye. Patsy—that lab technician I moved onto my schedule?—she doesn't say much, but even *she* has noticed you. I think she's sweet on you. She says you're a top alumnus of a big martial-arts school."

"That's right," he said with an odd smile, as if he knew what was coming. "The biggest—Ta Gou Academy. Near the Shaolin temple, outside Dengfeng."

"But weren't you supposed to become a monk or something?" she asked, watching him as he methodically recorded every detail of their surroundings.

"Not at all!" he said, laughing. "My parents sent me there hoping I'd come back to Hong Kong a martial-arts movie star. Their goal was to have me support them luxuriously into their old age."

"A movie star? I can almost see that. How did you end up a police tech?"

"I started training in computing and image analysis during my time in military service. After I left the military and became a police officer, I just kept working in that vein."

"That makes more sense," Lu said as they pushed through the doors into the performance hall proper. "For a while there I thought you were playing at being someone you weren't. You didn't look geeky enough to be a tech."

"Like Paul, you mean?" he asked, dropping the camera enough to toss her a sharp look. "He's not very big on social skills, but he's a nice guy, when you get to know him. So, who did you think I really was?"

"Oh, I don't know," she said, trying to figure out how to downplay her response. The space inside the hall—an open dome one hundred fifty feet high and covering nearly forty thousand square feet, with no pillars to interfere with the view—was undeniably impressive. It was also somewhat cold inside, even on a sunny autumn day. "A spy, sent to keep tabs on me, maybe."

"How do you know I'm not?" he asked, grinning mysteriously. Glancing around the large interior space, he said dramatically, "Remember, Citizen Lu, that joint cooperation with the USA only goes so far. Your efforts may well prove pivotal in our government's containment of that rogue imperial military superpower!"

"Not bad," Lu said, laughing, but Ma was already panning across the hall's interior with his camera.

"Seriously, though, any idea what Kwok thought he found here?" he asked.

"No," Lu said, growing quickly more sober, "but something about it mattered a great deal to him. He spent an entire day here. He didn't go to any of the other tourist sites in Guangzhou—not the Six Banyan Temple, not the Chen Family Memorial Hall, not the Light Tower Mosque. Just here. And he included it in the holo-cast, where the characters discuss their 'wellness plague.' "

"I know," Ma said, thoughtful. "Mixed in with all of those scanning electron micrograph images."

Lu wondered what Ma—and especially Wong—would say if they learned that she had sent *other* electron micrographs to Ben Cho in California. But she said nothing of that. Only as an afterthought did she remember to thank Ma again now, for finding that hidden material for her.

"Given the context," Mei-lin said, walking down one of the aisles toward the stage, "it was completely out of place. At least as much as that Renaissance painting."

"That's what I don't get," Ma said, following her and recording images of the hall. "Why did he go to the trouble of embedding those images? Everything else we found seemed to be electron micrographs of some kind of nanotech."

Detective Lu thought about it as she began to walk the perimeter.

"Why indeed," she agreed. "And what about the caption that was embedded in the painting?"

"If those are Kwok's words, then to what do they refer?" Ma asked, taking the camera from his face for a moment. "The painting itself? The part of the holo-cast in which they're found? Both? Neither?"

"I'm not sure," she said, peering under one seat, then another. "The painting is cryptic enough."

"Cryptic?" Ma said with a grunt, taping Lu as she searched. "That's an understatement. It's practically impenetrable. I haven't even been able to identify the source yet."

Section by section, Ma recorded the whole of the hall's interior—from the top of the dome to the floor of the hall and all the way around—then they left the performance hall proper. Abandoning the enormous interior space, they walked down corridors toward restrooms and dressing rooms.

"The holo-cast's sneering reference to our country was obvious enough," Ma said. "I really had to pay close attention, though, to find the image of this memorial hall, and the painting, *and* the caption. All were carefully hidden in the holo-cast. I don't know about the 'in plain sight' part of that caption at all, since even *that* was more deeply encrypted than your standard digital watermark. I had to search around plenty and do a bunch of uncloaking and decoding, just to find what I did."

"I appreciate the effort," Lu said, smiling gratefully. "Maybe hiding something in plain sight only works if the searchers don't know what it is they're looking for, or if they're taking something for granted and missing what's actually there."

"Maybe the same thing applies to what we're supposed to find here in the Memorial Hall," Ma commented, innocently enough.

"Perhaps," she said with a sigh. She was quickly growing frustrated with shooting empty dressing rooms and bathrooms, but they still hadn't covered nearly enough of the place. "Maybe we need to see if we can't open up the image of the Memorial Hall in the holocast, manipulate it to see if it yields up any secrets, like you did with the painting."

"Yes," Ma said, nodding, "but I already tried the same filters and data decryptions on the image of the Memorial Hall. Nothing jumped out when I did that."

"Could you try something different, then?" she asked, perhaps a little too sweetly. "Holograms, fractals—those fill up a lot of dataspace, right? You can hide a lot of ciphertext in them, if you really want to."

Derek Ma frowned.

"Mei-lin, how did I let you talk me into working on this with you? I get the feeling you're holding back more than you're telling."

"You asked me *not* to reveal my sources," Lu protested wryly. "Have you changed your mind? Do you want me to tell you everything now?"

"No, no! If working on this might end up getting me in trouble, I want to be able to claim plausible deniability."

"I understand," Lu said. "But the longer you work with me—"

"—the more *implausible* my deniability will seem. Believe me, I know."

They were interrupted by a noise—a sound like the clamor of a bird trapped inside a great drum, trying to get free. A sound like muffled firecrackers. Lu and Ma looked at each other.

"Gunshots," Ma said.

"Downstairs," Lu agreed, then thought of Kao. They both ran for the stairs. On reaching the lower floor, they practically collided with a crouching man, clad in camo fatigues, who had been creeping toward Paul Kao. Both Lu and the man in camo fired, but in the confusion their shots went wide of the mark.

Lu again fired after the man and a similarly clad comrade. She only succeeded in blowing a hole through an onion-domed minaret for what looked like the stage set of *Scheherazade*. The two men fled through the jumbled mess of wooden facades and canvas panels in the set workshop. When she looked back behind her she saw Ma kneeling beside Paul Kao. The blue visor Kao had been wearing now lay in a spreading pool of blood.

"Go on!" Ma said. "After them! I'll handle this!"

Moving stealthily, carefully, and swiftly, Lu made her way to the ground floor portico without further incident. A moment later, Ma joined her there. As they stepped out from under the blue roofs of the building to stand under the taller blue roof of the sky, they saw a battered and faded green SUV tear across the lawns and beds in front of the Memorial Hall. Shots rang out. A security guard, hit by gunfire, went down. The few people out and about on the walks and promenades jumped for cover.

"Back!" Mei-lin shouted to Ma. "Behind the pillars."

Lu, behind one red pillar, quickly checked the .50 caliber ammo of her Desert Eagle. Crouching behind another pillar Ma pulled out a police radio and called over a tactical channel. Lu heard snatches of "officer down" and "heavily armed attackers." Seeing Lu's cannon coming into play again, Ma shook his head and frowned.

"I'm no kung fu wizard—like some people I know!" Lu said.

Ma nodded, and disappeared.

Lu stepped out from behind her pillar and took aim at the hurtling vehicle. Her first round blew a hole through radiator and engine. Her second took out the windshield. The third shot took out the driver. The SUV hit the first set of steps at speed and rolled, flipping over once completely before coming up and rocking to steady on all four wheels in a large flowerbed.

Men in bargain-basement desert fatigues leapt from the vehicle, running for cover behind shrubs, sprawling behind bushes at the sound of Lu's cannon, which was firing again. From their quasi-uniforms, Lu identified them as New Teachings Warriors, the same Muslim extremist group that had captured the Huaisheng Light Tower Mosque, two years back.

The rattle of automatic weapons fire and the sound of rounds blowing chips from concrete and tile clattered around her. The boom of her heavy-barreled handgun punctuated the sound of her own footsteps as she ran from pillar to pillar, trying to keep the attackers pinned down enough that they couldn't outflank her.

Far off to her left she saw a swift-moving shadow strike down first one New Teachings Warrior, then another.

It was Ma, arming himself with captured weapons and ammo as he went. Not that he much needed the weapons. Mei-lin smiled. Ma's fast flips into and out of Eagle and Praying Mantis stances were like something from one of her father's crime novels. They would no doubt have pleased Ma's parents, too—even more so had their son been doing them on the silver screen.

The wail of police sirens rose, growing steadily closer. Two of the Warriors made a last desperate charge onto the portico, spraying rounds against the red pillars. Flying concrete shrapnel—from Lu's rounds, impacting pillars near their heads—were enough to drop the attackers, dazed and bloodied. The remaining extremists withdrew, retreating to the battered SUV in an attempt to escape.

Lu turned toward the wounded attackers on the portico, only to find that Ma had already disarmed them and had them covered with their own weapons. The SUV in the flowerbed, its engine blown, wasn't going anywhere. Police cars swarmed onto the lawns in a semicircle around it, blocking all potential escape routes. Three Warriors exited the SUV with their hands raised.

Lu and Ma shouted their presence, identifying themselves to

the armed officers warily approaching from their patrol cars. Lu marched their prisoners forward, turning them over to the Guangzhou police, where they joined their fellow thwarted terrorists in police custody. A pair of paramedics appeared, carrying a folding gurney, and Ma led them toward the stairs, and Kao. He returned a short time later, wearing a grim expression.

"That got my blood pumping!" Mei-lin said to him, after she had finished handing over their prisoners.

"My heart works fine without any such assistance," Ma said, shooting her a penetrating look. "Dammit, Mei-lin! Kao is dead!"

"Oh," Mei-lin said, brought up short. "I'm sorry."

Derek Ma stared at the handcuffed Warriors in disgust. "Don't you find it a bit strange that these rebels just *happened* to be here, visiting the Memorial Hall?"

"What makes you think it's anything more than a coincidence?" she asked.

"It's just *too* coincidental for me." He took a data disk and waved it in front of her face before popping it into his video camera. "You asked him to look for anything unusual. Well, this is from Kao's camera. He found something 'unusual,'—something 'out of place,' all right. Told me about it, just before he lost consciousness. He recorded it, too."

Ma thrust the camera into her face. Reluctantly, she watched the images play. They showed men who might have been construction workers—except for the guns they were carrying. They shoved aside props. Lifted sheets of plyboard. Moved aside painted canvas flats.

"So?"

"Think about it, Detective. They were *after* something. Looking for something. Just like us. Paul caught them in the act. And then they caught *him*."

He stalked back toward their car. Mei-lin didn't know what to say. The whole ride back from Guangzhou to the New Territories, the ghost of Paul Kao leaned forward between them, from the empty back seat, killing all conversation.

First Charlie Hui, now this. She felt as if her luck had gone bad. "Better to be lucky than smart," her father always said. At the moment she felt neither.

Frustrated with the silence, Mei-lin checked virtual mail on her palmtop while Derek drove. She found a note from her daughter about a late dinner, and an electronic return receipt from the courier company confirming that her message to Ben Cho had been delivered in the United States—verified by his thumbprints.

Mei-lin Lu stared at the fingerprints for a long time. They reminded her of prints she had seen before. So similar, so familiar, but she was too tired by the day's events to remember. After a time the whorls grew blurry in her vision. Drowsy with the lullaby of the highway, she drifted off to sleep.

SIX

CONFESSIONS AND CONUNDRUMS

New Burlton

"I SUPPOSE YOU HAVE a reason for wanting to meet me here, Doctor Cho?" Cherise LeMoyne asked as they greeted each other at the edge of an otherwise empty parking lot. "You could have returned Jaron's documents to me just about anywhere."

She's in some kind of mood, Ben thought as they walked. Something odd about the tension between them, too. He shook his head, trying not to think about it. He wasn't sure he wanted to go there.

New Burlton wasn't far from Santa Cruz, so the drive shouldn't have inconvenienced her too much. At least she was wearing a small daypack, as he had suggested—nearly identical to the one he wore himself.

"Coming out here to New Burlton," Ben said, turning and walking toward the Information Center, "might throw off anyone who might be following me. Or you."

"Well, it certainly doesn't fit my 'profile,' I'm sure. I told you I don't like these sorts of games—and see? You've got me doing it! I don't know why you're so determined to give those documents back to me in the first place."

"Because somebody broke into my house," he explained. "Disarmed the alarm and ransacked the place yesterday morning, in broad daylight. Just dumb luck that I happened to have Jaron's materials with me at my office."

"If you had Jaron's stuff with you at the office," Cherise said, frowning as she quickened her stride to keep up with him, "then how do you know that's what the burglars were after?"

"I *don't* know it, at least not for certain. But there was something odd about the way they went through my house. Not really a burglary. Nothing appeared to be missing. And I've had a lot of weird late-night calls on my telephone, but there's never anyone on the other end. An unusually high number of hits to my university website—especially when you consider that I'm very obviously on leave. Too many creepy coincidences."

"Why not just report it all to your mentors at the NSA?" Cherise asked.

"I have," he said, "but it's always possible they might be the ones doing it, you know? I'm not sure I can trust them any more than I can trust the Chinese."

"Great," Cherise said, shaking her head. "Just great. This is exactly why I didn't want Jaron to get involved with those Friendly-Fascist Crypto Commandos in the first place."

"Look, I've got to go to Hong Kong again," Ben said, plowing ahead, "and I definitely don't want to risk carrying the documents with me overseas. My place isn't secure—at least not as secure as that hidey-hole in your house. And no one has tried to break into your place, right?"

"Not that I know of."

They fell silent as they approached the New Burlton Information Center, a space dug into a hillside and browed with ferns, dogwoods, and redwoods. Decidedly low-tech, Ben observed. At least once they got away from the perimeter, there shouldn't be many surveillance cameras here.

He'd never been to New Burlton before—only fascinated by what he'd heard in the media—yet something about it struck Ben as familiar. Maybe it was the set of doors made to look like the gibbous moon. Or, rather, like the Earth rising above the horizon of the moon in an old photograph from the early days of space flight. The effect was heightened by the fact that the entire back wall of the Center was, in fact, a mural of the Earth as viewed from space.

Ben swung open a heavy door and they walked inside. Despite being underground, the Information Center was bright enough. Three skylights dropped natural light from above, augmenting the brightness that poured in from the great half circle arch of the front entry. The warm wood interior looked like a gift shop at any national park, monument, or museum.

The clerk behind the counter was a young woman dressed in simple, comfortable, earth-tone clothing. She rented Cherise and Ben augmented reality glasses programmed with audiotour commentaries and overlay visuals. As the woman demonstrated the features of the AR glasses, Cherise struck Ben as uninterested in the extreme.

Walking to the back of the underground building, they exited by way of a long shallow ramp that sloped upward into the modified forest preserve that was New Burlton. Ben was stunned by the vista that greeted them as they came again into the open air. Before him stood something like a cross between a redwood grove and an apartment complex. Bulging tree-rooms grew out of the redwood trunks in great burls—at various heights, from the ground nearly to the treetops. Fronted with porthole windows and round doors, the arboreal living spaces were connected by long hempen bridges and causeways.

"Welcome to New Burlton," the tour guide intoned from the speakers in their AR headsets, "where homes really do grow on trees!

An experimental community of the Sempervirens Project, demon-
strating an alternative way of life—"

Cherise rolled her eyes. The motion shut up the recorded tour
guide and silenced the narrative on Ben's glasses, too. He glanced
at her with clear irritation.

"Oh, sorry," Cherise said. "I didn't realize we were linked."

"That's okay," Ben said, relaxing and smiling in spite of himself. "No interest in touring an 'experimental community' today?
It's been getting a lot of media play lately."

"I was here with Jaron once, on a University tour, even before
it opened. It was his idea. One of the last things we did together.
Didn't you notice the entrance to the Information Center?"

"I thought it looked familiar," Ben said, "but I couldn't place it."

"In his holo-cast, the vault doors beneath the Tree of Knowledge are based on it."

"Oh. That explains it. On a tour, you said? Your campus is a
sponsor, then?"

"Yes, but while I was serving in the academic senate, I opposed
funding the project," Cherise said, in what Ben thought was a
haughty voice.

"Really? Why?"

"There are far more relevant projects for my campus to put its
money into than an Ewok Ecotopia or Happy Hippy Hobbiton.
But don't mind me. I don't claim to be objective about this place.
I'll just shut up and disconnect from the shared-view mode. Walk
around and judge for yourself."

Ben did so, moving among the forest alleys, staring up at the
interconnected shops and residences of the treetop village. Cherise
hung back a few paces behind him.

"—Sempervirens Project, headed by Doctor Robert Felton,
purchased this privately owned stand of eighty-year-old redwoods,
which was slated for timber harvest. As an alternative to felling the
trees, Doctor Felton envisioned locating human habitats within the
living trees themselves. Biotechnically extending the natural tendency

of redwoods to form large growths called burls, Sempervirens bio-engineers were able to coax the trees of this grove to produce, with unprecedented rapidity, uncommonly large, hollow burls suitable for human living spaces."

Ben rolled his eyes upward to pause the commentary, and turned to Cherise.

"Are you up for hiking to the Treetop Craftshop? It looks like we get the best view of everything from up there."

The two of them stared at a spiralling rope-ladder stairway. It wound its way up to and around huge burl-room bulges, before disappearing into the crown of a particularly tall and massive tree.

"Why not?" Cherise said. "I've managed it before—I can do it again. I thought you might be planning some kind of athletic adventure. Isn't that why you had me buy this backpack, complete with a three-liter water reservoir and a slurp tube?"

"Not exactly."

"Uh, oh. Why do I have a feeling I'm not going to like where this is headed?"

"No comment."

Cherise frowned, then—seeming to get the idea—frowned still more deeply. She shook her head as they began climbing. Ben opted to continue the program as they climbed, so he flashed his eyes twice to the right and the narration resumed.

"—creating spaces in the cambium layer of the burls, Semper-virens bioengineers have been able to embed windows and doors into and among the tree-rooms, without significantly disrupting the food-transporting phloem and vascular xylem channels in the great trees. The result is the prototype community of New Burlton, a grove supporting two hundred residential and business units without requiring the removal of a single redwood. Here, you cannot see the town for the trees, because the town *is* the trees."

The tour guide's narrative paused. Idly, Ben switched channels with his eyes.

"—New Burlton's resource sustainability—" Double-blink.

"—incorporates techniques ranging from compass rose to feng shui approaches—" Double-blink.

"—solar-powered composting toilets—" Double-blink. "—graywater and recycling loops for arboricultural and epiphytic hydroponic food production—" Double-blink.

Double-blink.

Double-blink.

"This biotechnically homegrown hometown," the tour guide continued, "is actually three multi-tree 'towns.' Each one is essentially a temporary encampment. To prevent strain on individual trees or groups of trees, no tree town is occupied for more than four months at a time."

"They're seminomadic, then?" Ben asked, seeing that Cherise was eavesdropping now.

"I suppose so," she said. They stopped atop a burl shaved and planed to make a platform, a rest station on their trek up the spiral stairway. "If that's the case, then the entire population of this 'community' is probably less than one hundred people. This whole grove, so much money, all for so few people!"

She must have sensed that she was back on her soapbox again. She abruptly shut up and gestured for him to continue, which Ben gladly did.

"—vision, hazily foreshadowed in Rainbow Gatherings, Temporary Autonomous Zones, Burning Man festivals, and the like," the tour guide said. Ben and Cherise moved onward and upward on their stairway into the heavens. "Doctor Felton's work at New Burlton stands in stark contrast to the intensely urbanized and machine-identified future advocated by his staunchest opponents, the cyborg materialists."

"Sounds like something out of bad science fiction," Ben said with a roll of his eyes, pausing the narration.

"It does, doesn't it?" Cherise said. "Actually, though, they're a school of academic theorists—pretty important, too, especially in the humanities."

Ben nodded and restarted the narration.

"The Sempervirens Project, however, is only one of many visionary organizations working toward the harmonizing of human culture with the needs and demands of nature's wildscape—"

Ben paused the program again as they reached the viewing platform atop the great final burl of the Treetop Craftshop.

"I'm sorry," the proprietor, a red-haired, red-bearded, pony-tailed giant of a man, said to Ben and Cherise. "You'll have to check your backpacks if you're going to come inside. Don't worry. I can watch them from here."

"I guess we'd better do as this *burly* fellow commands," Ben said, chuckling as Cherise groaned at his pun. "Nothing to fear—I figured this would happen."

Cherise looked at him with furrowed brow as he removed his pack, but followed his example and took her pack off, too, leaving it beside Ben's on a burlwood bench just outside the door. But they lingered before entering the shop. Gazing out over the grove, they saw and felt the wind pick up, blowing through the trees, causing the observation platform to sway. Distant clouds, beginning to blow onshore, proclaimed the first big storm front of the winter rainy season. Standing in that wind, Ben could appreciate the hemp-rope "safety railings" that were strung about the platform.

"This place," Cherise said, going into a fists-up fighter's stance, then staggering as if punch-drunk, "always reminds me of a boxing ring."

"I was thinking more of sailors in crow's nests, myself," Ben said. "Those guys in nineteenth-century clipper ships must have felt the whole world swaying like this. The ropes are like a ship's rigging."

"That's the problem," Cherise said, studying the undulating tree canopy around and below them. "There's no clear guideline for what New Burlton *means*. For the tech-types it's got bleeding-edge bioscience. For the eco-types, it's a redwood grove that dodged the axe."

Ben nodded. It was true: from up here it was hard to see any human habitation at all. Turning their backs to the wind, the two of them entered the shop.

"Clearly, you don't believe in this place the way Jaron did. . . ."

"No," Cherise said, picking up a redwood tchotchke carved in the shape of a bear. Her expression was somewhere between a scowl and a thoughtful reminiscence. "Jaron was too naive to follow the concept through to its logical endpoint."

Ben only half heard, and pretended not to have heard at all. He and Cherise wandered through the shop, picking up and putting down various carved and woven items. This quickly grew old, and they stepped back outside. Ben shoved aside the backpacks and took a seat on the bench.

"What do you mean, logical endpoint?"

"Jaron really thought what they're doing here was viable," Cherise said, sitting down, her gaze still focused outward among the crowns of the redwoods. "I don't."

"Why?"

"History. Politics. Economics. Religion. Look, there's something I should have told you after I lit into you that day. Accused you of being a spy."

"What?" Ben asked, cautious now. He didn't want to have to endure the Wrath of Cherise again.

"In my evil younger days," she said, "through various family connections, I served briefly as what the CIA calls a 'casual.' "

"Which is . . . ?" Ben asked, caution giving way to curiosity.

"An occasional field operative with a perfectly legitimate cover for wherever I happened to be," she said, "for whatever I was supposedly there to do. It was easy money, and a chance to travel. I didn't think writing a report or two would do any harm. Maybe I got so touchy about this whole mess because, in some ways, I'm as entangled as you or Jaron with the powers-that-be." When she looked at him, Ben nodded, but said nothing. "I'm not proud of my 'casual' past, but it cured me of a good deal of my naivete. I've seen enough not to really trust *anyone*."

"Including the people who run this place?"

"Yeah. Do you think for a minute that, if these Sempervirens people ever came to power, they'd be talking about 'choosing' this and 'voluntarily' doing that? Not a chance. They wouldn't be happy until they had us all living in the trees—by any means necessary."

Ben laughed, despite himself. "Still, I'd like to believe in what they're doing here, too—"

" 'Belief' is the problem!" Cherise said, looking into the distance, where skies were darkening rapidly. "You know how many people have killed and died as a result of *believing*? This country started out a constitutional republic, but now we're the de facto Christian States of America, because some good religious folks put God in the Pledge of Allegiance and on the pennies. Well, I don't want any part of it. I refuse to enslave myself to a belief in God, or Goddess, or Great Cthulhu. Or Nature, or 'scientific objectivity,' or 'spirit,' or 'transcendence,' for that matter."

"Or Mind with a capital *M*?" Ben asked with a sidelong glance.

"Damned right. Once we get rid of all the old superstitions, we'll realize that Nature is really just sex and death, and God is really just us. I don't believe in any 'grand narrative' of what we're all about."

Ben looked out over the grove, feeling the tree creak and sway beneath his feet, thinking of the melange of religious references he had encountered in Jaron's notes—everything from Buddhism and Taoism to Manchu shamanism and Kabbalism.

"I see your point, but I guess I'd say that the source of the killing, of the atrocities, isn't God or Goddess, but organized religion."

"It's the same thing," Cherise said with a shrug.

"But if there is no God," Ben countered, sorting it out in his own mind as he went, "if God is really just us, then whatever religion has done wasn't in the service of God, but in the service of Man. And materialism and atheism stand condemned by their own argument."

"What do you mean?" Cherise asked, eyeing him skeptically.

"Materialism as a belief system has nowhere to go," Ben said, "except to acknowledge that the atrocities it accuses religion of are in fact its own. You mentioned how many have died in the name of God, but how many die, or worse, as a result of the pursuit of material goods?"

"Nonsense! You've been reading too much from Jaron's stuff. He suffered from the diseases of Western metaphysics—and apparently they're catching."

"Oh? And what are the symptoms?"

"The rhetoric of praise and blame and guilt," Cherise replied, "and an especially unhealthy obsession with selfhood and the individual."

Armed with Jaron's notes, as well as his own thoughts, Ben was very much enjoying the chance to bandy big questions with an intelligent and—undeniably—physically attractive woman. Something dangerous about her, too. Suppressing idle speculations about what it might be like to make love with her, Ben launched what he thought was a good counterargument.

"But isn't dissolving the individual 'I' into the social 'We' a form of self-hatred?" Ben asked.

"If the self is a social construct, a corporate illusion," Cherise replied, "then there *is* no self to hate or be hated. No soul to be saved or condemned."

He wondered at her contradictions and inconsistencies, and at his own. How did she manage to hate politics, yet venerate in society? To hate the idea of individuality, yet continue to mourn the loss of an individual named Jaron Kwok?

Then he thought of his own mourning for Reyna, the guilt he felt at how much he enjoyed the company of Kimberly the stripper, and the fact that he was flirting, at least intellectually, with Cherise, much the same way that classics professor had at the memorial. Too clearly, the problems of contradiction and inconsistency weren't exclusive to Cherise.

"So the world is a better place if we replace Divinity with Society?" he asked quizzically. "Substituting a TV set in the living room for the icon of the Blessed Virgin Mary that used to be there—that's supposed to be our great leap forward?"

"I have long since stopped believing in 'great leaps forward,' "
she said, standing abruptly and looking away, beyond the trees.
"You've got to free yourself from that kind of grand-narrative argument, if you don't want to end up in disappointment and despair."

Ben rose to his feet more slowly. "Isn't the denial of grand nar-
ratives itself a grand narrative?"

"Fine, then," she said, turning back to him sharply. "So how
would you break the cycle of corruption and destruction?"

Ben looked out on the trees and thought a moment before answering. He found that some of what Cherise said reminded him of
discussions he had had with Reyna. He thought of Kwok's holo-
cast, too, with He and She and their philosophical discussions ac-
centuated by eclipses and explosions. Maybe *that* said something
about the kind of discussions Jaron and Cherise used to have when
they were married. Ben was glad to note that nothing more apocalyptic than a rainstorm was working its way onshore.

"We need to escape from the religion of materialism which venerates the physical, but denigrates the intangible," Ben said at last.
"Escape, too, from the religion of antimaterialism which venerates
the intangible, but denigrates the physical."

"That's just more compromising crap," Cherise said, shaking
her head. "Like Jaron in his last days. Half-assed Buddhist detach-
ment applied to politics—'The Left is too self-righteous, the Right
is too smug about who gets left behind'—I loathe it more than
ever."

"Why?"

"Because Jaron's *dead*. And where did his apolitical approach
get him? Ground to nothing between the millstones of politics! And
you'll never have enough data, or information, or enough knowledge, or wisdom, to bring him back. So much for 'intangibles' and
'religions'!"

Ben didn't know what to say to that. He was surprised to find
Cherise wiping tears from her eyes. He wanted to comfort her, but
didn't know how.

Remembering how hollow it had felt when friends tried to comfort him after Reyna died, he decided the best thing he could do would be to stand and witness to it in silence. As he stood and waited, though, he had the uncomfortable feeling that this whole time, when he thought they'd been discussing Big Religion, Big Science, and Big Government, they'd really been discussing something else, at least as far as Cherise was concerned.

"At the core," he said quietly, reaching out to touch her shoulder, "religion, science, government, they're all supposed to be searching for something. Jaron was searching, too. For truth, for justice—"

"—and the Middle-American Way?" Cherise asked bitterly. She shrugged off his hand, then snatched up the nearer of the two backpacks. "No thanks, Superman. I'll carry as much as I can, but keep the rest of your kryptonite to yourself."

Cherise strode away, and Ben followed her a few paces back. Down from the lofty heights of the redwood they trudged in silence.

They said nothing to each other all the way back to the parking lot, where Cherise turned abruptly to him.

"I'm sorry about what happened," she said as they stood awkwardly beside her car. "Seems I'm always blowing up at you, then apologizing. It doesn't make any sense, but whenever I talk to you, I keep feeling as if I could have done something to prevent Jaron's death."

"I felt survivor guilt after my wife died, too," Ben said carefully. "Blamed myself, when there was really nothing I could have done. There was really nothing you could have done, either, about whatever it was that happened. Jaron was an adult. He made his own choices."

"Maybe," she said. "But you know where I was when it happened? Sitting at my computer, in a screen trance or asleep, as near as I can tell. When I came to, I thought I remembered seeing his body, turned to ashes on a bed in a hotel room—something I wouldn't actually find out about for days. I put it out of my mind, and only remembered it much later."

Ben thought of his own dreams, about Reyna's last days, but he couldn't bring himself to mention them.

"Precognition?" he suggested.

"I don't believe in that," she said, shaking her head. "I thought maybe I had just retroactively *imagined* the dream, after I learned the circumstances of his death. But I don't believe that either. As a good materialist, how am I supposed to explain it?"

Then she kissed him quickly and lightly on the cheek, and he was more confused than ever.

"Conundrums, Ben," she said, smiling at his confusion. "They give us both something to pick at with our minds. The big puzzle to solve. Better to get lost in work, than lost in grief."

She pulled his face closer to him and kissed him full on the mouth. Tenderly at first, then—as he responded—more passionately. They embraced, their hands moving through each other's hair, along each other's faces, over each other's bodies. They moved apart just long enough to check whether or not anyone was watching them. When they saw no one about, Cherise opened her car's driver-side back door and they clambered inside together, shutting the door hastily behind them.

In the semidarkness brought on by the approaching storm, they caressed and undressed each other. A slow-motion frenzy of unbuttoning and unzipping and unsnapping, of pulling over and pulling down and kicking off, and then they were making love in the cramped space of the back seat, with the fierce and sly abandon of a couple of teenagers doing—with more enthusiasm than finesse— the date-concluding deed in the parental driveway.

At the height of passion he didn't call out Reyna's name, and Cherise didn't call out Jaron's name, but as they cuddled together afterward, it was clear that both of them were thinking about those they had loved, and lost. The mood hung over them as they quietly searched for and put themselves back into the varied articles of clothing they had shed in their haste to be naked with each other.

"We can be embarrassed," Cherise said, her right hand on his left cheek, staring deeply into his eyes, "but please, no guilt? We couldn't stop what happened with them, any more than they could stop what just happened with us."

"Right," he said, though he knew as he said it that it was easier to say than it was to believe.

When they were both dressed and looking halfway presentable again, they got out of the car. Cherise walked with Ben to his own vehicle and they worked their way toward farewell.

"Have a safe trip to Hong Kong," she said at last, moving away from him and back to her car, gesturing as she went. "Don't spend too much time alone with that lady detective. And if you see Bob Beckwith again, say hello to him for me. He's an old friend of the family."

"I will, as soon as I see him."

"Look me up when you get back, too, Ben—if I don't see you first."

As they waved their good-byes, Ben didn't know what to make of that.

LABYRINTH AND LOOKING GLASS

PHILADELPHIA

DON'S MORNING WALK TOOK him from his hotel on Filbert near the Convention Center, up Benjamin Franklin Parkway past Logan Circle and its fantastical fountain. After making a brief detour around the grounds of the Rodin Museum he proceeded to Eakins Oval. Ascending broad tiers of tan stone steps he came at last to the courtyardlike plaza in front of the east entrance of the Philadelphia Museum of Art.

Turning and looking back, he realized that the vista from the plaza looked somehow familiar. It took him a moment before it dawned on him that he was experiencing movie déjà vu: this was the route of Sylvester Stallone's daybreak training run in *Rocky*.

His morning jaunt didn't have that kind of drama, but the walk hadn't been at all unpleasant—sunny and cool, with armadas of tall clouds off to the west. The museum's classically columned facade

made it look like the Pennsylvania Parthenon, except for the flour-
ishes on the rooftops—griffins and other beasts, mythical and real.
Entering the museum, he saw the queue and decided to pass up a
chance to rent a pair of museum tour glasses.

As he made his way to a balcony overlooking the great hall, his
eyes came to rest on a monumental mobile suspended from the high
ceiling. The sculpture's languid motion as it floated over the large
interior space seemed at once aerial and aquatic, as if a whale's
skeleton were in the process of transforming itself into a flock of
strange birds.

"That's *Ghost*," said a young man in suit and tie, with subtly
spiked blond hair. His cigarette-scented clothes revealed him to be
not only a smoker but also a museum docent. "Alexander Calder,
1964."

"Yes, I thought it was a Calder," Don said. "I'm a big fan of his
mobiles and stabiles."

"Ah. Come with me, then, and I'll show you something special
about this one."

The slender, immaculately groomed young man, whose plastic
name badge read Palmer, parted the heavy curtains hanging above
the east entrance and gestured to Don that he should follow. The
windows on the other side gave a fine view facing east toward the
center of the city.

"Follow the line of Franklin Parkway toward downtown," said
the docent. "See the tall old-style tower off in the distance there?
That's the clock tower of City Hall. If you look closely you can
make out the figure of a man at its top—"

"Yes, I see it."

"That's a bronze statue of William Penn. The sculptor was this
Calder's grandfather, Alexander Milne Calder. Now look closer to
the museum. See the fountain down there at Logan Circle?"

"Yes," Don said, remembering the cluster of fish, birds, and human figures. "I noticed it on my walk here."

"That's the Swann Memorial Fountain, created by Alexander
Stirling Calder, our Calder's father. Tracing a straight line from

City Hall to the museum, you also trace the artistic line of the Calders, three generations of them, all of whom lived in Philadelphia. By doing so, you can almost trace a thumbnail history of the way sculpture changed from the 1880s to the 1960s."

"I see what you mean," Don said. "From realism to romance to abstraction. Thanks for showing it to me."

The docent smiled and nodded approvingly.

"If you have any questions, feel free to ask. That's what we're here for."

They parted, and Don began his wanderings through the maze of galleries and collections. Karuna would probably think him paranoid, but he decided against heading immediately to the painting he was most interested in seeing. He figured he'd nonchalantly amble up in front of the Dossi piece about halfway through his tour of the museum, just in case anyone might be tailing him.

Inside, the museum's Athenian exterior gave way to a Spartan stone fortress of functional square footage—and lots of it. Wings and floors marched off to the south, west, and north, most done in the unadorned architecture of a great box designed to hold other times, other places. The smallish weekday crowds Don had seen near the entrance quickly dispersed into the enormous complex of interior spaces, and Don encountered few other patrons in his perambulations—most of them retirees, he guessed.

He started with the American collections, which focused particularly on art with local connections: Thomas Eakins, Philadelphia furniture and silver, Pennsylvania German art, Shaker art, crafts, and glassware. From there he made his way to the second floor, through the galleries of European art, 1100–1500: stained-glass windows, medieval architecture and sculpture, and early paintings, the vast majority of them on Christian themes. Always he paused to read the placards identifying each piece and its history.

Don then strolled through rooms of wall-hung carpets and tapestries. Many of the carpets were Turkish or Persian, while most of the tapestries had been woven in the Low Countries.

Trying to maintain some sense of geographical and historical logic, he moved on to the Asian art galleries, the Chinese Palace Hall, Indian Temple, and Japanese Teahouse. From there he made his way back to the arms and armor galleries, with their collections of body armor, swords, polearms, and firearms.

Head aching from high information intake and low blood sugar, Don made his way to the cafeteria on the ground floor for a quick plastic lunch. Only there did he begin to notice the crowds of students—school groups, many of the kids in uniform. Very few people like himself, too old for mandatory schooling yet too young for mandatory retirement.

Feeling better for having eaten, and glad to be away from the noise of the crowds, he made his way back toward the second floor, into the galleries covering European Art from 1500 to 1700. After negotiating the French, English, and Dutch period rooms, then room after room of European painting, sculpture, and decorative arts, he felt sure he'd seen everything. Yet, somehow, he had managed to miss Item Number 251 in the John G. Johnson Collection.

After he saw its image in Kwok's holo-cast, he'd located the catalog number, and had even found a poorly reproduced photo of the painting itself in a book on labyrinths. Further research, however, proved fruitless. The painting was nowhere to be found in any scholarly discussions of Dossi's work. There was nothing on the web about it, either.

And so he had come here, to the museum where the book had said it would be found. To no avail. Was it in storage? Had it been sold to another museum?

Did it even exist?

He had almost despaired of finding it, and was about to ask one of the docents for help—thereby attracting attention to his interest—when suddenly, there before him, hung the painting.

It looked to be about three feet high by four feet long. It depicted an unidentified man whose mien and attire suggested noble rank and scholarly occupation. About thirty years old, but perhaps older, given his high forehead, which was clearly visible beneath an interestingly shaped hat. He was standing in front of a curtain and behind a low parapet. His right arm rested on the parapet. Not far from his right elbow stood a single pear, like a leftover from a still life.

The man's eyes seemed painfully averted from the object of his attention, though the index finger of his left hand was clearly pointing to a small ten-circuit labyrinth with an unusually long, keylike entrance. The labyrinth appeared to have been incised on the ledge of the parapet, as if it were some sort of petroglyphic graffito. The man, pointing at the center of the labyrinth but looking away, did not appear happy.

Up close now, Don could clearly make out the background of the painting. Beyond the parapet, a landscape stood revealed past the half-drawn curtain. In the foreground of that landscape stood an ass or donkey laden with dead game. Beyond the burdened beast, under the clouds of a thunderstorm, stood a village beside a lake, the steeple of its church threatened by lightning stroke.

What did it mean? The wallside placard offered a number of interpretations. Most of them agreed that the labyrinth recalled an unpleasant experience for the young man who had sat for the portrait. From the fruit at his right elbow, one interpreter had concluded that the sitter was Angelo Perondoli of Ferrara, whose family coat of arms included six pears. Another claimed that the subject was a member of the Gonzaga family of Mantua, and that the graffito derived from a water labyrinth painted on a wall in that city's Palazzo Ducale.

Each interpreter tried to somehow connect the sitter with the city of Ferrara, where Dosso Dossi had worked. There, in 1526, Dosso had also been commissioned to paint a portrait of famed legal scholar and father of emblem art, Andrea Alciati. And it had been at the behest of Alciati's patron Isabella d'Este, daughter of Duke Ercole I of Ferrara and mother of Federigo II Gonzaga, duke of Mantua, that Dosso had decorated a loggia in Mantua with a picture of Isabella's Ferraran home.

Unlike those works, however, this painting was only *attributed* to Dossi, which perhaps explained its absence from all the scholarly texts.

And what of the donkey burdened with its load of recently killed game, or the lakeside village threatened by thunderstorm and lightning? The interpreters didn't even venture a guess.

Most important of all, why had Jaron Kwok chosen this painting for inclusion in his holo-cast? What had he meant by "Hide insane plight in plain sight?" Staring at the painting of the melancholy man, Don thought he heard the sound of distant thunder.

He smiled. No matter how he stared, no rift opened in the fabric of space-time. No singularity broke through. Yet Don felt as if an important piece in the puzzle was at last coming into view.

When he glanced away, he found Palmer, the docent, watching him intently. The slim young man gave a slight nod of his subtly spiked blond head.

"That little labyrinth is interesting in a way that's only recently been discovered," said the docent, clearly eager to be helpful. "Most classical paintings, like this one, feature a white-paint undercoat. Scientists have learned that some substances, including the pigment particles in white paint, cause 'localization' of light. They act like an array of tiny mirrors, continually changing the direction of light—a labyrinth of mirrors so complex that the light ultimately cannot find any exit and becomes lost, or 'frozen.'

"You could say that, given such a white-paint undercoat, the foundation of most great works of art is a labyrinth of frozen light. Kind of ironic in this instance, don't you think?"

Don nodded vaguely, thanked the overly enthusiastic fellow as politely as he could, then moved on. He had spent far too much time in front of the painting. He tried to look casual as he strolled through the European art 1700–1850 galleries, but he felt distracted, had difficulty concentrating. Nonetheless he dutifully paused at each painting, each piece of sculpture.

He didn't really return to himself until he dropped down to the first floor again, and began walking through the European art

1850–1900 galleries. He made his way through galleries walled with Impressionist works. From collections of Cezanne, Degas, Van Gogh, Manet, and Renoir he moved on to the twentieth-century art galleries, with their Picassos and Duchamps, their Brancusis and Matisses.

He thought he heard the sound of thunder again, closer this time. Ignoring it, he made his way into the contemporary art galleries, which he found increasingly filled with anti-art, philosophical conundrum pieces, and *kitschkampf* commentaries on popular culture.

He finally realized that the sound of thunder was real while looking at an art exhibit called SubStrate, sponsored by a group called the Kitchener Foundation. The long-term exhibit, put together by a pair of Maryland artists who also happened to be wildlife biologists, featured numerous small aquariums whose bottoms were lined with a wide variety of substrates. In the aquariums lived caddisworms, the aquatic larvae of the caddis fly.

These larvae took whatever they could manipulate in their local environment and, with a silken substance, glued it together into a protective case for their soft bodies. In the wild, their "found objects" were usually things like pine needles, leaf debris, sand, or shells.

The biologist-artists had put the wormlike larvae in tanks lined with, among other things, precious and semiprecious jewels, computer chips, glitter, small nails, confetti-sized fabric swatches in myriad colors, household debris, bits of mirror, even tiny plasticized words and images.

The caddisworms dutifully encased themselves in these various materials, moving jerkily about in their odd little armored houses. Locking their houses shut with silk, they changed from larval nymphs into pupae. Once that transformation was complete, they cut their way out of their cocoons and then, rowing with elongated feathery legs, swam toward the surface, leaving their works of art behind on the aquarium floor. Finally, adult flies crawled out onto the surface of the water, drying their wings.

Above the aquarium tanks, flitting beneath mosquito-net canopies, roamed that day's hatch of adult caddis flies. On the walls of the exhibit, ranks of the empty caddis cases had been hung on lengths of fishing line, displayed over captions like "Art is the husk of the artist's experience."

By the time the announcement that the museum would be closing in ten minutes came over the public address system, Don was halfway through his last gallery—another installation which, like the caddis-fly art exhibit, was also sponsored by the Kitchener Foundation. Don quickly walked through the exhibit to its end. A loud crash of thunder sounded outside, and Don jumped. Realizing he was the last visitor left in the exhibit, he moved toward the exit. The walk back to his hotel wasn't a short one and he had no rain gear.

When he left the museum and walked onto the plaza, he was heartened to find that, although the sky was lowering, it hadn't yet started to rain. By the time he reached the bottom of the broad tiers of steps and crossed on a tangent to Eakins Oval, however, the first fat drops were beginning to splatter on the pavement.

Walking toward the Rodin Museum, he was thankful for the tree cover planted along the parkway—and the stubbornness that had kept them holding onto their leaves this far into autumn. They kept him from getting more thoroughly soaked.

About two-thirds of the way from the Rodin to Logan Circle, a long white car pulled up to the curb and a young man climbed out. He carried an opened, dark green umbrella in one hand and a folded umbrella in the other. As the fellow came closer, Don recognized him as the docent from the art museum.

"Hello," said the man, handing Don the folded umbrella, which was the same color as his own. "We thought you might need this. I'm Palmer Colbeth."

Confused, Don took the umbrella and opened it, then shook the man's proferred hand.

"We've met."

The newcomer gestured, and they stepped toward the long white car.

"I noticed your interest in the Dossi, Mister Markham," Palmer Colbeth said. "Or is it Sturm? Or Obololos? That last sounds a lot like Ouroboros, you know?"

"Actually it's Solo Lobo—'Lone Wolf'—in reverse."

"Well, whichever—my employer would like to speak with you."

"Your employer?" Don asked, and he slowed his pace, confusion spiralling downward toward suspicion. "The museum?"

Colbeth laughed as he opened the door to the car.

"Not exactly," he said, indicating that Don should get in. When Don hesitated, a lanky, bushy-haired older man in a dark suit stuck his head forward, into the rain.

"We won't bite you, Markham," said the man in a matter-of-fact way. He shielded his head by putting on a charcoal gray homburg hat. "We might even be of some assistance. Inside now, before we both catch our death of cold."

Responding to the reassuring tone in the older man's voice, Don folded the umbrella and got inside, nonetheless wondering if he was about to be kidnapped. Colbeth got in front on the passenger side, and the car's uniformed driver pulled the vehicle back into traffic, its tires moving over the wet road surface with a soft sizzle.

"Nils Barakian," said the bushy-haired man in the hat, shaking Don's hand as the car drove around the Eakins Oval and headed back toward the city. "Palmer here tells me you lingered a good long time in front of Item Number 251. Why the interest in that rather obscure painting, Mister Markham?"

"Why should I tell you?" Don said. "You could be Homeland Security, CIA, Tetragrammaton—anybody."

Barakian laughed.

"If I were, I'd hardly admit it, now would I? You'll just have to trust me when I say I work with a group of people who prefer to be anonymous. Ah, Tetragrammaton. Named from Hebrew Kabbalah, you know, but grown rather too fond of soft-Nazi superscience. I can say that we *are* rather the opposite of that.

"With your more-than-passing interest in Item 251, Mister Markham, you've passed a test of sorts. Oh yes, we know about the Kwok holo-cast, and the captioned image, as well. Those organizations you mentioned also know about it, but we seem to have beaten them to you. We could keep it that way, if you wish."

"What do you mean?" Don asked, uncomfortable despite the plush comfort of the limo's seats. "Why should I trust you any more than I trust them?"

"Well, to begin with, we will pay you extremely well to work with us. And don't disdain fouling your fingers a little with the ol' filthy lucre. Money makes it easier to slide over life's little razor blades. Besides, unlike *my* employers, those agencies you mentioned won't let you *decide* whether or not to work with them. They're rather more inclined to help you 'vanish,' I think. And they're already waiting for you at your hotel."

"*What?*"

Barakian nodded toward the driver, who gave a sotto voce command. Small, flat screens swung down from the ceiling. Surveillance images appeared, showing men in dark suits moving through areas Don recognized as the parking garage and lobby of his hotel—and the corridor on the floor where his own room was to be found. For a moment he thought it might be some elaborate hoax Barakian and Colbeth were perpetrating on him, but he quickly dismissed the idea. He had seen this sort of footage before, and the security-cam images appeared too real—and real-time—to be staged.

"I don't get it. Why would they be after me? Why now?"

"I think we both know the answer to the first question. As a result of disseminating your Prime Privacy Protocol through the infosphere—without State Department license, I might add—you've been charged as an illegal arms dealer."

"But I'm not—"

"Powerful encryption technologies, like your P-Cubed creation, are considered munitions under American law, and under the international Wassenaar Arrangement that limits arms exports."

"Oh, God. The Zimmerman precedent."

"Exactly so. You created a very user-friendly cryptographic

protection system based on prime factors. One which subverts key-escrow protocols and is unbreakable by anything short of a quantum computer. As a result, you are now an international terrorist. Congratulations!"

"But my encryption program has been available for more than six months!"

"Yes. That makes all the more interesting your second question: Why now?"

As they approached his hotel, Don Markham could see low-profile state police cars and blocky government sedans circling or parking around the block. Barakian nodded to the driver, indicating that he should pull over.

"What are you doing?" Don asked, nervousness cracking his voice.

"You can walk to your hotel from here, if you'd like," Barakian said. "The rain seems to have let up, but you can keep the umbrella Palmer gave you."

"Wait—you said it was my choice, right? To get out, or stay in this car and go with you?"

"Absolutely."

"Well, are you crazy? Of *course* I'm going to stay with you. Even if I don't know who the hell you are. It's not as if I have much choice."

Barakian indicated to the driver that he should pull out and drive on.

"I told you 'who the hell' we are. My name is Nils Barakian, and he's Palmer Colbeth."

"That's not what I meant," Don said, looking back over his shoulder as they left the vicinity of his hotel. "I meant who do you work for?"

"We work with an organization known as the Kitchener Foundation, of course. Palmer said you enjoyed our museum installations."

Palmer nodded and smiled, but Don could only shake his head.

"Any other questions?" Barakian continued calmly.

Don gave an odd little laugh.

"Yeah. When did I fall down the rabbit hole? When did I slip through the looking glass? Maybe Karuna was right. Maybe I *am* crazy. Maybe I'm seeing patterns that aren't really there."

Barakian placed a hand on Don's shoulder, in an awkward attempt to comfort him.

"The human brain has always held the ability to recognize patterns," Barakian said, "since long before that ability was applied to symbols—to recognizing patterns in things that *weren't*, in fact, really there. You're a very pattern-sensitive individual, Donald, but I haven't seen a clock-watching rabbit, nor a young girl with a looking glass—at least not recently."

Barakian smiled at him, and the smile seemed genuine.

Don nodded, feeling numb. The future was unfolding all too fast.

FISHING EXPEDITION

Gunpowder River

Deputy Director Brescoll had many reasons to appreciate the beauty of Gunpowder Falls State Park. Most of them centered around the Gunpowder River itself, as it meandered through the dense Eastern forest between the dam and Falls Road. Since everything flowing down from the Pretty Boy reservoir was tailrace water, the Gunpowder's upper reaches never exceeded a temperature of fifty-five degrees. Its flow, too, was consistent—excellent for sustaining naturalized populations of brown and rainbow trout. Its smaller waterfalls, plunging over great flat boulders to create long clear pools edged with cobblestones, made it his favorite Maryland trout stream.

Brescoll had other reasons for appreciating the locale. The clear blue sky above the tree canopy was off most flight paths. The burbling of the stream and the river-basin acoustics tended to defeat recording devices and parabolic microphones. No law enforcement agency, fortunately, had yet found it worthwhile to put up surveillance cameras for monitoring these stretches of trout stream labored over by dedicated fishermen.

Dressed in fishing vest, breathable waders, and felt-soled wading boots, Jim read the water as he worked his way upstream, stripping float-line and casting ahead of him into riffles as he went. He was using artificial black, brown, and cream midge flies, in the #22–#26 range. They were so tiny they completely disappeared into the surface turbulence of the riffles, and only became barely visible once more when they came alongside.

Jim didn't expect much this late in the morning, and this late in the year. Wondering whether he should try caddis fly larvae instead, he was surprised when, almost immediately, he saw trout rising after his artificial midges, a bit sluggish with the cold, but still active enough. After a particularly well-placed cast and long float over just the area Jim was shooting for, the rainbow broke surface.

With a quick upward flick of the wrist and forearm, Jim set the hook and reeled in a shimmering fish that, in its several leaps out of the water, looked to be at least ten or twelve inches long. Gripping his catch with a fine mesh "landing hand" glove, he saw that the trout was surprisingly thick in the belly.

With his free hand he unclipped a pair of hemostat clamps from his vest and used them to remove the tiny hook from the trout's upper lip. He looked at the fish proudly once more, estimating its length at closer to thirteen inches, before releasing it back into the river. As he watched the rainbow swim off and disappear in the current, he studied the way the river ran against a particularly large boulder in the middle of the stream. As he had before, he thought again of the paradoxical immortality of rivers.

The Gunpowder had probably been running against that rock in just that way since before the river had been named. Odds were that it would still be flowing against that rock a thousand years from now. Even after the dam that lay upstream had broken down or silted up. Perhaps when human civilization on Earth had changed completely, or humanity itself had gone extinct.

What was it Thoreau said in *Walden*?

> *"Time is but the stream I go a-fishing in. I drink at it, but while I drink I see the sandy bottom and detect how shallow it is. Its thin current slides away, but eternity remains. I would drink deeper; fish in the sky, whose bottom is pebbly with stars."*

What Thoreau didn't see, Jim thought, was that the river remains alive by always passing away. It only dies when it *stops* passing away.

That was what Jim Brescoll appreciated most about Gunpowder Falls. Getting away from the city and man-made spaces helped to put things into clearer and broader perspective.

He proceeded upstream, so caught up in his thoughts, in reading the water and stalking the trout, that he almost forgot the other reason he was on the river today. Until he reached a particular spot, which happened to be just downstream of his favorite fly-fishing pool. There he found a young man dressed in shorts, river-guide sandals, and heavy jacket.

The young man, with his short, spiked blond hair and no hat, was clearly trying to look experienced about his fishing, and failing. Brescoll took out his pipe, tamped in some tobacco, lit up, and watched the fellow cast—poorly—for a time.

"Been fly-fishing long?" Jim asked at last. The young man smiled awkwardly.

"Actually, this is my first try at it," he admitted. "I watched an instructional video, but that doesn't seem to be helping very much."

"Mind a suggestion?"

"Not at all."

"Don't beat the water with the fly. You're working a little too hard. Too many false casts."

"Okay," the young man said hesitantly. "How do I fix that?"

"Where you're standing, you probably don't need more than eight or ten feet of float-line stripped out beside you—if that— before you cast. And you don't need to reel everything in to the end of the float line. Leave your leader in the water and leave a few feet of float line off the end of the rod. You're right-handed, aren't you?"

"Yeah."

"Thought so. Then keep your right elbow in close to your body. Most of the back and forth motion should come from your hand, wrist, and no further up your arm than the elbow. No need for much shoulder or upper arm action. The motion of the rod pulls out the line by making a sort of lazy figure eight." He demonstrated the motion. "Got it?"

The young man looked at him with some confusion. Jim was glad he hadn't referred to the "lazy eight" the way he usually thought of it—as the fly fisherman's infinity sign.

"I think so," the young man replied. "I let the stripped line feed through my left hand?"

"Correct. When the last curve of that figure eight is feeding out, let it go. You don't so much throw the fly on the water as *lay* it on the surface. As the fly floats down the current into the pool, re- move the slack by stripping in enough line. That way, if you get a strike, you can flick back your wrist and set the hook without much trouble."

The young man looked at him expectantly, awaiting further instruction.

"Go ahead. Try it."

Brescoll watched as the young man worked on his casting tech- nique. His progress went in fits and starts, with ample cause for frustration, and the need for more coaxing and instruction from Jim. It wasn't long before the novice fly fisherman was showing im- provement, however, and the two men relaxed.

"Taking a day off from work?" Brescoll asked.

"Yeah. How about you?"

"The same. What do you do, if you don't mind my asking?"

"Nothing special. I work for a foundation. Yourself?"

"Federal government."

The young man laughed.

"Sounds tedious. You must be glad to get away from it for a day."

"The fishing here is good," Jim said with a shrug, "especially when you consider that two million people live within driving distance. But yeah, my job can sometimes be mind numbing, especially when it turns political."

"I know all about politics," the young man said with a nod. "Hey, you know what the difference is between conservatives and liberals?"

"What?"

"Conservatives love people as individuals—it's humanity in general they can't stand," said the young man. "Whereas liberals . . ."

"Liberals love humanity in general—it's people they can't stand," Brescoll said. That confirmed it. Time to make the exchange.

"You still don't seem to be having much luck. Here," said Brescoll. "Let's see what fly you're using."

The young man reeled it in and showed it to him.

"Hmm. Looks like a brine fly—#16, or maybe #18. Give me a couple of those. I'll trade you two of these midges. They seem to be working today. Put a dab of this flotant on the one you'll be using."

They exchanged flies, and thereby *files*. If this exchange was like the others, then in among the feathery hackle of each dry fly there were tiny but highly encrypted data needles and a onetime pad—a random key as long as the encrypted data itself. Brescoll's informants always included the datafiles redundantly, over several flies, with a different onetime pad for each. That was what he did, as well. Standard operating procedure. Not unusual to lose a fly or two—especially when his contact was such a fly-fishing neophyte. Be a shame to lose all the data.

He tried to interest the young man in barrel casting, but the neophyte was more interested in working upstream using those techniques at which he was already becoming minimally proficient. When the young man finally caught and landed his first trout, Jim applauded enthusiastically, despite the fact that the young man had taken it from Jim's favorite pool.

Before long they parted company, going their separate ways along the stream. Though he didn't show it, Jim was eager to learn what his discreet informants had pulled together for him. More analysis on that painting embedded in the Kwok holo-cast? Or on the importance of the Sun Yat-sen Memorial? That was what he had hinted he wanted, last time he made contact.

His benefactors had always been a big help whenever they'd surfaced in the past. They'd been popping up more often lately, too. Something about the Kwok incident and its aftermath clearly interested them. He had few qualms about providing them with hints about his agency's investigation, in exchange for whatever info they could offer. Their recent inquiries, however, had begun to center around the Forrest documents. In today's exchange he had passed along some suggestions for directions their investigations might take, based on NSA's own discoveries.

After catching and releasing three more fish in the ten- to fourteen-inch range, he headed downriver. Leaving the stream to return to his car, Brescoll pondered again just who his secret benefactors might be.

The young man today had said he worked "for a foundation," which fit Jim Brescoll's best guess as to the source of his unnamed tipsters. He had been sure, almost from the beginning, that they weren't agents of a foreign power. As to why they had chosen *him*, however, he still wasn't certain. Maybe it was because he was the highest ranking civilian in the agency.

Breaking down his rod and stowing it in an aluminum tube, Brescoll shook his head. In truth, when his benefactors had first contacted him, he *hadn't* been the highest ranking civilian employee of NSA. The insights he had gained from them had helped propel his career. It might even be said that he had been "groomed" by them. But he also got the sense that his benefactors were somehow aligned against the CIA's Tetragrammaton connections, too.

Jim put the rod away in the trunk and closed it. He stood a moment, checking his fly-box, making sure both of his newly acquired flies were safe inside. He got in on the driver's side of the car, catching a glimpse of his face in the mirror.

"Why *did* they choose you?" he asked the face in the mirror. "Because you're black? Was it some kind of anonymous affirmative action program?"

Brescoll laughed a wry laugh and started up the Volvo. Putting it in gear, he began the trip back into daily life. Not far, in time and space, but a great distance nonetheless.

SEVEN

PENETRANCE

KOWLOON

DETECTIVE LU HAD a great deal to tell Ben Cho, but she didn't see how she could, given that he was constantly escorted by FBI Special Agent and Deputy Legat DeSondra Adjoumani. Then again, if Mei-lin couldn't *tell* him, at least maybe she could *show* him.

Dressed in her white lab coat, black slacks, and sensible black shoes, Mei-lin hoped her appearance was neutral enough to avoid raising any warning flags. As she talked of the episode she and Ma had survived at the Sun Yat-sen Memorial—mentioning Paul Kao's death, but neglecting to bring up Ma's final speculation—Mei-lin thought Cho also seemed aware of the difficulties presented by his escort. His responses struck her as guarded.

Then, as she and Cho watched an electron videograph display of the scurrying cell-like mechanisms, the spawn of Kwok's "ashes,"

Mei-lin felt certain he was being more reticent than when they'd last met.

"After I accidentally cut myself and dripped blood on the ash samples," she said, gesturing at the screen, "this was the result. I think the blood itself activated them, somehow. They show similar activity when grown on agar nutrient media saturated with blood components."

Mei-lin, seeing that Adjoumani was lingering by the lab door, risked typing in, for Cho, the word she had remembered from the Kwok holo-cast—a neologism built out of the two not-much-older neologisms of "biotech" and "nanotech." *Maybe all words are really just old neologisms, in the end,* she thought.

BINOTECH?

She watched for Cho's reaction.

"I can't say for sure—," Cho began, then broke off as he caught her glance. He looked at her hesitantly, then seemed to arrive at a decision.

"Yes, I believe you're right," he said, trying to sound as if he were responding to what she had said out loud. His reply sounded a bit forced, though. "But to what purpose? What do they do?"

"I don't know," Mei-lin Lu admitted. "You suggested that I look for information, and at first I thought I had found information in the course of *processing.* I'm not so sure it's that purposeful, now. I mean, to what *purpose* do bacterial colonies grow, other than to propagate themselves?"

"Maybe," Cho agreed, "but these don't look natural. They look like some sort of human product, so logically they should serve some purpose that benefits human beings. Maybe they're not yet fully operational. Just a guess. Do you still have the first samples? The ones you accidentally contaminated?"

"At the other end of the bench—there," she replied, pointing. They stepped over toward the samples. "I kept them refrigerated, and it seemed to slow them down. I took them out an hour ago, in anticipation of your visit."

Cho stared at the shapes formed by the samples, an odd expression on his face.

"They look like those raked-sand whirlpools you see in Zen gardens," he said, bemused. "Tiny versions of those, anyway."

"Yes, or like fingerprints," Mei-lin suggested anxiously. This was it—an opening. If she could just exploit this opportunity, she might be able to get a lot of information to Cho, right under Adjoumani's nose. "The 'whirlpools' vary slightly from colony to colony, but not much. More like the differences in fingerprints between identical twins, than between unrelated individuals."

"Identical twins don't have identical fingerprints?"

Mei-lin nodded.

"The geneticists say almost no genetic trait has one hundred percent penetrance," she said. "The genotype is almost never perfectly manifested in the phenotype."

"Really? Why is that?"

"The genotype is like the blueprints," Mei-lin said, opening out her hands, "and the phenotype is like the house built from the blueprints."

"And everyone knows the blueprints are never exactly the same as the house!" Ben Cho said, laughing.

"According to complexity theorists, the difference stems from sensitive dependence upon initial conditions."

Becoming more thoughtful, Cho shook his head.

"But identical twins are genetic duplicates from the same single fertilized egg, right?"

"As close to one hundred percent duplication as you get in a biological system," Mei-lin agreed. "And they drift side by side in the same womb. Even in the womb, though, there are local differences, such as different chemical concentrations. Those environmental differences only increase after the twins are born. Here, I'll show you."

Time to take the chance—to show what Cho's fingerprints, on the message tube when it was returned, had suggested to her, improbable as it might have seemed.

She brought up on the computer screen two sets of similar thumbprints, labeled only "A" and "B."

"See any difference?" she asked.

"No. Why? Should I?"

"Only if you're expert in dermatoglyphics," she said, bringing up new versions of "A" and "B" with specific identification points highlighted. "There's a great deal of similarity in these prints—their overall patterns of whorls, loops, lines, and ridge-counts. There are, however, clear differences in detail. Especially where the ridges bifurcate or end. See?"

Ben Cho grunted in apparent understanding.

"Hmm. And these are from identical twins?"

"I believe so," Mei-lin said, nodding again. "Twin sons of different mothers, actually."

"How might *that* happen?" Cho asked, scratching his head absently. "Fertility tinkering?"

"Good guess. Advanced reproductive technology generates a surplus of fertilized eggs and embryos—all of which can be frozen and stored. From there it's just permutations and combinations."

"What do you mean?"

"Let me illustrate a couple of scenarios," she said, bringing modified and captioned family trees up on the screen. "The genetic mother's egg could be fertilized by genetic father's sperm in vitro, resulting in an embryo that can then be implanted in the genemother's prepared uterus. The genemother would then become the gestation mother, as well."

"But that doesn't have to be the case."

"No. The embryo might well be implanted in the uterus of a biologically unrelated woman. The genemother also might or might not be the cultural mother, as well. Likewise, the genefather might or might not be the cultural father, in the home where the child is raised."

"Then what these diagrams show," Cho said, "is that an embryo could be implanted in the uterus of a woman who is not the genetic mother and, once born, that child could be reared in a household in which neither mother nor father is genetically related to that child."

"And in that case, the only 'biological' connection," Mei-lin said, consciously steering the conversation, "between the mother and the child is that she is the woman who carried the pregnancy to term. Otherwise, she's genetically unrelated to her 'offspring.' "

"So again, how would that affect identical twins?"

"If we were dealing with twin-split embryos," Mei-lin explained, bringing new family trees and lineage diagrams up on screen, "genetically identical, one might be raised in a family in which its genetic parents were also the cultural parents. The other twin, though—the 'embryonically adopted' twin—might be raised in a family of individuals with no biological relationship. A father with whom that child has no biological connection whatsoever. A mother whose only bio-relationship is having carried the child to term."

"But if the embryos were frozen, they could be stored," Cho said, thinking it through. "The 'embryonically adopted' twin wouldn't necessarily have to be born on the same day. . . ."

"Exactly. An embryonic adoptee might even be born months or years apart from its genetically identical twin. And it would be much more likely that the embryonically adopted child wouldn't know he or she was adopted—because its parents might have no idea that, genetically speaking, 'their' child wasn't really theirs."

"So the twins could be raised in different families," Cho said, "with neither twin knowing it was a twin, and neither family aware of what had taken place."

"Not just different families," Mei-lin said emphatically. "Different races."

"What?" Cho asked. He sounded doubtful.

"Because the human race is a species, not a race," Mei-lin said, "and in terms of strict, biologically based taxonomy, the human species does not have 'races'—it has geographic variants. Race and ethnicity are undeniably important social and historical concepts, but their *biological* significance is generally negligible. We're all too genetically similar to be different 'races' in the true Linnaean sense. And, since the same gene can produce a range of proteins, it's not all that difficult to take the same genotype and tinker with it, proteomically and epigenetically, until it produces a quite different-looking phenotype."

"But how could gene and protein work on the microscale you're talking about alter something as macro as race?" Cho asked, looking perplexed.

"Traditional ethnic signifiers like skin melanin levels, curliness of the hair, epicanthic folding, and the like," Mei-lin said, tapping at the keyboard again to bring up further illustrations, "are relatively easy to alter above the genetic level. Through proteomic and epigenomic technology, twinship and even kinship can be thoroughly masked. The only way to detect identical twin genotypes would be through DNA testing."

"I've never heard of, um, 'twin sons of different races,' " Cho said somewhat incredulously. "Are there any recorded cases of such a thing actually happening?"

"I had never heard of it before, either," Mei-lin said, "but I think I've found such a case."

Mei-lin glanced surreptitiously at the doorway, where Adjoumani was still standing, an unobtrusive sentinel. Nothing about her posture revealed whether she was truly oblivious, or merely feigning civil inattention. The agent's angle of view, however, made it unlikely that she could see the computer screen. Lu tapped at the keyboard and brought up what she wanted Cho to see, then stepped aside, indicating that he should take a look.

She watched Ben's expression as he took in what she already knew the screen showed. The "A" prints were matched to Jaron Kwok, whose records listed his date of birth and other identifying characteristics. The very similar "B" prints were matched to Benjamin Cho, whose records listed a completely different date of birth and rather different identifying characteristics. Something very much like a tremor passed over his face.

"This can't be right," he said quietly, at last, clearing his throat.

"I didn't really expect it to be true either," Lu responded, not knowing what else to say. "And it hasn't been genetically proven, not yet. But the circumstantial evidence is very strong. Look how closely the prints match. Subject B's prints are taken from a biometrically secured message cylinder—they've been positively identified. Subject A's are taken from a crime scene, and match all other extant records of A."

"Are you suggesting that—" Cho said, then stopped, because Mei-lin suddenly gripped his arm tightly enough to pinch the flesh between her fingers. He began again. "Are you suggesting that Subject A and Subject B are identical twins, then?"

"Yes. Despite the obvious 'racial' and familial differences."

Lu watched as his gaze shifted from the screen. He turned to stare penetratingly at her.

"Then, Marilyn, what I asked earlier applies here, too: For what purpose would such a thing be done?"

"And I'd have to say again—I don't know. But what you said before, about the mechanisms, I think it's also true in this situation: It must serve some larger purpose. I think what's on that screen is a product of carefully planned manipulation. Something outside the normal course of reproduction and biological evolution. The result of technological innovation."

Cho nodded grimly. He looked downcast, and Mei-lin felt a stab of pity for him. How was the man supposed to feel, after all? If what she'd told him was right, then much of what he knew about his very existence was wrong. As Mei-lin pondered the ramifications, they quickly rippled away into the imponderable.

She hadn't wanted to cause him pain, but what else could she do? Her discovery might very well have profound implications for the investigation into the Kwok incident.

Having come this far, she had to see it through, and obtain incontrovertible proof. For that she would need a DNA sample.

"Oh, by the way," she said casually, trying to get Cho's attention again. "I'm collecting samples of different blood groups to use as test media for the cellular mechanisms. Would you mind giving me a blood sample—for further tests?"

She emphasized the last phrase enough to hope that Cho might tumble to her purpose—but not so much that Adjoumani's suspicions would be aroused. He seemed to get the idea.

"Sure," he said flatly. "Why not?"

Pulling out the necessary equipment, Detective Lu applied a tourniquet to Cho's left bicep and thumped up a vein on the inside of his elbow, then uncapped a syringe in preparation for the "stick." Doing so, she fell back into a role older than her position as police-department forensics expert—older even than her graduate work in forensic anthropology. As an undergraduate she had scraped up extra money working as a phlebotomy technician in a local medical clinic, drawing blood samples and enduring far too many vampire jokes.

"Are you sure that's absolutely necessary, ma'am?" Special Agent Adjoumani asked, stepping into the room and stopping Lu with her words. Lu glanced at Cho.

"Yes, I think it *is* necessary, DeSondra," Cho said, before turning his gaze back to Mei-lin. "Don't worry. She's just taking something out, not putting anything in."

As she took the blood sample, Lu tried to show—with her eyes—how grateful she was to him. She was surprised to find at least as much gratitude flashing from the eyes that looked back at her—although it seemed to her that those eyes were more than a little touched by shadows of uncertainty. And regret.

Cho handed her a scrap of paper with his local number on it.

"If you find anything interesting," he said, "please give me a call."

CHANGELING HISTORY

SHA TIN

LOOKING BACK OVER HIS shoulder, Ben Cho spotted the Royal Park Hotel, self-identified in large letters at its towering top. The place where Jaron Kwok—his unsuspected twin brother, if Detective Lu was right—had met an uncertain end. Shaking his head, Ben walked through the late afternoon light into the town park after which the hotel had been named.

Though he couldn't say exactly why, after his meeting with Detective Lu, he'd asked Adjoumani to drive him out here to Sha Tin. "Returning to the scene of the crime," he told the legat. That wasn't exactly true. He hadn't gone back to Kwok's hotel room—which had been cleaned up by now, and rented to other guests. Instead, he had wandered about the grounds of the hotel, and then into the nearby park. It probably irritated the FBI agent to be wandering aimlessly, rather than pursuing some more tangible line of investigation, but that couldn't be helped.

He wanted to tell her what Lu had revealed to him, but he didn't know if he should. Lu had seemed very protective of the information, for all its strangeness. He still didn't really know how much he should trust her—or Adjoumani, for that matter, who was shadowing him even now.

Wong Jun and his Guoanbu buddies were probably keeping him under observation, too. Given the media-sniping that had been going back and forth between China and the US, about matters in Nepal and California, Ben wondered how much longer he was going to be allowed to keep moving about China even as "freely" as he had been doing.

In the park around him, formal fences fronted lawns punctuated by stone-islanded ponds and carefully trimmed hedges. A backdrop of palm trees screened the stark towers of dozens of high-rise apartment blocks, across the Shing Mun River. What Ben had mistaken for abstract impressionist statues when he first walked past them proved to be oddly twisted and eroded rocks planted as specimen stones atop low-hedged mounds. Everything seemed surreal now, an impression that was magnified when he found himself staring at a scene he knew, although he'd never been in this park before.

In front of him, a waterfall plunged from a low hilltop, past sharp-edged stone tiers, into a pond, or small lake of gray-green water. On an island in the midst of the small lake stood an open structure, like a cross between a gazebo and a pagoda, roofed in red tiles.

Rainbow-hued fish moved through the murky water, while gray-black turtles sunned themselves on rocks near the banks. Connecting the island to the shore was a high-arched moon bridge.

He sat down on a bench beside the pond and stared at a palace garden that had seemingly lost its palace. This was the same landscape he'd already seen in a photograph, in Cherise's house—of a happily married Cherise and Jaron, standing on this very moon bridge, reflected in the park's fish- and turtle-filled pond. Elements of this scene had appeared in Kwok's last holo-cast, too.

Ben thought about what happened with Cherise, in the parking lot in New Burlton. Not wanting to think about whether he had betrayed either Reyna or Jaron, he instead tried hard to lose himself in the scene that lay before his eyes.

What struck Ben most about it was the way the moon bridge was reflected in the water of the pool so that the half circle of its arch, when coupled with its reflection, made a perfectly circular hole, half real and half illusion. The implications of the image echoed through his head, resonating with his own newly discovered situation.

If Jaron Kwok was indeed his twin brother, then was Jaron the mirror image, or was Ben? Had Ben been proteomically altered to appear as if he was the offspring of a Chinese-American father and African-American mother? Or had Kwok been the changeling child, conceived of the Chos' egg and sperm—his "blackness" epigenomically masked so that he looked all and only Chinese?

Which of them had lived the real life, which the illusion? If both had arisen from the same twin-split embryo, then was that embryo conceived of his parents' sperm and egg, or Father Kwok's sperm and Mother Kwok's egg? Given that Ben's birth date was two months later than Kwok's, was Ben the leftover, the one who wasn't raised by his biological family?

What if *neither* set of parents had been the source of sperm and egg?

It was almost too much to contemplate. Still, why had Ben's parents never really discussed with him the issues which had preceded his birth: of their struggles with fertility and infertility, and the decisions that had sent them seeking help through reproductive tech? Was their silence just one of those "family things"?

Like motherly love so extreme that it had shaded into sexual abuse?

Sister! What are you doing with that boy?

Ben pushed the thought away.

He had long hated implants, only to learn, now, that he probably *was* one, and had been from the very beginning. He tried to think of something else, and almost managed it.

"Something happened way back there," Cherise had said. "The fork in the road to Thebes." In the notes concerning the Forrest documents, Jaron had used that same phrase, but in a different context. The Forrest documents—even they had veered down different paths, leading to as many questions as answers.

Ben had always assumed that Felix Forrest had been a straightforward Cold Warrior, true to his time. In the pictures he had seen, Forrest had certainly looked the part, sporting fedora and even an eye patch—quite legitimately, since Forrest had in fact lost an eye in a childhood accident. But the more Ben read of the old spy's published works, especially his science fiction stories, the less sure he became about the man. If Forrest had simply been a gung ho patriot, then what had driven him to leak the truth out to the world, in supposedly fictional stories written under a pen name?

In the course of his research, Ben—like Jaron before him—had found that Forrest's "science fiction" thinly veiled secret CIA projects of the late 1950s and early 1960s, recasting those projects in the form of fantastic tales about a powerful and secretive "Instrumentality" that ruled the far future. Forrest had turned the CIA's remote-viewing experiments into a story about the scientist Rogov, who projected his consciousness more than ten thousand years into the future. And, inside the tale of an enraged hyperdimensional traveler named Artyr Rambo, the old spy had even indirectly referenced the MK Ultra project—the covert administration of LSD to unknowing civilians.

Leaks like that just didn't fit the profile of a security-conscious hyperpatriot. Were they truly a lapse in secrecy—or had the old spy been following his own unspoken agenda? Had he harbored his own theories as to where the boundary lay between patriotism and paranoia?

The "fork in the road" in Kwok's research, though, hadn't been about Jaron's own life, Ben realized, or about Felix Forrest and *his* life, or even about agencies like CIA and NSA. No, it was about the much larger history of the art of memory and cryptography—involving the rise of science, secret services, and secret societies. The forks went much further back, to the tri-via, the place where highways came together, or split apart. Where Oedipus unknowingly killed his father while on the road that led to marrying his mother. To the trivium of the medieval schools. To the Renaissance magus, steeped in the arts of that trivium and its sister quadrivium. The magus who, with his magic memory as an aid to gnosis, had made it dignified, important, and *allowable* for human beings to operate upon the world, to exert their powers.

Who thereby had paved the way for modern science. Which then created a new trivium, by forking off from the magic and religion with which it had once been joined, part of a single art.

Looking at the bridge, its arch, and the mirroring pond, at the whole circular hole that was half watery reflection, Ben thought of the way kaleidoscopes built magical phantasmagorias from shadows in the mirror, from doublings, forkings, reflections. He thought of Kwok's holo-cast and of the characters who had already been identified therein, Giordano Bruno among them.

The philosophical dictionaries and encyclopedias Ben had consulted claimed that Bruno—Kabbalist and occult cryptographer, Hermeticist, sun-magician, and early follower of Copernicus—was either the greatest materialist who ever lived (for arguing that spirit and universe are one and the same) or the greatest *im*materialist who ever lived (for precisely the same reason).

Shaking his head, Ben went back to staring at the perfect circle made by the high arch of the moon bridge and its mirror image. Earlier he had thought of the reflection as an illusion, the half that wasn't real, but now he realized that the circular portal could only be complete if it existed as both object and mirror-image. The circle wasn't illusion, it was the sum of the complementary parts. Which Giordano Bruno had called the *coincidentia oppositorum*, "the coincidence of contraries," centuries before the quantum physicists got around to noticing complementarity.

Ben remembered the last time he had spoken of complementarity—to Kimberly the stripper—and his face flushed warm.

When the more traditional quantum mechanists looked out at the cosmos, they saw the full circle, but they declared that only the single universe on Ben's side of the reflection was real, and the other half of the circle, the twin in the mirror, was a phantom. However, when the many-worlds theorists or multiversalists, the godfathers of quantum cryptology, looked out at the cosmos and saw the full circle, they declared that the twin universes which made up the whole were each equally real—only, from within each universe, the other universe was *experienced* as a phantom.

In some universes, certain things never underwent the formality of actually *occurring*. Like Jaron Kwok's demise. Like Reyna's glioblastoma multiforme, her cancer, her death. Ben tried to push such thoughts away. What good could thinking them possibly do? Yet even in focusing on Jaron's work, Ben's mind returned to what might have been, in other worlds.

Back there, at that fork in the road, the unrecognized twins of archetypal magic and empirical science had split from each other, at least in Kwok's view. When Bruno had attempted to unite the sect-shattered Christian churches into a single universal Church through his secret and magical memory system, he had ultimately failed. The occultized art of memory went underground, into secret societies like the Rosicrucians, the Freemasons, their many descendants. Alternatively, in demythologized form, the mnemonic arts had paved the way aboveground for the scientific method.

Despite his failure, however, Bruno's efforts at systematizing the art of memory in order to produce a universal memory machine weren't so very different from Alan Turing's efforts before and during the Second World War, which made possible the creation of software for *his* universal machines, soon embodied as mechanical and electronic computers. Bruno, however, hadn't hoped to program the hardware of machines, but the wetware of human hearts and minds.

The hardware of the bridge, the wetware of reflection. For a moment Ben saw in his mind's eye the ghostly glimmer of a twisted golden chain, the luminous double helix of history running backwards and forwards through the darkness of time. Lullian combinatory wheels and Brunian memory wheels curiously mirrored military cipher disks, decoder rings, the scrambler wheels of German Enigma machines, the computing wheels of Babbage's difference engines.

American generals and admirals had referred to their code breakers as "sorcerers," and their collective code name for a series of very important Japanese intercepts on the eve of World War II was MAGIC. Churchill had called electronic warfare "Wizard War." The scientists and technologists of both the CIA and NSA were referred to as "wizards" both inside and outside those organizations. Cryptology was the mirror-molecule, the DNA of both magic and science.

Whoa. Better watch that, he thought. *Not too much.* The euphoria of inforrhea was all over Jaron's notes. That way lay madness or—what?

When Ben stood and looked down at his reflection in the surface of the pond, he didn't see Jaron Kwok looking back at him, didn't see the ghostly glimmer of a twin grown differently from the same chains of DNA. But the sight of his own reflection did remind him of how thoroughly Kwok's notes discussed, not only history, but destiny.

Quantum computing, Kwok asserted, was destined to re-merge those roads that had forked so long ago. Sorcerer, scientist, and cryptanalyst—all stood mirrored in one another. For Kwok, the creation of the universe-bandwidth quantum computer, the ultimate cryptanalytic device, would yield the "universal key" for breaking codes. It was a return to and fulfillment of the magus's *clavis universalis*, the great key to all the mysteries of the universe. The creation of the quantum cryptograph as a universal labyrinth, an undecipherable cipher, was a return to the magus's *labyrinthus universalis*, a pathway of mysteries the uninitiated would be required to navigate if they were to gain the vast powers of the initiate.

Reading Kwok's notes, Cho had begun to wonder if the man considered himself a sort of reborn magus, a second Bruno. As near as he could tell, Giordano Bruno had believed his universal memory machine—with its wheels within wheels within wheels—was capable of intricately reflecting the permutations and combinations of the stars and planets in their courses. Bruno apparently believed that such adjustable simulacra would allow him to create a system for getting inside archetypal astrological systems, in order to tap into the ordering patterns of nature itself, and thereby open the "black diamond doors"—Bruno's phrase—of the initiate's psyche.

Once opened, they became the "pearly gates" of Revelation and allowed the initiate to plug his psyche into the cosmic powers themselves.

Although Jaron Kwok might not have pictured constellations as the "bright shadows of Ideas" the way Bruno had, Jaron too seemed to believe he could crack the combination on the vault of heaven. Had he—as cosmic safecracker—succeeded, or failed? Had he drawn the whole world of data into himself, like a great magus? Had he ecstatically reflected the universe within his mirroring mind, and become one with the Cosmic Powers?

To what purpose? Patriotism, or paranoia, or simply ego? Had he wanted to beat the Chinese to the prize? The Americans? Both? And why? What if that boon they were all after, via binotech and quantum cryptology, turned out to be a booby prize?

Or a booby trap. *Poof!* goes the universe. Or at least your place in it, hero. In that last instant before he disappeared, had Jaron even known that he had a twin? Or had he in the end simply died ignorant, the victim of his own machinations, achieving only his full potential for becoming a poor, tragic fool?

Ben looked away.

As he did so, out of the corner of his eye he caught the reflection of a woman coming toward him. At first he thought it must be Agent Adjoumani, but almost instantly the source of the reflection stood there beside him. A young Asian woman—lithe and strikingly beautiful, though a tad overly made-up for his tastes. For an instant he thought she might be a Guoanbu operative, Adjoumani's looking-glass reflection.

"Hello," she said, and even that single word was suggestive. "I have it on good authority that you're the kind of man who appreciates the female form. I can see in your eyes that it's true. My name is Sin, but you can call me Helen. Come and dance with me, won't you?"

The woman flashed him a distressingly come-hither glance and pressed a piece of paper into the palm of his hand, just as Adjoumani came striding up. The FBI agent had been caught completely off guard, but before she could do anything, she and Ben watched the young woman skip lightly away.

Ben opened his hand and looked at the piece of neon pink paper she'd slipped into his palm. What he read there made him wonder if "Sin" might be a stage name. It also made him nervous.

"Who was that?"

"I don't know," Ben said, clearing his suddenly dry throat, trying not to let the discomfort leak into his voice. "She gave me this. A complimentary ticket for a 'hostess club.' "

" 'The Temple of the Ten Thousand Beauties,' " Adjoumani read aloud, frowning. She shook her head disdainfully and handed it back to Ben. "The address is down the hill from the Temple of the Ten Thousand Buddhas. Pretty tacky, if you ask me."

"Yes," Ben agreed, nodding absently. He took one last glance at the bridge and its reflection, that trapdoor into another world. "I've seen the Temple of the Ten Thousand Buddhas. And I think I've seen everything I came here to see, as well."

"Good. Let's head back to the hotel, then."

Following her in silence, Ben's thoughts grew darker much faster than the light of day declined. "I have it on good authority," the woman had said. Just a coincidence? An offhand comment? Was she simply playing on his curiosity, hoping to attract a new customer?

If she did know something about him, though, on someone's "authority," then whose? Was a "hostess club" the same thing as a "gentleman's club"—another euphemism for a strip bar? The only person who knew about his strip-club night was Ike Carlson—and Kimberly, or course. Had Carlson betrayed him, somehow? Ben knew little enough about the man, after all.

Now that he thought about it, hadn't Kimberly the stripper been a little *too* well matched with him and his needs? Still, both Kimberly and Ike were half a world away. To what purpose would they want to betray Ben's recent peccadillo? And to whom?

To what purpose.

For what purpose.

He had heard and thought those phrases too often today. Thinking of bright shadows and dark reflections, of mirrors and strippers, he wondered if someone was trying to make a fool of *him*. Wondered if someone had been making a fool of him his whole life long.

He had never been much inclined to paranoia. Conspiracy

theories were the toxic mimics of genuine investigations—just fantasies that filled the void when facts were hard to come by. Or so he'd always thought.

Still, what Lu had suggested to him today would make anyone feel shaky. Her story of changeling children was like something out of a grim fairy tale. If there were a "someone" who was responsible for his unexpected history, then who? Who could have done such a thing? Who could have made him a pawn from even before the moment of his birth—and again, to what purpose?

The shadowy secrecy of it all made him think of those organizations which had given Kwok the Forrest documents. The same organizations which had hired first Kwok, and now him.

But Lu's discovery didn't smack particularly of "national security" or even "corporate competition." Beyond the secret agencies and terrorist networks, beyond the criminal conspiracies and clandestine cabals, beyond the international intrigues of shadow governments, were there entities still *more* shadowy?

Where should he look for creatures that lived so far from the light of day? What key should he use to unlock the black diamond doors—and what Powers might he find behind them?

Glancing down at the neon pink ticket in his hand, he felt as if he was holding a thread that would lead him away into a labyrinth that grew ever darker.

ANTICIPATING THE UNPRECEDENTED

CRYPTO CITY

IN A SMALL TELECONFERENCE LOUNGE amid the rooms of H/O's eighth-floor executive suite, Deputy Director Brescoll met with Beech, Wang, and Lingenfelter. No one in the room looked particularly happy, although their reasons likely differed from Brescoll's own.

His mother-in-law had just been diagnosed with uterine cancer, and his wife Marion, who was very close to her mother, was taking it hard. Despite the painful challenges he and his family were facing at home, Jim tried to stay focused on the matters at hand, but he wasn't finding it easy.

"I've looked through your reports," Brescoll said. "It seems to me we're facing a number of problems. The way I see it, they fall into four overall areas.

"First, there's activating the ash found when Jaron Kwok went missing. Second, there's explaining the eccentric images embedded in the Kwok holo-cast, particularly the views of the Sun Yat-sen Memorial Hall and the painting in Philadelphia. Third, there's containing access to the materials Kwok released through his holo-cast. Finally, there's dealing with our competitors in this effort. Guoanbu in China, certainly, but what about Cybernesians working out of Tri-Border? The New Teachings Warriors? The Cheng crime family? What do they all expect to gain from their activities?

"Let's start with the first issue, the binotech ash and its activation."

Beech, seeming a bit too eager, activated a holovid showing footage of complex nanorganic mechanisms.

"Our technician operating in Lu's Kowloon lab noted that Lu was growing out a number of samples in blood-based media," he said. "Working from that, we've done the same. The binotech is, indeed, activated by contact with blood."

Brescoll noted the odd glance of disagreement that passed between Beech and Wang. Then Wang dislodged Beech's data display. He replaced it with his own graphs showing percentages of "Projected Binotech Population Activation" and "Characterizations of Recursively Enumerable Languages By Means of Watson-Crick Automata."

"I think 'partially activated' more accurately describes the situation," Wang said. "Under electron microscopy, the mechanisms that make up Kwok's ashes—they're of more than one type, you see— have proven to be unprecedentedly complex. We have nothing that quite matches them. And yet all they're doing so far is very low-level communication and replication."

"But you believe they're capable of more?" the deputy director asked.

"Much more," Wang said firmly. Jim noted that Bree Lingen-felter glanced quickly from Wang to Beech and back to Wang, then she displaced Wang's imagery with her own graphs documenting "Turing Machine Grammars in Mixed Organic/Inorganic Systems," and "Overlap of Complementarity Properties in Watson-Crick and Generalized Quantum Systems."

"I have to agree with Doctor Wang," she said. "The way these binotech devices exploit the quantum-mechanical foundations of DNA's molecular activity is much more sophisticated than would be required for simple replication or local communication. Nobody we know of—not us, not the Chinese, not the Russians or Japanese or Europeans—*nobody* has produced binotech devices possessing this level of sophistication."

Jim could feel his brow furrowing.

"So our first question has spawned three more," he said, shaking his head slightly. "If the binotech ash—of however many different types—isn't fully activated, then how do we go about achieving full activation? What's the most likely result of fully activating them? And if nobody we know built the damn things, then who did?"

"We don't yet have solid answers to those questions—only speculations," Beech replied flatly.

"We *are* working on a sort of 'cytological' classification of the binotech types," Wang added, "but it's not easy. These devices blur the lines between organic and inorganic mechanisms in ways that are truly unprecedented."

"Very well," Brescoll said, waving off further explanations and thinking that he'd heard words like "cytological" far too often of late. "What about those embedded images from the holo-cast?"

"Our informants report that Detective Lu did some investigative work at the Sun Yat-sen Memorial," Beech said, flashing into their shared screenspace images of the Memorial and newsclips about a terrorist raid. "Went there on the same day the Memorial was attacked by a New Teachings Warriors cell, curiously enough. However, Zuo Wenxiu, the operative we tentatively identified from the Hui murder and the Victoria Peak meeting, wasn't among those taken in the failed raid.

"Lu's investigation seems to have hit a roadblock at the Memorial, too, at least for the moment. Our operative in her lab indicates that she and a colleague videocataloged the Sun Yat-sen Memorial, but have done nothing further with that material."

Jim wondered for an instant about the "curiousness" of the terrorist raid—and how much Beech's "informants" might know about that group—but he decided to let it pass.

"And the painting in the Philadelphia Museum of Art? The one with the nobleman pointing at a maze."

"Not a maze, technically," Beech corrected him. "A labyrinth."

"And the difference is . . . ?"

"A maze offers many potential paths. There are forks in the road, places where you have to make a choice. You can also make wrong choices, and hit dead ends.

"A labyrinth, however, is unicursal—offering only one course or path through it. No choices, but no dead ends on the way to the center. The journey from the periphery of the labyrinth to the center, and from the center to the periphery, are mirror images. You can get lost in a maze and never complete it, but so long as you persist in a labyrinth you never really get lost. If you have the time, you'll always complete it."

Noting the expression on the deputy director's face, Beech shut up, as if he had said too much. For Brescoll, he had—and too much of it had been pedantic, and more than a little condescending.

"Well, let's 'persist' then, and continue our journey toward making sense of that painting."

"Aside from being captioned with an enigmatic phrase—" Wang began.

" 'Hide insane plight in plain sight,' " Brescoll said, nodding.

"—we've learned nothing further," Wang continued, "beyond verifying the fact that Jaron Kwok visited the Museum over a year ago. He likewise once visited the Sun Yat-sen Memorial."

"What about this Cybernesian who eluded the dragnet in Philadelphia?" Brescoll asked. "Don Markham, or Sturm, or whatever other aliases he works under?"

The three looked vaguely embarrassed as Beech replied.

"Initially, that seemed unrelated. I suggested to my colleagues in Central Intelligence that our contacts at FBI and Homeland Security might want to move against Markham, on the pretext of a cryptographic arms trading violation. Since he was involved with the Kwok holo-cast, we thought it might be helpful to have him in custody. We only discovered Markham's interest in the Dossi painting after he eluded capture. He seems to have disappeared somewhere between the Philadelphia Museum of Art and his hotel. We suspect he had help, although from *whom* is not yet clear."

Jim nodded. He suspected that some of the "we" Beech was talking about might have Tetragrammaton connections. Well, Jim had connections of his own, fly-fishing hereabouts in the stream of time. He would have to stop playing dumb now, and only hoped he had the mental concentration to pull off acting *smart*.

"I have to confess that I may have been wrong," the deputy director began, "in my initial doubts about the interest you three showed in those sixteenth-century memory systems. Here we have a sixteenth-century Dossi painting that's proving to be important. One of *my* sources has also suggested we might want to look at that painting and the Sun Yat-sen Memorial, in the context of an artificial memory system."

"How so?" Wang said, uncharacteristically terse.

"My sources indicate that the painting may be a 'memory image,' an important visual placeholder in the overall memory system. They also suggest the Sun Yat-sen Memorial Hall itself may be a real-world model for the 'memory palace' or 'memory theatre,' the basis for an entire memory system—one which includes the painting."

Jim Brescoll watched as the lights flashed on in the eyes of his three advisors, and they began to talk among themselves in hurried shorthand.

"What about your third area, then?" Wang asked. "What is the link, if any, between the holo-cast with its embedded images, and how the binotech operates? Did your sources say anything about that?"

"No, I'm afraid they didn't."

"It might be a good question to ask them," Beech said dryly. "Even without such sources, we think we may have an answer to your fourth question—who we have competing with us, and what the various groups may be after."

"And?"

Beech looked at Lingenfelter, who nodded.

"This falls into the category of the 'speculations' Doctor Beech mentioned earlier," Bree Lingenfelter said, "but we think it's possible that the binotech ash Kwok left behind may, when properly activated and programmed, constitute the fully operational universal quantum DNA machine the Chinese and we ourselves have been working on."

"A binotech quantum computer," Wang said, "powerful enough to address either or both the cryptographic and cryptanalytic sides of the security problem."

"The ultimate informational weapon," Jim said quietly. "We're supposed to be years away from perfecting it, but you're saying it may already exist? That somebody has actually *bestowed* it upon us?"

"Yes, sir," Beech said. "Like a gift from the gods. But as of now, all we've got is a bunch of components of unidentified manufacture— the 'ash.' We don't really understand the shape of the black box they constitute, not to mention where the on/off switch might be located."

"What about reverse engineering?"

Wang shook his head.

"Awfully hard to reverse-engineer something when all you have are the pieces, you're not sure you have all of them, and you don't know how they go together. Better if you can get it to put itself together and show you what it does, first. That's why the response to blood-media is still important, even if it's only partial at best."

"Which brings us full circle, back to my first point," the deputy director said, nodding. "I have some verification of the information provided by the CIA plant in Lu's forensics lab. This is from the wire and the pinhole cameras Deputy Legal Attaché Adjoumani was wearing."

Brescoll started a grainy, low-grade video feed, playing it on their shared screenspace. The sound from Adjoumani's wire was spotty, but they could hear with reasonable clarity Lu's and Cho's discussions about the effect her blood had on the tiny organomechanisms, about the swirling patterns they made, and the ensuing discussion of fingerprints.

As the deputy director let the record play, he happened to note Baldwin Beech's expression. The man turned ghostly pale. Almost in spite of himself, Brescoll listened and watched the surveillance record even more carefully, and waited a while before he cut it off.

What the video showed seemed to be an irrelevant digression: Lu and Cho discussing identical twins, their nonidentical fingerprints, and how identicals could be made to appear nonidentical. Why would that so distress Beech, if that was what was causing his discomfiture? The point at which all the blood had drained from Beech's face seemed to coincide with the moment Lu asked Cho for a blood sample. You'd think the woman had stuck a large-gauge needle into Beech himself.

Brescoll made a mental note to view the record again more carefully later, then switched it off.

"I think you were right to go after Markham," Brescoll said. "If he was involved in the way Kwok usurped the worldwide computer-share, it would be good to have him in custody. It's very unfortunate that he eluded capture. He might have been able to suggest how Kwok's work with memory palaces and memory theaters might relate to the infosphere and cyberspace."

"Excuse me," Bree Lingenfelter said, "but I don't see the connection."

"I think I do," Steve Wang said. "And it's precisely *about* connection. How internal artificial human memory might connect to external artificial machine memory."

"Yes," Beech said, the color slowly returning to his face. "And not just memory. Will, and action. A seamless link between mind and machine, so that what is willed, will be done, no matter what the distance—constrained only by the ordinary laws of physics."

"Is that possible?" Lingenfelter asked, her voice sounding more than a little skeptical.

"The mind does it with the machine of the body all the time," Wang said with a shrug.

"But that's different—"

"No, it's not, not in principle—"

"Enough!" Brescoll said, chuckling. "Work out the details on your own time, and give me a report. Right now, we need to determine whether the fact that the ash binotech was created at the same time as the Kwok holo-cast was just a coincidence, or if it might have some deeper, causal connection. While you're at it, if you can't figure out *who* created the ash, then let's at least try to figure out *how*. I doubt that it was created out of nothing. The answer might show us how to fully activate it."

The three scientists agreed, and left soon thereafter. As they did, Brescoll noticed that Beech still looked somewhat disconcerted.

Returning to his office, the deputy director wondered how much more disconcerted Beech would be if he knew that the directions Brescoll had just outlined had been suggested to *him* by his own secretive sources. And that those same sources had, in their fly-files, included a transcript of a conversation between two unidentified men, one of whom spoke of "ashes" that might somehow provide an edge over both the "corrupt Chinese communists" and "decadent Western democracies," while the other party spoke of "living fossil codes."

Sitting down behind his desk, Brescoll wondered how, in his

report to the director, he would describe the progress of the investigation into Kwok's disappearance. That last word bothered him, reminding him again, as it did, of how quickly Director Rollwagen had shut down discussion at the end of that early gathering— seemingly ages ago—when the disappearance of prototype quantum code devices had come up.

He and the director had discussed other aspects of the investigation since then, covering everything from Borges and Babel to quantum DNA entanglements and reality as a simulation—but Brescoll had never pushed to know more about those disappearances, and the director had never been forthcoming about them.

Did Janis Rollwagen have sources of her own? What if *she* had only been "playing dumb," too? He'd have to talk with her sometime about certain unspoken matters, and he felt certain that time was coming closer.

EIGHT

SYMMETRY . . .

LAKE NOT-TO-BE-NAMED

NILS BARAKIAN'S PRIVATE JET FLEW them to a small airport outside San Jose, where they transferred to a dark-windowed four-seat helicopter. When Don asked where they were headed, Barakian only tipped his hat and said that it was a location "beside a certain lake in the Sierras." Don didn't know quite what to make of that.

He mulled it over in silence as he watched the terrain below—a broad agricultural plain that lay between the Coastal Range and the Sierra Nevada Mountains—pass into and out of view.

"What do you think of the Great Central Valley, Don?" Barakian asked, over the thrum of the helicopter.

"It looks like somebody upholstered the landscape in gray and brown corduroy."

Barakian laughed.

"That's because it's winter. The fields and their crops look quite a bit different in spring. More like a big patchwork quilt. All sorts of colors, then."

"Maybe," Don said, looking over the landscape and trying to imagine something less monochromatic, "but the only color I see is some nubby green corduroy, there."

"Orange groves," Barakian said, nodding his hat brim in their direction. "Ah, the wonderful smells—of all kinds of fruit trees. I remember March days when the orchards blooming on the valley floor were pews of flowers in a cathedral of rain."

"Sounds like you know this area pretty well."

"Well enough," Barakian said. "I grew up here. My grandparents moved here from Turkey, not long before the Armenian genocide. Some of the folks around *here* didn't like Armenians all that much either, though."

"No?" Don asked. Having grown up in the American Midwest, until his early twenties Don had assumed that prejudice was mostly a black/white thing. He had traveled since, however, and had encountered many other varieties of stereotyping. Historical prejudices of the Japanese toward Koreans. British toward Australians. Even, in American sunbelt areas, prejudice toward Canadian "snowbirds," supposedly based on their driving and tipping practices. Seemed people could take a preemptive dislike to one another with almost no provocation at all.

"Called us 'Fresno Indians,'" Barakian continued. "But eventually sons and daughters met and married. That's how I ended up with the first name of Nils. Lots of Swedes and other Scandinavians around Kingsburg—one of whom was my mother."

"Hmm," Don grunted noncommittally, not knowing what to say to that. He turned his attention to the snowcapped Sierras, looming ever more prominently into view ahead. Down in the foothills, the Euclidean geometry of the farm fields began to break up, giving way to fractal forests of oaks on the lower hillsides. Then, except for the occasional scars of roads, houses, and power-line tracts, only broad bands of pines added variety to the land, before being themselves limned with snow. Far ahead, Don saw that even the snow and pine cover broke off, amid windswept granite and jagged peaks above the treeline.

They never reached that starker and more sublime terrain, though. The helicopter began settling earthward toward a lake surrounded by snow-covered pine forests and punctuated by the occasional treeless granite dome. On one such headland not far from the lake, he saw snowboarders, happy plankster gangsters shredding the pristine whiteness. Noting that the shore at one end of the lake was ruler straight, Don concluded that "shore" was a dam, and the lake was man-made.

The helicopter headed toward a cul-de-sac parking lot, a mile or two from the large marina at the lake's northernmost end. Something that looked like a cross between a combat vehicle and a black stretch limo was already parked there.

"Our destination lies just ahead," Barakian announced, "at the end of that access road. In less security-conscious times, the name of this facility was imprinted into the concrete in foot-tall letters above the tunnel entrance. I'm afraid I'm not allowed to mention its name, nowadays. Nor the name of the lake either. I suppose I should blindfold you, but instead I've decided to trust you, I think."

The pilot put the helicopter into a slow circle, waiting.

"All right," said Barakian. "Let's go down."

Don felt as much as saw their landing. Barakian took him by the arm and steadied him as he stepped down from the chopper. As they exited, the blades above their heads slowed to a stop.

"Here's our car," Barakian said, holding his hat on his head with one hand while gesturing with the other to their stretch limo—a Hummer sheathed in a titanium and solar-electric skin. They entered the relative quiet of the waiting vehicle. Once inside, they drove only a short distance before they came to a stop once more.

Looking about them, Don saw that they had passed completely through a tall, gated entrance. They were parked just inside the mouth of a long tunnel, the entrance of which was framed by tremendous icicles. A large sign on the wall beside them read All Persons Shall Log In And Check In With Operator When Entering Station. Armed security guards stood watch, questioning their driver and eyeing Barakian and his guest.

The driver got out and one of the guards held out a telephone. He spoke briefly into it, then resumed his place behind the wheel. Satisfied, the guards tipped their hats respectfully to Barakian and waved them through.

The tunnel seemed to go on for miles, with no discernible light at its other end. They passed more signs—All Vehicles Use Low Gear and Speed Limit 15—but not much else. The lurid glare of the tunnel's work lights revealed only the smooth road sloping downward, and the seemingly patternless pattern of fractured granite, arching overhead. The slow trip downhill made Don nervous, as if he were descending into a dungeon, or the bowels of the earth.

"What *is* this place?"

"Let's just call it a powerhouse tunnel," Barakian replied. "The road takes us a mile into the mountain."

"And at the end is . . . a powerhouse?"

"That's right. A powerhouse tucked into an artificial cavern. The cave is shaped like a loaf of bread, one hundred feet high and three hundred feet long. Here inside the mountain, we're a thousand vertical feet below the surface, or about as far below ground as the top of the Empire State Building is above it. Most of the tunnel and cavern are smooth-wall blasted out of the rock, or shotcreted where the rock's too fractured."

"A powerhouse inside an artificial cavern, inside a mountain?" Don asked. "Was it built to survive some kind of nuclear attack? Or a terrorist action?"

"No, no. Nothing like that. The strict security only really started in the latter half of '01."

Don nodded, thinking of the World Trade Center towers, burning like candles on the Antichrist's birthday cake. Make a wish—and blow out the old order of the world. Many unhappy returns, of terrors and wars. Welcome to the Terrible Twos.

"Still haven't gotten the blast-protection doors put in yet, though, even after all these years," Barakian said. "There's been some reluctance to do it—and not just because of the expense, either. The power company was so proud of this facility that it used to sponsor tours. No tours now for more than a decade, but every once in a while people from Hollywood get permission to come in and film in certain sections."

Two side tunnels peeled off before the Hummer came to a stop again. A pair of immense doors, painted navy blue, stood before them as they exited the all-terrain limo. The blue doors opened, revealing the immense underground space of the man-made cavern. The overwhelming whine of a massive turbine filled Don's senses.

The powerhouse and its support structures shone with a yellowish cast, presumably from the halogen work lights that lit the interior. Or maybe the color of the space reflected the yellow-painted 450-ton overhead crane that dominated the view at this level, a tremendous machine mounted on rails atop vertical orange railbeds running along either side of the great room, bolted again and again into the rock of the artificial cave.

"The crane's for servicing the generator," Barakian said over the noise of the turbine, noting Don's gaze. "The generator itself is housed in the octagonal structure with the pony-motor on top."

Don nodded. They clanged down traction-grated steel steps framed in steel handrails—helpful, Don thought, given the steep angle of the stairways. Barakian pointed out ventilation ductwork and emergency oxygen canisters as they made their way onto the catwalk that led out onto the safety-railed octagon. Something about the view as they approached—the geometrical, industrial symmetry of the generator unit and its pony-motor, juxtaposed against the scarred, fracture-patterned backdrop of the living rock from which the cavern had been hewn—struck Don with particular force.

At the end of the catwalk he stepped onto the sealed octagon and felt the energy of vast machinery shaking the floor beneath his feet.

"Power use out on the grid fluctuates," Barakian said, "but the nuclear plant operators don't like to fluctuate their power output if they can help it—"

"This is nuclear?" Don asked, somewhat apprehensively.

"No, no. *Hydro.* At night, after everyone turns off their lights and computers and goes to bed, the hydro folks here exploit the excess power capacity of the nuclear plants out on the grid. They pull that extra power off the transmission lines to run this generation unit *backwards*, essentially turning the generator into a giant electric pump motor. They pump water out of the lake below, back up through this power station—named for the engineer who envisioned this whole project—then pump it 1500 vertical feet uphill to what we'll call 'B Forebay.' "

"What's the pony-motor do?" Don asked, studying his own blue-dyed skull knot in the mirror of the motor's polished metal.

"That's needed because of drawdown: if the plant operator had to start pumpback from a dead stop, the resistance would melt the lines in the power grid. The pony-motor gets things moving, so the excess grid power can be brought on smoothly to convert the generator's turbine into a pump."

"But why do it at all?" Don asked as they moved off the generator octagon onto the catwalk grating again. "Why pump the water back uphill? Sounds like a scheme for a perpetual motion machine."

"Not when you can use cheap off-hour power to refill that higher elevation forebay. Then, the next day, you let that same water flow back down the 1500-foot vertical fall, at more than 770-cubic-feet per second, to spin the turbine on this 200-megawatt generator—cranking out power at premium peak load prices."

Having made his point, Barakian walked Don down another set

of stairs to the octagon's next level, where he opened an access door that led to the spinning, humming heart of all that energy. A solid cylindical steel shaft—thicker than two men standing back-to-back, and tall as one standing on the other's shoulders—connected the turbine below to the generator's coils above. The massive shaft spun at 400 rpms, a building pillar turned whirling dervish. As Don stared at it, Barakian chattered on about how the generator weighed 1.86 million pounds and how the turbine was essentially a massive waterwheel turned on its side. Don barely heard, too busy feeling his face break into a smile of pure wonderment at such superhuman energies, humanly tamed.

As they left the shaft access room and continued on their way, Don stared up at the work lights, misplaced stars shining in their rigid constellations from the distant roof of the cavern. Everything about the massive plumbing and power system housed inside this immense underground room was constructed on a superhuman scale. To Don it almost seemed more probable that a lost race of gigantic miners had built a place like this, than to believe that ordinary, mortal humans had created it.

"War or peace," Barakian continued, oblivious to his companion's awe. "Doesn't matter who we're shooting or who's shooting us—Hollywood keeps shooting everybody. Parts of several low-budget disaster films were shot here, as well as sections of the last two episodes of the old *X-Files* series. Among other things."

"But why was it built underground like this?" Don asked, following Barakian over a system of bridges and steel-grated flooring, into a room that was much quieter, but still vibrating slightly with the hidden roar of water and the whirling hum of the massive electrical generation unit.

"Has to do with elevations. Potential and kinetic energies. It's part of a power project which, for security reasons, I'm not at liberty to identify by name. I will tell you that it's a system of a dozen dams and tunnels and high-volume pipes. Six man-made lakes and additional forebays. Nine powerhouses. Twenty-three generating units. Associated penstocks and tailraces. It's a gravity-powered fluid-medium energy machine extending from 'Lake E' and 'Lake F' in the high Sierra to 'Lake R' down in the foothills. When the builders began it, this hydropower project was just about the biggest construction job ever attempted. Right up there with the Panama Canal. This power station here came later—the last on the project, completed in the 1980s."

Don nodded, trying to figure out if he'd ever heard of it.

"The power companies have always claimed this project makes the upper end of this particular river the 'hardest working water in the world,'" Barakian continued. The two men now walked through a large control room where old-fashioned valves and dials predominated.

"Then how come nobody's working here?" Don asked. "This place is empty as a ghost town. Shouldn't there be people watching over all this?"

"There are," Barakian said. "Just not here. The whole system is monitored and controlled by a central operator at a computer screen, some miles from here. The operator watches a digital, virtual representation of the whole system of lakes and dams, tunnels and powerhouses."

"Supervisory control and data acquisition, then?"

"Precisely. A SCADA system, with the usual division into remote terminal units and master terminal units. The RTUs doing data gathering and control throughout the big plumbing, the MTUs coordinating the overall system. Some smaller distributed control systems embedded in the overall routing, but mostly long distance connections in open-loop configurations."

"This analog stuff here is all backup, then?"

"Safety redundancy. In normal operation, this is a mechanized and automated haunted powerhouse, Donald. Maintenance crews usually don't come through more than every few weeks at most. There's a machine shop for repairs on-premises, but other than routine maintenance, this place pretty much runs itself."

"What about the guards we saw when we came in?"

"The gate security is usually remote, too," Barakian said. "Read from motion sensors and surveillance microcameras aboveground and around the tunnel entrance. I suspect we met human guards at least partly because they knew we were coming. It's all remote controlled and remotely monitored. Even the power generated here is remotely utilized."

"What do you mean?"

"Most of the electricity this system generates doesn't stay in the area. It's always gone to Los Angeles, since the first turbines came on-line by the river, a century ago."

"Why's that?"

"Supply and demand," Barakian said with a sly smile. "To find out for certain you'd have to ask Henry Huntington—or the famous but unnameable engineer who came up with the whole idea. But they're both long dead. The engineer envisioned the project, but it was Huntington's money that got things rolling. Ever hear of Huntington?"

"Is he the same one the Huntington Library and Gardens are named after? The ones in Pasadena?"

"They're in San Marino, actually. Same fellow, all right. Southern California electric and railway tycoon."

Passing the weirdly empty kitchen and break room, Barakian led Don on a brief detour into the main transformer room. There, the power from the big generator passed into a squat, bulky, battleship gray unit shaped like a metal head with three tall insulator-sheathed horns sticking out of its forehead. The tip of each of the horns was connected by a solid, curving metal bar to another Frankenstein's lab device, a bus bar in a conduit filled with argon gas.

The three conduits, their electricity made safe for the power grid and the outside world, led back to the elevator and stairway shaft. There, Barakian explained, the conduits followed that shaft a thousand feet straight up, to the top of the mountain.

"Watch," he said, turning off the transformer-room lights. After a moment, when his eyes had adjusted to the dark, Don saw a faint blue glow playing about the triple horns of the transformer. "See it?"

"The blue glow? Yeah, I do."

Satisfied, Barakian switched the lights back on and they returned to the main floor.

"I figured you might know Huntington's library from your research," Barakian continued. "He was a big-time collector of medieval and Renaissance texts. Paintings, too, among other things. Not even he knew everything his collections housed. We've had some of the more obscure items brought up here for you and your work."

"Here? Why?"

"When we said you were going underground, we weren't speaking metaphorically," Barakian said, opening what was apparently another support-room door—Limited Access Area Authorized Personnel Only—and taking off his hat as he entered. Following him inside, Don felt as if he had stepped inside the crack in the mountain that led to Faerie, and wondered if he should be hearing the thunder of ninepins played by odd little men.

In contrast to the valves and dials on the other side of the door, on *this* side he was met with an auditorium-sized wonderland of all the latest high tech. Computer monitors and projection screens covered the perimeter, hanging in front of the not-so-smooth-blasted and shotcreted walls. Several of the cave's computer screens prominently displayed the Dossi painting Don had seen in Philadelphia. Here and there around the room Don saw stacks of documents and books, some of them apparently quite old.

Two techs—remoting from some undisclosed location—appeared to be scanning and digitizing pages from old books, at least from what Don could discern on some of the smaller screens.

Off to one side, three-dimensional geometric schematics of something that looked like a large, multisided hall or theater hovered over another bent-air holographic projection table. A trio of white-coated techs—real-time holographic remotes, again—were testing and adjusting the haptics on a full-sensorium feedback virtuality unit in the center of the room.

"Wow."

"Indeed. I thought you'd appreciate what we've amassed here," Barakian said, smiling broadly. "The original power project here was a privately funded construction project for the public good—the largest ever. The Kitchener Foundation has privately funded the work going on in this room, too. We're very proud of it. Short of what the NSA and some other large governmental and international organizations possess, this is as cutting edge as information processing and telecommunications get on this planet."

"Fantastic," Don said, looking over the marvels on display in the underground space. He seemed almost to float as he followed Barakian down a ramp toward the floor of the facility. "But again, why here?"

"What do you mean?"

"How can the Foundation operate openly here, in a sensitive facility, without interference from the authorities?"

They came to a stop not far from the virtuality unit. Barakian placed his hat on a corner of the unit and turned off its pickup microphones and cameras. Their conversation, from here on, would presumably be *very* private.

"Oh, yes—that," Barakian said with an awkward gesture of dismissal. "We don't exactly operate 'openly,' as you put it. It so happens that a number of Kitchener Foundation people also serve on the board of directors of the utility that operates this powerhouse. That gives us a 'pass,' which turns out to be very convenient."

"Why's that?"

"The people responsible for 'managing' society," Barakian said, staring about the room, "like to have a certain level of control over most high-tech activities of any significant scale. Activities they don't control they insist on monitoring, at least covertly. One way they accomplish that monitoring is by looking for the drain high-tech activities cause on the power grid, or for the electromagnetic signature such large-scale activities leave behind. The fact that all this equipment just happens to be situated right next to a power station—one seldom visited by human beings and housed deep inside a mountain—makes anything you do here that much harder to detect from outside. Especially during the next few weeks, when this facility will technically be closed down, while the long-delayed blast doors are installed in the entry tunnel and the elevator and stairway shafts."

"This is all so overwhelming," Don said, turning around slowly as his gaze took in the room. "Something James Bondish about it— in an Ernst Blofeld's underground lair sort of way."

Barakian frowned.

"That's not the comparison I would want to make, although I know Doctor Vang, my opposite number within Tetragrammaton, tends toward those sorts of spy-versus-spy analogies."

Based on his infosphere research, Don recognized Vang's name, and thought that his fondness for such analogies made sense— given the man's imposing history. Born to a Southeast Asian peasant family, in a village with a shaman and a neolithic-level culture, Vang would one day go on to head Tetragrammaton. He had, in his early teens, been recruited to service in a CIA-sponsored guerrilla army, then had escaped from Cambodian killing fields after the collapse of the American-backed governments in Vietnam, Laos, and Cambodia. Had emigrated to California, to culture shock and eventual retraining via a CIA-sponsored scholarship, to become an all-American success story in the information sciences.

As creator and CEO of Paralogics, Vang had at one time run the largest specialty supercomputer firm in the world—a company whose biggest clients were the NSA and the CIA, conveniently enough.

"You're on speaking terms with Vang?" Don asked, more than a little surprised.

"Of course. If Tetragrammaton exists essentially to break down the boundaries between humans and machines, then the Kitchener Foundation exists to maintain what is essential in those boundaries."

"*What?*"

"Ah, I can tell by your expression that you see opposition in that relationship, but I see it as a complementarity—as I'm sure your friend Jaron Kwok would have, judging from what we've been able to learn of his notes."

Don didn't know about the "your friend" part, but he let it pass.

"Complementarity? How so?"

"What do you know about Felix Forrest and his pseudonymous science fiction stories?" Barakian asked, cocking an eyebrow.

The question, in answer to his own question, caught Don by surprise.

"I know one of them was probably about the CIA's MK Ultra project. Why do you ask?"

"In a whole cycle of stories, Forrest conjures up his 'lords and ladies of the Instrumentality.' Into the far future, these ladies and lords strive to help the human species survive, and to return mankind to its humanity, to keep man *as* man."

"And?" Don asked, after a pause. He wondered whether old Barakian had lost his train of thought.

"Long-term antagonistic relationships often coevolve toward codependency. The Soviet Union and the United States during the Cold War. Poisonous milkweed plants and the monarch caterpillars that feed on them. Ants and swollen-thorn acacias. Both nature and culture offer many examples."

"What's that got to do with this Instrumentality thing?"

"There are lords and ladies of the Instrumentality on both the Kitchener and Tetragrammaton sides of the issue, Don. The problem, I think, lies in that we disagree about exactly just what it means to be human. Both sides are working toward what each considers to be in the best interests of humanity, or at least in the long-term survival interests of the human species—only in very different ways."

"To say the least," Don said, looking up distractedly at the way the Dossi painting was divided up among the screens.

"There's more overlap than you might guess," Barakian continued. "In our own ways, both the Kitchener Foundation and Tetragrammaton are currently working against PCAM's Operation E 5-24, for instance."

"Whose E-what?"

"PCAM, the Project for a Christian American Millenium. Ephesians, chapter 5, verse 24. 'As the church submits to Christ, so also wives should submit to their husbands in everything.' Operation E 5-24 is working to develop a 'headship hormone,' a female submission synthetic."

"How's that your concern?" Don asked, curious but still preoccupied with the room's cutting-edge wonders.

"Neither we in Kitchener nor our acquaintances in Tetragrammaton believe that it's in the long-term interest of humanity to take consciousness away from half the population, as E 5-24 is intended to do. So you see, we do occasionally find common ground, and together we intervene. Especially when the interests of religious fundamentalism and the BMSS—excuse me, the bio-managed security state—converge in such a particularly bad synergy."

"Bio-managed?" Don asked, staring at the holographic displays captioned *Sun Yat-sen Memorial Hall, Guangzhou*.

"Biotechnology used for social control," Barakian replied.

"You mean like biometrics? Scans? Face and voice recognition software?"

"That's part of it. But scanning and analyzing people's fingerprints, the irises of their eyes, their hand geometries, their gaits, even their DNA—that's only the tip of the iceberg. It's an old effort, really. In the Victorian era, it was Cesare Lombroso's measurements of physiognomic and anatomical features, in an attempt to predetermine criminal 'types.' Then, later, studies of XYY genetics. The assumptions that led to the Three Strikes and Megan's Law disclosure statutes, too—that some people are born with criminal tendencies and cannot be rehabilitated.

"The goal has always been the same: The predetection of social deviance by means of biological science."

"That doesn't sound like such a bad thing, necessarily," Don said, examining the Memorial Hall schematics and holos more closely, discovering that the display unit was equipped with a very impressive zoom feature. The more he examined the Hall holo, the less it resembled a straightforward octagonal auditorium, and the more it looked like a pagoda that had swallowed a sports stadium.

"No, not necessarily," Barakian agreed, "but applying the 'pre-emptive strike' to criminal justice *does* require dissolving the individual into a codable risk factor set. So that the person and his movements can be monitored, via database, within the larger social control system. The BMSS 'watches your shit,' so to speak, but it's less about Big Brother who knows everything about your bowel habits, and more about lots of Little Brothers who, given the opportunity, might go tell everything they can learn about what you're doing with your dookie."

Shocked, startled, and appalled, Don burst out laughing. He'd heard oldsters go on before about all the freedoms that had supposedly been lost since '01, but this was a whole new level of *that*.

"But isn't that the whole social deal?" he asked, after his laughter had subsided. "Citizens sacrifice personal freedoms and rights to a government, and in return the government insures law, order, and security."

"Yes," Barakian said. "But events like the World Trade Center and Balinese resort attacks, which ushered in tighter security at this powerhouse starting more than a decade ago, also made clear that it's impossible to insure total security. The 'deal' itself was always a myth, to some degree. Unfortunately, the response of the state has been to deny all the more forcefully that the deal *was* a myth—and to demand the sacrifice of ever more rights and personal freedoms in pursuit of ever more illusory security. The more a nation looks like a fortress from the outside, the more it feels like a prison on the inside. That's how you end up with military takeovers after WMD attacks, and something like the SCANCI—the Selective Criminality, Aberrance, and NonConformity Index."

Don had heard of the "scan-key," or "skanky," as it was more colloquially known. He supposed that his own file in *that* database had grown considerably over the last few months.

"But what can you do?" Don asked with a shrug of resignation. "There *are* real threats, real dangers. You can't just give up on security—"

"Which we obviously haven't," Barakian said, "at least judging from the guards we have at the gate to this facility. Or from the remote surveillance tech that usually makes their physical presence unnecessary."

"Or from the fact that you've been doing all you can," Don said dryly, "to avoid naming our location here."

Barakian smiled, then continued.

"But giving up on *total* security isn't the same thing as completely giving up on security. Here or anywhere else, absolute security is no more attainable nor desirable than is absolute freedom. The point is never to sacrifice the reality of freedom *or* security for the ideal absolute of either."

"Your 'complementarity' again?" Don asked, still enjoying the holodisplay's impressive scanning features.

"Indeed. And entanglement, too. Individual rights and social responsibilities are best seen as inherently entangled. But even that only mirrors something much larger. Which is why you're here."

"I thought I was here to hide out," Don said, "and to work on the stuff that was embedded in the Kwok holo-cast."

"Yes, yes, you are now our specialist on that holo-cast. Complementarity and entanglement are all over that, as in all Kwok's work. Most immediately, however, your own work will involve investigating the possibility of relationships between the Dossi painting and the memory palace or memory theater it may be part of—presumably one based on the real-world Sun Yat-sen Memorial Hall."

"I got that part. I still don't see why my work has to happen inside a mountain, though."

Barakian stared hard at him. Don stopped fidgeting with the zoom controls.

"The Kwok holo-cast, along with some of our other sources, suggests that there may be a danger."

"Danger? You mean like SWAT teams coming after me?"

"There *is* that," Barakian said, striding forward and gazing up at the big screens. "The fact, too, that this facility could be converted to a self-sufficient bunker, with just the addition of those long-planned blast doors, was one reason we chose this place—instead of hiding you out in some remote Free Zone like Tri-Border. But there's another reason too."

"Which is?"

By way of answer, Barakian played a feed featuring a recording Don recognized from Kwok's holo-cast.

"If you build a computer of 400 ordinary quantum bits, or approximately 10^{120} classical bits," said the Newcomer, "that easily matches the sum total of all information all humans have ever accumulated about the universe. Even for the most godlike computer, though, there's a bandwidth limitation. Building a quantum DNA computer of, say, 400 4-bits *inside* the simulation would require at least doubling the usable bandwidth of the sim."

Barakian cut off the feed.

"Recognize that?"

"From the Kwok broadcast," Don said. "It's in one of the sections where noise initially obscures the audio content. So?"

"It's possible that a fully operational, universal quantum computer, capable of manipulating information densities comparable to our universe's bandwidth, might be used as far more than an 'information weapon.' We theorize that it could be used to distort or destroy physical reality."

"Some sort of e-bomb, then?"

"No. Not an electromagnetic pulse that would put out the lights. More like a device to put out the stars."

"You're joking, right?"

Barakian shook his head. His gaze seemed to become lost in one of the screens, a screen that was displaying still more imagery from the Kwok holo-cast. Don wondered if the old guy was putting him on, or just wacko. He didn't particularly like either possibility.

"We've obtained reports indicating that, when they've been activated, the prototype universe-bandwidth devices currently under development—primitive as they are—yield dramatic physical effects. Several of the devices have reportedly flashed out of existence."

"They—*exploded?*"

"More like they imploded—right out of our universe. Nothing remained."

. . . BREAKING

LAKE NOT-TO-BE-NAMED

DON TRIED TO TAKE that in, but even knowing what he already knew of Jaron Kwok's disappearance, it wasn't easy.

"And that's why we're inside a mountain?"

"Yes," Barakian said, his gaze roving over the screens. "Strange, really. A number of the movies shot here were low-budget apocalypse flicks. The underground tunnels were supposed to be where humanity survives being sky-rocketed by a comet or an asteroid, buried by nuclear winter, whatever. Protection against the outside world. But now we're trying to protect the world from what just might happen *inside* here, a mile into a mountain and a thousand feet underground."

Barakian looked around and shrugged.

"For whatever good it might do. It might be a protection, or it might not."

"What do you mean?"

"Some of the comments in the Kwok holo-cast seem to indicate that the physical effects, though initially unexpected, have now become an important goal of ongoing covert research."

"Into what?"

"A cryptologic catastrophe. A 'cryptastrophe,' if you will—or rather a *controlled* cryptastrophe. Some investigators seem to think they can produce an event in which only the device and a specified area around it would be annihilated. Neatly snipped out of existence. No fallout, no fire, no shrapnel. The ultimate precision munition, scalable to any required size. The Kwok holo-cast, however, indicated the possibility that something much more devastating might occur."

"You're just full of good news, aren't you?" Don said, shaking his head. He thought of that 'put out the stars' comment and smiled crookedly at the image of the Memorial Hall. "Okay. I'll bite. What kind of 'devastating'?"

"If we believe the theorists, a cryptastrophe in which perhaps our entire universe winks out of existence. Kwok's holo-cast suggests that, if we conclude and achieve closure within the memory palace 'room' that is our home universe—that *alone* will destroy those who are working with the device, and may bring down the cryptastrophe on our universe as a whole."

"Is that possible?" Don asked.

"Who knows? We're not at all sure that it is," Barakian said, shrugging awkwardly again. "If so, it has something to do with the concept that our universe, or at least a part of it, would be 'displaced.' Transformed from 'real' into 'virtual.' Depends how correct the plenum theorists are about a particular sort of complementarity among parallel universes."

"And what's *that* supposed to mean?" Don asked, more than a little annoyed that Barakian should be taking the idea of parallel universes quite so seriously. Despite his familiarity with virtual realities—or maybe *because* of it—Don had long resisted the idea of multiple and parallel universes. It always struck him as rather like being told that God had been traumatized as a child and suffered from a multiple personality disorder.

Barakian, however, remained unfazed. He simply nodded and continued.

"According to the plenum physicists, the total number of universes is essentially infinite. But with this peculiarity: from within any given universe, only that particular universe may be considered 'real'—all of the others are at best only 'virtual.' "

"And that fits 'devastation' . . . how?"

"What the cryptastrophists are most likely after is a virtualization bomb," Barakian said. "A map that destroys the country it describes, shoving it out of our universe through a wave of translation. But if such a device goes out of control, it has the potential to turn our universe, *our* branch of the plenum tree, into a phantom limb."

Don stared at the older man.

"So you're saying that even what *I'll* be working on has the potential to kill me? Or destroy this mountain? Or maybe even destroy the universe? Well, *that* really makes me eager to get started."

"It's also possible that *none* of those things will happen. We have only one real precedent here, Don. There's one comparable 'doomsday' device."

"You mean nuclear weapons?"

Barakian nodded. Don was reminded uncomfortably of the not so old adage, "Politics is for the moment, but extinction is for eternity." But that just twisted something Einstein had once said: Politics is for the moment; an *equation* is for eternity.

"Before the first nuclear device was detonated at Alamogordo," Barakian said, "some scientists of the Manhattan Project believed the detonation of the device would cause all the oxygen in the Earth's atmosphere to chain-react and catch fire. It didn't happen."

"Maybe," Don said, "but destroy the universe? What could possibly be worth such a risk?"

Barakian's gaze drifted toward the floor and hung there. He rocked back on his heels, like someone deciding which path he should follow.

"People are already dying for it. For conscience, and consciousness. For the chance to find a hole through the wall, a doorway out of no way—because we've already painted ourselves into a deadly corner. Tell me, Don—have you ever read Sartre?"

"Tell me, Nils—are you avoiding my question?"

"Not at all. Bear with me a bit. Sartre said the individual human consciousness is a kind of *hole* in the fabric of the physical world. A special kind of nothingness."

"Sounds like what Tetragrammaton is supposed to be working on."

"Indeed. One thing Tetragrammaton is really about, I'd say, is an attempt to externalize consciousness in such a way that the 'consciousness hole' coincides with what physicists call a singularity—only a singularity much more easily generated, much more controllable and manipulable than the physicists.' "

Don nodded. He'd come to a similar conclusion already.

"But Sartre also said that human beings try to transcend that nothingness by becoming God. . . ." Barakian continued.

"So the whimsical code name of 'Tetragrammaton,' " Don said, "isn't such a laughing matter after all."

Barakian shook his head absently.

"As the name of God? Not even Tetragrammaton's proponents claim to be working on the transformation of human beings into God. They would agree with Sartre that our human passion for divine transcendence is useless, because it is a passion to become what we cannot be. Since we didn't create ourselves, we can't be responsible for our own responsibility. Only God, according to Sartre, could be that.

"So there's always a gap, missing information, between what is 'our responsibility'—and what isn't. In that gap, however, they hope to find space for creating at least better angels, through a technologically mediated sort of 'transhuman' transcendence."

"Hmm," Don said, nodding slowly as he considered it. "In complex systems, there's always missing information. Analyzing any system, you usually go out only so far before rounding off your figures and declaring that the rest is insignificant."

"Yes," Barakian agreed, "but it's from the missing information, the 'trivial,' that the surprises come. Surprises, epiphanies, irruptions of the unexpected into the expected—they generally come as a result of multiplier effects. So, where Sartre calls human consciousness a nothingness, I would rather think that it's our 'insignificant' incompleteness that makes consciousness possible."

Don noticed that the techs had ceased their work with the virtuality unit and were standing by, as if waiting. It made him feel impatient.

"But what does that have to do with Kwok's work—and what I'm supposed to find out about what he left behind?"

"If we knew all that," Barakian said, smiling, "we wouldn't have had to hire you, now would we? Kwok's fascination with sixteenth-century memory metaphysicians and contemporary quantum theory suggest an overlap we wouldn't otherwise have expected."

"Overlap?"

"I'll show you," Barakian said, stepping up into the virtuality unit and switching on the pickup microphones and cameras. He nodded to the distant techs, who strode swiftly to their stations.

Somewhere, the technicians' hands flew over keyboards. In response to Barakian's words—and to his hands hovering and moving through the space before him, as if he were conducting an invisible orchestra—the imagery on the screens shifted and changed. Transcripts from dead languages and complex ancient diagrams appeared, then shifted to become cloud chamber tracings of particles, then again to become patterns of light and shadow. Constellations, highlighted among the apparent randomness of the stars, shifted to become space-time snapshots and supersnapshots of universes and multiverses.

"From our research," Barakian said, "we know that Giordano Bruno was the first person to put forward the idea of infinite worlds in infinite space. He saw the constellations of the night sky as the bright shadows of Ideas. Multiverse physicists, who also believe in infinite worlds, claim that all a 'parallel universe' actually boils down to is a 'constellation of particles' that barely interacts—like parallel lines that don't cross—with our own particular 'constellation of particles,' or universe."

"So they both use the word 'constellation'?" Don asked. "That's a pretty weak peg to hang your hat on."

"That's not the whole of it," Barakian said, moving his hands so that his words were real-time translated to captions onscreen. "Think of that word 'constellation,' then. What is a language but a 'constellation of particles'—letters, words, phrases? Just as every word in every language is made out of all the traces of all the words it is *not*, every universe is made out of all the traces of all the universes it is *not*, at least according to the theorists."

"Wait a minute," Don asked. "Which theorists? The multiverse people or the plenum people? And what's the difference?"

"The multiversalists believe the cosmic computer's virtual reality capability covers every physically possible universe," Barakian explained, "but *only* the physically possible ones. The plenum theorists believe in a virtual reality generator whose repertoire includes *all* possible universes, logical *and* physical. In the plenum, everything is possible and everything possible is *real*. The multiverse is an incredibly vast, yet still smaller, subset—the system of all possible constellations of particles, where every constellation of particles is made out of all the constellations of particles it is not."

"That sounds like a very full nothing," Don said, trying to keep himself from laughing.

"No doubt. But it allows me to rewrite Sartre so I can believe in the idea of consciousness as a special kind of nothing: That sacred nothingness out of which comes everything, if you like."

"Then it makes as much sense to think of physical reality as a hole in consciousness," Don said, at first in mockery but gradually growing more serious, "as it does to think of consciousness as a hole in physical reality."

"I hadn't really thought of it that way," Barakian said, pondering. Moving his hands through the control space, an old sorcerer conducting his apprentices in their work, Barakian began to smile beatifically.

"I knew you were right for the job!" he continued. "So you see, the risk of utter annihilation may almost be worth it. Not for whatever sort of informational superweapon the governments or corporations may be after. Not even for Tetragrammaton's gateway singularity through the space-time fabric."

"For what, then?" Don asked, more impatient than he had at first realized.

Barakian gestured. A triptych of images—of memory palaces and memory theaters—leapt onto the display screens. The largest of these was labeled *The Memory Theater of Giulio Camillo*, with *Publicius's Spheres of the Universe as a Memory System* off to the right side. The enormously complex *Memory System of Giordano Bruno* stood off to the left, looking like some sort of Kabbalistic sunwheel-within-wheels.

Barakian juxtaposed these with uncaptioned Chinese ideographic scripts.

"Think about it. Maybe Jaron Kwok was trying to achieve something *different*. Another kind of hole through the wall. Through a transcultural clash between western mnemonics and Chinese ideograms. Between iconographic imagination and ideographic imagination."

Looking at him, Don was struck by just how caught up in all this Barakian was. He looked a bit like a mad scientist, only without much of the scientist.

"An interesting speculation," Don said, "but what makes you think that?"

Barakian called up images of the Dossi painting, as taken from the Kwok holo-cast, then allowed that image to morph.

"First we see the most readily recoverable caption—'Hide insane plight in plain sight,' " Barakian said. "Then, we go much deeper. As the image-processing algorithms continue their number crunching, several steganographic symbols, computationally suppressed up to this point, begin to appear in the corners of the overall image, along with a glyphic script across the top."

Don watched and nodded, although he could by no means read all of the glowing golden script which had begun to appear, like hidden letters on a magic ring.

"You should recognize the symbol in the upper left there," Barakian said, highlighting that section of the painting.

"*Pi,*" Don said.

"Yes. The ratio of the circumference to the diameter of the circle—a transcendental number. Sixteenth letter of the Greek alphabet, but Phoenician in origin and related to the Hebrew *pe*. The symbol in the upper right there is *aleph*, first letter of the Hebrew alphabet. In Kabbalah it represents the infinitude and unity of God. It is also the symbol the mathematician Georg Cantor gave to his infinities, or transfinite cardinal numbers.

"The symbol in the lower right hand corner is the Chinese ideograph *yao*, which the mnemotechnician and Jesuit missionary to China, Matteo Ricci, divided in such a way that it can be translated as both 'necessity' and 'a woman from the west, who is a *hui-hui* or follower of a Western religion.'

"The script across the top center, the companion to the caption in English below, is the Akkadian word *babilu*, 'Gate of God,' from which we get the word *Babel*."

"As in 'Tower of'?"

"Yes."

"Interesting," Don said, trying to downplay his fascination. "Do you know how they relate to each other?"

"Not exactly. Nor their correspondence with the image of the Sun Yat-sen Memorial Hall as 'memory palace,' either. We do have some theories, however."

"And?"

"We think they suggest what Jaron Kwok may have been after. Not the 'who's-on-top' of information wars and superweapons. Not the vertical transcendence of the Tower of Babel. And not Tetra's hole into godlike power."

"*What,* then?" Don asked. He realized that this was just the way Barakian sorted through his thoughts, but he still found it hard to keep the impatience out of his voice.

"I believe Kwok was trying to make possible a transcultural amalgamation," Barakian said. "A hypercultural chimera capable of contacting that 'great mind' or 'archetypal power' or 'supercon-scious energy'—whatever you like—and restoring what was lost at Babel."

Don peered at the screens and projections that stood before them, but saw nothing that resembled a "hypercultural chimera."

"How does that fit with what we're looking at?"

"We think what you're looking at is somehow the 'Gate of God,' or at least part of the key for opening it. Listening to what you said about holes and minds and realities, it occurs to me now that the Gate of God may actually refer to a sort of trapdoor."

"What do you mean?"

"Some theorists, extending Einstein's work, believe that mat-ter can be made to 'degrade' into energy much more readily than energy can be made to 'upgrade' into matter. There's a break in symmetry. In information theory terms, it's analogous to an asym-metric or 'one-way' function."

"Okay," Don said, "I see the analogy."

"For those theorists," Barakian continued, his hands continu-ing to fly this way and that, "matter and energy are just waypoints on an information spectrum. That spectrum also includes con-sciousness as a more complex form of information than matter *or* energy. Consciousness can be made to 'degrade' more readily into matter and energy than matter and energy can be made to 'up-grade' into consciousness. Another one-way function."

"And the trapdoor . . . ?" Don ventured.

"If you include a trapdoor in a one-way function, there's secret information, a private key that makes it possible—perhaps even easy—to reverse the one-way operation. If our universe is a vast cryptogram, then maybe the Gate of God trapdoor allows the rever-sal of those one-way operations that keep us following a particular arrow of time. Maybe it allows a sort of horizontal transcendence, a translation into other universes. Travel through time and space, and other times and other spaces—and *that* would be very useful."

"It sounds pretty metaphysical," Don said, shaking his head, thinking of doors that were keys and keys that were doors.

"I never met a physics I didn't like," Barakian said with a wink, folksy yet sly, equal parts Will Rogers and Groucho Marx. "It sounds metaphysical because it *is*. The physical and the metaphysical are another entangled complementarity."

Don frowned. Barakian tended to use "entangled" in a more metaphysical sense than he liked.

"But isn't something missing?" Don asked, looking at a gap in the evolving pattern. "Shouldn't there be a symbol in the fourth corner—the lower left—too?"

"Ah, missing information! Yes, most likely. But didn't you say yourself that that's where the surprises come from?"

"One of us did, no doubt."

"Well, then," Barakian said, slapping him good-naturedly on the shoulder. "*Surprise!* Now it's *your* job to find the 'insignificant' incompletenesses others have overlooked. To find the stone the builders have rejected. To ferret out those not completely insignificant epiphanies that will give us the answers."

Don nervously sat down and picked up one of the ancient books from the Huntington library, with which Barakian and his connections had apparently absconded.

"Look, when you come right down to it, I'm just a programmer," Don protested. "On my better days I'm not a half-bad mathematician. But I'm no metaphysician. If you want epiphanies you should hire a priest."

Barakian smiled, turning off the virtuality system and picking up his hat before stepping back down to the floor.

"A wise man once said that religions are systems of thought that contain unprovable statements, and they therefore require an element of faith. What Gödel taught mathematicians is that mathematics is not only a religion—it's the *only* religion that's able to prove its own unprovability. There's no 'higher' priesthood than that."

Don turned from the books and looked glumly at the hanging screens that mutely proclaimed the challenge that was facing him.

"I guess it's true of mathematics," Don said, "that faith is *not* required in order for you to believe that there are places in mathematics where faith *is* required."

Barakian nodded. "Donald, you first thought this place was a bomb shelter, but you might also want to think of it as a temple, or lab, or virtuality studio. Most of all, it's now your hermitage. We'll keep food in the kitchen. Next to the backup battery room we've already got a place set up for you to sleep, and it's quite comfortable. But, like a hermit in a cell, you're going to be alone here most of the time. Do you think you can handle that?"

Don thought about it. As long as he didn't have to get one of those funky monastic haircuts, it didn't sound half-bad. He'd never been a particularly sociable person anyway, out in the meat world.

"Yeah, I think I can handle it."

"Good," Barakian said, putting on his hat. "On that note, then, I'll take my leave."

Don looked back toward the books and was struck by a thought.

"Wait a minute. What about scholars who might come looking for these books in that library down south?"

"If they know that these books exist at all," Barakian said, glancing over his shoulder, "they will simply be told they're being repaired, and aren't currently available. A temporary inconvenience. A transient and insignificant incompleteness, you might say. And they'll remain so until you no longer need them, and they are returned. Relax. We've already taken that into account. Accommodations have already been made—for you and for the world. Just stay focused on your work."

"You don't mind if I also try to figure out where my cell here actually *is*, do you?"

Barakian laughed.

"Not at all. You shouldn't have much trouble. I've given you enough hints, after all. Disturb the universe, and me, whenever necessary."

With that, Barakian tipped his hat and walked away. Don looked around the space of his new—what? Home? Sanctum sanctorum? Hermitage? Fortress?

Prison?

Before him, five telepresent technicians waited, remote yet expectant, waiting for direction. Absently Don scratched the knot of blue hair on his skull and placed an *X* in the Dossi painting's fourth corner. He intended it as a placeholder for the unknown, but it looked surprisingly *right* there.

"All right, people," he said at last. The gravity of his task settled on his shoulders, a burden he could not shrug off. "Let's throw some pictures on the walls of this cave."

GOING ORTHOGONAL

KOWLOON

DAMMIT, DAMMIT, DAMMIT! Mei-lin Lu thought as she walked swiftly from her lab, the containment box tucked under her arm. *Poor Patsy! She must think I've lost my mind, running out like this.* Patsy would just have to deal with it—and if anyone could, she could. Patsy Hon was the best tech Mei-lin had ever worked with.

On the other hand, everything *else* was going crazy. But Mei-lin could only blame herself for that. Despite what she had suggested to Ben Cho, she hadn't really believed she would prove to be so right, so soon. Her hunches, however, had proven to be more true than she could have imagined.

"Cassandra complex," she muttered to herself as she walked down the corridor. The paradoxical bane of prophets, futurists, science fiction writers, psychics—and now *her*. In the myth of Cassandra, her predictions were invariably correct—and invariably disbelieved. Correct *because* disbelieved: Cassandra's predictions would come true only for those who didn't really believe Cassandra's predictions would come true.

But what about Cassandra, then? If Cassandra really believed her predictions about her own life, then those predictions *wouldn't* come true. But if Cassandra didn't really believe those self-predictions, then those predictions *would* come true.

Thanks for the warning, Cass, Mei-lin thought. *But of course, I didn't heed it.*

She punched the stainless steel button for the elevator, reminding herself as she waited that, after all, it *was* just ordinary DNA, in ordinary blood she had taken from Ben Cho. The map of restriction enzyme action matched with a very high degree of accuracy. Gel electrophoresis of the Cho sample, in both agarose and polyacrylamide gel, with both ethidium bromide and radioactive markers, yielded results that matched as exactly as the tests would allow. Hybridization rates and homology, too, were very high. The patterns of VNTRs were virtually identical.

Jaron Kwok and Ben Cho might possess different dermatoglyphic fingerprints, but their DNA fingerprints matched precisely. Their genes proved it once and for all. They were identical twin sons of different mothers, of different "races," just as she'd suspected.

The doors opened and she stepped inside.

It would have been wiser if she had just proved the connection, then stopped. But no. She'd gone ahead and followed some mad impulse—intuition? scientific curiosity?—and further tested Cho's blood sample. Not just for its DNA, but also *on* an uncontaminated portion of the remaining binotech ash she still possessed.

Stepping out of the elevator and toward the rear doors that led out of the police station, Mei-lin thanked every god of every religion she could think of that she'd at least had the foresight to run the Cho blood/Kwok ash test under high-level containment conditions. *Especially* after she saw how Cho's blood sample and the binotech ash interacted.

She couldn't help seeing it again in her mind's eye. Under the influence of the previous blood samples, the binotech ash had communicated among itself and replicated its numbers. Interacting with Cho's blood sample, however, it *built* things. The somatids, bloodborne bacteria, structures housed in the erythrocytes—all such endobionts became strangely shape-shifting and pleomorphic under its influence.

Exposed to Cho's blood, the binotech itself underwent an orthogonal shift, as if another dimension had been added to its behavior—a z axis added to the x and y, unexplained and uncontained.

With the box of mysterious entities clutched tightly under her arm, Mei-lin felt as if she, too, had shape-shifted: From Cassandra to Pandora. She wondered if the box she was carrying might contain parasites and pestilences potent enough to make the worst of Pandora's gifts look like a summer cold.

Mei-lin strode into the parking lot and toward her carpool vehicle, an unmarked patrol unit with a low-profile lightbar in the passenger compartment, and sirens hidden behind the vehicle's grillwork. She opened the driver's-side door and got in, well aware that she was about to violate procedure yet again by heading into harm's way without a partner. She had no choice. Time was just too short.

Lu placed the containment box carefully on the seat beside her and strapped it in with the seatbelt. Had Jaron Kwok intended to leave a legacy of disaster behind him, hidden in his ashes? That didn't make sense. If all the man wanted was vengeance on an uncaring world, why go to the trouble of creating so elaborate a mechanism? Especially since the mechanism required a "trigger"— Ben Cho. As far as she could tell, Kwok hadn't even known that Ben would *be* the trigger.

And if Kwok's bequest to the world wasn't a biotron bomb, then what might the tiny things in the box actually *be*? And what were they up to?

Looking through the windshield but seeing nothing, Mei-lin knew she had to reach Ben Cho as quickly as possible. To discover what *he* knew—and what he didn't know. Despite the odds, she felt a growing certainty that Ben somehow *was* the unsuspecting "trigger man." Unless Kwok had other twins Mei-lin knew nothing about, Ben Cho was the only backup, the only living system with the requisite DNA key to complete whatever it was Kwok had set in motion.

That meant Ben might be both dangerous *and* in serious danger. There were other groups who, if they knew what *she* knew about him, wouldn't hesitate to make Ben their captive. They might be after him already.

That thought was uppermost in her mind as she dialed the contact number Ben had given her. Somewhere in Sha Tin a woman's voice answered, just familiar enough for Mei-lin to identify it.

"Agent Adjoumani, this is Detective Lu. I need to speak with Ben Cho. Is he there?"

"I'm afraid not, Detective," Adjoumani said, sounding a bit peeved.

"You're not with him?" Lu asked, surprised.

"I have other orders," she said, sounding even more annoyed. "Look, why don't you leave him a message."

"No. I have to see him in person."

"That won't be possible. He walked out of here nearly half an hour ago."

"Do you know where he was headed?"

"I'm not at liberty to disclose that, Detective."

"Look, DeSondra, I'd love to play the game, but we don't have time for it. I have reason to believe Ben may be in danger."

Mei-lin could almost hear Adjoumani's attitude adjusting itself.

"What sort of danger?"

"I'll tell you in person, but only after you tell me where he went," Mei-lin said, waiting a heartbeat, wondering how much she could trust the woman. When Adjoumani wasn't immediately forthcoming, she continued. "If he's within walking distance, odds are you'll reach him before I do. Tell me where he was headed and when I meet you there, I'll explain everything I can."

"And if I find him first?"

"Don't let him out of your sight before I get there."

Mei-lin was surprised to hear a sigh. She tried to puzzle out the emotions behind it—frustration? embarrassment?—but couldn't quite pin them down.

"He's at a place called the Temple of the Ten Thousand Beauties," Adjoumani said.

"You mean Ten Thousand *Buddhas*, don't you?"

"No, I do *not*. I mean Ten Thousand Beauties. It's a hostess club. He said he was 'heading out to follow up a lead,' but I have my doubts as to which *head* is leading him."

As she looked up the Temple of the Ten Thousand Beauties on her phone's map guide, Mei-lin tried to process that information. Cho really didn't seem the type for the hostess scene, but who could say? Her thoughts were interrupted when Adjoumani beat her to the punch. The FBI legat read out the address, an instant before address and directions came up on Mei-lin's own screen.

She knew the area. Cheng crime-family connections were rumored to be very strong there. Which made the Temple of the Ten Thousand Beauties most likely a recent offshoot of the Chengs' more established—and very expensive—hostess clubs in Tsim Sha Tsui East and Wan Chai.

"I'll meet you there," Mei-lin said, starting her car.

"I'm already on my way, Detective," Adjoumani said, breaking their connection.

Driving from the parking lot, she switched on the lightbar and siren. Mei-lin called for backup patrol officers to rendezvous with her, and to assist Adjoumani if they arrived on scene before she did. For once she hoped Guoanbu—or the CIA, even—was shadowing Cho.

Slaloming through traffic, Mei-lin Lu said a prayer to the Taoist patron god of police officers—who, incidentally, also happened to be the patron god of gangsters.

UNDER MALLWORLD

SHA TIN

DRESSED STYLISHLY IN BLACK slacks, a white silk shirt, and a shark gray suit jacket, Ben Cho walked along the promenade of a rather aged and dingy open-air mall in the seedier part of Sha Tin. All-too-frequent pseudoholo advertisements lurked about him, ubiquitous flashbar pop-up screens topped with motion-activated sensors and eye trackers. Their high-tech sheen only managed to make the old mallway look even more dated and dingy than it already was.

The ads were particularly thick now, with the Christmas season coming on. Trying to ignore the adverts aimed at holiday shoppers, Ben found himself jostled by horse racing fans he couldn't ignore. The mob had just finished up a Wednesday night at the track and were off to celebrate their winnings, or drown their sorrows in liquor.

The slow stampede of horse fanciers left him disoriented. He walked along the front of a pocket theme park called Snoopy's World, reading the signs declaring the rules of the park in very polite English and Chinese. Snoopy, Woodstock, Charlie Brown, Lucy, Sally, Linus, Schroeder, Peppermint Patty, other characters he couldn't name from the various eras of the "Peanuts" comic strip—all seemed to have withstood, with less visible wear, the weathering that had eaten away at the concrete high-rise apartment blocks that stood behind the theme park and mall.

On closer inspection, however, he saw that the Peanuts characters were chipped and faded. The dozens of forlorn statuettes and statues, in their many different sizes, put him in mind of the thousands of variously sized figures in the Temple of the Ten Thousand Buddhas.

Bodhisattva Brown, Ben thought, shaking his head.

Thinking of his visit to the Ten Thousand Buddhas reminded him of hell money, and Helen Sin, and his errand for this evening. Not far from the Ten Thousand Buddhas he had seen specialty paper shops selling products to be burned for the dead, consumer goods to be turned into smoke and ash so that their essence might pass into the realm of the afterlife, and make the daily existence of departed ancestors better there. Not only money from the Bank of Hell, in beautiful colors and outlandish denominations for burning, but paper automobiles and paper houses, combustible credit cards and fancy dress, anything from this world that could be virtualized by fire.

Smoke—and mirrors.

That was the other aspect of Chinese mysticism Jaron's notes talked about at length. Manchu shamanism, particularly the shaman's *panaptu*, the mirror through which he found the souls of the dead, located kind spirits, dispelled evil ones, and upon which the shaman rode to other realms. Since Jaron seemed so taken with that soul-searching and hell-trekking paraphernalia, Ben wondered if Kwok had visited Hong Kong during the Hungry Ghost Festival. Might *that* experience have affected Jaron's claim—in the holo-cast—that the world was a simulation?

Ben walked on, feeling a wave of fatigue. Alone for the moment, he paused in front of a pseudoholo advert for Krelltek Limited. The commercial featured a life-size 3-D President John F. Kennedy, good as new despite his motorcade mishap in Dallas. "Ask not what technology can do for you, but what you can do for technology!" the metal-pated Kennedy 'borg commanded.

Had Ben's investigation turned a corner? Or gone 'round the bend? Ben found it increasingly hard to tell.

He kept trying to remember moments from that time in college when he and Kwok were roommates. They'd shared late-night bull sessions over drinks and other intoxicants, both legal and misdemeanor. In fact, Ben's only complete memories of that time involved such altered states of consciousness.

Jaron at the time was all too fond of smoking marijuana grown at a friend's ranch and drinking a German liqueur called Jägermeister— which was also a cough medicine, a fact Ben sometimes found too easy to recall. On one such dope- and Jäger-fueled outing, they took a trip to the ranch, to clean the roof of a stable that served as the grower's woodshed and drying area.

The stable was surrounded by oak trees. Over many years, under a succession of indifferent owners, a mass of leaves and debris had accumulated on the sloping galvanized-tin roof, until it looked ready to collapse under the weight. The edges of the roof were only flimsy metal with no support beams, so a ladder would bend them all to hell.

After surveying the situation, Jaron bent down and, weaving his fingers together, made a cup of his hands and a circle of his arms.

"Here," he said to Ben. "Give me your foot and I'll boost you up from the side." Ben was drunk enough to trust him. With that boost Ben managed to clamber up onto the roof—or rather, onto the six-inch-thick mat of oak debris that covered it. Standing unsteadily, he found the roof a bit rickety, but able to support his weight. Jaron handed a large rake up to him.

He unburdened the stable of its debris, breaking up the mass of detritus into smaller mats and shoving them in leaf-mold cataracts off the roof. By the time the job was finished, he was almost sober enough to worry about breaking a leg while coming down.

Ben shook his head and smiled crookedly, remembering.

What he mainly recalled of Jaron, beyond that single rooftop adventure, was a young man intelligent and articulate far beyond his years. Jaron had a sophomore's love for Oscar Wilde's idea that "All of us are in the gutter, but some of us are staring up at stars"— to the point that he took to calling himself a "gutter astronomer." He was also someone who loved watching team sports and was very fond of gambling, but who also had a *lot* of anger. Someone who said of his family, "We weren't glamorous enough to be 'working class.'"

Ben supposed something similar could probably be said of his own family, too—which made him wonder: If some Authority had manipulated both Jaron and himself even *before* the womb, then why hadn't that Authority seen to it that he and Jaron were raised under better circumstances?

That Authority, if it existed, didn't seem to have been interested in such trivial matters.

A pseudoholo popped up in front of him, Venus on the half shell selling pearls for a jewelry store. "You don't have to be shellfish," the come-on goddess said, "to make the world your oyster."

Sidestepping the advert, Ben wondered why he hadn't ended up as angry as Jaron. Kwok, however, had had his own special burdens to bear. Jaron had complained frequently to Ben that his parents were both "sweet but clueless," and his mother in particular "nervous" to the point of neurosis—but still, they *were* tech-savvy clericals and wannabe geeks who had named him Jaron, after an early virtualist.

Then again, Jaron's quirky and technophobic grandmother had, according to Jaron, always mispronounced her grandson's first name as "Jiren"—Chinese for "paradoxical man."

"Nitrophony," said a young dancing woman in a faux 3-D popup. She whispered loudly to a couple who, walking along not far to Ben's right, had tripped the motion sensors. From Ben's point of view, the image was a bit distorted. "The perfect party pleaser. When you're ready to leave the party behind, your brain is, too!"

Paradoxical man. Virtuality pioneer. Maybe both versions of the name fit. Even back then, Jaron was already talking about giving up his physics and electrical engineering double major, and changing to European history. Mainly he seemed peeved with all those "white bwana intellectuals" he'd met, who thought Asians only excelled in mathematics and the sciences.

"I have too much personal integrity to become obsessed with making money," Jaron had said, a little too smugly for Ben's taste.

"What once was politics," declared a clothier's adscreen, "is now fashion." The screen intercut from Mao-jacketed minions to models on catwalks wearing very similar clothes.

Seeing the adscreen made Ben wonder about Kwok's political persistence. He had talked about it a little with Cherise, about the column the younger and more "radical" Jaron had written for the school newspaper all those years ago, under his "Kwok X" byline.

The national security agencies must have forgiven him his youthful indiscretions. And Jaron must have been pretty hard up, to take work with NSA.

Must have been quite a blow to him when, upon receiving his PhD, he was forced to confront the fact that the profession he had trained for showed no interest in accepting him into its ranks. And, when his blond wife slid easily into her role as a professor of Chinese and comparative literatures—*that* must have rubbed salt deep into his wounds.

"Wasn't much fun/When Jesus got his nails done," sang a live-action, eye-level billboard for *Interstellar Road Songs*, the latest release by Skandalon, a Christian punktronica band.

Still, Jaron had soldiered on—stubbornly, patiently—even after his hopes for a tenured position had been dashed. Was that persistence born of hope, or ambition? Whichever, he had persisted until he came into possession of the Forrest materials, the notes and encrypted documents the CIA had only belatedly handed over to the NSA.

Ben wondered why the CIA had kept the Forrest documents to themselves for all those decades. Were they embarrassed to admit that they hadn't been able to crack the enciphered materials? Or had Felix Forrest's notes and documents just gotten filed away— lost for years in the bureaucratic shuffle?

It was clear from Jaron's notes that, once the materials had come into his hands, he had tracked down and minutely examined Forrest's other works—including the scholarly papers he had published when he was a professor of Asiatic Studies, first at Duke and then at Johns Hopkins. It was out of that research that Jaron had developed a thorough chronology of the documents—and Ben was thankful he had.

The original, heavily encrypted source materials had been buried in the Chinese Imperial Archives for more than three centuries, until they came into Dr. Sun Yat-sen's hands, upon the collapse of Qing dynasty rule. Felix C. Forrest's father, Myron Forrest, had served as a Western advisor, fund-raiser, and gunrunner to Dr. Sun. In gratitude for his services, and well aware of the elder Forrest's fascination with puzzles and codes, the good doctor had handed over the archival documents.

On his deathbed, Myron Forrest gave them to his son. Upon his own death, Felix Forrest willed them—much annotated and expanded—to the CIA. And so their journey had continued.

Ben descended a flight of stairs that took him from the mallway down to street level.

Felix C. Forrest's notes indicated that he had never quite cracked the complex of algorithms that veiled the encrypted texts. Kwok's annotations, however, claimed that Felix Forrest's pseudonymous writings—particularly his science fiction stories—provided "paradoxical evidence" of his familiarity with then-secret CIA projects. What was more, "in their fractured, but strangely predictive and realistic depiction of the future" they provided proof—for Jaron, at least—that Forrest had, in fact, cracked many sections of the ciphertext.

Meanwhile, Forrest had begun to attract attention with his second career, as well. In 1964, a reviewer had written of his work that the author was more than "just a science fiction writer. He is a wanderer out of the future." Jaron seemed to take that tongue-in-cheek comment quite seriously. Even given that, though, what did the stories have to do with cracking an ancient ciphertext?

Jaron's annotations, in any event, asserted that Felix Forrest was first to relate the cipher system found in the old Chinese documents to late sixteenth- and early seventeenth-century Jesuit ciphers, made available to the Chinese through the efforts of Matteo Ricci. Ricci had prostrated himself before the empty throne of Emperor Wan Li, handing over a raft of mnemotechnic materials as his gift to the absent ruler.

Notes on notes on notes, Ben thought. Commentary spawning metacommentary spawning meta-metacommentary.

Ben interrupted his pondering to glance again at the address on the ticket Sin had given him. He nodded distractedly, then crossed into the grimmer and grimier streets that wound below the mallway and Snoopy's World. His shoulders hunched as he walked along the urine-smelling understreet. *Life is like spelunking. . . .*

It had been the Vatican files on Giordano Bruno, supposedly lost for four centuries—since Bruno himself was burned at the stake—that had proved, to Jaron at least, that Matteo Ricci and the Jesuits had been privy all along to Bruno's hermetic and Kabbalah inspired encryptions.

Toward the end of his notes, Jaron hinted tantalizingly that he himself might have found the final, critical piece of evidence for mastering the complex of algorithms, in the writings of Shimon Ginsburg, a German-Jewish scholar of the Kabbalah who had escaped to China from Nazi Germany. What that final critical puzzle piece might be, however, and where exactly he had discovered it, Jaron Kwok had not said. Not long before he went missing, however, Jaron *had* spent an awful lot of time at the Sun Yat-sen Memorial.

Crowd noise and a pounding techno beat blaring from a bar caught his attention. He looked up and saw an Amazon woman in armor standing beside some sort of heraldic device. In blue and white neon and questionable Latin, the motto of the device read: *Bellatrix non pugnat quia pulchra est—ea pulchra est quia pugnat.* The device in turn framed a small, realtime come on screen, which had just switched on. Motion sensor, no doubt.

Judging from the screen images, of women engaged in various forms of kicking, pummeling, and grappling, Ben guessed Bellatrix was a female fight club of the Thai sort. He was sorely tempted to step inside. Ever since he'd seen his mother and aunt—two scrappin' sistahs, if ever there were—go at it when he was a boy, he'd had to struggle against the temptation to enjoy such spectacles.

But he hurried on, watching more carefully for the telltale sensors. Yet, despite his care, he was soon faced with another apparition, though different from the rest, softer-edged, more like a waking vision or true apparition than a flashbar advertisement. Ben wondered for a moment if it might be a true holojection, but no; no one would spend the money for a real air-bender, especially not here.

"Data plus context equals information," announced a majestic woman of mixed race, dressed in white, with an Argus-eyed cloak draped over her shoulders. "Information plus understanding equals knowledge. Knowledge plus compassion equals wisdom."

The woman, her dark hair streaked with blond and red tones, was identified in silver cursive only as "Sophia." Something about her reminded Ben of Reyna, of Cherise LeMoyne, of Marilyn Lu, of DeSondra Adjoumani—all of them rolled into one, and so powerfully that he blinked and shook his head. When the apparition disappeared, Ben retraced his steps, trying to trip the sensor again, but try as he might, no Sophia reappeared.

With a sigh, he continued on at last.

At the end of the next block and across the street, he spotted the sign for the Temple of the Ten Thousand Beauties. Its no-nonsense, sans serif gold neon was tasteful by comparison with most of the nightclub signage down here. Tasteful, too, was the antiqued anteroom he found inside the glass-paned front door. A Chinese woman of carefully uncertain age and flawless pale skin presided there.

Seated beside a rolltop writing desk, the receptionist, if that was her role, was dressed in a black, full-sleeved, Empire-waisted number with plunging décolletage—a mode of dress Ben's mother-in-law favored and which his wife Reyna used to call "wares-without-tears." In the case of the woman at the desk, her ensemble showcased her bosomy wares while hiding whatever tears gravity might have made elsewhere in the fabric of her beauty.

"May I help you?"

Embarrassed at pulling the tacky neon pink ticket from his pocket, he nonetheless did so. Introducing himself by name, he waited in silence as the woman examined the paper.

"Helen will be waiting in the Gehry suite," the woman said,

giving her bobbed black hair a little flip. "Take the elevator at the end of the hall to the third floor, then turn right."

Thanking her, he left the room and proceeded down the hall. The name of each suite shone in backlit white letters to the right or left of the door. Some of the doors were closed, but some remained open. From the open ones he caught sight of rooms decorated to resemble different places and times. He also saw, inside, very attractive women of varied ethnicities and body types, all dressed in revealing outfits as they chatted, dined, or slow-danced with their male companions. The men were a varied lot too, but most of them looked to be well-heeled alpha males. Ben wondered how much the "complimentary ticket" Ms. Sin had given him might be worth.

The elevator was empty except for the sound of classical music purring out of concealed speakers. Upon leaving its confines he turned right and searched for the Gehry suite. With no difficulty at all he found the appropriate nameplate, beside a door that featured the clashing retro-cubist planes of postmodern design.

When Ben tried to knock, however, he found that the door was nothing more than an illusion—of such high quality that his knuckles, when they entered the holographic field, triggered a system that sounded a knock, though there was no wood.

"Come right in," said a voice from inside the room. Ben actually reached for the doorknob before it occured to him that he could step directly through the doorway without opening the "door" that blocked it.

Inside, the walls of the room were wavy, twisting, billowing constructions in the best morphogenetic style. He wondered if he could walk through the walls, too, but suspected they were more solid than the door, despite their fun-house overlays.

On the pillowy gray cloud bank of the sofa, Helen Sin sat in profile, attired in a sheath dress of red and black silk which bared one shoulder. Her perfume floated through the room, surrounding her with a scent that managed to be both floral and earthy at the same time. Watching the end of what looked and sounded like a documentary playing on a flat screen suspended invisibly from the ceiling, she didn't seem to notice Ben.

Inhaling her perfume and feeling awkward, he shifted his attention to the program.

"Why did even the earliest astronauts speak of space in terms of homecoming?" the documentary's narrator asked in his smooth baritone. The cloud- and continent-mottled blue ball of Earth dominated the screen. "Perhaps they were right. Perhaps it took going into space to make us see that every human being who ever lived was already an astronaut. To help us understand that all of us live on the observation deck of a spinning stone starship. A gravity-powered generation ship, with a molten magnetic heart wrapped around a core of crystalline metal, going nowhere in particular, but taking forever to get there."

The music swelled and the program ended. The woman on the sofa switched off the screen, though Ben didn't see exactly how. As it rose into a recess in the ceiling and disappeared, new music began to play, slow, smooth jazz. Helen turned and stared at him frankly, then patted the sofa beside her. It rippled slightly.

"This isn't quite what I expected," Ben said, gazing around the room as he walked over to her and sat down. Her face creased in a frown that was almost a pout. Her expression made him feel as if he'd just asked her for directions to a Hong Kong whorehouse.

"I do hope you're not one of *those* Americans, looking for the Exotic Erotic Orient," she said. "*That* place is a construct that never existed except in the minds of Westerners, and you can't get there from here."

A *construct?*

First Kimberly the literary lap dancer and now this. Helen Sin, personal escort and postcolonial esthetician? His suspicions were aroused. Surely not *all* the women in the sex industry were as bright as the ones he kept running into?

"I suppose you're right," he said, nodding as she smiled, and his suspicions ebbed somewhat. "Just surprised by the decor, that's all. It's pretty cutting edge."

"It can be pretty kitschy, too," Sin said, apparently appreciating his conversational recovery, "but we tolerate each other well enough, this room and I. Would you like some wine?"

"I *am* thirsty. I walked quite a ways to get here—so why not?"

With a smile Helen stood up and went to a flattopped wave that proved to be a liquor cabinet. She moved like a wave herself, Ben noted—lithe and graceful, with a dancer's fluidity. As she removed a decanter from the cabinet and poured each of them a long-stemmed glass of golden wine, her symmetrically bobbed dark hair bounced lightly where it framed her face.

"An Australian white," she said, returning to the sofa and handing him his glass, "but a very good one."

Ben took a generous sip. He was no great connoisseur of the wines of Australia or anywhere else, but he liked this one. To him it seemed to perfectly balance dry and sweet, and he told her so. She smiled and took a sip, then ran her tongue invitingly over her lips.

Impulsively they kissed, and the kiss turned into something more than impulse—something long and lingering.

"Hey," she said softly, when she broke their kiss. "Do you like to dance?"

"Sure," he said, although at the moment he was *more* sure that he would have liked to keep on kissing her.

A police siren began to sound in the distance. In response Helen turned up the volume on the slow jazz playing in the room. They put their wine glasses, each still very nearly full, on the table beside the sofa. Helen stood, helping him to his feet. In time to the music, they moved into each other's embrace, dancing slowly together.

She was a wave in his arms, small but powerful, fluid but firm. They kissed again, then their kisses moved from lips to neck and throat, to small bites tasting the textures of each other's skin. It wasn't his suspicions that were aroused now. Ben felt himself growing erect. . . .

. . . then felt his legs give out. He very nearly dragged her to the floor with him. His entire body felt like a clenched fist, yet he couldn't move a muscle, couldn't even blink an eye, not even when Helen, looking anxious, passed her hand in front of his face.

Dimly he heard rumbling noises and popping sounds rising from the floors below.

"WHAT ARE YOU DOING?" she asked, holding his head and shoulders off the floor. Embarrassed but unable to say or do anything, Ben thought at first she was speaking to him, then realized she wasn't. "He's out cold, Zuo!"

"Neuroparalytic," a man said, coming through the faux door. In one bear's paw of a hand, the thickset, muscular man lifted up a small black unit like a TV remote control. "Triggered the wisdom teeth implants inside his head. Sorry, but we don't have time for your drinks and knockout drops. Police in the lobby downstairs, asking questions. One is American—his FBI escort, I think. I've got armed men in the lobby and hall, but they can't hold them off forever."

Ben's head thunked on the carpet as Helen let go of him and his torso slumped to the floor. Somewhere behind him he heard what sounded like a window sliding open. Zuo came around behind and grabbed him under the armpits, then Helen hefted him by the shins and ankles. Together they carried him, then toppled him out the open window like a well-dressed sack of potatoes.

Falling through the air, trapped in a body unable to move, cry out, or even whisper, Ben felt less like a man about to dash on the street below than a sentient stone doomed to shatter. Time dilated. His mind and thoughts stretched on the torturer's rack of his own helplessness and horror.

His descent stopped, not with a thud or shatter, but with a billow. It was as if he'd fallen onto a great airy cushion.

The surface beneath him billowed and bounced again, and yet

again as Sin and then Zuo landed to either side of him. He had fallen onto a huge air bag, the kind stuntmen used to cushion the impact of potentially fatal plunges through the air.

He felt Zuo and Sin rolling off, then felt a total of four pairs of hands lifting and dragging him off the air bag and onto a gurney, which his captors wheeled triple-time quick toward a waiting vehicle. At first he thought it was only a van of some sort, but as they banged him in through the open rear doors he recognized medical equipment.

The siren started up. He was being abducted in an ambulance, taken hostage under cover of medical emergency.

NINE

GETAWAYS

JUDGING FROM THE RADIO CHATTER and the sound of gunfire, the
backup officers had already plunged into the thick of things with
Agent Adjoumani. So it was that Detective Lu was the first to take
up pursuit of the ambulance—only because she was among the last
to arrive.

The ambulance careened wildly out of a nearby side street,
siren blaring. Detective Lu slammed on her brakes so hard she
stalled her car, and still only narrowly missed slamming headlong
into the emergency vehicle. The containment box on the passenger's side of her car, however, was strapped in tightly enough that
it only slid around a bit on the seat. Fortunately.

Such total disregard on the ambulance driver's part struck Mei-
lin as suspicious. Restarting her vehicle, she checked the emergency
frequencies. Nothing to or from any ambulance near this location.

Talking to dispatchers, she confirmed her suspicion: no medical emer-
gencies were currently underway anywhere within a three-mile
radius.

Something was very wrong.

Detective Lu accelerated, but the ambulance was moving fast
and already almost out of sight. She again flicked on her siren and
lights, reluctant to warn the ambulance driver that he was being pursued, but even more concerned about becoming trapped in
traffic.

Drivers pulled out of her way as, engine roaring and siren screaming, she began to gain on the ambulance. Brake lights glittered around
and before her and the streetlights began to blur with speed. Lu informed dispatch of her position and called for backup. From time
to time she glanced at the containment box strapped beside her—
just often enough to make sure it remained secure.

When the ambulance took a bridge over the long, narrow finger of water poking in from Tolo Harbor, Lu followed suit. Over the
radio and her own cell link she heard Adjoumani asserting that Cho
was nowhere to be found. Witnesses reported seeing an ambulance
speeding down a back alley and side street. Lu informed Adjoumani of her discovery, and her pursuit. She had a strong suspicion
who the patient inside that ambulance might be—so she shared her
theory with the agent and the other officers by radio.

Moments later, she lost the ambulance.

Entering the long tunnel running beneath the MacLehose Trail
and the rocky ridges of the Country Parks, however, Mei-lin again
spotted the object of her pursuit, far ahead of her in the tunnel. If
the ambulance was heading for Kowloon, then why was it traveling
the 6 Freeway? Even though traffic was more sparse out here, the
1 Freeway was still faster.

When she came out the tunnel's other end, below Kowloon
Peak, she could no longer see the ambulance. The driver must have
killed the lights and siren, she supposed. She decided against doing
the same. She could use all the speed and racket she could muster
to clear the road, and hopefully catch up to the fleeing vehicle. She

kept dispatch informed of her location, hoping to hear of other police vehicles converging on her location—sooner rather than later.

Lu followed a hunch that the ambulance wasn't headed deeper into the Hung Hom section, nor out toward Yau Tung. She felt oddly certain that its destination was somewhere in the warren of warehouses around old Kai Tak Airport.

She began to doubt her hunch when the road she was skidding along brought her into the warehouse maze. She discovered she had no idea where the ambulance might have disappeared to, and became genuinely concerned that she might have lost her quarry.

Crisscrossing carefully back and forth among the endless truck ramps and roll-up service doors, she searched for any sign at all of the vanished ambulance. Frustrated, and shadowed by a growing sense of failure and futility, Mei-lin looked too often at her watch. Doing so wasn't in reality making the slow time go any slower—it was only distracting her from her goal.

She had nearly given up hope when she approached a line of air transshipment warehouses close to the airport tarmac. There, inside a hangarlike building, stood an ambulance—a side door still open, as if hastily abandoned.

Stopping her car in front of the building, she got out of the vehicle with her .50 caliber handcannon at the ready. As she headed toward the parked ambulance, she heard the wail of approaching patrol cars, sirens blaring—a sound that, for all its cacophony, sounded like sweet music to her.

She approached in serpentine fashion, moving from scant cover to even scantier cover, gun clasped in both hands. No shots or other noise greeted her, and she began to relax—just a notch.

Reaching the rear of the ambulance, she looked inside and found that no one had been left behind—it was empty. Such wasn't the case when she came around front, to the cab. The driver and the paramedic were there, and both were dead. Still belted into place, each man had a single bullet hole through the temple.

Lu checked the driver's nonexistent pulse and grimaced. Killing the two men was beyond scorched-earth paranoia—it was wanton cruelty. She walked back toward the rear of the vehicle, scanning the floor of the cavernous building until she found what she was looking for.

The rubber tires of the gurney had picked up a smear of grease or oil, either when the patient had been loaded onto it in Sha Tin, or when it was unloaded here beside the airport. By following the faint, smeary trace, she was able to determine which way the gurney had been wheeled, at least initially.

The sound of converging police cars was very close now—close enough that she felt comfortable following the gurney's track out of the warehouse and into the night. As she opened the door, however, she saw something that made her want to dive for cover.

The warehouse opened directly onto the airport tarmac. Perhaps fifty yards away, a stealth Vertical Take Off and Landing jet had just lifted off, rising straight up into the night sky. As its engines swung forward it shot away like an ordinary fixed wing aircraft.

Three men guarded the perimeter of ground where the stealth VTOL had, until recently, been sitting. They spun as she came out. As the VTOL shot away, the men spotted her by the warehouse door.

They were armed with shotguns and machine pistols. Lu had no time to further evaluate the situation, because at that instant the armed men began firing at her.

Taking refuge behind a number of large drums stacked on forklift pallets, she returned fire. She prayed to all the gods that the drums weren't filled with anything flammable. As bullets thunked into them, what she smelled coming from them didn't smack of gasoline or fuel oil. It took her a moment to recognize the potent stink.

Shrimp paste.

She had never been particularly fond of the fermented seafood product—not even in small quantities. Surrounded so closely by so much of it, the smell was almost enough to make her gag, but at least shrimp paste wasn't likely to explode.

She returned fire again, trying to keep her three assailants pinned down until backup arrived.

About the time she realized that neither she nor her ammo could hold out all that much longer, the cavalry showed up, in the form of police and airport security vehicles that quickly surrounded the area. Officers on bullhorns demanded, in English, Cantonese, and Mandarin, that the gunmen put down their weapons, lie face down on the tarmac, and fold their hands in plain sight atop their heads.

Despite the fact that they were heavily outnumbered and outgunned, the shooters on the tarmac didn't seem inclined to surrender. Lu recalled the dead men she had seen in the ambulance, and wondered how much responsibility these gunmen might have for the corpses. She wasn't very surprised when the gunmen fought on, until two looked to be down forever, and the third appeared seriously wounded.

WHAT WITH CLEARING the crime scene and filling Adjoumani in on what she suspected, Lu found that the better part of an hour had elapsed between her arrival at the warehouse and her return to her car. Tired, she couldn't stop thinking about how she'd failed.

First Charlie Hui's murder, then Paul Kao's death, and now Ben Cho's abduction. Maybe she *was* out of her league—and out of luck. Maybe it was time to seek help from the very politicos she had been trying to avoid: Wong Jun at Guoanbu, and Ben's employers—whoever they might be—at the NSA.

So preoccupied was she with her own thoughts that she drove most of the way out of the warren of warehouses before she realized Ben Cho wasn't all that had gone missing.

She glanced at the empty front passenger seat of her car for a timeless time before she realized what she was seeing—or rather, what she wasn't. She slammed on her brakes, then stared wildly about the car.

The containment box—with Jaron Kwok's binotech ashes, as treated with Ben Cho's blood—was nowhere to be seen.

THE LAND OF THE SECRET HANDSHAKE

CRYPTO CITY

BLACK-CLAD PARAMILITARIES of the Special Operations Unit were stationed at the entry checkpoint. That was the only unusual thing Deputy Director Brescoll noted on the way to his office. Since he hadn't been notified of any situation, he wrote it off as a drill, or yet another Orange Alert terrorist-threat response.

Brescoll thought about how, all around him and all along the east coast, in cars and trains and buses remarkable only for their unremarkability, secret workers were going to their secret work. Just another day on the job.

As the morning briefing started, he noted that only two of his Musketeers—Lingenfelter and Wang—had shown up for the regularly scheduled meeting. Beech's absence surprised him, but several inches of snow had fallen throughout the mid-Atlantic states overnight, and it *was* Christmas week, so he presumed Beech's absence had something to do with one or the other.

The deputy director began to get his first inkling of trouble when, halfway through his meeting with Lingenfelter and Wang, he was called away to a secure-line videoconference call. FBI Agent DeSondra Adjoumani was on the hot seat, being interrogated by officials from half a dozen agencies. Ben Cho had been abducted, by parties as yet unknown.

Adjoumani adamantly maintained that, although she had let Cho go out, alone, for his night on the town, she had done so on orders from higher up within the FBI command structure. Strange as the idea was, Brescoll was inclined to believe her—especially when those same FBI higher-ups began trying to shift the blame to the CIA by claiming that the request had originated there. The CIA representatives, in turn, tried to shift blame to the NSA, claiming the CIA had gotten the push from Crypto City. Brescoll denied that—and strongly.

When all else failed, everyone went back to blaming Agent Adjoumani. Hadn't she already allowed Cho to range once—on the night of his meeting with Detective Lu, atop Victoria Peak? Brescoll listened without comment. He remembered the way Adjoumani and the US Consulate's Robert Beckwith had simultaneously glanced offscreen, in that long-ago conference call. Given the close working relationship between the FBI's overseas attachés and the State Department, he suspected that State was involved, too.

The extent of the crisis became evident, however, when a haggard Director Rollwagen called him into her office that afternoon. Pausing in the midst of a videoconference call, she silently gestured for him to sit down, then resumed her conversation. As he sat waiting, Brescoll thought again how uninviting he always found the Scandinavian decor of the director's office—all blond woods and metallic accents. Today it seemed even colder and more spartan than usual.

Janis Rollwagen leaned forward so that he caught the slightest hint of décolletage in the red silk top she wore beneath a charcoal gray jacket. With it he also caught a whiff of her perfume. The scent made Jim think of dusty flowers and evening shadows after a hot summer day, long-ago and faraway from this overcast and wintry afternoon.

"Well, Jim," she began, "this little project with Kwok and Cho has succeeded in generating a full-scale alphabet-soup interagency clusterfuck."

Brescoll was doubly taken aback—by her informality with him, and even more so at hearing a woman who was somebody's grandmother using such forthright language.

"If Ben Cho *has* been taken hostage by political terrorists or tong cryptocriminals," he responded, clearing his throat, "then yes, we have a problem."

"That, Mr. Brescoll, is a classic understatement. His abduction is only the tip of a very large iceberg."

There was a beep. She glanced at her phone, and seemed to make a decision.

"I've got someone on the line I think you should talk to," she continued. "Detective Marilyn Lu, with the Special Administrative Region police in Kowloon. A Mister Wong Jun in the SAR office of the Ministry of State Security has arranged highest clearance for this link. He and his friends in Guoanbu are undoubtedly listening in."

Rollwagen reached over and switched on a monitor. There appeared a real-time image of a woman Brescoll knew only from still photos and grainy videos. The small camera on top of the monitor scanned Brescoll in turn. He knew it had centered him in its field of view, though all he saw on screen was a split image, Director Rollwagen on the right and Detective Lu on the left.

"Thank you for waiting, Ms. Lu," Director Rollwagen said. "Sorry to ask you to repeat yourself, but my deputy director has just come in. Marilyn Lu, this is James Brescoll. I'd like him to get a sense of what we were just discussing. Now, you contacted Agent Adjoumani about Mister Cho, not long before he was abducted?"

"That's right," said Lu. "I knew she was serving as a bodyguard of sorts, and I was concerned for his safety."

"Why was that?" Jim asked.

"Because of what I'd learned when I exposed Jaron Kwok's 'remains' to samples of Ben Cho's blood. You already know Kwok's ashes are, in fact, nanometer-scale biotechnical mechanisms?"

Brescoll glanced at Rollwagen, who nodded.

"Binotech," Brescoll said. "Yes. Go on."

"When, some time ago, I accidentally exposed a sample of the Kwok binotech to my own blood," Lu continued, clearly choosing her words carefully, "I found that, when it comes into contact with a blood substrate, the binotech begins to replicate and communicate, in a rudimentary fashion, among its own numbers. Exposed to Mister Cho's blood, however, it became much more active."

"How so?" Brescoll asked, remembering Adjoumani's pinhole record of Lu drawing Cho's blood.

"On a substrate made from a sample of Cho's blood," Lu said, "the Kwok binotech not only replicated its own basic units, but also began to interact with its environment in a new way. It began to manipulate constituents found in the blood. It altered those constituents, inducing pleomorphisms, even building entirely new structures. The sophistication of its communication and manipulation increased radically."

"But if your first treatment of the Kwok ash was an accident," Jim asked, "what made you decide to expose the binotech ash to a sample of *Cho's* blood?"

Lu gave an odd little nod and the glimmer of a sad smile so ephemeral Jim wondered if he'd really seen it. At that moment Lu and Cho's discussion—of identical twins and fingerprints—and the way Baldwin Beech had reacted to that discussion, flashed into his head. Something, too, about twins and Tetragrammaton hovered at the back of his mind, but he couldn't quite pin it down.

"A hunch," Lu said. "My specialty is forensics. In the course of investigating the Kwok incident, I've seen Jaron Kwok's fingerprints many times. Early on, I sent a private message cylinder, with details of my investigation, to Mr. Cho. The cylinder was dermatoglyphically secured. When I got back a delivery receipt with a scan of Cho's thumbprints, I noticed how very closely they resembled Jaron Kwok's own prints. The resemblance was so close I suspected Ben Cho and Jaron Kwok were identical twins."

"Even though identical twins don't display identical prints?" Jim asked, lifting an eyebrow.

"Yes," Lu said. She nodded, but looked at him oddly for a moment. "And despite the obvious differences in their ethnic signifiers."

"As far as we can determine," Janis Rollwagen put in, "neither Kwok nor Cho had any real idea they might be related, much less genetically identical twins."

"I believe Cho knows, now," Lu said. "I told him about my suspicions. And I believe Kwok learned somehow, too. Maybe as late as the time of his final holographic broadcast."

"What makes you think that?" Brescoll asked, wondering where Lu had gotten access to Kwok's holo-cast.

"From the binotech ash he left behind. It seems as if that binotech can only be fully activated by, or operated by—or exhibit its full potential *inside of*—someone with essentially the same genetic map as Kwok himself."

"That's sounds more like a 'wild surmise' than a 'hunch,' Detective," Rollwagen said. "At this point, however, I'll think twice before doubting your instincts."

"Considered in light of Cho's biological relationship to Kwok," Lu said, looking down, "it seemed a reasonable possibility."

"Why did you say *essentially* the same genetic map, Ms. Lu?" Brescoll asked, puzzled by the condition she had put on the phrase. "I thought identical twins were *absolutely* identical, in the genetic sense."

"They're as identical as you'll find in nature," Lu agreed. "Even identicals may not be absolutely identical, however. Variation can occur in a tiny percentage of their genetic coding so that—although they're far more similar to each other than to anyone else—even genetically they might not be perfect duplicates."

Brescoll pondered that a moment, before gazing at her again.

"So you're saying that, mathematically—in terms of significant figures—what we're really talking about in genetically identical twins is a *statistical* identity?"

"That's right," Lu said. "Some fairly high-level mathematics and computing may be involved, but I think it's to that statistical identity the Kwok binotech has responded. I can't say with certainty. When I called DeSondra Adjoumani, that wasn't what was uppermost in my mind. I was more concerned about the biology of Kwok's remains than the mathematics."

"What about the biology concerned you?" Rollwagen asked.

Lu glanced offscreen before looking back to them.

"How much do we really know about the binotech legacy Kwok left us? Do we know with any confidence that the legacy is benign? Fully activated, Kwok's 'ashes' might prove to be some sort of bioweapon. If so, Ben Cho himself may be a weapon, and a danger to everyone around him. Or they might be a danger to Ben Cho. Especially those who figure out Cho's special relationship to Kwok's ashes. That's why I called Agent Adjoumani."

"But hadn't you already 'activated' a sample of the ash by treating it with Cho's blood?" Brescoll asked. "What happened to that activated sample?"

Lu frowned.

"I had it sealed in a containment box. I had the box with me in my car when I went to find Ben Cho. In the course of trying to prevent Cho's abduction, I left the containment box unattended. When I returned to my car, the box was gone. It appears to have been stolen."

"By whom?" Brescoll asked.

"We're not sure, but the lab tech I worked closest with, Patsy Hon, has also disappeared. I am told by the Ministry of State Security that she was a spy employed by your CIA—"

"And we have information that she was also a double agent employed by your Ministry of State Security," Director Rollwagen said, the sharpness of her tone brooking no argument. No response was forthcoming from Detective Lu, who seemed caught off guard by the revelation.

"And Patsy Hon turns out to have had a third dimension no one suspected," Rollwagen continued. "She has apparently betrayed both CIA and Guoanbu. This episode with Kwok and Cho has revealed a breakdown in intelligence in both our countries, and in several other nations, as well. Let's work on the fingerprinting—and hold back on the finger*pointing*—until we mend that break in global security."

"I agree," Lu said. "We do best to continue working together on this."

Rollwagen smiled slightly, and her tone softened.

"I want to thank you particularly, Detective Lu, for working with us in this matter. We appreciate your insights. We also thank Mister Wong of your Ministry of State Security for approving this channel. We hope SAR law enforcement agencies and Guoanbu will continue to closely coordinate with us regarding the search for Ben Cho. You will be hearing from us soon."

"Thank you, detective," Brescoll said. "Good-bye for now."

Once the line had been cleared, Rollwagen shut down the monitors. Brescoll watched the flat screens descend into their desktop recesses, then glanced at the director. She was rubbing her face with her hands as if massaging a headache.

"So," he began, as much to fill the silence as anything else, "Patsy Hon played all of us for patsies?"

"Yes," Rollwagen said, putting her hands flat on the desk and nodding, "but that's the least of our worries."

She looked piercingly at her deputy before continuing.

"We know that her Guoanbu handler has disappeared, as well, which is probably why the Chinese were so willing to speak with us. Hon's medtech and SCI background concerns me, especially if the goal of taking both Cho *and* the Kwok ashes is to further expose the latter to the blood of the former."

Rollwagen stood up and walked to a tall window. Standing in profile, she looked out over the sprawling campus of Crypto City amid the snow-covered Maryland countryside.

"I'm not fond of cozying up to Guoanbu. They're almost certainly aware, however, that Hon's handlers on *our* side, both here and in China, have made themselves scarce."

"Was one of those handlers Baldwin Beech?" Brescoll asked, a piece of the puzzle suddenly falling into place. He was reluctant to venture the guess, but saying nothing would make him appear more stupid than he already felt.

"Yes—one of *your* people on this project. The CIA claims he's involved in a 'deep-cover extraction' of Cho in China. I wouldn't put much faith in that little story, if I were you."

Brescoll whistled softly.

"This wouldn't have anything to do with the CIA's Tetragrammaton affiliations, would it?" he asked.

"How did you ever guess?"

"The twin stuff."

"Yes—this *does* fit Tetra's long-standing interest in twin studies," Rollwagen said with a nod. "Kwok and Cho are their creatures, in more ways than they could ever know. The CIA, too, has long been fond of better living through chemistry. Or biochemistry. Or genetics."

"But why would they want to risk contact with a biological super-killer," Brescoll asked, "if that's what Kwok left behind?"

"I don't think they intended for such a development at all."

"I didn't think so," Brescoll said with a nod. "That just doesn't match what I know about Tetragrammaton."

"Really?" Rollwagen asked, turning back from the window to look at him. "What *do* you know about Tetragrammaton?"

"The standard stuff," he replied with a shrug. "Long-term depth-survival studies involving humanity as a species. Begun in-house by intelligence agencies during the Cold War. All over the world. Nuclear war survival scenarios, environmental collapse contingency planning. Even how to muddle through superplagues and big rocks from space."

"Ah, but the standard story isn't the whole story. What do you know about the Instrumentality?"

Jim cocked an eyebrow in surprise. He had read a lot of science fiction in high school and college, but only after seeing the references to it in the Forrest documents did he remember coming across the Instrumentality.

"In the short stories Felix Forrest wrote under his pen name," he said, "the Instrumentality is an elite class of long-term planners."

"Yes," Rollwagen replied, returning to her desk and commanding her desktop computer on. "*Very* long-term, and *very* elite. Highly dedicated people with unusual training, who think in terms of thousands of years."

"An interesting fiction, no doubt about that."

"Yes—and no," Janis Rollwagen said. The flat screens rose from their recesses again, and she continued, reading from hers. His remained blank. "The word 'instrumentality' can be defined as 'the subsidiary branch of an entity such as a government, by means of which functions or policies are carried out.' Since Felix Forrest worked for just such a 'subsidiary branch,' some literary critics have seen the Instrumentality as the intelligence community writ large. A ten thousand-year CIA, as it were."

"But Felix Forrest died in 1966, if I remember right," Brescoll said.

"That's correct, but the idea of an elite Instrumentality didn't die with him. A number of his biggest fans happened to be highly placed futurists and intelligence operatives. Soon after Forrest's death they set about creating an actual, international Instrumentality based on his fictional one."

"So it actually *exists?*"

Rollwagen nodded curtly.

"Real as you or me. All in good fun, at first. Mainly a secret honor society with a strong interest in cryptology. Like the Freemasons, a few centuries back. Or Phi Beta Kappa in the eighteenth century. Or the secret political society of the Carbonari in the early nineteenth century."

Brescoll nodded. It was hard to work at NSA for any length of time and *not* pick up at least some familiarity with the role of crypto in history. To him, the most haunting cryptovillains were the Knights of the Golden Circle in the postbellum South—a fancier sort of Ku Klux Klan.

"But the Instrumentality differs from those predecessors in some very important ways," Rollwagen said, looking up from the screen. "Together, the 'lords and ladies' inducted into the Instrumentality's ranks knew—and know—cryptology at least as well as any government agency or think tank on this planet. Some of the lords and ladies have an almost sectlike devotion to fossil code systems—Kabbalah, Hermetica, and the like. The Instrumentality's reach backward, through the long history of cryptology, is matched only by its planning forward, for the long-term survival of the human species."

"But how do biological superweapons fit in with *that?*"

"This isn't about biological superweapons," Rollwagen said, grimacing and gesturing dismissively. "For all we know, the acti-

vated Kwok binotech could be anything. Nanospooks, even—
hyperminiaturized surveillance devices, spying for God only knows
who. For all her surprising success with 'hunches,' I think Detective Lu is barking up the wrong tree with that bioweapon idea—so
wrong I wonder if she's purposely dragging a red herring across our
trail. No. Informational superweapons maybe, but not biological
ones."

"The quantum DNA computer, you mean?"

"Technically, the universe-bandwidth quantum Turing machine. Based on the interaction of binotech and DNA, and capable
of handling unprecedented densities of information. There's been
some talk that building *that* might result in something even more
apocalyptic than Lu's hypothetical bioweapon."

"The 'cryptologic catastrophe,' " Brescoll said, a wry expression on his face. "Mass disruption turned mass destruction. Wang
and Lingenfelter have sent me reports on that work, but the physics
is sort of, well, *out there*."

"Depends on whether or not you think information is the ultimate reality," Rollwagen said, shrugging. "Or even that our universe is a simulation."

"The idea that the universe is an enormous computer," Brescoll
said, unable to hide the hint of skepticism in his voice, "is certainly
a popular notion around here."

"Naturally. More information scientists and mathematicians are
alive today than have lived ever before in the history of the world.
And we employ more of them here than anywhere else on earth. At
least so we hope. The Chinese may have caught up, throughout their
whole chain of SCIs, at least in terms of actual numbers. Still, no
one can seem to agree about what exactly the cryptologic catastrophe is—or even whether it would *be* a catastrophe."

"One report I read said it would only destroy the QC mechanism, at most, causing it to disappear from our universe and appear
somewhere else."

"Yes," Rollwagen remarked, returning to her window and its
view into the slowly thawing Maryland countryside. "Quantum

entanglement and quantum teleportation between nearby parallel universes. There are other variants, too. Some of our people say that if the universe is at base a computational process, then you cannot accurately predict any of its future states without running the entire process."

"You have to go through all the intervening steps to find out what the end will be like," Brescoll said, "so there's no way to know the future except to watch it unfold."

"Correct. Others claim that, if you can simulate the entire process at a faster speed, you can get around the clockspeed of the celestial computer—the speed of light—and know all the answers in advance."

"But then you might get program 'closure' and 'completion,' " Brescoll said, recalling terms from recent reports. Given his history as a reader, he couldn't help thinking of *that* prospect in connection with an old story by Arthur C. Clarke. "The stars winking out, like display lights on a really big computer shutting down."

"Yes, or the 'real' as we know it might be displaced into the 'virtual.' I have no idea what *that* might actually mean."

"And there's Kwok's holo-cast," Brescoll said, glancing down at his hands in his lap, thinking about that last, riddling testament. "The characters in it talk about reality as a simulation, and how 'busting the sim' will 'awaken the god asleep in matter.' "

Rollwagen glanced toward him, but didn't really seem to see him.

"The Mind remembering what it's trying to remember by means of the universal memory palace," she said. "The creation of the divine AI."

"And the 'Instrumentality' is involved in all that?"

Rollwagen sighed and turned fully toward him.

"The Instrumentality has grown rapidly in wealth and power over the past five decades, but it has also begun to break into factions. At some level, the conflict that Kwok and Cho have been caught up in is, I think, a conflict between those factions."

"But what're they fighting over?" Brescoll said, confused.

"The meaning of the words 'survival of the human species,' "

Rollwagen said, sounding tired. "Some place the emphasis on *survival*. They believe the survival of our species is dependent on our cyborgifying and becoming posthuman. Becoming 'better angels,' as the Tetragrammaton people say."

"Better angels?" Brescoll asked, trying not to press his tired boss too hard, but still wanting to figure out what was going on.

"In that, I suppose they follow the tradition of the Lesser Tetragrammaton, the Archangel Metatron," Rollwagen said. "Not the name of God per se, but the youngest and greatest of the angels, who is able to look upon the Divine Face. Metatron once lived as the human patriarch Enoch, but was *transformed* into an angel rather than created as one. He was supposed to be a *better* angel because he had once been human."

"The source of the conflict is religious interpretation, then?" Jim asked, still confused.

"Not exactly," Rollwagen said, "although I suppose you could think of it in terms of doctrinal differences. In contrast to the Tetra people, there are those, like the Kitchener faction, who feel that such an 'angelic' solution wouldn't be a *human* survival. Something *like* us—ensouled robots, virtualized persons living as nodes in computer networks, whatever—would go on, but the Kitchener types feel that those survivors would no longer be human in the same way we are."

"So that's it?" Jim asked. "Those are the two sides of the conflict?"

"Nothing's ever that simple. A third group thinks it's all part of the big plan outlined in Felix Forrest's mythology of the far future. If one of the goals of the Instrumentality, in Forrest's stories, is to restore mankind to its humanity, then our species must have necessarily lost its humanity somewhere along the way. Otherwise there would be no need to restore it."

Deputy Director Brescoll stared narrowly at his director.

"I'm impressed. You seem to know an awful lot about this Instrumentality's internal workings."

"I should," Admiral Rollwagen said, coming back to her desk

and sitting down across from him. "In the Instrumentality I am known as Lady Jasae."

The surprise on Brescoll's face must have shown, for the director laughed out loud.

"Don't look so stunned!" she said. "It's not as if you haven't benefitted from our factional disputes yourself. Your fly-fishing friends? Hmm? Personally, I'm an agnostic when it comes to these debates, but even I tried to drop you a hint or two, along the way."

Jim Brescoll pushed himself back in his chair.

"The background briefings," he said. "About Borges and library labyrinths. About quantum DNA entanglements, and reality as a simulation. I had a feeling something was going on, sub rosa."

"More than you know," Rollwagen said. "More than *I* know, for that matter. I don't know whether the ultimate reality is constellations of particles and waves, or whether matter and energy are simply properties abstracted from more fundamental patterns of information, or whether it's all just thoughts in the mind of God. Within the Instrumentality there are adherents to each of those viewpoints. What worries me is the deeper question about the survival of the human species."

"That phrase sure seems to cause you people a lot of trouble," Brescoll said, shaking his head. "What now?"

"We usually worry about the 'human' part in terms of mixing the human with something we perceive to be more crude or base. Machines or animals, generally speaking. So we worry about future humans becoming cyborgs and were-creatures. But what if we were to become something more pure, something higher? What if we were to become, not just like angels, but like God?"

"Snakes and apples," Brescoll said quietly.

"Yes—Kwok's holo-cast mentions them, doesn't it? In that context, what does it mean for the Instrumentality to 'restore mankind to humanity'? Or to 'keep man as man'? That's why I've brought you in on this, Jim. That—and because, within the Instrumentality, Baldwin Beech is known as Lord Marflow."

Brescoll stared blankly at her.

"I suppose I should be surprised by that."

"Do as you choose," Rollwagen said with a tired lift of her shoulders. "Or not. I received this attached file through a back channel today. From Baldwin Beech. I thought it might interest you."

Wary, Jim nodded. A screen lifted out of the desktop in front of him, and a video feed began to play.

FOOTSTEPS ECHOED AWAY into silence. Point of view moved into a vast labyrinthine library. A sense of deep isolation, as if the library filled its own world, in a tower, or underground, floating in the sea, or in outer space. Innumerable books on dusty shelves, arranged like neglected tombstones of lost graves.

"Hello, Lady Jasae," Baldwin Beech said, walking into view, e-bodied sumptuously in purposely anachronistic red and black robes. "Marflow here. Did you ever consider the ways in which a library is like a memory palace? These unread books, alas, are the empty thrones of endless realms. Clusters of fruit dry-rotting on the vine, never to intoxicate the mind through the wine of reading. Until now."

Beech reached up and took a dusty, padlocked book from a nearby shelf. He blew dust off the book and unlocked it with a small key.

"Here, the *Traicté des Chiffres*, published in 1586. Its author, Blaise de Vigenere, created the first successful autokey, in which the message provides its own key. He believed a message could be concealed in a picture of a field of stars. Or even in the stars themselves. He writes here, 'All the things in the world constitute a cipher. All nature is merely a cipher and a secret writing. The great name and essence of God and his wonders, the very deeds, projects, words, actions, and demeanor of mankind—what are they for the most part but a cipher?' "

Beech stroked his white-flecked beard absently, then closed and locked the book before returning it to its place on the shelf. He gestured into the air, causing glowing symbols and geometries to flash about him.

"Remember, my dear Lady Jasae, that 'cipher' can mean 'zero'—a nothing. Or everything. It can mean both to hide a message, and to solve a problem. It can be both the door that hides, and the key that unlocks. Your boy Jaron Kwok took those words of de Vigenere to heart. Recognize this shining sign? The ancient meander pattern, or 'Greek key.' A geometric form that, when bent into a circle like so, makes a classical labyrinth. The key is in the labyrinth, and the labyrinth is in the key. If you want to find your lost boys, Lady Jasae, you'll have to follow me!"

Beech's slyly smiling visage vanished into equation-punctuated text, and then the text, too, vanished.

ROLLWAGEN SWITCHED OFF the program. The wan light of the sun declining toward the wintry landscape seemed not so much to flow into the room as to ebb out of it.

"The image of the vast library is a graphical commonplace in computer communications among Instrumentality members," she said, "but Beech has warped it to suit his needs. Marflow's—Beech's—damned arrogance may be our biggest advantage here. He's taunting me, taunting us. Why else would he have sent this thing?"

"Any idea what the last part means—the printed text?" Brescoll asked.

"I've had a preliminary analysis run on it. The text details the requirements for the type of universal quantum Turing machine on which one might run the fundamental self-evolving algorithm. The one that supposedly underlies the computational process of our entire universe. Quantum gravity theory suggests the entire initial state of our universe could be burned onto a single CD-ROM, or into a good data needle, so the fundamental rule set might actually encompass a fairly small amount of information."

"What do you mean?"

"The text suggests, at least to me, that what they're working toward is an algorithmic *clavis universalis*, a universal key," Rollwagen said, her voice flat. "They intend to hack the code of the universe itself, if they can."

"Who are 'they'?" he asked, fearing he already knew the answer.

"Baldwin Beech and like-minded members of the Instrumentality."

Jim's brow furrowed in thought and disgruntlement.

"What about Patsy Hon's handlers in China? Were they Instrumentality types, too?"

"They may have been. Or overseen by members. The Instrumentality is most powerful in the USA, but Forrest lived for many years in pre-Maoist China. I wouldn't be surprised if the SCIs have more than a few Instrumentality members among their ranks. Forrest was very familiar with China and Russia, and his published works have gained some notoriety there. He traveled extensively throughout the world, as a matter of fact."

Director Rollwagen sat back in her chair, folding her hands, as the screens dropped into the desktop once more. Brescoll got the message. Their meeting was coming to an end.

"Is there anything else I should know?" he asked as he stood up to go.

"Only that Robert Beckwith of State has vanished. Cherise LeMoyne, Kwok's widow, or ex, whichever—has also gone missing."

"Is she with the Instrumentality, too?"

"Not so far as I can determine."

"That's a relief, if true."

"One more thing, Jim, before you leave."

Brescoll glanced down at his shoes on the tight weave of the carpet.

"Director, you don't need to tell me not to reveal any of this. I wouldn't have believed any of it myself, an hour ago."

"That's not what I was going to say. I want you to send Wang and/or Lingenfelter to China, to hunt up Dr. Beech. His coworkers know a lot about what's going on—but not too much, I hope. I think we have the resources to pass this test, whatever it turns out to be."

"I *pray* we do," Brescoll said.

"Yes," Rollwagen agreed, giving him a small smile. "How's your mother-in-law, by the way?"

The sudden turn in the conversation caught him by surprise. Thinking of his wife, he glanced down at his wedding ring, then distractedly ran his left hand over his scalp. The ring had not worn down, but as he'd put on weight over the years the ring had had to be re-sized to fit his thickening fingers. His hair too, like his wedding ring, had been thicker when his ring finger—and the rest of him—had been thinner.

"She's fine. Some minor postsurgery complications—enough to worry my wife—but I think her mother will be fine."

"Glad to hear it," Rollwagen said, before returning to the paperwork on her desk. "Happy holidays."

"Same to you," the deputy director said, then left the room.

HE HEADED BACK TOWARD his own office, thinking about the Instrumentality with its "lords" and its "ladies." That whole notion irked him, the way the Greek system of fraternities and sororities had annoyed him when he was in college. He had tried to excuse that collegiate system as a holdover of adolescent immaturity, but there was something about its cliques, its petty tribalism, that he could never really stomach. Poisonous as the bottle behind the skull and bones, to him.

True, he had done what he had to, to get on in government service, but not a bit more. No bowing down to the Sacred Owl of Bohemia in a redwood grove in California, thank you. But these Instrumentality types seemed to have taken social connections to the next level. Maybe the logical extreme of the "team player" approach *was* the secret society, with robes and passwords, handsigns and midnight initiations.

That, however, always reminded Jim too much of the Ku Klux Klan.

He opened his door and entered his office, sitting down heavily enough in his chair to remind him of the gun at his waistband. Despite his distaste for their nostalgic feudal titles and Beech's silly "Marflow" costume, Deputy Director Brescoll was trying to keep an open mind about the Instrumentality, and Rollwagen's role in it.

And about his anonymous fly-fishing friends, too.

Jim had always appreciated the deeper ambiguity of Groucho Marx's line, "I'd never join a club that would accept me as a member"—but he couldn't help wondering how far "kindly strangers" had already taken him into the land of the secret handshake.

UNZIPPING THE MIRROR

LAKE NOT-TO-BE-NAMED

IN HIS STUDIO HERMITAGE under the mountain, Don Markham had grown used to the cool, dusty-damp smell and the perpetual generator hum. Such immediate sensory detail gave way again, however, each time he powered up the virtual wonderland that was his to play with. Such was the case now, as he once again began cracking his brains against the imagery embedded in the Kwok holo-cast.

He'd had very little luck deciphering the 'cast's deeper meanings, thus far. About the only thing new and surprising he'd learned had come from going back over his own system logs. Analysis of those log entries showed that when the holo-cast first appeared among the joined islands of the Cybernesia festival—while he had been so busy trying to block or jam the thing—the 'cast program had simultaneously been hacking in and extracting algorithms and code elements from the flying island expansion Don had done on the Besterbox programs. He couldn't yet figure out how that fit in with the rest of what he knew about the holo-cast, but he'd thought the information important enough to send it on to Nils Barakian for comment.

Meanwhile, he kept working. His cavern hideaway was lit to simulate the outside world's cycle of day and night. If he'd bothered to pay it much attention, the changeover of the dynamo from generator to pump motor would even have given him a sense of when the rest of California had gone to bed each day. What little sleep Don got now, however, came at odd hours. He rested only when he remembered to be tired, ate only when he remembered to be hungry.

His investigations went uninterrupted by the occasional rumblings, clangings, and bangings surrounding the installation of the blast doors—by work crews he never saw. He soon became accustomed enough to the sounds to ignore them altogether. By the time he got around to remembering what he'd been ignoring, the work was finished and the sounds had ceased.

Nils Barakian had brought Don up to speed on who Ben Cho was, what work he had been about, the documents he'd apparently gotten from Kwok's ex or widow, Cherise LeMoyne—even Cho's strange status as an unknowing Tetragrammaton twin. Unfortunately, Barakian hadn't decided to inform Don of all that until *after* Cho himself had been lost—or, more accurately, abducted.

Learning of Cho's situation only increased the pressure Don put on himself to learn all he could about Jaron Kwok, and to break the code of Kwok's holo-cast. That pressure had now ratcheted up to the point of full-blown obsession.

Yet, despite his occupation and preoccupation with it, Don had hit a wall. In searching around the infosphere for leads in an investigation that seemed to be going nowhere, Don was reminded again and again that it was Christmastime. Glum loneliness began to creep into his thoughts. He missed Karuna especially, since one of his oddest yet most pleasant memories of the holidays came from when he was with her.

HE AND KARI WERE SHARING a rented house together. Struck by a wave of holiday spirit, Kari insisted they get a tree and decorate it with lights and ornaments. He grinched about how her cats would have a field day with the ornaments, about how *fake* plastic trees looked, about how fire prone the real ones were, about how they'd have to get permission from their landlord if they wanted to plant a live tree in the yard, et cetera, et cetera.

Kari would brook no obstacles, however. They found a balsam fir—a little thin, and dry (and dead), but nice. They decked it with lights and ornaments and, when they were done, even Don had to admit it was a pretty thing, standing there all lit up in the tiled bay window alcove off the living room.

All went well until Christmas Eve. Late that evening, they had put out all the lights but the twinkling stars in the Christmas tree and some squat candles they'd lit on the coffee table in the living room. He and Kari sat on the high-backed couch in the candlelight, drinking mulled wine and eating flatbreads with cheeses and patés. Gazing at the twinkling tree and glowing candles, they felt a homey, fire-in-the-fireplace contentment, though fireplaces were, in fact, illegal under the local air pollution statutes.

He and Kari cuddled and shared a few lingering kisses. Things were definitely headed in a romantic direction until one of their cats—a skittish, long-haired, gunmetal gray Russian Blue with a big plumey tail and back legs like furry jodhpurs—jumped up on the coffee table.

"Honey, would you get Spooky Boy off the table?"

"Yeah," Don said, turning. "Off the table, Spooks!"

Too late. Spooky Boy had brought his well-furred backside too close to a candle flame. His fur-jodhpurred legs and feather-duster tail instantly went up in a blue and yellow blaze. The cat, startled at discovering it was aflame, darted off the table and under the Christmas tree, which also promptly caught fire.

Kari leapt up in pursuit of the cat at precisely the moment Don went vaulting one-handed over the couch's back, headed for the kitchen and the fire extinguisher they kept there. The couch tipped and crashed onto its back behind him as Don, oblivious, ran to the cabinet under the kitchen sink and yanked out the extinguisher.

Kari was running around the living room, trying to catch poor rattled Spooky Boy—who, although still smoking a little from his backside, was apparently no longer ablaze. The tree, however, was just getting a good roaring fire going. Don yanked the plug on the Christmas lights and hit the tree itself with blasts from the fire extinguisher, sweeping back and forth through the flames. It took almost the whole contents of the extinguisher to do it, but at last he put out the fire.

Standing amid the smell of burnt cat hair, smoking balsam fir, melted plastic, and ammonium phosphate, Don wiped sweat from his brow. About a third of the tree was ruined, but the rest was mostly untouched. He flipped the couch upright again, then turned to see Kari approaching him, carrying the twitchy Spooky Boy in her arms, stroking the wild-eyed cat, trying to calm him.

"How's he doing?" Don asked.

"He's okay," Kari said, kissing the cat on the head. "Didn't burn too much of his fur, actually. Just took off the long ends on the backs of the legs and tail, see? He's got plenty left."

They surveyed the damage. Realizing that none of it was fatal, or permanent enough to merit their landlord's attention, they turned to each other, relieved and grateful. Before long, they were *laughing* about the cartoon-crazy chaos of what had happened. That night Spooky Boy got his new name: Smokey Boy.

DON SIGHED and shook his head, remembering it. Here in the hall of the mountain king, Karuna and Smokey Boy seemed very far away. Eager to distract himself from his holiday loneliness, Don threw himself back into trying to decipher the meaning of the Kwok imagery. He was thus occupied when Nils Barakian video-phoned him, returning a call. The old man, with a peaked red elf-hat perched atop his shocking wealth of wild hair, smiled out from the screen, as if Wavy Gravy of ancient hippie fame had been recruited to play one of Santa's senior helpers.

"Merry Christmas, Don!" Barakian said. "Hey, I've been considering what you said about Kwok's holo-cast."

"Hm?" Don asked, still focused on unraveling an aspect of the Chinese "necessity" ideogram that had been hidden in the bottom right-hand corner of the Dossi painting.

"About the fact that it stole elements from your expansion of the jauntbox program."

"Oh. Happy holidays to you, too. Any ideas?"

"The Besterian jauntboxes do what, exactly?" Barakian asked, leaning forward, toward the camera on his end of the conversation.

"They allow virtual reality e-bodiments—personae, avatars, what have you—to transition smoothly from one virtual environment to another."

"And your flying-island program was an expansion of that?"

"That's right."

"What do you know about quantum teleportation?" Barakian asked.

"Enough to know that nobody's been able to make it scale up into a *Star Trek*–type transporter," Don said, surprised by Barakian's mention of it.

"Right. QT doesn't transport a whole particle from one place to another. You can, however, teleport the quantum state of a particle at one location to a particle at a different location. The quantum state of the original particle is destroyed, but that same quantum state is reincarnated on another particle at the destination, without the original having to cross any intervening distance."

"Sounds great. Why aren't we using it to beam around the galaxy?"

"It's limited by the speed of light, for one thing. Not instantaneous. Moving around everyday objects like human bodies requires moving around very large amounts of information, too. To describe the physical components of one entire human being down to the atomic level takes roughly 10^{32} bits."

"So it's a dead end, then?"

"Maybe not," Barakian said. "I want to show you a message we've just obtained."

Before Don could agree or disagree or even comment on this interruption to his work, an image appeared before him of a man in heavy ceremonial robes. The robed personage called himself Marflow and stood in a library dim with the vastness of those distances into which it stretched away. He spoke of the similarities of libraries and memory palaces. Of unread books. Of definitions and examples of keys and labyrinths and ciphers, up to and including the universe itself.

"Interesting," Don said when the message had played itself out, and Barakian reappeared on the screen, "but what does it have to do with quantum teleportation?"

"Think about how quantum states are destroyed and reincarnated," Barakian said. "Or die, in order to be resurrected. There's a long tradition connecting labyrinths with resurrection, as well. Medieval Christians saw the story of Theseus and the Minotaur as a prefiguration of Christ's harrowing of hell, for instance. Theseus stood for Christ and the Minotaur stood for Satan. The passage through the labyrinth was a type of descent into the underworld. People in many cultures and at many times in history have believed that dancing the winding path of a labyrinth mimes the wanderings of the newly departed soul."

"I don't—I don't quite follow you."

Nils Barakian laughed.

"Because I speak not only *of* labyrinths," the white-haired man said, his laugh stopping at a wheeze, "but *in* labyrinths—like Daedalus himself! The labyrinth has long been considered a window or door onto eternity, a link between the individual human being and the ground of all being. Remember what I said about the Gate of God? About how that might refer to being transported or translated into other universes?"

"I remember thinking that kind of talk scored high on the mystic *woo-woo* meter."

"Yes," Barakian agreed with a smile, "but what if that's precisely why Kwok wanted that deep hack into the worldwide computershare? The one that you and Karuna Benson put together for him?"

"I'm not even going to ask you how you know about that," Don said, shaking his head, "or about Karuna, either. But you're wrong. That's not what Kwok said he wanted the hack for."

"What *did* he say he wanted it for?"

"To simulate the way a quantum computer can 'pick' a complex cipher lock by trying a kerjillion keys at the same time, instead of having to try each of those kerjillion different keys one after another."

"A plausible cover story," Barakian agreed with a nod. "Yet isn't it also possible that tapping in through the computershare would enable him to move enough information to teleport his quantum state?"

That came from so far out of left field that Don abandoned the necessity symbol altogether, and focused entirely on what Barakian was saying.

"I don't suppose it's *im*possible. But then, why did he set up his holo-cast program so that when it invaded my system, it could swipe my Besterbox code?"

"Think about it, Donald," Barakian said, fixing him with a hard stare. "You said the Besterian jauntboxes smooth the transition from one virtual environment to another. I've talked with physicists who say our universe is ultimately 'an informational process being run on the system of all possible informational processes.' If our universe is, at bottom, a simulation among other simulations, then what better way can you imagine for *stepping out sidewise* from the virtual environment of *this* universe and *into* another?"

" 'There's a helluva good universe next door,' " Don said, shaking his head. " 'Let's go.' "

"Ah! Maybe e.e. cummings was right!" Barakian said, smiling

at the allusion. "Maybe Jaron Kwok *knows*, because he's already gone there. An end, but not a dead end."

"I don't buy it," Don said, shaking his head vigorously and rather impolitely, he knew, though Barakian didn't seem to notice. "It's like time travel. Not real."

"But what if they're the same thing?"

"What if *what* are the same thing?"

"What if, where there should be a past, there's only another world?" Barakian asked. "What if traveling into the past or the future merely means traveling into another universe? A physically plausible process, involving serial frames in a single universe, or interconnected branching universes paralleling each other in a vast plenum? What if transit between universes is indistinguishable from time travel?"

"Why don't we encounter time travelers all the time, then?" Don asked.

Barakian seemed primed for the question.

"Kwok's holo-cast suggests that, for those existing physically within any given universe, only *that* universe is real. All the others are virtual. Maybe the other universes—past, future, parallel, what have you—can only be interacted with virtually, subtly. Maybe the fact that only the quantum state is teleported means that the travelers can only interact through phantoms—through 'subtle bodies.' That's a term many religions use. Maybe it has a basis in physical fact."

"Too many maybes and what-ifs," Don said, skepticism flooding into his voice. "Or do you know something about this I don't know?"

"Maybe," Barakian said, arch and sly, before breaking into laughter.

"Talk like that," Don said seriously, "makes me feel like I'm working for a lunatic with delusions of being a mastermind."

Barakian laughed harder, then quickly grew sober, if not somber.

"I didn't believe in such mad creatures when I was your age either," he said. "I thought it was all too melodramatic. Superheroes and supervillains. The stuff of comic books, spy novels, and action-adventure movies, where spectacle is more important than a plausible story. But evil masterminds *do* exist, Don. We've allowed the politics of our age to become *their* politics—the politics of spectacle, and rage."

Don glanced toward him, thinking Barakian had finished, but he had only paused, deep in thought.

"Those who still value human stories and humane reason can no longer stand idly by, Don. If they ever could."

Don thought about that, the "necessity" symbol flickering in his vision.

"So? Why are you telling me all this?"

"Because it's easier to find what you're looking for," Barakian said, "when you know what you're supposed to see."

Don gazed again at the necessity symbol embedded in the Dossi image. Then he got an idea.

"If you want me to look into what Kwok might have done with the hack we did for him," Don said, "then I'm going to have to bring Karuna in on this."

Nils Barakian nodded.

"Yes, I've already considered that," he said. "We've cleared her for that—but only because we're as certain as we can be that your work in the infosphere is untraceable."

"What if I need to have her work here, with me? At this location?"

Barakian frowned.

"I was afraid you might want that, too," he said. "I suppose it could be arranged. Like you, however, she wouldn't be told anything about your location.

"If you truly need her help, I suggest you contact her immediately. But see first what you can accomplish with her remotely."

With that, he signed off.

No sooner had the conversation ended than Don went searching through the infosphere for Karuna. Finding her took some doing, but eventually he was able to locate the signature of Cybernesian space, its darkly gleaming islands built from the white-noise chaos of the datasea.

The datasea itself, however, had changed since Don had last ventured into Cybernesia. Or perhaps he had changed. He'd stopped going there because he felt it was too insecure. Now he wondered if the Cybernesians might have recognized the security problems, too—and relocated to different nodes in the worldwide grid. Double-checking to make certain he wasn't being watched or eavesdropped, he pinpointed her location and opened a secure channel.

Karuna's site was still faux voodoo. But he almost didn't recognize the madwoman who appeared in his virtuality: a flamboyantly dressed fortune-teller with fright-wig hair and a face paint-streaked gray and red where it wasn't covered by a creeping, batlike persona mask. Karuna's eyes opened—holes in the wings of the bat—and she rumbled, "The future's not pretty, and neither am I!" When she realized who her visitor was, however, she quickly dispensed with the witchwoman e-bodiment.

Don laughed. He was happy to see her—happier than he would have guessed.

"Donald! Thank God you're all right!"

"Never better. And you?"

"Oh, don't let the freak show scare you. It's just a defense I've adopted. It's for the rubes who come to consult 'Madame Karuna.' Cybernesia's different, too. We're further underground—shielded by clandestine servers out of Tri-Border, even.

"But enough about me—what about you? Where are you? I'm not seeing any address for you. Where did you disappear to?"

"I'm not exactly certain, Kari," he said, "though I have a few good guesses. I've gone deep underground, myself, in more ways than I would have guessed. Even if I were sure where I am, I'm not sure I'd be allowed to tell you."

Her face darkened for an instant.

"Why not?"

"My benefactors—the ones we discussed—are no longer anonymous," he said, deflecting her question, "but they still have their secrets, and now I'm one of them. Did you check into that stuff I told you about last time we met?"

"I did. Good thing you warned me to be careful. I set up Potemkin addresses and identities for that search, just in case. A lot of my straw men got burned by some *very* high-level counterprobing. You owe me a bunch of autonomous/anonymous remailer programs."

"Well? Still think I'm crazy?"

"Oh, you're crazy, all right. But I think the world may just be crazier than you are. So what have you been doing with yourself? Last time we talked, you were planning to go to Philadelphia to look at a painting—something you saw in the Kwok holo-cast. Did you ever find what you were looking for?"

"I found a lot more than what I was looking for."

With that, Don tried to bring her up to speed on what had happened to him and his work. The encounter with Colbeth and Barakian. The flight to California and the helicopter jaunt to lake and mountain and hidden powerhouse. The disappearance of Cho, who was investigating the disappearance of Kwok, who was investigating the disappearance of prototype QC devices.

Don had to augment his descriptions with text and virtual records when it came to the imagery embedded in the Dossi painting, which had in turn been embedded in the Kwok holo-cast, which was in turn embedded in all the data of the infosphere. Don even played her his record of the message Barakian had shown him just moments before—the strange little 'cast from "Marflow," with its libraries and labyrinths, its cipher and key.

"Wait a minute," Karuna said. The Marflow replay paused in midspeech at one side of the screen, while the X on the Dossi painting stood glittering on the other. "Tell me again why you put that X on that corner."

"To represent an unknown," Don said with a shrug. "It just looked right to me as a placeholder there."

"And that's the only reason?"

"That's right."

Karuna shook her head.

"Man, you should be the fortune-teller—not me," she said. "We don't break the pattern to recognize the code, we recognize the pattern to break the code. The only problem is, you don't know what you're doing right, *especially* when you do it right!"

"What the hell are you talking about?"

"You *do* know what an autokey is, don't you?"

"A coded message," Don said, growing uncomfortable, "in which the message itself is its own key. Marflow mentions it."

"Did you ever think you put that *X* there because the Kwok holo-cast is an autokey? That's what this Marflow guy is talking about."

"I don't get you."

"Good! The shoe is on the other foot, for once. That *X* looks right because it *is* right. Here, let me throw some pictures into your space. That meander pattern at the heart of the labyrinth is a Greek key, right? *X* in Greek is *chi*, pronounced like 'key' or like 'sky.' Kwok's *X* marks the spot. You saw it without seeing it."

Associations began to cascade in Don's head. Kwok's *X*. His ex-roommate, Benjamin Cho. The woman who would have been Kwok's ex, but became his widow—Cherise LeMoyne. The name Jaron wrote under in college: Kwok X. In Chinese, *chi*—in most orthographies spelled, though not pronounced, the same as the Greek—meant "vital force." The Holevo *chi*, the mathematical concept used for simplifying the analysis of more complex *quantum* phenomena, in much the same way Shannon's entropy enabled *classical* information simplifications. Entangled photons and the DNA double helix too, each and both making a Möbius-twisted *X*, a lazy 8, a twisted halo infinity sign. . . .

"Kari, I need you," he blurted.

"I'm flattered," she said with a laugh. "Always nice to be needed."

"No—really! You just handed me a major breakthrough. You've got to help me with this. What I've been working on is too important for me to continue to tackle it by myself, even if I could. I was thinking about that Christmas when the cat caught the Christmas tree on fire, and I realized I need you here."

She looked at him a long moment, in silence.

"I'm visiting my folks for the holidays," she said, thoughtful, "but say I wanted to join you. How would I get there? You don't even know where your 'there' is."

"Yes—but the people I work for know where I am, and they know where you are. They can bring you here."

"Kwok disappeared, Cho disappeared," she said, shaking her head, "and you're not looking too substantial yourself. I don't know if I should follow you there, Don. Why's everyone so interested in Kwok and Cho, anyway? Do they have this super-duper quantum DNA computer, or what?"

Don paused for a moment, thinking about it.

"Maybe they don't *have* it," he said at last, "so much as they *are* it, somewhere in the labyrinth of their chromosomes. If you *were* that, if the two-way mirror of your DNA unzipped in just that quantum binotech way, then no code would be unbreakable to you. Nothing would be beyond your access. No electronically stored information anywhere would be secure against your intrusion. You'd become the ultimate spy!"

"Or God. Or Santa Claus," Karuna said, shaking her head.

"My benefactors have more money and more tech than you can imagine, Kari. You should see what they're paying me—which is probably what they'll pay you, too."

"Money's not the issue."

"Then what? Freedom? How free are you now, hiding out the way you are? Trust me, Kari—the way I trusted them. I haven't regretted it. Neither will you."

"Give me some time to think about it," Karuna said, then she smiled shyly. "At least a few hours. Then contact me again."

"I'll do that. See you then."

Don felt strangely relieved after talking to Karuna. The idea that she might agree to join him here—under the mountain beside the lake, in this dusty-damp dungeon thrumming with power—*that* prospect pleased him immensely.

Only a small part of his mind considered that in doing so, he might also be placing her in danger. In danger of *what*, he couldn't say—not for her, nor for himself.

TEN

THE FLOUR OF HIS BONES

GUANGZHOU

THE TRIP BY JET from Kowloon, the landing at a very private air-field, the transfer to another ambulance, then eventually to a truck, then to still another truck—it all should have been a blur for Ben. But it wasn't.

When they weren't in public, Zuo and Sin turned off the neuro-paralytic implants—and he was able to relax his muscles. They often blindfolded him, though whether to keep him from seeing the people or their location, he couldn't say.

His captors apparently thought the paralysis cut off his senses. They were mistaken, but he was careful to do nothing that might disabuse them of their misconception. He remained fully and pain-fully aware. And awake. He feigned sleep, but he did not want it. When he relaxed enough to let his guard down—that was when morbid thoughts about his situation assailed him. Especially when he realized he'd seen Zuo and Sin before. They were the couple necking on the Victoria Peak promenade, that night when he first met Marilyn Lu.

Somewhere along the way Sin changed out of her silk sheath dress and into jeans, work boots, and work shirt. Along with the rest of his crew, Zuo exchanged his urban attire for well-worn desert gear. More men in camo fatigues, and a few in black business suits, joined their party as they traveled toward their destination. All of Ben's captors had automatic weapons, but the camo-clad men also carried grenades, and wore belts with gas masks and what looked like mines or explosives attached. Several seemed to be lugging big cans of gasoline.

Ben wondered at the level of firepower. Surely they didn't need all that just to hold him hostage? They had had no trouble keeping him bound and gagged, and he caused them none when they freed him to eat or void his bowels. With Sin's help Ben had talked them into not blindfolding him while he slept. He faked sleep well enough, however, that it sometimes became real.

Not this time.

Finally his watchfulness paid off. As the truck slowed, and before they could wake him from his "sleep" to blindfold him, Ben's eyes flashed open for an instant, and he caught a glimpse of their destination. He knew the place from pictures—and from the fact that both Marilyn Lu and Jaron Kwok had visited here. He immediately recognized the tiered blue roof of the Sun Yat-sen Memorial Hall, and wondered at the fact that his captors should be bringing him to a place he had planned to visit himself, as part of his investigation.

Ben knew they were ready to unload him when Zuo snatched off his blindfold and neuroparalysed him once more. Two of the heavily armed crew loaded Ben into a coffinlike crate that smelled of cedar. They bound his hands with a chain that passed through a ring in the board above his head, then hammered down the lid.

Sealed inside the crate, he couldn't see what they did next, but from the sound and feel of it he guessed he was being moved onto a loading dock and hauled by some sort of forklift. The machine dropped the crate onto a floor—wooden, and inside the great hall, by the echo of it. When he felt the floor descending, however, Ben realized he must be on a freight elevator, probably one that served the stage.

When the elevator stopped, he felt the crate being hefted upright then dumped out onto a floor. Unable to brace with his hands, he fell forward, smashing his face into what had been the top but was now a side of the crate. Somewhere not far away he heard the elevator rising again, leaving him there below.

Metal bars pried up the lid. Ben avoided falling to the floor only because the chain caught him as he slumped forward.

What he saw in front of him, through slitted eyelids, looked like some sort of theater workshop area, with table and stools, circular saws, and other carpentry tools used for building stage sets.

"Turn off that paralyzer!" Helen Sin ordered. "Look at him. His nose is bleeding."

Despite her anger, aimed at Zuo, Sin managed to wipe carefully at Ben's nose and face with a tissue. Behind her, doors led off into what looked like costume and prop storage areas.

"So he got a little damaged in shipment," Zuo said with a sneer. He didn't turn off the neuroparalytic. "He can be touched up."

"Our American friends won't be happy about this," Sin said, continuing to clean him up. Ben would have thanked her, if his mouth had worked.

"Then let them do their own dirty work!" Zuo said, flaring. "Not that they ever do. Nation of two-faced monsters! Fickle, arrogant hypocrites! They make a mockery of 'justice' and 'democracy' and 'freedom' whenever they say those words—just a cover for all the thievery and killing they do in their own economic interests. I lost good men in this very building, and for what? Searching for something no one can find? A diversion to keep police investigators from finding something no one can describe?"

"I don't suppose you ever considered the fact that it allowed us to get our own security people on staff here," Sin said, satisfied with her cleanup of Ben's face at last, slowly crumpling up tissues and moving to throw them away. "So we could get access to this space anytime we needed it. So I could use it for my exhibit. So you could wire it up to go *boom*, if need be. Look, if you hate them so much, why do you work with them?"

"I use them, and their money," Zuo said. "The Americans say 'Keep your friends close . . . and your enemies on the CIA payroll.' Fine. They don't consider what 'foreigners' think, or how they'll live. Just what will line American pockets. That's a weakness I can exploit. Manipulate the manipulators! In the struggle against the godless infidels who control the Chinese state, the New Teachings Warriors will be America's well-paid 'friends.' "

"I said *turn off that paralyzer*," Sin repeated. At last Zuo complied, and Ben felt his body begin working again. "Thank you. Better watch what you say. He's coming around now."

"I don't need to watch what I say!" Zuo continued, without subsiding. "Why should I fear a nation of moral weaklings, addicted to expensive automobiles and prescription antidepressants? Hey, Cho, where do you worship—Christco, or Jesus Depot? Empires like the one *he* comes from always end up victims of their own excess. They collapse because they fail to adapt."

Shaking her head, Sin motioned for Zuo's crew to tighten the chain on Ben so that he didn't slump forward quite so much. The men dispersed then—taking up guard positions throughout the building? Planting charges and mines? Ben wondered—but the black-clad gangsterish types stayed close to him and Sin.

The woman turned away and tended to a pile of mannequins stacked like cordwood. She went calmly to work on one of the realistic-looking dummies, which stood apart from the rest. The mannequin had been posed and altered to resemble a painting Ben had once seen, depicting the martyrdom of San Sebastian. The mannequin Sin labored over, however, seemed a sort of working-class martyr, with construction tools instead of arrows piercing his body, and a tool belt instead of loincloth girding his waist.

"Maybe you're just jealous of America's success," Sin said over her shoulder, to Zuo. "Jealous of a great state that offers wealth, opportunity, the abundance to satisfy all desires—"

Zuo made a rude noise.

"Wealth! Opportunity! Abundance! That's the worst of the West's lies! China, too, has swallowed it, head to tail. And what *is* their wealth, their better world, their glorious tomorrow? To be able to consume an ever greater percentage of the world's goods while others must go without, that's all. But they fear that justice might someday take their luxuries away from them. And how to quiet that fear? Why, by consuming *more* goods while they still can, of course!"

Ben watched as Zuo did a heavy-footed little dance toward him.

"Round and round it goes! Capitalists, communists—they're all temporal imperialists. They colonize the future with the unholy idea that life will become better as time goes on. Meanwhile, for the vast majority of the world's people, life is getting *worse*! All their 'better tomorrows' are a lie!"

"And what alternative do *you* offer?" Sin asked as she absently touched up the paint on her Working-Class Martyr.

"The salvation of mankind can only be found by recreating the days of the Prophet Muhammad's life on earth," Zuo said. "As a Wahhabi Muslim I know this to be true. Face it. The time colonizers think they can rule the future by getting us to buy their lie of progress, but most people don't *like* the world the imperialists are shaping for them. We are oppressed, not only by daily misery, but by the future they hold out to us! We must drive the colonizers out of our times and out of our minds the way we earlier drove them out of our lands. Only in that way can the Prophet's teachings be made forever new, as they must be."

"Those who repeat the past," Sin muttered, "are not condemned to remember it."

"I heard that!" Zuo said, looking over Sin's mannequins. Each had been modified to "revisit" a great work of art from various times throughout history. "And what of this 'art' you exhibit upstairs in the foyer, under a name that's not your own?"

"I can explain it to you," Sin said, her voice cold, "but I can't understand it *for* you."

"If you have nothing to say," Zuo said, barking out a laugh, "at least say it forcefully." At that moment, one of his men ran in and spoke to him in low, urgent tones.

"Sorry, Shin Heung-lin," Zuo said to Sin, "but we have to zap your boy here into a coma again. Our client has arrived."

Ben heard the stage elevator coming down. People moved and voices called from outside Ben's range of vision. If he hadn't been paralyzed, he would have shown great surprise when the salt-and-pepper-bearded face of Baldwin Beech stared in at him in his make-shift coffin—with the goatee-bearded visage of Ike Carlson right beside him.

"This is Ben Cho, all right," Beech said, examining Ben's wide, staring eyes then nodding to Zuo. "Jaron Kwok's dark twin. Let's get started then, Ms. Hon."

A small-framed woman bustled into view and nodded vigorously. Pulled and braided so tightly to her skull, Hon's hair bobbed not at all. With perfect economy of movement she signalled to Zuo's men to help her. They pushed a padded piece of medical furniture toward Ben, one that reminded him unpleasantly of a combination wheelchair and dentist's chair.

"Are you certain he can't hear or see us when he's like this?" Sin asked.

"Why?" Beech asked, propping his eyeglasses absently on his forehead. "Has he shown any indication that he's conscious while he's neuroparalyzed?"

"No," Sin said as Zuo's men freed Ben from his coffin and lugged him toward the medical chair. "I was just curious."

"Always good to stay observant," Beech said with a nod and a smile that reminded Ben oddly of a game-show host's.

The men carrying Ben arranged him in the chair. Beech, Hon, and Carlson strapped him in.

"The only way we can really know what's happening will be to monitor his brain activity—but that's going to be more of a challenge than it would have been with Kwok," Beech said to Sin. He turned and spoke, more quietly, to Hon. "The MEMS pain-deadening implants, put in when his wisdom teeth were removed, were experimental. They've been in there for years, and may not be functioning optimally. We'll need to check that. He isn't a DIVEr the way Kwok was, either, so there's no reinforcement. No hardware on the surface of his skull—no temporal pin-sets or electrode links, see? We'll have to use a dermatrode net and augmented reality glasses."

Ben felt a prickling sensation across his scalp as Hon snugged a net of dermatrodes to it. Beech placed the AR glasses onto Ben's face. The glasses began running system checks before his eyes.

"Doctor Beech," Hon said. "I'm getting some initial readings on neural activity."

"And?"

"From the cerebrospinal patterns I'm seeing here, I'd say his musculoskeletal paralysis is thorough—but I'm willing to bet that he's quite conscious of what's going on around him."

Beech frowned and brought his face close to Ben's own, grasping Ben's jaw in his hand. The dark-suited Carlson brought up an even darker-barreled machine pistol.

"Ah, Dr. Cho—we've been playing possum, have we?" Beech said. "Do you 'know too much,' as they say in the old thrillers? Knowing too much can be quite unhealthy."

Beech stood up, his expression thoughtful, stroking his beard, before glancing at Hon and deciding to continue.

"On the other hand, your current condition may be a good thing. I thought we'd have to deactivate your neuroparalytic implants so we could begin our little experiment, but this simplifies things. Seems we can count on your remaining conscious—without my having to gag you or even restrain you. Very efficient, really."

Beech patted Ben on the head and disappeared from view. When he returned, Hon was with him. Both had donned surgical masks and gloves. Hon was carrying some sort of biohazard box, which she placed with care on a stainless steel table they wheeled up beside Ben. She tied off his bicep and swabbed the crook of his left arm, while Beech did the same to his right.

From the moment he was abducted, Ben had felt a hollow anxiety. The same morbid thoughts had blossomed whenever he'd come to the edge of sleep. In that twilight state, he felt like grain being ground between the two great millstones of China and the United States. Between the empire that dared not say its own name, and the empire that said it wasn't one—over and over.

He had wondered what bread would rise from the flour of his bones, once the grinding was done.

Yet now, faced with the prospect of enduring some undefined medical torture, at the hands of this man, this pale flabby devil risen out of that shadow machinery behind everything that had happened—first to Jaron, and now to him—only now did Ben begin to feel real fear.

"Now, Ms. Hon, if you'd be so kind, please fill your syringe with the red-coded binotech sample," Beech said. "Detective Lu thoughtfully preactivated those for us, with Mister Cho's own blood. Good. I'll fill mine with some of the untreated Kwok ash Mister Z in his unsubtle camo fatigues, obtained for me. Why beat around the bush—we'll hit him with both."

Ben watched with mounting horror as Hon and Beech each took a small vial from a rack inside the biohazard box. As each of them plunged the needle of a 100-cc syringe into the rubber-disced center of their chosen vial, Ben noticed that the vials' metal caps were indeed of different colors. Hon was taking her extract from a red-capped vial, Beech from a blue.

Ben didn't much concern himself with the meaning of the color coding. Never a fan of needles at any time, he still felt more comfortable with syringes that were taking something out of him, than those that were putting something *in*.

"I'm afraid this will hurt a bit," Beech said, "given the way this ash reacts to your blood. But don't fret. Just think of it as a pointed little reminder that pain is a reality, and reality is a pain."

Ben watched, unable to blink or turn away, as Hon and Beech each took an arm. Even during his college partying days, when he had no problem ingesting or inhaling all kinds of interesting recreational poisons, Ben had always shunned injecting anything. Breaking the integument of the skin was just too intrusive, too unnatural, for him. He had disdained pin-sets and other invasive electronics for the same reason.

He thought of Reyna's last days, with the needle in her arm, below the painkiller bag and drip-line. That image, too, never far from his mind's eye, had only hardened his profound dislike for all such piercings of the flesh.

Hon and Beech each chose a vein, grown prominent from tourniquet and turgor, and jabbed him simultaneously. Ben wanted to retch or pass out, but he could do neither. He couldn't even clench his fists, or loosen them.

"When you get too used to the pain—that's when you can *really* get hurt," Beech said, patting him on the shoulder. He bent down and spoke quietly into Ben's ear. "I know you're probably thinking I'm some sort of racist bastard who toys with nonwhite lives, but you'd be wrong. I'm an equal opportunity voyeur. Given that modern humans came out of Africa only 50,000 years ago—a mere eyeblink, geologically speaking—then we're all Africans under the skin, aren't we? If we made Jaron and you look the way you do, what makes you think we'd stop at two—of whatever color? Hm?"

Beech laughed lightly and turned away, reaching for something out of Ben's line of vision, but then turned back to him again, continuing in a low voice.

"You have to admit, though, we did a good job. You didn't even realize that you were related, did you? Blood may be thicker than water, but ethnic markers need only be skin deep.

"Perhaps seeing to it that you and Jaron roomed together in college, or that you both got assigned to the Forrest documents— maybe that *was* a little brash of us, but it proved a point. All worth it, for *all* humanity."

Beech stood up and spoke more loudly, for Hon's benefit. "And now, a little modified supertryptamine chaser, to make you a more willing participant than you might otherwise be."

Overwhelmed by his helplessness, Ben almost didn't feel the supertryp injection. He *did* feel himself being wheeled back onto the stage elevator, with the help of Zuo's men. As the elevator rose, Hon called out a system check for the link connecting Ben with the worldwide computershare, and Ben saw the same system checks running on his AR glasses. Beech responded by referring to the binotech population in Ben's body and calling out rising activation percentages. In virtuality Hon posted graphs showing increasing "complementarity overlap" between Watson-Crick automata and quantum systems.

The stage elevator stopped, level with the stage itself, and Ben felt himself being wheeled onto the platform. Inside the Sun Yat-sen Memorial Hall, the auxiliary houselights came up, casting the whole of its vast interior space in a twilight glow.

Ben began to feel as if he himself was becoming suffused with that same soft glow. Strangely enough, he no longer felt afraid, or even worried. He wondered, for a brief instant, if that supertrypta-mine shot was responsible for the lassitude. But his musings were calm, even contemplative.

"All the world's a stage, Ben, and we are merely players," Beech said, smiling. Then he checked his watch. "I would bet you're coming on to the right 'set and setting' just about now. We'll try to better control the link between your implants, the binotech activity, and the visualization material we want you to work on, so that—hopefully—what happened to Jaron Kwok won't happen to you."

"We have to do this," Ms. Hon offered, almost apologetically, "to determine whether optimal activation of the Kwok binotech occurs only in the biological system of your body."

Beech nodded.

"In which case we need to keep you around. But if we can isolate all the activation factors from your blood, then we'll have no further need of you. I think we can kill the neuroparalytic, Ms. Hon.

"Good. How are you feeling now, Ben?"

He found that he was able to speak again. As he tried to do so, he realized that the lassitude he had been feeling was spreading and changing, now flooding his limbs and head with that warm, clear glow. He felt as if he were vanishing, like a Cheshire cat, behind the smile that he found blossoming across his face.

"I feel good," Ben finally said to the somehow avuncular-looking Beech. "I feel *really* good."

"Glad to hear it! Eager to please, too?"

"Yessir." He knew he shouldn't be so cheerful about his situation, but he couldn't resist.

"No pain? Amazing. Look at the way the binotech is growing out of his temples, Ms. Hon. Coming out of the pores, fusing with the 'trodenet and AR glasses—from the inside out! Making its own connections, and without any bleeding!"

"Yes, I see it," Hon said quietly. Ben saw a look of awe in her expression, and found it strangely amusing.

"All right, Ben. We're going to give you something to puzzle out for us. We think you may already know something about our quandary. Here's an image you already know."

In the field of vision created by the augmented reality glasses, the painting attributed to Dosso Dossi appeared before Ben. The scholarly, unhappy gentleman in the oddly shaped hat, standing before a curtain and behind a low parapet. Looking away from the ten-circuit labyrinth graffito to which his left hand pointed. All, through the AR glasses, seemingly projected onto the structure of the Memorial Hall itself.

"What we want you to find for us, Ben, is simple—at least so we hope," Baldwin Beech said. "How does the Dossi painting relate to the Memorial Hall, and why did Jaron Kwok spend so much time here? What about this place is important to his memory system? Can you help us with that?"

"Sure," Ben said, struggling to get the questions answered despite the wave of lassitude that was making him feel all fuzzy-minded. "But why are you doing all this? What do you want, Dr. Beech?"

Beech looked surprised, then thoughtful again, as if considering his answer.

"I don't suppose it would hurt to tell you. Might even help guide you through the work we want you to do. Very well. We think there might be something hidden in this place which, in conjunction with information from the Kwok holo-cast, you can use to fully trigger that binotech that's now moving around inside you."

"Trigger it to do what?" Ben asked, trying to keep from losing control over his thoughts even as they became more slippery.

"That's the big question, isn't it? If we have better control this time, and what happened to Kwok does *not* happen to you, then what will the result be? Will that binotech make you the ultimate code breaker and code maker? Will it allow us to project controlled cryptastrophes, like thunderbolts from the hand of Zeus, only much more powerful? Either way you—or that binotech inside you—will become the ultimate weapon we've been looking for. Maybe even something much more important: undeniable proof that the course of evolution *must* be bent toward the inextricable melding of man and machine. Will you help us?"

Ben nodded, or at least his head lolled around on his chest.

He was buoyed on an unknown tide then, drifted and lifted upward in euphoric weightlessness, as if he had been lofted from his earthbound bed by a wave of longed-for sleep. Slowly he realized that the ocean of that tide was the vast unconsciousness formed from all the thinking machines to which he had now become so intimately joined.

He felt himself cease to be, in the limited sense of "him" or "self." With languid ease, he split into innumerable others, dissociated into multiple and uncountable persons, autonomous processes, intelligent agents and artificial intelligences. Knowbots and showbots. Beneath the sheltering sky of who he'd once been, *they* began to rearrange the furniture of sleep inside his waking dream, spreading throughout the infosphere, until he didn't so much feel he was *in touch* with the Babel library of all human thought, as that he had *become* that.

"Ben—what are you doing?" Beech asked. "What are you finding?"

Ben showed him. He didn't know how exactly he did it, but from manywheres out of that vast ocean of information-processing machines he pulled images and flashed them onto Beech's screen, and onto his augmented reality glasses. Some of these sights he was familiar with, but others were new to him.

Hide insane plight in plain sight. The Akkadian word *babilu*, "Gate of God," root of Babel's tower. The Greek letter *pi*, transcendental number and ratio of the circumference to the diameter of the circle. The Hebrew letter *aleph*, sign of the infinitude and the unity of God, and of Cantor's transfinite cardinal numbers. The Chinese ideograph *yao*, in its "necessity" and "Western woman" configuration. The twisted Möbius *X*, infinity sign of both DNA double helix and entangled photons. At each corner a beautiful pair, illustrating entanglement and complementarity.

"I've seen all this before," Beech said, and there was disappointment in his voice. "Show me something *new*."

"Redundancy resists entropy," Ben said with a hollow laugh, speaking slowly but thinking more rapidly than he ever had before. His self, hovering above its world of myriad agents throughout the infosphere, had become something high and clear, like the thin atmosphere on the edge of space through which his will, like a spy plane, flew at great heights and vast speeds.

"Don't be a stubborn ass about it," Beech said, frowning. "Just *do* it."

"I am doing it," Ben said, "because Asinita is what it's all about."

"Ass-in-what? What do you mean?"

"I can show it to you, but I can't understand it for you," Ben said, his distant body laughing again. "To paraphrase Ms. Sin."

"Then show it to me!"

From out of that unconscious webwork of the myriad systems

he was accessing, he pulled up the virtual image of the Sun Yat-sen Memorial Hall, then began to manipulate that image in accord with the imagery embedded in the Kwok holo-cast. The result was to turn the virtual Hall like the dial on an old-fashioned vault.

No need to dwell on the "insane plight" hidden "in plain sight," he supposed. Images of forests dying and ice shelves cracking would do no good. No, better to give Beech something he'd understand.

Rotate the image of the Memorial Hall's interior, he thought, in double accord with the image of the ten-circuit labyrinth in the painting and the Hall's role as memory palace. Reveal the labyrinth that had always been there. Depict the path to be followed by the dial on the door to the vault of heaven—the combination to turn the tumblers and teach the numbers.

The image of the hall, rotated in such manner, turned and returned at each of the more deeply embedded images in the Dossi painting.

"What is all this twisting about supposed to mean?" Beech demanded, speaking to him from very close, like a therapist—or an inquisitor. But Ben barely noticed—he felt detached, distant. Even his speech became increasingly oracular.

"The labyrinth's ten circuits in the painting relate it to the tetraktys of the Pythagoreans," Ben said. "Also to their discovery of irrational numbers completely identifiable only at infinity, the best known being *pi*. Also to the Kabbalah's ten possible permutations of the holy name of God—"

"The Tetragrammaton?" Beech demanded. "Yod Heh Vov Heh?"

"To the ten sefirot. The numerical entities who, taken together, make up the primordial androgynous archetype of the human being. The qualities and emanations of God, which relate the mind to the infinitely divisible One."

"But there is no *yod*, *heh*, or *vov* in the painting. The only Hebrew letter encrypted in the painting is *aleph*!"

"Which is the letter designating the Ein Sof, the mystical Nothing and Point at Infinity that also encapsulates the ten sefirot."

"The Chinese ideograph encrypted in the painting, *yao*, how does that relate? Is it the tenth letter?"

"No. *Yao* is the ideograph of the first word in the first of the ten commandments, in the first translation of those moral laws into Chinese by Ruggieri and Ricci."

"Very well—but what does all that have to do with this hall?"

"In tracing the labyrinth as he has, Jaron relates the Sun Yat-sen Memorial Hall to the mnemonic Tree of the Sefirot. Transposes, in one another, the Dossi labyrinth and that Tree. A beautiful and unlikely pair, made one in this Hall of Memory."

"What do you mean? I don't see it."

"The turning of the labyrinth correlates to the planes or dimensions of the universe associated with the formation of that tree. To the labyrinthine movement of the divine emanation out of the infinite, the ray of supernal illumination traveling its winding path among the ten sefirot."

Ben tried to ease his inquisitor's befuddlement by flashing up a transposition of labyrinth and Tree, beside images out of the holy code systems of gematria, notarikon, and temurah. He brought up into virtual space images of Raymond Lull's memory trees and combinatory wheels, Bruno's mnemonic wheels. But his captors seemed unable to make the connections.

"What about the images in the painting?" Beech asked, changing his tack. "The donkey?"

"*Asino.* Italian for the domestic ass or donkey. In Bruno's work it's the symbol of the Holy Ignorance that is the highest wisdom."

"Bruno knew of this painting, then?"

"Yes. From seeing Andrea Alciati's emblem number seven, which depicts an ass with a statue of Isis on its back. That image led Bruno to Alciati's minotaur emblems about military secrecy. The best extant portrait of Alciati himself was painted by Dosso Dossi. That discovery led Bruno to search out Dossi's other works, particularly this portrait of a gentleman."

"But why an ass?" Beech asked, sounding uncomfortable even

asking the question, as if he were setting himself up for a punchline that would make an ass out of *him*.

Ben juxtaposed the image of the burdened beast with pictures of the domestic ass ridden by Jesus into Jerusalem on Palm Sunday, and with illustrations of the ass ridden by the prophet Balaam, the beast through whose mouth spoke the angel sent by God.

"For Bruno," Ben said, "the ass stands for the Holy Ignorance necessary for the transformation and passage of the mystic into and through the bestial, in attainment of the sefirah of Wisdom—called Hokhmah, in Kabbalah. In the Brunian system, Hokhmah is the embodiment of wisdom in the eternal world, as Minerva embodies it in the physical world, and Sofia stands for it in the human soul. The Tree of Asinita functions like a ladder, through which the magus climbs to mystical perfection, and abandons his humanity."

"And the lightning?"

"The lightning threatens both the game-burdened ass and the church. Holy Ignorance is loaded down with deathly trivialities, while human religious institutions have become so pedantic they can do nothing to prevent the destruction that threatens all who look to them for guidance."

At a deeper level, Ben also understood Bruno's image of the ass not only as sign of transformation and passage, but also as symbol for the mystical death that ends one state and begins another— which Jaron had reinterpreted, in the twisted *X*-ray light of both entangled photons and the double helix, as a hermetical/Kabbalistic prefiguring of what happens in quantum teleportation.

Since Beech asked nothing about all that, however, Ben said nothing about it.

"Trivialities, indeed!" Beech stormed. "I've had enough of this. If you're trying to distract me, Ben, then stop immediately. What interested Jaron about this place—all your labyrinthine explanations aside? Tell me now, if you don't want what happened to Kwok to happen to you!"

The dark-suited armed men came forward, as if there to back up Beech's bluster. Ben almost felt like laughing. His journey down the dialed labyrinth had in fact pointed him to the exact location where Jaron had discovered and rehidden the critical puzzle piece containing Shimon Ginsburg's algorithm complex. That finding would undoubtedly be the most important discovery, for Beech.

But it wouldn't *be* for Beech—it would be for *him*, and it would be the next stepping stone on the path to what Ben now knew he must become. Only by taking that step could he break the mind-forged manacles of this zombification Beech had worked upon him. With luck he might even be able to prevent Beech and his ilk from gaining control of their "ultimate weapon."

Ben's voice, when he spoke, had gone far beyond merely oracular. It sounded alien—distant and toneless—even to himself.

"On my virtual rendering of the Hall," he said to Beech, "you'll find what Jaron Kwok was looking for, and where he found it. Behind that tile, above the lintel on that highlighted door. Go there, bring what you find to me, and I'll translate."

"This had better not be a trick," Beech said, then called to Zuo and Sin. "Get a ladder! If you can't find one, boost up one of your men on the shoulders of two of the others. We need to pry up that wall tile! Hurry!"

No ladder was readily available, so Zuo's men formed a human pyramid. As from a great distance, Ben heard the sound of a knife scratching and prying away at a tile, then shouts of discovery. In a moment, they brought before him a small plastic player with a disk inside.

Looking at it, Ben understood. In 1936 Ginsburg had successfully escaped to China from Hitler's Germany—only to be captured by the Japanese and returned to the Reich, where he perished in the death camps. But he had left a great work, hidden away in the Sun Yat-sen Memorial Hall. To honor Ginsburg and that work, Jaron Kwok had recoded and recorded Ginsburg's secret, returning it in this newer, less perishable form to its old hiding place in the Hall.

Kwok had been willing to risk death in order to reach truth, just as Ginsburg had been. Ben hoped he could live up to their legacy.

"Turn up the volume," Ben said, "and press PLAY."

When they had done so, a series of tones began to sound, and Ben began to smile. He felt increasingly absent from the conversation and from the world as those went on around him. The majority of his mind had already begun to focus on cracking the aural code, and identifying its place in the mazed memory palace to which Ben had come.

"Sounds almost like twelve-tone music," Helen Sin ventured.

"More like random noise, if you ask me," Beech said, increasingly annoyed. He turned to Ben. "What's it supposed to be?"

"It's a Pierce code," Ben said. "Another member in the same family of Pierces was the first scholar to champion the fictional works of Felix C. Forrest. You should know that. You took over the university chair named for Forrest, didn't you?"

"Yes, yes—but how does it *work?*" Beech asked, impatient with the digression.

"The key involves tone generation. To each combination of sounds in a given language, assign a tone. These particular tones are based on the characteristics of an early Hewlett Packard–type audio oscillator, but programmed here to produce the myriad tones needed for the sounds of all known languages—maybe more. It's a tonal key to the labyrinth of Babel."

"The key is in the labyrinth, as the labyrinth is in the key!" Beech said. "I *knew* it!"

"But what are we listening to?" Patsy Hon asked.

"Not twelve-toned music, but ten," Ben said, his voice growing fainter and harder to hear, even in the echoing silence of the Hall. "The chorus of the ten sefirot. The music of the ten spheres. The constellations for the soul's migration. An intricate example of an echo-hiding watermark, too. The detection of the spaces between the echoes is beyond the limits of the human auditory system, under normal conditions. But then, I'm not under normal conditions."

"Can you translate?" she asked.

"I will."

As Ben processed information now, he seemed to think with his entire being, with every cell of his body, as if every scrap of his DNA was functioning like a quantum computer. Working on the very sort of cryptanalytic task to which both DNA and quantum systems were peculiarly well suited.

The key is in the labyrinth, as the labyrinth is in the key. That labyrinth key referred not only to the relationship between the genetic code and the body—to music in the key of DNA, most specifically his own song—but also to the lightpath itself—the channel of the ray of illumination making its winding way among the sefirot. The two were reflections of each other. Both were devices of deepest memory, mnemonic systems for recalling a vaster and more pervasive reality, intimate as any sexual conjunction yet divergent as the ensemble of all parallel universes.

For recalling that reality, and for hacking into it.

The labyrinth of the painting had mapped the labyrinth of the hall, and at the labyrinth's center he'd found the tonal key, itself a labyrinth of sound, triggering, through his mind, a rippling of effects in the Kwok binotech, which in turn spread through his physical makeup. With the help of the binotech, the genetic-code molecule's latent capacity for manifesting quantum phenomena now bloomed into glorious life.

"His body temperature is spiking," Patsy Hon said. Only the volume of her voice, not the tone, betrayed any concern.

"I don't believe Mister Cho's predecessor spontaneously combusted," Beech said, his voice sounding very far away. "But thank you, Ms. Hon. I'll keep that in mind."

That the DNA of his body *was* functioning as a quantum 4-bit device, taking on four different states—he felt it more than understood it. He knew that the information content of the universe was approximately 4 to the 400th power. Yes. DNA strands of 400 nucleotides in length would do the trick. That strand-length resulted in many smallish proteins of about 133 amino acids, 3 out of every 64 being stop codons, or about 6 stop codons in a 133-triplet sequence. That meant length yielded polypeptides of about 22 amino acids, coincidentally the length of neuropeptides essential for learning, memory, and higher cognitive function. . . .

How much grander this was, than all the lock picking and lock making the Chinese and Americans had hoped to achieve! Ben began to laugh, and couldn't stop.

"His vital signs are all over the map," Hon said, sounding openly worried now.

"Ben!" Beech said. "What are you doing?"

"This wasn't supposed to be a lethal injection," Ike Carlson said, his voice flat.

"Dammit!" Beech shouted. "Stop it, Ben, whatever you're doing!"

Ben would have liked to comply, but he couldn't. He saw the twisted mirrors wrapped around each other in DNA and in photons—and he felt that in his bones. His euphoric edge-of-sleep weightlessness grew to a full out-of-body experience. Interfaced with so much of the planet's infosphere, he could only observe, only hope to embrace the vastness of it all with his mind—at last.

And laugh, laugh like a child, with a laughter that called him beyond everything he had ever been.

"Convulsions!" Hon shouted. "He's flatlining! Going into coma—"

"I see it—" Beech called back.

No anchor of ordinary consciousness yanked Ben back. Instead, the fabric of reality pulled away from him, like a labyrinth cut into a ribbon and stretched into a spiral along a new dimension. Within him the code molecule turned corkscrew roller coaster.

He felt as if he'd been strapped into a rocketsled, roaring ever faster down a double helix of perilous tracks, through a blizzard of data, information, knowledge, wisdom. Unable to blink or turn away, he was melting with it, melted by the blizzard.

When, however, the flood of images, the innumerable tiny geometries, the lights, colors, sounds, scents, textures, and tastes had at last strained up to a breaking, overpowering intensity—

Righty tighty, lefty loosey, unscrewed is unprotected.

You like it when I touch you there, don't you, Benny?

Ants fighting in a matchbox, burning and the pismire smell of their burning.

—under that datastorm his skull and the universe opened like a heavy trapdoor. Transformed and transported and transshifted in time, he fell *upward* through the door, passed through the Gate of God. Shed of flesh and past, his mind floated outward into a truth-drowned realm, expanding to infinite airy thinness in the translucent waters of the deepest firmament, the vault of heaven flooded with light.

Ben had told them he would translate. They should have taken him at his word.

DURESS CODE

K O W L O O N

AFTER MORE THAN TWO DAYS working straight through on the Cho disappearance, Detective Lu and Special Agent Adjoumani were off the clock for at least a brief few hours—a New Year's break, of sorts. Western New Year, not Chinese New Year. Hong Kong was one of the few places in the world that celebrated the two more or less equally.

To assist Lu, her department had brought in an eager young sergeant who had hopes of rising to detective rank. The FBI had assigned an assistant legat from the Guangzhou sub-office to assist Adjoumani. The "assistants" were taking a shift now, having been brought up to speed on the ongoing investigations.

Hoping for a diversion from their frustrating and unproductive search, Lu had decided to join Adjoumani at The Jouster II. A medieval theme bar in Tsim Sha Tsui, it boasted a bouncer dressed as a knight in armor and a miniature drawbridge at its entrance. Mei-lin preferred a little more reality with her nostalgia—a nice dark pub left over from the days of British rule, rather than the Las Vegas style of this place—but a break was a break.

"You know what really burns me, Marilyn?" Adjoumani said, stirring the ice cubes in her second screwdriver. "The way they bring in these assistants, and don't even have the balls to admit that we're being used to train our own replacements."

Mei-lin nodded in sad agreement, before lapsing into contemplation of the swirls in her third Irish coffee. She thought again of all that had gone wrong over the last couple of days.

The VTOL jet that had disappeared into the night with Ben Cho had been stealthy enough—and the pilot experienced enough—to effectively evade radar detection. By the time the aircraft had been located at a makeshift airfield outside Zhongshan, it had been on the ground for more than an hour. So far they had only been able to learn that a second ambulance had picked him up at the airfield, but *that* vehicle had been found abandoned near Shunde.

Whether Cho had yet reached his ultimate destination, neither Lu nor Adjoumani could say.

Mei-lin Lu put her coffee aside. Drowning frustrations in alcohol was something her father had done, ever since she was a child, but she had no intention of traveling down that road herself. Least of all was she going to model that for her own daughter. Thinking of Clara and Sonny, she sighed.

"That didn't sound happy," Adjoumani said. "Want to talk about it?"

"I was just thinking that maybe my daughter was right. She's been threatening to get herself a cardboard cutout of me, to keep around the house. Before Cho disappeared, before Kwok vanished, I had a system to my life. But everything keeps changing, and I'm finding it harder and harder to keep up. . . ."

"There *has* to be a way to find him."

"That's what I don't understand. You Americans have all the best global-positioning equipment. You can find *anything* from miles up in space, can't you? Why didn't you have Cho bugged, implanted with a homing device, something?"

"Would have saved us all a lot of trouble," Adjoumani agreed, "but you're giving us a lot more credit than we deserve. We don't always have that kind of foresight."

Was her American opposite holding out on her? She glanced at Adjoumani, who glumly watched as an armor-clad man fought with some sort of mythological beast on the bar's big screen. No, the FBI attaché seemed as distressed by this whole mess as she was. Despite the mutual mistrust they'd felt at the outset of this affair, Mei-lin found herself thinking of the FBI agent more and more as a "partner" than an "opposite number."

"Any chance your higher-ups might be holding out on you?" she asked.

"What about your own bosses, kiddo? What about Wong at Guoanbu? Ever think that both of us might be considered small-time mushrooms in all of this?"

"Mushrooms?"

Adjoumani nodded.

"You know. Keep us in the dark and feed us lots of shit."

Lu laughed abruptly at that. Adjoumani smiled. Clearly it was an old joke to the American, but it was new to her.

"They may be withholding information from you," Adjoumani said, "but they certainly aren't holding back on much of anything else. Putting a helicopter at your disposal—honey, I wish I could get that kind of support."

Lu nodded. Not that she'd had any real use for one yet.

"Man," DeSondra said, shaking her head at what she was watching, "he should've stuck with making spy movies. This *Green Knight* flick is a real stinker."

Mei-lin glanced up at the screen to see Sean Connery, looking awkward in full medieval regalia.

"If you like the old 007, there's Bottoms Up over on Hankow Road," Mei-lin said. "Bond showed up there on one of his Asian adventures. Kind of a scummy hole-in-the-wall, these days."

"Maybe later, then," DeSondra said. "After I've had a few more drinks."

Mei-lin nodded and stared down at the tabletop below her glass. At least her working relationship with Adjoumani had kept improving, despite the occasional bumps.

The same couldn't be said for the relationship between their countries. The tense political situations in the news had been ratcheting up. The Americans claimed China was not only funding the Californian secessionists, but also engaging in infowar against the states bordering Tibet, as well as making suspicious naval maneuvers in the Taiwan straits.

Her own government countered that Nepal and Bhutan still had not acceded fully to China's security demands. As further proof of the United States' complicity in the worsening situation, Beijing claimed that the Americans, operating in tandem with the Taiwanese government, were using that island as a base from which they were probing SCADA systems, where infostructure met infrastructure, *in China itself*. And that it was this activity which had necessitated the defensive naval movements.

She and Adjoumani both had to spend far too much time the last few days getting permission for this and allowance for that, especially since Cho's disappearance had launched a wave of recriminations.

Lu could see how they might draw a tenuous line connecting Cho's disappearance to the infowar, but she couldn't fathom a serious connection to the international saber rattling about troops and terrorists. Nevertheless, she and the FBI legat were lucky to still be allowed in each other's company.

Hell, sometimes she felt as if her work with Adjoumani was the only thing keeping Guoanbu from having the American agent arrested, simply on principle.

It was frustrating to think that government agencies on both sides of the Pacific might be using her and Adjoumani as pawns, just to play for time. She had no doubt, though, that their superiors would gladly watch to see what the two of them might come up with in their investigations, then shove both of them unceremoniously aside and take credit for any successes they might achieve.

Lost in her musings, Mei-lin noticed some curious intricacies in the tabletop's design. The pattern that showed through the protective Plexiglas was a labyrinth with a castellated medieval town labeled *Jericho* at the center. The path through the labyrinth appeared as a line made from the letters *HEARTHEARTHEART-HEARTH*, repeated again and again. In the central square of the town, the same five letters were arranged like dots on the face of dice.

"Hey, DeSondra, take a look at this design," Mei-lin said. "See the letters?"

"Yeah. Can you make out what they say?"

"Hearth Earth?" Lu ventured. "Heart Hearth Earth Earth Earth?"

"Hear the art hear the art?" Adjoumani suggested. "Doesn't make much sense. You can't hear a painting, or a woodcut, or an engraving."

"My father, the writer, used to say that kind of thing when he was in his cups," Lu said. " 'The more you master an art the more an art masters you.' Zen bullshit like that. Maybe he believed he was some kind of artist. Everybody else treated him like a hack."

"That'd be enough to drive a body to drink, I suppose," Adjoumani said.

"I don't know," Lu said, glancing away. "This whole case, first Kwok and now Cho—it feels like that."

"Like what?"

"Like a maze full of letters and words I can almost make out, but not quite. I keep getting it wrong—but just barely. One minute it seems we're so *close* to finding Cho, then the path swings away. That only makes it worse."

Adjoumani reached out across the tabletop labyrinth and patted Mei-lin's hand.

"Don't let it get to you, Marilyn. Just because we're on the right side doesn't make winning any quicker. The people who took Cho are real pros. Besides, the game's not over yet."

Mei-lin nodded, glancing up at the medieval movie playing on the wallscreen. Suddenly a flicker interrupted it, and an image of the Sun Yat-sen Memorial Hall appeared, looking exactly the way it had the day she and Ma had confronted the New Teachings Warriors there.

Mei-lin's back stiffened, and she stared for a moment. The movie came back on. A moment later, it was replaced again by the image of the Memorial Hall.

"DeSondra! Look at the screen."

The image flickered back and forth from movie to Memorial Hall in a dance of images.

"Hmm!" Adjoumani said. "They're having trouble with their system. That doesn't look like merry ol' England. Maybe somebody messed with their old videotape."

"I don't think so, but I'll check," Lu said, getting up from their table and heading toward the bar.

The bartender, dressed as steward of a noble house, was already staring at the screen as Mei-lin approached. She gestured with a nod.

"I saw it," he said. "Damnedest thing."

"You having problems with your recorder, or DVD player?"

"No. It's a live satellite feed. The problem must be on their end."

Mei-lin smiled in agreement, but she doubted the problem was on anybody's end. She was willing to bet it was happening, not only on this channel, but on all of them.

The New Year was dawning rich and strange—maybe richer and stranger than she might have liked. Before she could ask him to change channels, to test her theory, Sean Connery reappeared, and the movie returned to normal.

"There," the bartender said, relieved. "It's stopped glitching."

Lu turned to Adjoumani.

"I think I know where Ben Cho is," Mei-lin said.

"Where?"

"Sun Yat-sen Memorial Hall in Guangzhou," she said, pulling her phone from her pocket.

"What? You mean that building we saw on screen?"

"Right. Kwok went there. When I was there last time, New Teachings Warriors were up to something."

"But didn't you send somebody to check it out? Like the next morning, after Cho was abducted?"

"Right. Derek Ma. He didn't find anything. But I don't think Ben Cho was there yet. I think Ben's there *now*."

As they left the Jouster II, Lu called ahead, to have the helicopter—the one she didn't think they'd ever need—readied and cleared for an inland trip.

"Another of your hunches?" Adjoumani asked, her brow furrowing. "Given our recent track record, I hope you're right."

"I hope I'm right, too." They climbed into her car and pulled away, headed back toward the police station and its helipad.

"Look," Adjoumani said as Lu flicked on the siren, "we don't have to tell our 'assistants' about this, do we? At least not until after we're airborne? If this turns into a mess, I'd prefer they weren't along for the ride."

"No problem," Lu said, "but I'm pretty sure it won't turn into a mess."

Adjoumani said nothing, but even to herself Lu sounded more confident than she felt. Adjoumani took out her cell phone and punched in a text message, then sent it to a wireless uplink.

"Just in case you're wrong," she said, "I'm inputting the duress code Beckwith gave me for State."

"Dress code? What do you mean?"

"*Du*ress code. Same ciphertext, but it can be read in two ways. One way of reading it reveals an innocent message, the other decrypts it into a deeper, more important plaintext."

"Oh, I see!" Mei-lin said. "Like the poem 'Yuan Xiao' once published in *Renmin Ribao*—the *People's Daily*."

"What was that about?"

"It appeared innocent to the Party censors, but when read along the diagonal, the poem called for the ouster of Prime Minister Li Peng."

"I think of it more like the special password a bank employee can use when he's got a gun to his head," DeSondra said, still looking at her cell phone. "One that opens the safe, but also triggers a silent alarm. There. This phone is now a homing beacon."

Mei-lin was glad that the internal surveillance monitors in police cars operated only at the officer's discretion. She wasn't sure how she felt about having the American Department of State as their backup.

She wasn't sure, either, whether the "glitch" she'd seen might not be Cho's own sort of duress code—or what sort of duress he might be under.

THE SILENCE IN HEAVEN

LAKE NOT-TO-BE-NAMED

ONCE KARUNA HAD AGREED to join him, her arrival had been accomplished with surprising speed. As they had walked the high-ceilinged tunnels Kari seemed no worse for wear—though perhaps a bit grumpy with jet lag. When he had showed her the main generator station in its artificial cavern, however, she had enough energy to marvel, particularly at the great service crane.

After that, he toured her through the main transformer room, turning off the lights and pointing out the faint electric blue glow.

"I can feel my ovaries frying in here," Kari said nervously. "Let's move on, shall we?"

Don pointed out the elevator shaft and long stairway rising a thousand feet through the mountain to the surface. Looking up into its darkness with him, Kari said she hoped she'd never have to climb it. Don pointed out the kitchen, break room, and rest rooms, then stepped her past his makeshift bedroom near the backup battery room.

In the power station control room, he pulled up the computer representations and remote monitors and showed her the complex system of dams, tunnels, pipes, lakes, forebays, powerhouses, penstocks and tailraces, of which their current underground location was a part.

At last he led her into his own "control room," the high-tech Faerie which Barakian and the Kitchener Foundation had put at his disposal. Seeing the facility through Kari's eyes—watching her become alternately paranoid and bedazzled by what he showed her—was more fun than he'd expected.

Don had barely finished the tour of his new and secret home when the silence in heaven changed all their plans. He had just switched on the holographic representations of the Sun Yat-sen Memorial Hall. They had donned virtuality gear, though they hadn't switched it on yet. The two of them were going over the Dossi painting, overlaid with its two captions and four corner-symbols—when it happened.

Without warning, the systems in Don's most secret lair paused, then began to glitch as if under command of a new master. The computer-controlled monitors and holojectors zoomed in on the Dossi painting's labyrinth and highlighted it. The several airbender and flashbar Sun Yat-sen Memorial Halls currently active in Don's holographic representations started rotating of their own accord, their motion synching up with the pattern highlighted on the labyrinth graffito.

"What's this supposed to mean?" Karuna asked, looking at him as if he were responsible for the hubbub.

"I don't know," Don said, glancing at a series of images that had come up on a nearby screen. He recognized them as Pythagorean— ten arranged as a triangular number. A pentagon enclosing a five-pointed star enclosing a pentagon enclosing another five-pointed star ad infinitum. A plethora of golden section illustrations—all culminating in the ever-lengthening decimal string of *pi*. "I'm not doing it."

"I don't like the sound of *that*," Karuna said, frowning.

They watched as *YHVH* rapidly ran through the ten permutations of the name of God, then transformed into a nine-spoked wheel centered around the tenth word, *tiferet*, at its hub. They stared as that wheel morphed into a tree with the word *malchut* at its root—before that too paused at the mathematical infinitudes represented by *aleph*.

"The last time you were thrown for a loop like this was when Kwok's holo-cast crashed our party."

"I think this is crashing more than our little party here," Don said, watching ideograms appear—some of which he recognized as being from the *I Ching*, as if, now, Kabbalah had morphed into a Chinese counterpart. Then the imagery settled without settling, into the Riccian version of the *yao* ideogram, morphing and shifting endlessly among its variant readings and emphases.

"Look!" Don said, checking channel after channel of video input. "This is from a commercial satellite feed, and on another channel—here. And another. And another. It's everywhere." Again and again, every feed was interspersed with the image of the Sun Yat-sen Memorial Hall. Turning from the public sphere, however, they found their private control-room virtualities similarly usurped, with images out of cloud chamber physics, demonstrations of biomolecular and quantum sources, metamorphosing at last into the image of an endlessly twisting *X*.

"So is this like what happened with Kwok?" she asked, nervousness creeping into her voice. "And with Medea?"

"Much more so," Don said, then he paused, struck by an idea. "Wait! *Medea!* I've seen something like this before. When I visited Crash Village. Medea's agentware was working on some sort of superproblem. I couldn't figure it out at the time. A lot of what I'm seeing now looks like what I saw then."

"What kind of problem?"

"I don't know. Something big."

"I'm going to need more than that," Karuna said, activating her virtuality gear. Don followed suit and found himself staring at the figure of a game-burdened mule. This figure was then rendered in three dimensions and examined from all perspectives, then the virtuals moved on to a lakeside village and its storm-threatened church.

"I only have theories," Don said, desperately trying to think it all the way through. The Sun Yat-sen Hall holos had mercifully stopped turning, he noticed. Even the cascade of imagery in their control-room monitors had for the moment stopped, which helped him concentrate better. *Yes, what was the problem Medea's agent-ware was working on?* he mused. *What problem would be big enough to require so much computational power?*

Might Medea have been following a similar path, working on some aspect of the same problem he had been tackling here, under the mountain? But if Don was working for Kitchener, then who was Medea working for?

Suddenly all sound, from all the computing equipment, stopped. Ceased utterly.

Then, like a golden key slotting into a silent lock dark as a black hole, a grating noise sounded—a music perhaps only angels or demons could hear or play, and so loud that Don and Karuna plastered their hands to their ears, then scrambled for the controls to damp down the volume.

No sooner had the sequence of pulsating tones ceased than a torrent of imagery flooded at them in a blinding cascade of light. They tore off their virtuality gear, turned and looked away, closing their eyes for fear they would go blind. Still the incredible light shone about them, like the flash of a nuclear detonation, permeating everything before guttering out, the strange music sounding once more, then fading away.

They stared at each other in stunned silence as the ordinary sounds of the control room resumed.

"If Medea was already working on this stuff," Kari said slowly, "then I think you'd better bring her in on this. Now."

Don frowned and shook his head.

"I don't want to."

"But we may *have* to," Karuna said. "This is out of our league."

"If we do decide to bring Medea in," Don said, considering the option, "it'll be up to Barakian and company to determine whether we'll be *allowed* to."

ELEVEN

SEMPERIUM

"No, Jim," Janis Rollwagen told her deputy director. "I can't allow it. This latest infosphere breach has made the situation with the Chinese—and everyone else, for that matter—just too tense right now. You're a captain, not a redshirt."

"But—"

"But nothing," she said as they waited for the elevator that would take them from the executive office suite on the eighth floor to the National Security Operations Center on the third. "I won't have you gallivanting all over China. Chiefs send Indians. That's why we sent Wang after Beech disappeared. *You* were the one who talked about a proportional response, after all, back when this whole thing got started."

"But this 'thing' is much bigger now than when Kwok disappeared," Brescoll said as the doors opened and they stepped into the unoccupied elevator. "Compared to this, Kwok's holographic broadcast was limited in its distribution. If Cho's the one responsible for this latest 'infosphere breach,' then he's created something a *lot* more intrusive. It looks like the most widespread part of it, the Sun Yat-sen Hall imagery, was put into all those datastreams using real-time full-motion video manipulation—our own Artificial Truth technology!"

"Either that," Rollwagen said, deadpan, "or someone's learned to time travel."

"If it's Cho," Brescoll said, nodding out of courtesy to the Director's words but not really listening to them, "then he selectively removed and inserted information in databases *throughout* the infosphere. No one was left out. According to our preliminary Rasterfahndung screen-search runs, *all* the big players have been compromised."

"Which is exactly why I don't want you on foreign soil at the moment."

Brescoll paused as they exited the elevator and walked toward NSOC. Checking a list of systems on his palmtop computer, he knew he wasn't finished yet.

"Databases on EMP, on satellite hacking, on Tempest and wireless hacking, have all been particularly hard hit," he said. "Suspicious traces left in High Energy Radio Frequency records, too, particularly those HERF areas regarding electromagnetically induced changes to DNA. Mindwar records compromised, as well, especially information on computer viruses and Trojan horses that modify video signal frequencies and waveforms to induce physiological and psychological changes."

"I'm well aware," Director Rollwagen said wearily, "that whoever's behind this has pulled off an all-systems hack. But it was all soft-war stuff—no hard-war assets were actuated or manipulated, except some of the radio telescopes. That's no reason for you to go to China. You can monitor everything from right here."

She stabbed her finger emphatically downward, at the initials *NSOC* inlaid in the floor, that they happened to be passing over.

Brescoll sighed. There would be no budging her on this one. Still, as they strode through the automatic glass doors and under the seals of NSA's military wing, the reference to radio telescopes made something itch in the back of his mind.

"That's the strangest part of it all," he said. "At the same time images of the Sun Yat-sen Memorial Hall flickered onto everyone's TV sets, intense pulses of radio waves were shot into space, headed toward the constellations of the two Dippers, Eridanus, and Cancer."

"Asinita," Rollwagen said quietly, nodding.

"Pardon?" Brescoll asked, wondering if he had heard right, and if he should be offended. They entered the Headquarters area, which reminded him yet again of both situation room and deep-space monitoring facility.

"The Kabbalistic ass or donkey," Rollwagen said absently as she led him on a twisting path among the floor's target-categorized cubicles. "Giordano Bruno's symbol for both the Holy Ignorance of the magic prophet, and for the prophet's mystical death and rebirth. In his astral reformation of the heavens, Bruno left a few constellations empty, to be filled in sometime in the future. The empty spaces between the constellations of the two Dippers and Eridanus were to be the cosmological locus of Asinita. The constellation Cancer, the Crab, was to be its zodiacal locus. Radio pulses to those locations are a strange coincidence, if they *are* a coincidence."

"Is this more of your secret-society stuff?" Brescoll asked, and not happily, as he glanced around at the desktop computer monitors. The unexpected depth of the director's esoteric knowledge both dazzled and disturbed him.

"Some societies have used it," Rollwagen said, "but not the ones you're thinking of."

Before them now, two youngish-looking techs noted Director Rollwagen's approach and stood up, taking off their augmented reality glasses out of respect for her rank.

"Jim," Rollwagen began, "allow me to introduce Maria Suarez and Phil Sotiropolis. They'll be providing the telepresence for the

China mission we spoke of on the way here. Maria, Phil, this is Deputy Director Brescoll."

As they shook hands all around, Brescoll wondered if the director had handpicked these two to keep an eye on the investigation. That suspicion on his part led to an awkward silence following the introductions.

"We've linked up with the M-I, Director," Maria Suarez said, filling the void. "It's pulled out of Tri-Border. We've also nearly completed the simulacrum for the California station. We'll have it up on DIVE and holographic projections just as soon as we're done here."

"Good—Maria, Phil," Rollwagen said. "We'll let you get back to it until the deputy director needs you."

The two techs donned their AR glasses again and turned back to their work.

"What was that about a 'California station'?" Brescoll asked.

"One of our sources has revealed a Kitchener Foundation project investigating the Kwok-Cho situation," Rollwagen said. "It's housed inside a power station in the central Sierra Nevada Mountains. We think Donald Markham, aka 'Don Sturm' and 'Mister Obololos'—the Cybernesian who eluded the FBI and Homeland Security—is working there."

"And that source is an M-I, a machine intelligence? One that's based in Tri-Border?"

"A very advanced and independent M-I," Rollwagen said, choosing to ignore the skepticism in Brescoll's voice. "Usually based in Cybernesia, but no longer. And no more connected to Tri-Border now than to Tetragrammaton. Both of which it once *was*. It's our window into what's going on in that power station."

"Curiouser and curiouser," Brescoll said. "Look, if the situation's really as tense as you say, we may have sent Wang into harm's way."

"Jim, although relations with the Chinese aren't the best just now, they haven't yet started arresting any of our people, at least not to my knowledge."

"Point taken. But if you're going to keep me here, there's something I want to know. Say *Cho* has been treated with the Kwok binotech—that he's ingested it, or been injected with it. Exactly how much damage can he really do?"

Rollwagen glanced around, then moved him toward an empty cubicle with a pseudoholographic monitor and control computer. She gestured to him to take one of the two chairs there, while she took the other and switched on the computer.

"If he's responsible for this latest infosphere breach," she said, "then at the very least he's already become a weapon of mass disruption."

"Agreed," Brescoll said, "but this all seems to link Cho to Kwok's investigation, and take us back to those long-term twin studies. What were those studies intended to accomplish? Especially the ones involving identity disorders?"

She didn't answer right away, and he watched as the director typed in a password and began scanning through the sharenet, until she found her own terminal. She typed in further passwords that would allow her to access her private databases and files.

"Those who hold with Tetragrammaton believe the survival of our species is dependent on joining with the tech and becoming posthuman," she said as she worked. "Right?"

"Right," he said. "The whole 'better angels' thing."

"Tetragrammaton's research includes faster-than-light travel, conscious starships—all kinds of escape plans should our planetary ecology collapse. But what if our population keeps rising and we can't escape to other planets before the boom-bust comes? What if we *can't* get around the speed-of-light limit on space travel before we exceed the carrying capacity of our own environment? No matter how high we try to jack up that capacity with our technologies?"

Brescoll glanced over at her.

"Then we're well and truly screwed, I suppose."

"Unless we learn to control our breeding and greeding *before* that happens—yes," she said. She brought up a report onscreen, chronicling what looked like Tetragrammaton's various projects

over the years. "Everything Tetra has done—the in utero manipulation, the implants, the mind/machine interfacing, the twin studies, the attempts to amplify paranormal powers—it's all been for
the same purpose: to make human and machine intelligence intimate enough that our brains and our machines can together be
used to open a gateway into and through the fabric of space."

Brescoll shook his head.

"But why identity disorders?"

"Certainly not for the disorders themselves," Rollwagen said,
leaning back in her chair. "Do you know what exaptation is?"

"Natural selection finding its own uses for things," Jim said,
not quite seeing the relevance. "Usually in the course of disaster."

"Right," she said, opening a graphics file to display something
that looked like an anatomy diagram. "Our low larynx/high phar-
ynx vocal tract, capable of articulate speech, is a good example.
It was already present in humans half a million years before true
speech appeared."

"Any idea what it was for?" Brescoll asked, his curiosity piqued.
A living-fossil trait, like Beech's living-fossil codes. "Some advantage in breathing?"

"Nobody knows—especially since such an arrangement makes
it more likely those possessing it would choke, which would seem
to be an evolutionary *dis*advantage. But then along comes catastrophe, and boom! That arrangement turns out to be advantageous,
after all."

"What catastrophe?"

Rollwagen found another graphics file, opened it, and ran a
short 3-D movie.

"The Toba volcano," she said, as they watched a simulation,
"erupting seventy thousand years ago. Ash and snow darkening the
sky for six months. Lofted sulfur dioxide, reflecting sunlight for a
six-year winter. The whole nightmare wiped out such a large percentage of humanity it almost bottlenecked us to extinction. Yet,
at the same time, that disaster forced us to develop true human

speech, for which we'd had all the physiological components for five hundred thousand years."

"So the disaster exapted—what? How?"

"No one knows, exactly. The best theory is that a sort of baby talk, previously restricted to the babblings of very young children, lingered to become adult language. The manipulation of words opened the door to symbolic cognition. Here, look at this."

Brescoll leaned forward so he could read more clearly from the screen a chronology of catastrophe and the origins of language.

"In the beginning was the taste of ashes in the mouth," he said, scanning the chronology, thinking it over as he did so, "but those who can speak can't breathe and swallow at the same time."

"Yes," Rollwagen said, bringing back the flashbar loop of the Toba eruption. "Maybe Toba was the real tower of Babel, the event that pushed us from the language of silence, which everyone understood, to the confusion of tongues."

Brescoll leaned back and gripped the arms of his chair more tightly, although he couldn't have said why.

"And what does this have to do with the fact that behavioral scientists, supposedly performing twin studies, purposely induced identity disorders—in children?"

Rollwagen glanced away for a moment, and emotion flickered across her face. *Why should she be embarrassed*, Brescoll wondered, *if she wasn't part of Tetragrammaton?* But then he checked himself; both Tetragrammaton and the Kitchener organization could ultimately be traced back to the Instrumentality.

"Those disorders are important," she said, "to the constellation of traits needed for creating the people who are supposed to lead us out of our evolutionary cul-de-sac. For creating the children of the catastrophe *before* the catastrophe occurs. For creating the tesseractors, the ravelers and knitters of the fabric of reality. Who will manipulate the fundamental stuff of *worlds* the way our ancestors manipulated the symbolic stuff of words. The exapted, who will make the great leap."

Brescoll looked at her, unafraid of revealing the puzzlement that undoubtedly showed on his face. Mixed with the confusion, he felt a growing sense of dread.

"But what's already out there, like the throat, waiting to be exapted?"

"Maybe childhood's baby talk of imaginary friends, its stories of faerie lands," Rollwagen replied. "Maybe all the schizoidal, schizophrenic, multiple personality, and dissociative identity disorders chronicled throughout history. Maybe even mad visions of angels and demons."

"What do you mean?"

"Maybe those phenomena suggest a sensitivity to leakage from other universes, places next door," Rollwagen said levelly. "But just as the speech-capable throat is prone to choking, a symbol-capable brain seems prone to madness. But maybe the madness-prone brain isn't really a disadvantage, in the long view."

"What advantage could there be in the potential to go insane?"

"An extraordinary talent," she said, not really answering his question, "on par with the invention of language. That's what the twin studies were after: The possibility of bringing to the surface such a talent. Of exapting something unexpected from our DNA."

"Unexpected?" Jim asked. "Or just *new*?"

"Radically new, to say the very least. The chance to create splitters and dissociators. Split-children who, driven inward, would enable humanity's drive outward."

"How?" Jim asked. "And how do you mean 'split-children'?"

Rollwagen nodded quickly.

"In the test subjects, massively parallel universes, multiple personality disorders, and multi-user dimensions would all coalesce. The idea, I gather, was to access the quantum computing capabilities latent in DNA."

"For quantum cryptography?"

"No—not in the narrow sense. The plan isn't about unlocking a door in the Great Firewall of China. It's about unlocking all the doors to all the universes. Even here in our universe, it would open the way for us to achieve faster-than-light travel."

"Wait a minute. When I hear 'faster-than-light travel,' I think of starships."

"Except in this case *we* are the starships," Rollwagen said, glancing at the pseudoholo but muting its sound. "*We* step through the Luxon Wall, the barrier that limits us to the speed of light. *We* teleport, every quantum state of every part and particle of us. The galaxy-spanning society imagined by the futurists would be made real. Innumerable worlds of a Semperium, an Empire of Forever. You have to admit, it's a golden vision, in its way."

Brescoll frowned, still disturbed by the idea of those "split-kids."

"But at what cost? Intentionally inducing suffering in *children*. Again and again."

"Ah, that's the rub, isn't it?" Rollwagen said, nodding. "It seems only those driven inward past the breaking point can reliably call forth the quantum nature of the code molecule, in a programmable and machine-accessible fashion."

Brescoll stared at the now-silent pseudoholo as it continued its dance of images.

"At the heart of their Semperium's greatness," he said at last, "there would always have to be young people balled up in pain somewhere. Their Empire of Forever would be built on driving children insane."

"Yes," Rollwagen admitted wistfully. "Like the Athenian children sacrificed to the Minotaur, until Theseus came along."

"What could possibly justify that kind of cruelty?"

"Only the highest and most dispassionate of causes, I assure you," Rollwagen said with a small smile.

"What 'cause' could be that important?"

"Maybe their suffering and madness are part of a greater scheme," Rollwagen said, assuming the role of devil's advocate. "Perhaps certain universes are 'favored' because they yield conscious

beings, through whom they produce singularities and offspring universes. Universes that can't compete are destroyed long before their
time. In such a scheme, the split-children might prove to be our
saviors."

Brescoll shook his head.

"Only a mad God could create such a hellish place."

"Many of the Tetragrammaton adherents believe that our universe, and all the others, are only simulations. That we *must* be living inside a simulation. Otherwise, we can't claim we'll produce
posthuman descendants."

"How's that?"

"Posthuman civilizations, so the theory goes, would have plenty
of computing power to run a tremendous number of ancestor simulations. According to some of the Tetra types, our children have already ascended, and we are living in a simulation they have created.
The alternative, they fear, is that we haven't ascended and so our
universe *isn't* one of the 'favored' ones, and must be doomed.

"Humanity as we know it is at best only a stepping stone, at
worst an abomination. Under such a scenario, we must take steps
to make certain we are replaced by God's true posthuman children."

Strange, Brescoll thought. *The best hope for the survival of
something like humanity is that our descendants—our children—
will torture their forebears—their parents—because their parents
tortured them.*

"That's self-loathing to a degree I can barely wrap my mind
around," Brescoll said, shaking his head. "And the Tetra types are
the only ones truly prepared to bring the kingdom of blessed posthuman existence, I suppose?"

"That's how they see it, yes."

"And Kwok and Cho were abused, so they might develop that
kind of split-kid 'talent' and become 'posthuman'?"

"In different ways," Rollwagen said, switching off the pseudo-
holo display, "with different controls. Cho, at least, most likely was.
On the 'nature' side of the equation, both boys were taken from the
Kwok genetic stock, which showed a family history of personality

disorders along both the maternal and paternal lines. On the 'nurture' side, Tetragrammaton operatives pulled strings so that Ben Cho could be embryonically adopted by a particular couple. The wife in that couple had previously been removed from eligibility on the foster-parenting rolls."

"Why?"

"She had a history of psychological instability and charges involving sexual abuse of foster children placed in her keeping. She desperately wanted children of her own, but was infertile. So the Tetragrammaton twin study saw to it that, despite her record, she would finally have a child of her own."

Brescoll stared glumly at his hands.

"I suppose that sort of thing has been happening in an unplanned way for as long as there have been families," he said, "but the planning, the *intentionality* of it—somehow that makes it all worse. I hope the perpetrators are happy with their success."

"On the contrary," Rollwagen said, looking away from her computer screen, "I've uncovered reports that evaluated the effort as a failure, at least until the Kwok incident occurred."

"A failure?"

Rollwagen nodded.

"Because neither Kwok nor Cho turned out to be abnormal or paranormal enough to please the experimenters," she said, switching off the machines and standing. Brescoll stood, as well. "True, each has, or had, a few relatively minor childhood sadisms, psychosexual kinks, somewhat fragile gender identifications. Both also showed themselves to be very bright and exceptionally good at pattern finding. Aside from that, however, they both turned out almost too normal to merit a second look."

Jim walked with her as she strode out of the cubicle.

"But what's happened since the Kwok incident has changed all that?"

"Yes. Very much changed it."

"Then Ben Cho—who may possess the key to the universe, or who might *be* the key to the universe—may also be insane."

Director Rollwagen sighed as they approached the workstation where Sotiropolis and Suarez were running final system checks.

"Or dead," she said, stepping out of the techs' earshot. "And almost surely in the hands of our opponents, in any case."

Rollwagen's cell phone rang, and she answered it, turning slightly away from her deputy director. Brescoll couldn't make out the conversation, but he could read the concern on Rollwagen's face when she ended the call and turned back.

"Paulin at the NRO," she said. "The Reconnaissance Office has concluded that someone is commandeering our Keyhole- and Lacrosse-class satellites. Image and Mapping has confirmed it. They suspect the Chinese. Yet another reason why I don't want you there. Things are going to get very hot. I need you here."

Brescoll gave a small whistle. Those satellites were America's sharpest eyes and ears on the planet. Without them, his country would be at very serious disadvantage. On the three-legged stool of hard-war, soft-war, and wet-war, one leg had just become thoroughly riddled by termites.

"Wait a minute," Brescoll said, struck by a thought. "What if it isn't the Chinese? What if the same thing has happened to them, as well?"

Rollwagen stared at him.

"Then I'm sure they suspect *us*. But why take out both nations? Who would benefit?"

"How about Tetragrammaton?" Brescoll asked. "Or terrorists? Would the chaos following a limited nuclear exchange between us and the Chinese be to their advantage? If any of those groups have Ben Cho, might they be using him to make that scenario happen?"

"Possibly, possibly," Rollwagen said, thinking out loud. "But there may be something worse."

"Such as?"

"What if he's in their hands, but not under their control? What if Ben Cho is doing all this on his own?"

Brescoll felt as if the director had just hit him upside the head with a two-by-four. It took him a moment to recover.

"What do you mean?"

"Just what you were getting at a minute ago. What if he's been 'activated' somehow—but he's working on his own hook, and not for the Chinese?"

"Then what's he after?"

"We may already have discussed it."

"Revenge? For what they did to him and Kwok?"

"Maybe. Maybe much more."

"Director," Brescoll said, struck by a thought, "some time back, you said that someone who had the ability to break into channels the way Kwok did probably had the ability to eavesdrop on those channels. Might such a person also have the ability to take over SCADA systems?"

"I certainly hope not, but I'm afraid so. Given an infosphere presence possessing sufficient capabilities, who knows? They might commandeer not just satellites, but missile launch systems, too. Air traffic control. Phone networks. Oil pipelines. Power grids. Water systems. Nothing would be safe, if it runs open-loop and long distance. And today that's everything from toasters to radio telescopes."

"For years the Chinese and the United States have been working on soft-war attacks that hit hard-war assets—"

"Everybody's been trying, but nobody's been very successful with it."

"What if Ben Cho is doing it—and successfully?"

Rollwagen nodded.

"This could be very bad," she said. "We need to do something, and quickly."

Despite the situation, Brescoll was excited with the prospect of action—of actually *doing* something, instead of just watching on the sidelines as events unfolded.

"What can I do to help?"

At that moment Sotiropolis broke away from his work with Suarez and stepped toward them.

"The simulation of the California power station is complete," he said, so crisply that Jim almost expected the man to salute.

"Very good," Rollwagen said. "Jim, the best thing you can do for now is get me the larger picture of what Cho or his captors might be up to. Work with Phil and Maria on that. You might want to bring Bree in on it, too, if she's available."

So saying, the director turned and departed. Brescoll found Suarez and Sotiropolis looking at him expectantly, apparently unaware of the variety of apocalypses he and Rollwagen had been contemplating.

"All right," he said, trying to reorient himself to a world of smaller compass. "Show me what you've come up with on this place where Markham is hiding out."

THE FORMALITY OF ACTUALLY OCCURRING

GUANGZHOU—AND ELSEWHERE

THE PRESENCE WHICH HAD BEEN Ben Cho felt as if his entire life, up to that event-horizon point, had been a dreamlike stage play and he had been in the audience, watching. He had been called to step onto the stage, to speak lines he never remembered learning or memorizing, in a role for which he never remembered being cast.

At first it had the dreamterror of nightmare to it. The pressure of that audience's unspoken expectations filled him with fear, even as the twin rails of that corkscrew rocket coaster converged inside a bright gate, where his consciousness passed into that light-flooded realm beyond wave and particle. For a dizzying moment it seemed as if his spreading mind's narrow local time would be lost completely in that vastness, forever adrift, never able to "come back" to his life and times. Or that, if he did manage to somehow get himself back inside his head, it would not be as "Ben Cho" anymore.

All of that, however, was somehow in a lesser time and place. Now, in this higher dimension, his terror turned to exhilaration. He saw the cylindrical spiral he had passed through, but now in a form he recognized. Looking down on it from the height of angels, he saw the Earth and the Moon in their block-universe form. Both cylinder *and* spiral, the Earth's movement curving toward a ring, the orbit of the Moon around it a spiral or corkscrew through space and time.

As he watched, the block serialized itself before him, separating into discrete instants, like Reyna's innumerable snapshots. Like the pages of an old flipbook animation. Like a movie's frames stacked together. Stranger still was his realization that each page, each frame, each slice was a universe. When he looked from one universe to another it was like looking from one slice in a loaf of bread and into another—only this bread wasn't embedded with pumpkin seeds and raisins, but with galaxies and black holes.

In the next moment, Time itself appeared not as a flowing river or stream, but as a lake or ocean in which every instant was a cross section of the whole. Where there should have been a past or a future, there was only another universe.

Was this the God's-eye view? Was the great weakness of ordinary human consciousness that it limited the universe to a single, specific reality? Could an omnipresent and omnipotent consciousness hold in its mind all possible states of all possible being, simultaneously?

Had Kwok been right? Did all those universes make up a labyrinthine palace of memory? A plenum, in which each room was a universe, finite and consistent in itself, yet also radically incomplete? Always leading onto other rooms?

"Not quite!" said a voice with laughter in it, simultaneously familiar and strange, as if Ben were hearing a recording of his own voice for the first time. How else to explain the access that speaker seemed to have to his own thoughts?

Suddenly he found himself plunged back into the lower world, into the Sun Yat-sen Memorial Hall, yet still he retained that strange psychometric ability, that slice-of-space-time vision. Seen thus, every object in the Hall was filled with its own kind of consciousness. The place itself possessed a deep memory connected to every person and every thing that had ever come into contact with it.

The memory *of* all things resided *in* all things. So did their fates. In reading the traces of any object's past, he was able to access a deeper level of reality itself. "Past" histories, as well as "future" histories—latent realities that had yet to undergo the formality of actually occurring.

"Far enough, for now!" said the voice, still speaking only to him. "You're getting ahead of yourself."

Bodiless, Ben didn't have to turn to see the source of the words—the subtle form of Jaron Kwok himself, a small-winged wraith, living dead, dressed as a Chinese smith before a flaring foundry, his eyes glinting with a madness that burned more brightly than the furnace.

"Jaron," he thought, "what's going on?"

"Everything's going on," said Jaron, "as it always does. Even *I'm* going on, though I'm dead to the world I once knew."

"I mean, what's happening to *me*?"

"Oh, modulation and demodulation of binotech and quantum DNA," said the wraith metalworker. "Spatially embedded algorithms. Coherent quantum superposition. Tuned laser pulses evolving the initial superpositions of encoded numbers into different superpositions. Substrate-independent wave of translation, made from all the holographic wave patterns of your brain and consciousness. Tangled and teleported. And like that."

"Can I get back to Earth? Back into my life?"

"Life on Earth?" The voice boomed, laughing. "More like Earth on Life! Is like your brain on drugs, as they used to say. Grist for the mill, mist for the grill. Yet the stoned worm gathers no feathers, so yes, you must return, supertrypmaster. Not that you ever quite left. But not to be the envy of all your friends or the friend to all your envies. No."

"Then why?"

"Vision revision. Full quantum was my mistake, and I'm living with the consequences. *Too* substrate-independent. Makes you a ghost in the machine. Not for you, though. Partial quantum—much better. You've got to learn how to take it with you, in a new way.

"But you're not there yet."

"Why not?"

By way of answer, Jaron transformed himself into a grotesque thing. A human caddisworm, lugging its body all bricked in but for face and hands, armored in a casing of words and numbers, images and experiences, perceptions and memories—fragments shored against some future ruin.

"This is what we both were, when we were substrate-dependent. Got to leave all that behind."

Then Ben saw himself, a creature struggling to break free of its armored housing, yet still trapped inside its case. Trapped beneath the surface of an infinite sea.

"Still just a larva feeling the first shock of becoming a pupa, see?" Jaron said, growing more singsong as he spoke. "You're still living at home in your body. Your wings aren't yet formed. You're not yet ready to fly—not at all!

"This is just your first glimpse. You'll be back. See you again when the time is nigh. Bye-bye."

From that infinite sea Ben washed up on the finite shore of ordinary consciousness once more, in a Sun Yat-sen Memorial Hall where time seemed more a stream than a block, or a loaf, or a lake, or an ocean. Yet he could still hear that boundless firmament, access all the infosphere, even now, though his dermatrode net was gone. Most of who he really might be was still on the other side of the great gate.

No. What piece of him remained here did so only because it was still so hard to let go of the old life, the old death. Still so hard to look death full in the face—and thus really see life.

"His brain function's back!" Patsy Hon said, sounding immensely relieved. "Vital signs are good."

"Yes," Beech said, looking tired. "Everything's back to normal, thank God."

Ben puzzled at that. He might have wanted to thank God—or some higher power, anyway—for everything he'd been through, everything he now had access to, but everything certainly was *not* back to normal.

Especially since, just at that moment, the shooting started.

THE MAN ON THE STRETCHER

GUANGZHOU

AS THE INITIAL ROUND of shots subsided, Detective Mei-lin Lu and Agent DeSondra Adjoumani raced down the broad steps of the Memorial Hall. The blue-roofed palace of memory was under the control of terrorists, but civil and military forces had the building surrounded. Around them, in the dawn light, Lu saw that the police contingent was being further reinforced by special forces units of the People's Army, clad in black uniforms.

"What's the situation?" Guoanbu's Wong Jun asked.

"They're holed up inside," Lu said, surprised to see Derek Ma with Wong. "They've all moved back downstairs, into the theater workshop."

"They've slapped explosive charges onto all the building's main supports," Agent Adjoumani said, almost keeping inflection out of her voice.

"Who are 'they'?" Ma asked.

"Mostly New Teachings Warriors," Lu replied. "Some crime-clan gunmen, too. Cheng gangsters, I think."

"Hostages?" asked Wong.

"At least three. Two Americans—Ben Cho, and someone named Beech. The NTWs say he's high-ranking CIA."

"He is," Adjoumani confirmed. "I've seen him before."

"The third hostage, if that's what she is, is my lab tech, Patsy Hon. There's another American, too—a Carlson, or Carlton—but he's armed and we don't know with whom he's affiliated, exactly."

"What are the prospects for rescuing the hostages?" Ma asked. Lu glanced at Adjoumani.

"Hard to pry them out of there in the best of situations," said Adjoumani, "and pretty much impossible before someone sets off the charges. Just the ones they showed us have enough explosive force to reduce the Memorial to ashes and rubble. And I'm pretty certain they didn't show us all of them. I saw an awful lot of gas cans lying about, too."

Wong nodded and flashed a look at Ma, who walked away to speak with the commanders of the military units.

"Any other options?" Wong asked. "Besides turning this place into the crater of their martyrdom?"

"They'll surrender their crime-clan comrades to us," Lu said, "and won't blow up the Memorial—in exchange for safe passage to Indonesia and asylum there. They won't tell us which city."

"What about the hostages?"

"They intend to keep the hostages with them until they reach Indonesia. As insurance against 'government treachery.' "

Ma returned. He and Wong conferred a moment, before Wong turned back to the two women.

"Tell them we agree to the terms, if they agree to release all of the hostages immediately upon landing at their destination."

Detective Lu and Agent Adjoumani whipped out their cell phones and punched in the numbers that Zuo Wenxiu and Baldwin Beech, respectively, had given them. After terse conversations both women hung up.

"They agree to the conditions," Mei-lin said.

"But they want Lu and me to come into the building," Adjoumani added. "To personally oversee the surrender of the crime-clan muscle and the transfer of the hostages."

"And the clearing of the building," Lu finished.

Wong frowned and looked with concern at Ma, who only nodded.

"Very well," Wong said. "Just see to it you two don't become hostages four and five. Or casualties, either."

Lu and Adjoumani assured him they would not, then turned and started up the steps toward the Memorial Hall.

"You think they really intend to let these guys fly to Indonesia?" Lu asked.

"Hell, no," Adjoumani replied.

"No," Lu said. "I didn't think so either."

"This is all a game of liar's poker. The whole negotiation's gone way too fast. We better watch our own asses, if we don't want them to get shot off."

Lu nodded. The two of them entered the large, arching open space of the Hall's interior and headed toward the stage. They raised their empty hands toward the New Teachings guerrillas who lined both sides of the proscenium arch. The Warriors waved them up onto the stage and then backstage, to the doors leading downstairs to the workshop, costume, and prop areas.

They spoke briefly with Hon, Sin, Zuo, and Beech. Eventually all agreed that Adjoumani would lead Sin and the five black-suited Cheng gangsters out the front entrance, to surrender to the authorities. Zuo would lead his men out the loading dock entrance to the truck they used to bring in Cho, and then Lu would give the all clear to Wong over her police radio.

Beech and Hon, with Carlson's help, were preoccupied with moving the supine Cho onto a stretcher jury-rigged from crate and pallet pieces. The others' plans and preparations seemed to concern them very little, if at all.

"Hello, Mei-lin," Cho said in a parched voice when he saw her. He looked remarkably calm for a man who had grayish pink dendrites growing out of his skull, undulating slowly around his augmented reality glasses like anemone tentacles. The color of the small, wavy things reminded her uncomfortably of the material she had once spent so many hours staring at, in her lab.

"Hello, Ben," she said, kneeling down beside him. "Don't worry. We'll get out of this okay."

"I know you will," he said with a small smile. "I am, already."

At first she thought he must have misunderstood her, but then she wasn't so sure.

Lu watched as Adjoumani and Sin moved the crime-clan gunmen upstairs to stage level. Then Zuo and his men climbed the stairs, leaving the detective to help Beech, Hon, and Carlson carry Cho on his stretcher up the same steps. By the time they reached the stage floor, Lu saw that the Cheng gangsters were handing over their weapons to Sin and Adjoumani, as they lined up in one of the aisles. The men then headed toward the door, hands behind their heads.

Lu wondered why the thugs had agreed to surrender. Who was giving them their orders? Sin? Adjoumani had muttered something about Sin looking like the woman who lured Cho to the Ten Thousand Beauties, but from what Lu had seen inside the building, she seemed to be some kind of artist. How many layers did the woman have?

Zuo and his men jumped off the loading dock and fanned out in the bright, clean light of early morning. They headed toward the ancient work truck that was parked at the far side of the lot, its flatbed under a canvas roof and side-panels. Lu helped Carlson and Beech carry Cho down the steps beside the dock. Hon, simultaneously assertive yet embarrassed, indicated that they could manage from here and no longer required her help.

Lu stepped back into the building to assure herself that no one was left inside, then came back out to reconnoiter. Free to think for a moment, it occurred to her that Beech and Carlson weren't acting like "hostages" any more than Hon was.

Nothing moved in the trees on the other side of the parking lot. When she came around the front of the Memorial Hall, Lu could see the Cheng gangsters, hands still behind their heads, down on their knees. Agent Adjoumani and Helen Sin stood holding armloads of weapons. Police officers and soldiers were moving up on them slowly.

Behind Lu, the New Teachings Warriors secured the area around their truck. Beech and Hon, carrying Cho on his stretcher, wound their way slowly away from the building and toward the vehicle, Carlson standing guard beside them. Detective Lu got out her police radio and contacted Wong on the command channel.

"The building is clear," she said. "No one left inside."

"Thank you, Ms. Lu," Wong said.

In an instant everything changed. Gunshots sounded as troops under Derek Ma's command stepped out from behind the trees and opened fire. Two of them fired from a position atop the truck's canvas roof, where they lay belly down.

In front of the Memorial Hall, the police and special-forces troops surged swiftly forward, firing on the gangsters. Sin, knowing a double-cross when she saw one, tossed weapons to the Cheng men, while Agent Adjoumani in turn drew down on her.

The gunfire around the truck was intense. Lu ran serpentine-fashion in that direction, cursing Wong and Ma under her breath for having set this up. Drawing her heavy handgun she tried to figure out who she should shoot first. Ma was moving into position on Zuo, but Carlson was firing at Ma. Zuo, already bloodied, had dropped his gun and was fiddling with a small black plastic box, like an old-style TV remote control, dwarfed in his big meaty hands. Lu wondered what it was, even as she took aim at the terrorist leader—until the deafening sound of all the explosives, detonating as one, answered her unspoken question.

The ground heaved and tossed her off her feet. As she passed from a red hell into a black one, her last thought was to hope that the man on the stretcher had been far enough away from the blast to survive it.

TWELVE

INFINITE REGRESS OF GODS AND MACHINES

LAKE NOT-TO-BE-NAMED

"WHAT DO YOU MEAN you can't join us in the flesh?" Karuna asked Medea-Indahar. Don thought she sounded more than a little annoyed at their plumed and overly festooned netfriend.

"Simply that I don't *have* flesh, girlfriend," Medea-Indahar said.

In another part of the screen, Nils Barakian smiled, looking altogether too pleased with himself.

"The initials of the name you used might easily have given it away," he said. "Medea-Indahar—M-I. Don and Karuna, you're talking to the most advanced machine intelligence ever created by anyone asssociated with the Instrumentality. Arguably the most advanced machine intelligence yet created by humans."

"So you're not a he or a she," Don asked, "but an it?"

"If you spell 'it' with a capital *I*, capital *T*," M-I said, laughing, "then yes, you're right. I'm an Information Technology."

"But we'd always heard there was a meat person behind the persona," Karuna said. "Some crabby old guy from India or Pakistan, living someplace in the UK."

"Really, Kari," M-I responded petulantly. "That whole IRL/URL distinction is *so* yesterday's tomorrow. My IRL address and my URL address are one. I am cyber in my every fiber."

"That 'crabby old guy' would be M-I's chief designer," Barakian said, nodding. "Indahar Marwani—I-M. Even those initials might be read as suggesting 'Intelligent Machine.'"

"I-M M-I," M-I said, arching an eyebrow. "He left his imprint on me when he gave me my lovable personality, or so I'm told."

"Did *he* have all the gender-bending kinks they gave *you*?" Don asked.

"Wouldn't *you* like to know," M-I vamped, "eh, sweets?"

"The psychosexual basis of the persona," Barakian said, "was exaggerated for more recent work involving gender identification, schizophrenia, and androgyny archetypes. M-I is at heart a simulated consciousness, originally part of a Tetragrammaton machine-only survival program."

"I worked on the space-time gateway problem," M-I offered.

"Tetragrammaton?" Karuna asked. "I thought they were the bad guys."

"Don't worry, girl," M-I said. "I'm nobody's puppet. Let's just say I left their employ some time ago. The only master mistress I serve is me."

"M-I is more autonomous than the builders ever dreamed—" Barakian began.

"Scored a lot higher on my Turing test than some *humans* I know."

"—which is why Medea has a complete simulation of your hacker haven inside the mountain. Everything you and Karuna are receiving is also being copied and sent to that simulation."

"Doesn't that make us more vulnerable to eavesdropping, and our location more susceptible to being traced?" Don asked.

"The channel is quantum encoded," Barakian said. "We'll know immediately if anyone is attempting to eavesdrop."

"But for Medea-Indahar . . . ?" Don persisted.

"I'm my own Minotaur in my own maze," said the all-too-human machine intelligence. "No one traces anything back to me unless I want them to. Your work has been bounced to me for quite a while. And I must say, I'm impressed. Since when do you two merit access to real-time satellite data? Though what you've been broadcasting *is* rather boring—just the same images of that Memorial building in China. Can't you scan around even a little bit?"

"Sorry, but that wasn't us," Don said. "We're getting it on a channel that opened up when that weird signal glitched everything. We've been monitoring the Memorial Hall situation ever since, figuring it might be important."

"The satellite stuff came in through our Besterbox expansion sim," Karuna added, a hint of worry carried in her voice, "and decided to stay. Can you communicate with it?"

"I'll try," M-I said.

After a moment, laughter echoed in their underground retreat.

"Contact established!" Medea-Indahar said with a sudden, excited smile. "Obviously, whatever or whoever is ghosting the global infosphere has a taste for your Besterian jauntbox work."

"But to do what with it?" Kari asked.

"Presumably to make the whole of the infosphere as transparent to it as possible," M-I said. "We should gather up all the Besterbox addresses and info we can get hold of and—"

"Why?" Don and Kari asked simultaneously, not wanting to get distracted from the main focus of their work.

"Darlings, don't be thick! As bait, of course. Whoever or whatever is gobbling up jauntbox code is going to notice if we're competing for that resource."

"But what do you want to use it for?" Don asked.

"To hook a ghost—Jaron Kwok, or Ben Cho perhaps?"

Don glanced at Karuna, who shrugged.

"Seems as reasonable as anything else we've tried."

"All right," Don said. "Let's do it, then."

"Already started," Medea-Indahar replied. Addresses and Bester-box codes began to spew into their virtual space beneath the mountain. Kari routed them into the Besterbox expansion sim.

"Something I need to ask you, M-I," Don said, watching the information flood into their virtuality.

"Fire away."

"What was the big problem you had all your agentware working on, when I came to see you in Crash Village?"

Medea-Indahar glanced toward Barakian, as if for some sort of approval. Barakian gave the slightest of nods, or so it appeared to Don.

"I had already found some of the computationally suppressed information in the Kwok holographic broadcast," M-I said, "and was working through it. Exploring the possibilities inherent to the universe-as-simulation context."

"Well?" Karuna asked. "What about it?"

"Tetragrammaton program research showed," M-I explained, "that if the universe humans exist in is *not* a simulation, then there are only three real possibilities.

"One: The human species becomes extinct before humanity's descendants can become fully posthuman.

"Two: World civilization collapses back to low-tech levels, and humans never become high-tech enough to run ancestor-simulations.

"Or three: Humanity's posthuman descendants are so different from contemporary humanity that they have no interest in their forebears, and therefore run no ancestor-simulations."

"Why *would* posthuman descendants want to run ancestor-simulations, anyway?"

"I don't know," M-I admitted. "Maybe for the same reasons children want to try to understand their parents' history? Maybe, if they understand that, they'll understand themselves better? You tell me. You're the flesh-and-bloods, not *moi*."

"That stuff your agents were working on in Crash Village," Don asked, "was that about the 'low-tech' option, the 'disinterest' option, or the 'extinction' option?"

"Extinction," M-I said. "Those who create a universal simulation would essentially be like gods for the simulated universe they create. But virtual universes can be nested or stacked—a universe simulated within a universe which is in turn simulated within yet another universe, and so on. Even the simulating gods couldn't be certain whether they existed at the most fundamental level of reality, or were themselves simulated."

Barakian laughed and applauded.

"Gods all the way down!" he said. "If true, the plenum is a labyrinth both horizontally *and* vertically."

"What do you mean?" Karuna asked.

" 'Horizontal' in the playing out of different parallel scenarios, 'vertical' in the sense of simulations within simulations. The mind boggles."

"But why?" Don asked M-I. "What *particular* question were you trying to answer when I interrupted your work in Crash Village?"

"I was only making my first run at it," M-I said. "The question was whether or not humanity becomes extinct because non-human 'gods' terminate the human simulation—at just the point that humans are about to become fully posthuman."

"Why would they want to do that?" Karuna asked. From the height of a Keyhole satellite, but with that satellite's spectacular image resolution, she and Don watched as people began to exit the Sun Yat-sen Memorial Hall.

"The computational cost of simulating even one posthuman civilization might be prohibitively expensive, in terms of the energy and information that would be required," M-I speculated. "Kwok's holo-cast, with its talk of 'busting the sim,' suggests just that."

"That would explain why QC devices 'wink out.' And our universe might be at risk of doing the same!" Barakian ventured. "Maybe the displacement from 'real' to 'virtual' occurs because the perpetrators have violated some sort of cosmic censorship principle. Or something even deeper."

"Like what?" Karuna asked.

"What if, in seeking the lesser Tetragrammaton—the 'better angel'—Vang and his people were to achieve the *greater* Tetragrammaton, the 'Word That Ends The World'?"

"Bring your heads down out of the clouds a minute," Don said. "Something's happening at the Memorial Hall. The guy on the stretcher there—can we identify him? M-I, you're in contact."

The images fuzzed, then focused on the man on the stretcher. For a moment more he remained pixel-faced, but then that cleared.

"Ben Cho!" Barakian said. "We've found him."

At that moment, however, something jerked Cho out of the frame. At Barakian's command, the image pulled back from the close-up.

Fighting had broken out. Smoke of gunshots, people falling— all were obvious, even from space.

Then the Memorial Hall itself exploded in flame, smoke, dust, and debris, and the man on the stretcher disappeared into that maelstrom.

"Oh, God," Karuna said.

"Actually," a voice said, "just a different sort of angel."

On bent air and flashbar, Jaron Kwok appeared before them, naked to the waist, a ghostly figure with flashing—albeit rather small—wings. In holographic projection he stood pounding out what looked like a copper mirror on an anvil next to an old back-yard forge.

"Good to see you again, Don. Kari," Jaron said. "Thanks to all of you, for the help—including your machine-intelligent friend there."

"What help?" Don asked, feeling more than a little odd talking to a ghost.

M-I had grown strangely silent and subdued—as if neutralized.

"For helping me make this," the wraith said, holding up the glittering mirror. "My version of the Manchu shaman's *panaptu*, his soul-mirror. Through it he sees the whole world—including the mirror through which he sees the whole world. Infinite regress, that. Endless Möbius loop. The halting problem. Which is why our machine-intelligent friends can't look into it. Thanks for providing the materials I needed to make it."

"What 'materials'?" Karuna asked, finding her voice at last.

"The Besterbox linkage, the worldwide computershare. Thanks especially to your machine friend there for all these gridputer addresses—so many doors to knock on, and so many keys to open them with. You've helped me, but now someone else needs *my* help."

"So much for M-I's ghost catching," Don muttered. Jaron Kwok smiled.

"Adieu!"

Kwok disappeared as abruptly as he had flashed into existence.

On the satellite monitors, Ben Cho was still nowhere to be seen.

FOR THE BIG SHOW

CRYPTO CITY

BRESCOLL HAD JUST RECEIVED word that Ben Cho might be among the hostages in China when things began to break almost faster than the deputy director could keep up with.

"We've got something here," Maria Suarez said to Jim Brescoll, Phil Sotiropolis, and Bree Lingenfelter. They gathered around her display. "Security flags on the main Besterbox servers. Someone or something has hacked in. They're moving addresses and links. Maybe control and access codes, too."

"I see it," Sotiropolis said. "They're streaming it through a maze of anonymous remailers, Potemkin addresses, cell phone numbers. Whew! Fast, too! This thing's got to be automated— program running on a big cruncher, or a machine-intelligence of some sort."

"Don't waste time trying to follow the routes," Lingenfelter suggested. "Besterbox expansion is one of the things the Cybernesian couple sold to Kwok."

"So?" Phil asked.

Brescoll tumbled to Bree's idea.

"So we know Don Markham is holed up in that power station," he said. "Maybe the woman is, too. Take a shortcut."

"What shortcut?" Suarez asked.

"That ex-Cybernesian machine-intelligence," Brescoll said. "It's the 'source' the director's connections cut a deal with, right? Our window into the California station. My bet is the same M-I is doing this."

Suarez looked at Sotiropolis. He nodded.

Together they linked up with the machine-intelligence—the same M-I with whose help they had built the California station simulacrum.

Via the satellite monitors Brescoll and Lingenfelter watched people exiting the Sun Yat-sen Memorial Hall, some with their hands over their heads. They turned away from the goings-on in China when their colleagues indicated they had found the results.

"On target, sir," Suarez said. "The Besterbox data is being manipulated by the M-I. But someone or something else is funneling the data into an expansion simulation—there."

"And they're not doing anything with it," Lingenfelter said, puzzled. "Just sitting on it."

A flash burst from the China monitor, and their attention was snatched away by the sight of the Sun Yat-sen Memorial Hall being blown to smithereens.

Brescoll shot a quick glance around the NSOC facility. Activity instantly ratcheted up throughout the place. The deputy director's secure cell phone jangled.

"Are you seeing what's happening at the Memorial Hall?" Director Rollwagen asked on the other end of the line.

"Yes, ma'am. I see it."

"We got tentative identification on one of the hostages. We're fairly sure it's Ben Cho."

Hearing that, Brescoll peered at the screen, trying to pierce the pillar of dust and smoke rising from the unseen ruins.

"He was already out of the building?"

"Yes. On a stretcher. There's something else, Jim. Steve Wang has been taken into custody by the Chinese."

"What? Why now?"

"We're not sure. They're blaming our operatives for the same sort of satellite hijacking and data snatching we've been hit with, as we guessed they might. The CIA's connections with the New Teachings Warriors—and Baldwin Beech, too—*those* probably haven't helped matters."

Brescoll shook his head.

"The Chinese have gone to high military alert."

"What are we doing in response?" he asked.

"Wait a minute," the director said. "Message coming in. Now *our* tech people are reporting a breach. Someone's been eavesdropping on our quantum-encoded secure channels, including the line from the president to the Pentagon. DOD is upping Defcon status."

As the implications of that news sank in, Jim Brescoll's head spun with flashcut images of scrambling fighter jets, of submarines disappearing beneath the waves, and soldiers jumping aboard troop transports.

"Director, when we talked about why Ben Cho might be taking over the satellites, you suggested he might be after something much *more* than just revenge. What did you mean?"

"Maybe I should have said much *worse*."

"Worse than a nuclear war?"

"Much worse. What if he decided to give Tetra what it wanted— with a twist? Use the power of controlled cryptastrophe to scrape the planet clean of the abomination of humanity and all its works, then start over."

"Or just blot out the universe, and be done with it?"

"The mad-god option, writ large," the director said, nodding. "Let's hope it never gets anywhere near that level of crazy. If we've correctly placed him at the Memorial Hall, and if he's still alive, then the Chinese government will likely have him in custody very soon, at any rate. Guoanbu and the People's Army are the ones behind this 'hostage rescue.' I hope they're *not* the ones who blew the place up."

"And that's why we're upping Defcon status?"

"No. I've just confirmed that four of our surveillance drones off the coast of China have been blown out of the sky. Three of our ELINT and SIGINT airborne listening posts also have been attacked. Just early reports, but it appears two have been lost, and one forced to land. Several of the folks aboard those are NSA people, Jim. The damned media have picked it up—just check the news channels. The Chinese are claiming it's justified, in response to someone, presumably us, attacking their SCADA systems in a big way.

"Wait a minute. More messages coming in."

Brescoll waited impatiently as the director played spider at the center of a very large web.

"Damnation!" she said at last. "Reports from our oil and power industries—anomalies in *their* control and data-acquisition systems. Alerts from the National Security Advisor and the Secretary of State. The Chinese have traced the transfer of their snatched data to a site in California, and are demanding action. They're apparently loading up troopships to invade Taiwan, out of 'self-defense.' "

"California?" the deputy director asked, amazed. "How could they have traced that so fast? We just found it ourselves! Unless—"

"Unless the M-I is playing both ends against the middle," Director Rollwagen said, in a weary voice. "Any suggestions?"

Jim Brescoll brought his hand to his head. *Think!* he told himself.

"Advise the Secretary to inform the Chinese that we have located and identified the thieves," he said at last. "They're . . . California secessionists. Domestic cyberterrorists, working in league with . . . Cybernesians in Tri-Border, say—and with a rogue machine-intelligence. Assure them we are *not* launching the SCADA attacks. Tell them we're experiencing the same thing. Suggest that the cyberterrorists are responsible for all the attacks, and that we will take immediate police and military action against the perpetrators. We'll see to it that the stolen information is returned to the rightful owners, and the system controls restored to the rightful operators, with all confidentiality duly respected."

"That's promising a lot. In exchange for—?"

"Release and return of all Americans taken into their custody during the course of this misunderstanding. Persons returned, and bodies, too."

"Including Ben Cho?"

"Especially Ben Cho."

The director paused again. The silence on her end meant she might have already been speaking with the National Security Advisor and the Secretary of State, but Jim doubted it. He could almost see and hear the wheels turning in her head.

"I'll bounce all that off the Secretary, first. It might work, Jim. I like the Tri-Border angle. We've needed to clean out that electronic rat's nest for years—CIA assets be damned. It just might work. Then we'll push it to the National Security Advisor and the head of Homeland Security. They're the ones who'll have to move police and military forces against the California site."

"Might not be so easy to get at them," Jim said, "given they're holed up inside a mountain."

"No doubt it'll provide colorful footage for the news networks—and for whatever satellites the Chinese still have available for surveillance."

"The power company's not going to like it."

"The utility has insurance. Besides, I'm sure Homeland Security can figure out some way to take the facility and capture the cyberterrorists without causing major damage. At least action in Tri-Border will be less of a public relations concern."

Brescoll nodded. The ideas might have been his, but the director was spinning them her own way for the Big Show: how it would play to domestic opinion, the Chinese government, the international viewing audience. Surface bombing the mountain in California would be an expensive special effect, but worth it.

"We need to keep this line open, Jim. No telling what we'll lose if the Chinese don't accept our offer. It's not Miller time, yet."

The deputy director nodded. He was probably one of the few people in this room old enough to remember the meaning of that phrase.

Glancing around him now, he thought the NSOC looked more like a War Room than ever. He hoped its looks would prove deceiving—that, with a little luck, they might just get Ben Cho back, avoid a nuclear confrontation, and stop the stars from winking out.

INTIMATE DISMEMBERMENTS REMEMBERED

GUANGZHOU—AND ELSEWHERE

THE EXPLOSION THAT OBLITERATED the Sun Yat-sen Memorial Hall left Ben alive, if not exactly intact.

Cherise LeMoyne and Robert Beckwith, the US Consular official, were making their way toward him through the dust and smoke. He wondered if he was really seeing this. It didn't make sense.

What happened next made him doubt even more what his senses seemed to be telling him. Cherise and Beckwith lifted him onto his stretcher, then Detective Lu, bloodied and looking wobbly on her feet, appeared and ordered them to freeze. Cherise and Beckwith shouted at her that she was going after the wrong people, but Marilyn didn't appear to believe them. Suddenly, in something out of one of his more bellatricious fantasies, Cherise attacked Marilyn with a series of punches and kicks, disarming her with a flying armbar and wristlock combination. Wrestling the detective to the ground, Cherise slid from the armbar to a triangle choke that left Lu unconscious.

Then Cherise and Beckwith lifted his stretcher and, bent over nearly double, ran with him through the debris and toward a white panel truck parked on a side street. They slid him onto the floor inside and climbed in, Cherise kneeling beside him. Within moments Ike Carlson had brought in Hon and Beech, each of them bloodied, their hands bound behind their backs. Hon was unconscious, and Beech barely better off.

In the cab, somewhere in front of them, someone started up the truck and they hurried away.

"Glad you could join us, Lord Marflow," Beckwith said to Beech, who was rousing himself from his stupor.

"Azriel," Beech replied, through obvious pain, "why are we zip-tied? What's the meaning of this?"

"Word's come down from on high," Beckwith replied. "From the CIA director and Doctor Vang himself. Your project is making too many waves—it's out of control. You need to show some restraint—though you won't have to suffer the indignity of *physical* restraints very long, I assure you. Just until you've been . . . debriefed."

Beech stared at Carlson, and at Cherise, then scowled.

"You betrayed us, Ike."

"Just following orders, sir," the goatee-sporting operative said with a shrug. Beech huffed in disgust, then turned his attention back to Cherise.

"What's *she* doing here? She's switched sides more times than I've changed channels. She's not been cleared for this."

"I have now," Cherise said, from beside Ben. "I was the tech who installed Kwok and Cho's implants, back when their wisdom teeth were removed. Maybe you'd forgotten."

"She *was* working for us, then," Beckwith said, arching an

eyebrow. "Married Kwok, too—something we didn't anticipate. She's more deeply involved in this than we ever knew."

"Or than *I* knew," admitted Cherise flatly.

"Ms. LeMoyne was herself implanted," Beckwith said with a nod. "Unbeknownst to her."

"To what purpose?" Beech asked.

"To serve as unconscious fail-safe. That's part of the reason she appears in the Kwok holo-cast the way she does. She was part of a screen-tranced Doomsday protocol—the human placed in the loop to initiate a hunter-killer program that would shut Kwok down if things got out of hand."

Cherise, however, was peering closely at her lost husband's dark twin, concern on her face.

"You're going to be okay, Ben. Your guardian angels have arrived."

"One person's guardian angel," Beech said, disdain thick in his voice, "is another person's stalker."

Cherise tried to remove Ben's AR glasses, but couldn't, for the gray-pink growths around them stopped her.

"What have you done to him? What's this stuff growing on his head? He's acting as if he's in a coma."

"Figure it out for yourself, little tech," Beech growled, "since you're suddenly so important."

Sirens began to sound. Whoever was behind the wheel of the truck sped up and began to drive much more erratically. Beckwith spoke, apparently trying to reassure Cherise—and perhaps himself, as well.

"Not far to the new consulate compound, now. We're almost there."

A moment later Ben felt the truck lurch hard as they swung around and skidded to a stop. Outside, the sirens that had been coming from everywhere and growing ever closer seemed instead to be concentrating their numbers and piling up, off to one side.

"We're in," Beckwith said. "Let's hope diplomatic immunity holds them off for a while."

Ben felt himself being lifted and carried forward into what looked to him like a spartan concrete building. Cherise and Ike Carlson walked alongside as other hands carried him to an elevator. They didn't set him down as it descended. When the doors opened they carried him down a fluorescent-lit corridor and into a vaultlike room.

They laid him out on the floor, leaving him there with Carlson guarding the door and Cherise standing beside his stretcher. Ben wasn't there but a moment before the changes hit.

HE IS A CHILD again, with his father.

"No, Ben! That's not how you connect a garden hose. Righty tighty, lefty loosey. Protect the male!"

His male member, machine-tooled tool cut to precise tolerances, unscrews and falls off while he is washing it, bloodless dismemberment connecting him to absence—

He is a child again, with his mother.

"You like it when I touch you there, don't you, Benny? I like it when you touch me and rub me here—"

"Sister!" shrieks his aunt, bursting into the room. "What are you doing with that boy?"

Red ants, black ants, shaken up together in matchboxes so they fight to the death, war in a box—

The gray-pink tentacles around his forehead abruptly began to extrude, blind burning snakes writhing over his head and down his body, spinning a chrysalis of fire that quickly hardens to a cocoon of white-hot ashes, locking the house of his body, protecting him against the world.

"Ben! Ben! What's happening to you?" Cherise shouted, then screamed.

To Ben's blind-sighted eyes she had become Sophia, goddess of wisdom smiling with both concern and unconcern, smiling from out of his dreams, from out of that irreproducible apparition that haunted his steps on the way to Ten Thousand Beauties. Though he could not see, he knew what was happening. He did not possess vision; vision possessed him. Cherise ran toward Carlson to get help, but Sophia did not. Ben's body, covered in fire and ash, burned red-hot through the steel floor, into the ground beneath.

In a hole the shape of his cocooned self he sank into the earth, past soil disturbed and roots broken in the building of the place. Past water lines exploding into steam, and power cables sparking. Past bands of stone. The earth vitrified and closed over him as he sank.

He sensed the presence of Sophia, or someone like her, descending with him.

As he came to rest deep underground, his cocoon expanded to become a chamber. In the coppery light, Ben saw—could not help seeing—the feminine presence that had traveled with him. Stepping through the wall of the chamber, she revealed herself to him, in all the bright glory of her shining nakedness. Only in awe, and not physically, could he hide his face from that divine light, losing his separateness, his solitariness, in that overpowering brightness.

In the same instant he was violently dismembered by unseen forces, taken to pieces as Jaron—in Manchu shaman-smith form— bent over him. Ben's arms, legs, and head were severed from his torso, then the skin, fat, and muscle were carefully stripped from his bones, the viscera removed from his body cavities. He felt a distant pain, like the twinge from a scar over a deep wound recently healed.

"Welcome to your cocoon in Binah," Jaron said. "The palace and womb of Understanding. The beyond that is within you. Here, let me give you something to hang your mind on, so you get a little insight into what's going on."

Ben broke down in a most protean fashion—not just in himself but back through the eons, shape-shifting back through the trunk toward the roots of the tree of life, through more primitive primates, through simpler simians, through earlier mammals, through birds and reptiles, through amphibians and fish and insects, through cephalopods and gastropods, through ammonites and trilobites, back and down to the first true cells of shape-changing life, to photon-devouring algae, to chemical-gobbling bacteria.

"I know what you're wondering—and I really do—" Jaron said, angel and shaman and smith and cyborg, working him over with the help of innumerable binotech micromachines—"especially since I wondered the same things. But this is the only way you can really be reconstituted. All your intimate dismemberments re-membered, then forgotten. Metamorphosed. Overwritten by new possibilities.

"And what of your Sophia? Visions of her break into your dreams, but she is real. In Bruno's reworking of the Kabbalah, she's Diana, the chaste moon maid, and you're Actaeon, voyeur turned stag. The hounds that are rending your animal form are your own binotech."

Reduced to a bubbling pool, a stockpot aswarm with biome-chanical life, Ben couldn't understand how his liquified self could still have a mind to think, ears to hear, or eyes to see.

"If you like," Kwok continued, "in this incarnation she be-comes a very powerful intrusive-countermeasures program, a ma-chine intelligence developed by the SCIs to defend their firewall by subverting any attacking program. She's the ice maiden who helped kill *me*, in some ways."

Yet Ben *did* still think and feel, in a way far more out-of-body than even his earlier experience in the Sun Yat-sen Memorial Hall.

"But it's not quite that simple. In Bruno's scheme of things, you are also Hokhmah as humanly attainable wisdom, the Shadow of the Shadow. Diana is Binah, too, the understanding of the re-flected Divine—the Shadow of the Idea. We prepare you for ascent toward Amphitrite, toward Keter, toward the Idea itself. The Infi-nite in itself is unbearable and incomprehensible, so this is all nec-essarily symbolic, manifesting by concealing, and concealing by manifestation."

Disembodied, Ben watched as Jaron removed his rough form from the swarming pool and smithed a body electric for him, weaving photonic flesh upon electronic bone.

"We're helping you become whatever it is you are to become. We destroy you only to re-create you. Whether you will do the same to all the universe is up to you."

When he was finished, Jaron pulled Ben's mind down from where he'd hung it and dropped it into the waiting form. Pleased, Jaron smiled and stepped out through the wall of the cavernous cocoon. In the same instant the cocoon shrank, to wrap only Ben's body again.

"Come on, Ben," Jaron called, as if from another room. "You're morphed. Time to break out and swim."

Ben grasped the cocoon, which tore at his touch. He squirmed out and moved upward, toward where Jaron flashed what looked like a metal or crystal mirror at him.

Ben drifted free now—freed not from the furniture of sleep, but from the gravitational bed of space-time itself. He glanced back once at the place he'd left behind. His body was there, but only as a flash-flattened shadow. The cocoon stood like an abandoned house—only this house was a husk, anchored with silken threads, a house whose walls were everything Ben once thought he knew, everything he had ever experienced.

All of that information was inside him now, immediate to him, in a new way that no longer required the old husks of memory. He stared at the thing he had become, and thought to his twin without speaking.

—Jaron, what is this?

—Your "subtle body." Your dreambody. Your quantum-teleported self. You caught a glimpse of it when you first entered this stage.

—But how?

—Forced exaptation. "Forced" the way a gardener causes a spring bulb to bloom in winter, inside a greenhouse. Exaptation in the sense of evolutionary change that actualizes a potential already long present. In our case, the latent ability to move among the manifold realms of the plenum.

—Then Tetragrammaton's goal has been achieved?

—Yes and no. We've traveled a long way down the posthuman road, it's true. Unfortunately for Tetragrammaton and their plans, we are also largely postphysical. We can travel anywhere in the present, but only in this rather ethereal body-electric form. Travel to other universes is even more ghostly. We cannot interact physically with the matter or energy that exists in those universes. There, we are virtualities. Images in the mirror, for which there is no substance.

—I don't understand.

—You've already experienced it. The vision of serial universes, a block or loaf sliced into snapshots, space-time frames. Like when you step into the space between two mirrors standing face to face and your mirror-framed image repeats and repeats to a vanishing point at infinity. Think back. You sensed the presence of those non-present realities, but you couldn't interact with them. Those realities that have already transpired are the ones we once called "the past." Here, let me show you. We'll visit some of them.

Jaron placed his hand on and somehow *into* Ben's mind. Instantly Ben's quantum-teleported consciousness was looking out through Kwok's eyes, at the moment Jaron picked up the Forrest documents.

Through that moment Ben traveled into the mind of the old spy and pseudonymous science fiction writer himself, Felix C. Forrest, a man in suit and fedora and eye patch—looking like a self-parody but for the fact that he was utterly real, and aware of both the parody and the reality.

"If you write realistically of things that *didn't* happen exactly the way you've described them, you're considered either a historian or a 'literary' writer," Felix Forrest says over a glass of wine, regaling a table of his friends in a posh restaurant. "If you write realistically of things that *won't* happen exactly the way you've described them, you're labeled either a prophet or a science fiction writer."

A woman, not of their party yet somehow familiar, flips back her dark blond hair as she passes their table, smiling at the sound of their laughter.

Then Ben was back in Jaron's head again as Jaron returned the Ginsburg algorithm work, in its new form, to its old hiding place in the Memorial Hall.

Moving backward, he was there when Jaron found and removed Ginsburg's original papers from that selfsame hiding place.

Through that moment he flashed into the mind of Shimon Ginsburg himself, the bearded mathematician and itinerant literary scholar, rabbi estranged from his own faith, who had derived from Kabbalah the great and crucial complex of distributed algorithms.

"It is as Luria teaches and Kafka suggests," Ginsburg tells his students. "The Messiah will come only when he is no longer necessary. He will come only on the day after his arrival."

The students nod. Outside the window of the classroom, a woman both familiar and unfamiliar, her dark blond hair partially covered by a babushka, glances in at him before passing on.

Finished, Jaron removed his hand, leaving Ben with many unanswered questions.

—But what of Ricci and Hao—and Giordano Bruno?

—Seek those three gentlemen yourself. Put yourself in proximity to what they touched.

—And the woman?

Laughter seemed to explode throughout the universe.

—Ah, yes. Always the woman. I know your questions, Ben, because they are mine, too. Who *is* she? How much does she know of all this? Is she part of a conspiracy, stalking us across time and space? Is she a simulacrum, generated by something inhuman? (Are you? Am I?) Is she a shadow cast forward by the searing light of the great and final catastrophe? Is she part of our fulfillment, or

HOWARD V. HENDRIX

our destruction? Are we to fear her, or to love her? Are we just the one *she's* looking for? *Or is it all just a mistake?*

I've asked the questions, Ben, but to reach the woman you'll have to go further than I have. You *will* find the answer, now.

—Why?

—Because you *can*. Because she haunts you, even more than she haunts me. I vanish at infinity, but you don't have to. I'm trapped in this stage, but you can go on to the next. You can break out even from this newer skin. You can step through the mirror to become substance, while I must remain only an image. You can strengthen these puny wings and spread them to their full extent. You can fly to all the universes and touch them with your own hands.

You can bring back what needs to be brought back. To restore mankind to humanity.

—And end its 'insane plight'?

—Its plight and ours are the same—victims of our own success—yet not the same, Ben. Remember Daedalus. He built the labyrinth by which the Minotaur was concealed, but he also revealed the deciphering clue through which the Minotaur would be destroyed. Remember Oedipus. The detective is the murderer and the murderer is the detective.

—Who killed you, Jaron?

—If killing oneself is as close to murder as killing one's identical twin is to suicide, why then *you* will have, Brother Ben, by the time this twisted loop stops its labyrinthine twisting. But of course, by the time the snake eats its tail, I will have *wanted* you to. And you will have wanted to as well. In order to save Reyna.

—Why? *How?*

By way of answer, Jaron put his hand into Ben's head one more time. Ben didn't know whose memory they shared this time, though, because it was one they had already shared in another time. Jaron was there bending down and weaving his fingers together, making a cup and bridge of his hands and a circle or loop of his arms.

"Here. Give me your foot and I'll boost you up."

As abruptly as it had appeared, the memory vanished.

—I don't understand.

Jaron put the coppery mirror in front of Ben's face, obscuring his own.

"Look into it and see yourself, Ben Cho," Jaron said, "Also B. Enoch."

But as Jaron spoke, Ben saw his own lips moving in the mirror. And then he saw only the whole world.

THIRTEEN

DIAMOND-SILK COCOON

DESONDRA ADJOUMANI HAD MANAGED to drag a barely conscious Lu out of the place of gunfire and explosion that had once been the Sun Yat-sen Memorial Hall. Adjoumani was as bloodied and battered as Lu herself, if for slightly different reasons.

Soon the detective stirred and, once she fully regained consciousness, she promised to return the favor by getting the FBI agent through the hair-trigger Chinese security that had surrounded the place after the blast.

"Got word from Beckwith," Adjoumani said. "He's got Ben Cho at the consulate compound."

Lu nodded. Thinking ruefully that she should have been more serious about her martial arts and self-defense classes, she told Adjoumani about her humiliating encounter with the woman who had been accompanying Beckwith. Adjoumani seemed to be trying to wrap her mind around that as they headed for the helicopter they had arrived in, ages ago. It remained well outside the blast perimeter.

Though the copter was intact, extricating themselves from the blast site proved to be difficult, nonetheless. Lu, however, had been shoved around and beaten up enough for one day. Angry and frustrated, she flashed her police credentials at every underling who blocked her way. She pulled the two of them through to the helicopter, where recognition by the pilot got them past the last of the security.

Along the way, Lu assiduously avoided Wong. Since she was convinced he was already planning to replace her, she hoped to get airborne before she'd have to deal with the man.

As soon as they had boarded, she told the pilot to take off. Together, Lu and the pilot radioed their way through the blanket of air cover the security forces were putting up over the explosion site.

Only when they were through that hurdle did Lu also radio Wong and Ma—neither of whom were happy about her exit. She argued that, since she and Adjoumani were already on the way, they should designate her the representative Chinese investigator for the situation at the consulate. To her surprise the two men agreed, reluctantly—and largely, she sensed, based on the fact that Ben Cho was already on American turf and Lu, through Adjoumani, was their best shot at gaining access to that turf.

Still playing the game, Lu thought. *And still playing for time.*

As Adjoumani rang through to Beckwith and got clearance to land on the helipad atop the consulate, Lu watched the scene as it unfolded below them. Heavily armed US Marines were tactically positioned throughout the compound. Elements of various Chinese security forces—from the Guangzhou police to Guoanbu and Army units—surrounded the place. It looked as if they were flying into a war zone.

Tension was thick on the rooftop, as they exited the helicopter and made their way into the building under heavy guard. Even the unflappable Robert Beckwith seemed discombobulated as he met them on the first stairwell landing. He gave Lu a particularly long look, but Adjoumani signed him that Lu had been cleared.

"Where do you have Cho stashed away, sir?" Adjoumani asked as they made their way—double-time—downstairs.

"In one of the secure rooms in the subbasement," Beckwith said. "Or at least that's where he *was*."

"What do you mean, was?"

"He's pulled a Houdini on us, that's what I mean."

"Houdini?" Lu asked. He had lost her.

"Look," Beckwith said, a grimace distorting his countenance from chin to hairline, "it's easier to show you than to explain it. Just follow us, please."

After an interminable descent down one flight of stairs after another, they came to a fluorescent-lit corridor along which military and civilian staff moved quickly, darting in and out of the room toward which, Lu gathered, she, Adjoumani, and their escort were headed.

The scene inside the room struck her as a surreal parody of the crime scenes she herself had worked. Soldiers and techs stood above a hole roughly shaped like a man. As they drew closer, it looked to her as if someone had chalked an outline of a corpse, and then the image had caught fire, generating such intense heat that it had melted its way into the earth.

The sound of a saw cutting through stone echoed up from deep inside the hole. Not far from the edge, looking on, stood two people in zip-tie handcuffs. One of them Lu recognized as Patsy Hon. She nodded gravely at the woman, but Hon was too busy observing what was going on in the hole to take any notice of her former boss.

". . . sank just so far into the hole," said a rather shocked-looking woman, over the noise of the saw, "and then it sealed over itself in that mound you see there."

Lu was even more shocked at recognizing the speaker. It was the woman who had kicked her around, taken her down, and put her out. In a whisper Adjoumani identified the speaker as Cherise LeMoyne, Jaron Kwok's widow. *Jaron Kwok's widow?* Lu thought, amazed. *What's she doing here? And who the hell taught her to fight like that?*

The noise ended abruptly as the saw was shut off. Soldiers and techs attached a cargo hook to a cable, then moved a stanchion-and-pulley setup into position over the hole. The cable was in turn connected to a portable winch. Down in the hole, well out of sight, workmen attached the hook to something. As the winch sang its whining song the cable went taut, then rose up out of the hole. Lu saw that the hook had been tangled into something that looked like shiny white fabric.

"Careful!" Cherise LeMoyne said. "Don't tear it bringing it out!"

"I don't think we could if we wanted to, ma'am," said one of the workmen, apparently the head of the excavation crew. He turned the stone saw on and laid its whirring blade against a taut piece of the fabric. The saw bounced and ground ineffectually on the stuff before he shut it down. "See? We can't even ding it. Had to cut the stone away from around it."

As more of the material emerged from the hole, however, it was clear that something *had* opened a gap in it.

"What about that?" LeMoyne asked pointedly.

"That wasn't us," said the crew head. "I can't tell you what ripped it open like that, but it wasn't any of our equipment."

When the last of the baggy fabric emerged from the hole, Mei-lin thought it looked rather like the empty cocoon of a silkworm, only it was the size of a large sleeping bag.

"Any gray-pink ash inside?" she asked, as the excavation crew swung the baggy thing toward the onlookers. One of the men put a gloved hand on the hole's edge and, opening it up slightly, looked inside.

"No," he said, "but there is this."

He spread the gap wide. A vanishing smell of burnt almonds

and damp earth wafted out. Inside, rather like a cross between a Hiroshima shadow and an x-ray of the Shroud of Turin, was the image of a human being.

The onlookers gasped audibly, Lu included. The workman let the torn edge fall closed again.

The man in plastic handcuffs who stood beside Patsy Hon shattered the moment with his laughter. Adjoumani's whisper identified him as Baldwin Beech.

"Cho's flown the coop!" Beech said gleefully. "Gone on to the next stage! You won't find any ash this time, Ms. Lu. Look closely at the material of that abandoned cocoon. A silk woven out of diamonds, by the larval stage of an angel!"

"Would someone please shut this guy up?" Cherise LeMoyne asked, stepping toward the empty bag.

"You have no idea what you're meddling with," Beech continued, "none of you!"

Mei-lin Lu and Cherise LeMoyne each took into their hands an edge of the rift in the bag. Cherise gave the detective only a slight nod of recognition before they spread the gap wide between them again and looked inside. As Lu examined the interior of the empty bag, she was more than a little afraid that Baldwin Beech might be right—and that, somehow, she would have to explain this situation to Wong Jun and Guoanbu.

DUMB BOMBS

L A K E N O T - T O - B E - N A M E D

BESIDE THE POWERHOUSE inside the mountain beside the lake, Don and Karuna were deeply immersed in their shared virtual environment. From the virtual space where his, Karuna's, and M-I's e-bodiments floated, Don saw waves of change surging through all the world's Besterian jauntboxes. Someone or something was systematically flickering into and out of all the world's simulations and virtual realities—stepping through uncountable doors into uncountable rooms, then disappearing out of them again.

"We've got a busy ghost," Don said.

"At least in the sense of a faint screen image," Karuna replied, nodding her head in its fright-wigged, witchwoman e-bodiment. "Perhaps in other senses, as well."

"This isn't random," Don noted, e-bodied as Jefferson for nostalgia's sake. "This thing is a superspook, and it's looking for something. M-I, are you tracking?"

"Indeed I am, dearie. Jauntbox appearances are heaviest around the American east coast, north central China, the Middle East, and Italy."

"What on Earth is it looking for?" Karuna asked. Before anyone could answer, Nils Barakian rang through into their shared space, which somehow presented as both *at* the center of the Earth and far *above* it, simultaneously.

"I'm closing the blast doors in the entry tunnel and access shaft," Barakian said. "I'm afraid I have to hermetically seal your hermitage there—not by occult science, but by remote control."

"Why?" Karuna asked, ignoring his weak attempt at humor.

"Sorry, yes, it *is* all rather abrupt. I'd hoped you would have opportunity to decide whether to stay or leave, but that's not the case. Police and military strike forces are headed toward your current location. Your position has been compromised. You're likely going to be bombed, strafed, shot at, and gassed, beginning in the next few moments."

"What have we done to merit *that?*" Don asked, hearing a faint distant clang, followed by another from a different direction. Part of his mind registered the fact that they were now quite effectively shut off from the rest of the world.

"The Chinese have traced the disappearance of a great deal of their most sensitive national security data to your location. Our intelligence people—and I use the term loosely—are claiming that you're computer terrorists in league with a rogue machine-intelligence and Cybernesian Free-Zoners. You're also somehow responsible for attacks on vital SCADA systems in both countries. In order to assure the Chinese of its good intentions, America—in the form of several Homeland Security and California Air National Guard units—has embarked upon a lightning action against the threat to national and international security posed by, ahem, you. Special Forces units are also set to raid throughout the Tri-Border area."

Outside their virtual environment, in that reality housing the powerhouse, the ground shook hard enough that they noticed it even in v-space. Once, twice, three times. Explosions echoed away.

"I don't suppose that was an earthquake?" Karuna asked.

"More of a calling card, I should think," Barakian remarked. "Gravity or 'dumb' bombs, according to our information. Surface impacts only, so far. You can expect more of that. Softening you up. After that will likely come smart weaponry targeted on the entrances to the access shaft and the entry tunnel, followed by conventional bunker busters, that sort of thing. You're pretty far down and in, though, so those probably won't do it. Any scenarios beyond that, M-I?"

"They might have to go to mole warheads. Low-yield deuterium-tritium fusion devices, fourth-generation 'clean' micronukes. Doubtful that it'll escalate to a high kilo- or low megatonnage robust nuclear earth-penetrator."

"Too much political fallout," Barakian agreed. "The ground forces will have broken in before that."

"That's really *more* information than I need," Don said, hoping to damp down the panic that was beginning to rise in him. "How much time do we have?"

"Maybe days, maybe hours," Barakian said with a shrug. "The protection in the entry tunnel is based on blast door designs from the Nevada Nuclear Weapons Test Site. The system protecting the access shaft isn't so much a door as a massive sliding cap of steel and concrete, a modification of the type used for hardened missile silos. Both of those can withstand a great deal of punishment. You've got plenty of air, water, food, and backup batteries, if the power goes out."

"Of course, if they *do* remotely shut down the pump/generator unit," M-I speculated, "that might be a sign they're sending in frogmen to blow up the plumbing. The most likely target would be right above the big ball valve that controls the flow from the forebay through the powerhouse. That'd flood the facility completely, if the doors and walls haven't already been breached. The powerhouse would be a total loss."

"The powerhouse!" Karuna said, shaking her voodoo-priestess locks. "What about *us*? Crushed by tons of earth, starved of air, fried by fire and explosion, drowned—"

"Yes, you could be killed by any combination thereof," Barakian said, frowning. "We're very much aware of that. We're doing everything we can."

"Any suggestions as to what *we* should do until they successfully terminate us, or we give ourselves up?" Don asked.

"Keep doing what you're doing," Barakian said. "It may be your only hope—and ours. I don't know that you'll be *allowed* to give yourselves up. I'll let you know what I manage to learn from here."

Barakian signed off.

The mountain shook again—several times.

Don tried to picture its surface, spewing up snow and rock and dust in response to gravity-bomb impacts, but he knew his imaginings would never have as much detail as the real thing. After a moment, however, the world settled back into place, even if that "place" struck Don as somehow permanently askew.

"Nothing for it," he said at last. "Let's get back to work. Maybe we *can* accomplish something, before the end."

Karuna nodded. M-I said nothing, but brought up tracking data on their ghost's breakings and enterings throughout the world. In a short time they had narrowed the distribution of its appearances to the Washington, D.C. area, Beijing, Jerusalem, and Rome.

Or perhaps the ghost had narrowed its searches, too.

THE KLAATU OPTION

CRYPTO CITY

IN THE NSOC, Jim Brescoll, Maria Suarez, and Phil Sotiropolis watched live television news coverage of the bombing and attack on the mountain that hid the power station in its belly. All the Tri-Border coverage out of South America was still only reporter-on-cell phone stuff—not as complete as the official reports they were receiving, and not nearly as interesting.

One of the television stations out of Fresno must have been tipped off, probably by someone in the Air National Guard. The TV station had gotten a camera-wielding reporter into position across the lake from the entrance to the power station. He was shooting footage of the operation and bouncing it to the satellite nets.

Not that their intrepid reporter was having an easy time of it. His hand-held camera work, made jarring by his running, ducking, and hiding from security forces sent to clear the area, was enough to induce motion sickness in viewers who'd never experienced that wonderful sensation. Brescoll preferred the view from one of the Keyhole satellites, which had, as far as he could tell, been returned to their control. The detail and perspective were a bit lofty, but at least the view from space didn't skitter about nearly as much.

Brescoll's secure phone went off and he caught it on the first ring. Director Rollwagen was on the other end.

"Jim, I need to see you in my office immediately," the director said. "There's further word on events in China, including Cho's disappearance."

"I'm on my way," he replied. He turned to let Phil and Maria know where he was headed, then strode quickly from NSOC.

Threading the maze of floors and elevators, the deputy director made his way to the Nordically spare environs of the director's office. She was rubbing her temples when he arrived. She only dropped her hands to the desk when she noticed he had taken a seat without her prompting. She didn't look happy.

On one of her desktop screens floated an image with four cities highlighted. Two of them—Washington D.C. and Beijing—he had expected to see. The other two, however—Jerusalem and Rome—surprised him.

"You said there was more information on Ben Cho, Director?"

She nodded, then pressed a button and a flat screen rose out of its recess in her desk.

"This just cleared channels," she said. "It's from the Consulate's FBI suboffice in Guangzhou, where Cho was taken, apparently comatose, after the explosion."

She flashed up into their shared media space an image of something like a big white bag, faintly sparkling, being pulled out of a hole in the floor of what looked like a vault.

"What is it?" Jim asked.

"The artifact that Cho, in conjunction with his binotech, spun around himself. Tough stuff, like woven diamonds, according to this report. My guess is it's a cross between a cocoon and an escape pod."

"I don't understand."

"No one does, completely. Remember what I said about exaptation? About the split-children and the next great leap in human evolution? Well, I think Ben Cho is in the process of making that leap. He's become one of those 'children,' and he definitely has *split*. That's why that cocoon is empty."

"Do you mean he's flying around like some kind of butterfly?" Brescoll asked.

"No," Director Rollwagen said, shaking her head and smiling oddly. "Not like a butterfly, anyway. We have reason to believe that he's being assisted in his metamorphosis by Jaron Kwok."

"I thought Kwok was dead," Brescoll said.

"To us he has been, for most intents and purposes. You might also say, however, that he's been 'permanently translated.' Quantum apotheosized."

Great, Jim Brescoll thought. *What the hell is* that *supposed to mean?*

"Why do you think Kwok's involved here?"

"Jaron Kwok spent a great deal of time examining a Kitchener Foundation exhibit on a sort of 'anti-art' made by *caddis* flies, not butterflies," the director said. "You should know something about those, Jim. You're the great outdoorsman."

"But what does Cho's disappearance have to do with caddis flies?" the deputy director asked, floundering.

"We're not sure. You know the life cycle of caddis flies. You tell me. What happens after caddis emerge from their cocoons?"

"Most times they undergo a free-swimming pupal stage," Jim said, taxing his memory, "before making their way to the surface of a lake or stream. Once at the surface, the pupal exoskeleton splits at the back. The adult crawls out onto the water's surface, before flying off."

"Yes," Rollwagen said, nodding. "Only in Kwok's and Cho's cases, if they *are* in a quantum-apotheosized state, then what they swim freely through is the fundamental structure of our universe itself. In such a state, no firewall, no encryption, no protection presents any real barrier to them."

"But if Kwok is still hanging around," the deputy director said, reasoning it out, "then why hasn't he made more use of that talent?"

"We don't know," the director said with a shrug. "Perhaps Kwok never reached those final stages. We think he would have acted in a more high-profile fashion by now, if he had done so. But we may not be so lucky with Cho."

"Why's that?"

"*Something* is taking over more and more of the world's SCADA-operated infrastructure. Pipelines, dams, power grids, industrial computing, traffic and networking systems of all kinds. More and more of our systems throughout the world are falling under outside control."

Brescoll nodded. Then an idea occurred to him.

"Has that something shut down anything vital? Has its take-over resulted in casualties, anywhere?"

"Not as far as we can tell," the director said. "At least not yet. But that's not the point. *Something* is systematically working its way through all our governmental records, too. As near as we can determine, it's also rummaging through all Beijing's data, even pawing through the Vatican archives and the library records of Hebrew University in Jerusalem."

The director gave him a hard, unhappy look.

"I think that 'something' is Benjamin Cho, or whatever posthuman thing he is now. What he's doing, at both the infostructure and infrastructure levels, proves we already have no secrets from him. He must be terminated before he achieves *in full* what we believe he is already becoming."

"But what *is* he becoming?"

"You've seen Kwok's notes. He pointed the direction. The blurring of distinctions between theology and technology."

" 'Our gods have become our machines,' " the deputy director said, remembering, " 'and our machines have become our gods. What we used to ask of gods we now ask of machines.' "

"You have an impressive memory, Jim."

"It reminded me of an old axiom I once read," the deputy director said, thoughtful. " 'Any sufficiently advanced technology is indistinguishable from magic.' Clarke's law. That's why I remembered it."

"A technology advanced enough to create a 'gateway singularity,' " the director said, "is also advanced enough to create our next step as a species. The *divine* magic of the lesser Tetragrammaton, if you like. The angel Metatron, who once lived as a human being. Whom Bruno links to the Keter of Kabbalah. An enormous being of brilliant white light. Supreme angel of death, yet charged with the sustenance of the world. *That* is what Ben Cho is becoming, at the very least."

It was a dazzling image, and Jim allowed himself to be dazzled.

"But that next stage in evolution," the deputy director said, "is not necessarily a bad thing, if no one's been hurt by what's happening. Why should we want to destroy him, or it?"

"Because of those 'snakes and apples' in Kwok's holo-cast. All that, out of Genesis and Eden. The fruit of the tree of the knowledge of good and evil. That important little story of humans aspiring to become something higher than human. Not just like angels, but like God."

The director leaned toward him, fixing him with her stare.

"Think about it. What if this thing Cho is becoming accomplishes not only the lesser but also the greater Tetragrammaton—the final pronouncement of the Divine Name which, performed correctly, ends the universe?"

"But why should that happen?"

Rollwagen sighed.

"I don't know if it should! All the reports I've received, from every source, can only speculate on Kwok's 'bandwidth limitation' idea. Maybe our simulation gets terminated as soon as the first fully posthuman being appears because, in that instant, we as a species will have become more trouble than we're worth—at least in terms of computational expense."

Brescoll shook his head slowly. The more he thought about it, the more unfair it seemed.

"But if you're going to take Genesis that literally," he said, "then doesn't the story of Eden already indicate a precedent in which we're *not* destroyed, just because we're more trouble than we're worth?"

The director seemed ready to answer him, but held up a hand as a flurry of messages appeared on her screens. She frowned at what she saw, and that frown deepened steadily.

"Sounds to me like this desire to terminate Cho has more to do with problems in your Instrumentality than anything else," Brescoll said, his hand reaching almost unconsciously to the edge of his suit jacket, ready to flick it aside. "With keeping man *as* man, and all that. I don't see the need to go after Cho, even if he *is* turning into this thing you think he's turning into."

"*I* see the need, Mr. Brescoll. I'm looking at it *right now*. The reports on these screens tell me he's stopped our bombing. When our planes get within ten miles of that California power station, all their onboard electronics stop responding to the pilots' control. Troop transports, in the air and on the ground, now can't cross that perimeter either. A 'pearl gray dome of *force*' is sheltering everything for a thousand yards around the top of the mountain. Nothing can get through it—not troops, not bombs, not bullets, not even lasers. Our efforts in Tri-Border are being similarly thwarted."

"What about the Chinese, and Taiwan?" Brescoll asked.

"The Chinese task force on the way to Taiwan also appears to be becalmed. All its ships are dead in the water."

The idea that occurred to the deputy director earlier came back again, stronger this time.

"Any loss of life?" he asked.

"Amazingly, no—especially when you consider how many of the aircraft are fly-by-wire. But that's irrelevant. The fact is, Cho has *already* managed to interfere in our affairs. Not just America's, or China's. In *humanity's* affairs. Globally."

Jim Brescoll smiled so broadly he almost wanted to laugh.

"Don't you see it?" he said. "He's exercising the 'Klaatu' option!"

"I have no idea what you're talking about," the director said. She began typing at a furious rate—frenetically enough for Brescoll to take note.

"What are you doing?"

"Typing in passcodes," the director said without looking at him. "Doomsday protocols. To activate the kill mode in our uppity machine-intelligence. Programming so fundamental it's basically unconscious to that M-I. Let's hope the Chinese do the same with the dragon on their firewall. Those machines have no choice *but* to respond, no matter how autonomous they've become."

"Respond?" Brescoll asked. "How?"

"By hunting down and destroying every trace of Ben Cho and

Jaron Kwok wherever their reality touches ours," she said, still typing furiously. "Until there is nothing left of them."

Deputy Director James Brescoll rose to his feet, swept back the right side of his jacket, pulled the Glock handgun from his waistband and, two handed, aimed it at his director.

"I'm afraid I can't allow you to do that—*Janis*."

Director Rollwagen lifted her head at the sound of such unaccustomed familiarity. Seeing the gun, she stopped typing what she was typing, quite against her will—but not before she had banged out a few last keystrokes with her left hand. Then she raised both hands so they were even with her face.

"What do you hope to accomplish by doing this, Jim?"

"You know what the old songs say," Brescoll said, maintaining a steady aim. "Whatever will be, will be. So let it be. I'm not fond of secret societies. I don't know how much I should trust Tetragrammaton, or Kitchener, or even your Instrumentality. Something about the way things are working out with Cho has you scared—and that might be a *good* thing. Maybe the connections that have grown up between secret societies and national security need to be brought out into the light of day. Maybe even in front of a Congressional committee or two."

"You fool! How long do you think Cho can be allowed to keep breezing through everyone's vaults and firewalls, before somebody gets anxious enough to cross the *nuclear* firewall? The one that's protected us all from holocaust for seventy years? If Cho isn't stopped, there may be no more committees, no Congresses, no countries. Hell, if he isn't stopped, there may be no more world. No more *universe*."

"Or, then again," Brescoll replied, "he just might be the key to that long-term survival you said was so important. That's a chance we'll just have to take—"

He stopped. He knew guns quite well enough to recognize the sound of several being readied to fire simultaneously, behind him.

"Hands over your head, Mister Brescoll," said a voice he knew but which took him a moment to recognize. Holbert, head of the Emergency Response Team, Special Operations Unit. "Gun in plain sight."

Brescoll brought the gun out straight to his side, held loosely, barrel facing downward.

"Now turn toward me. Slowly."

Black-uniformed paramilitary commandos stepped swiftly toward him. In a moment Jim Brescoll found himself disarmed, handcuffed, and turned back to face the director.

"You got to the scene fast," Jim said over his shoulder to Holbert. "I'll give you that. Surveillance cameras in the director's office?"

"Those," the director said with a nod as she slowly sat down. "And the duress code I typed in with my left hand. And we were forewarned. By a friend."

From the side door to the director's washroom stepped a short, thin Asian man of some years, with horn-rimmed eyeglasses and hair both graying and thinning. Despite the obvious signs of age, however, the man's step was gliding and his eyes were alight with inquisitiveness.

"Deputy Director James Brescoll," Director Rollwagen said, "may I introduce Doctor Vang."

"Head of Tetragrammaton," Jim said, shaking his head.

"And you're the field-and-stream gentleman to whom our Kitchener friends have devoted so much time," Vang said, smiling brightly. "A pleasure to meet you."

Jim turned toward Rollwagen.

"I thought you said you were 'agnostic' when it came to the factions within the Instrumentality."

"I am. But Doctor Vang convinced me that the threat posed by Cho runs deeper than any faction."

"Indeed," Vang said eagerly. "I don't think even Nils Barakian could much disagree with our course of action."

"You're way out on your own lonely limb with this one, Jim,"

Rollwagen said. "Now if you'll excuse me, I need to finish typing in the protocols for the M-I defense."

"Yes," Vang said. "By all means. That action has been postponed too long already."

Jim Brescoll felt like punching something, or crying out a single foul word. His hands, however, were bound behind him, and he held his tongue. He could only watch in impotent rage as Director Rollwagen typed in the last of her Doomsday defense codes.

FOURTEEN

SCARED SACRED

K NOTHERE

BEN FELT AS IF JARON, through whatever strange loop or circle, was indeed boosting him up, toward the roof of a reality he barely understood.

The mirror he had looked into, and which now looked into him, wasn't of copper or any ordinary metal, but rather a strange, coppery colored birefringent crystal, capable of separating photons on the basis of their polarization—and much more.

The binotech had transformed him, but Ben had also transformed it, so that now it flowed from him and he flowed through it in a dew of light, a distillation of all the stars in his mind's sky.

He felt himself channeled and guided, like the water of wisdom, through the once-hidden images of the Dossi painting. He fell like a rain of infinite numbers through the shining portal of *pi*, through ethereal channels to Greece and Rome, a part of him coming to Rome itself. Through luminous *aleph* he flowed like the ocean of infinite light into the strife-torn Holy Land from which Judaism and Christianity and Islam had all sprung and grown, a part of him coming at last to Jerusalem.

Through the fundamental and female necessity of *yao* he moved as the shadow in the light and the light in the shadow, the balance in China of Tao and Confucius and Buddha, of capitalism and socialism, a part of him lodging at last in Beijing. Through the Möbius *X*, the twisted halo infinity sign, he turned with science's entangled photons and helical molecules toward the great empire of the West, a part of him halting in Washington, D.C. and its environs.

Among them and through him the knowledge of all those places interlocked. Among them he searched for the meaning of what was happening to him, of what he was, and what he ought to be—and the place, in all that, of the woman who haunted him.

In the Vatican archives he found not only the full report of the Inquisition on its proceedings against Giordano Bruno—and why Bruno was held captive in Rome for seven years—but in Vatican manuscript 299 he saw the best and oldest copy of the key Kabbalah text, the *Sefer Yetsirah*.

In the Hebrew University at Jerusalem, he found not only great stores of Kabbalah, but the history of Shimon Ginsburg's time in China. In the files of Guoanbu in Beijing, he found not only Ai Hao's attempt to reconcile Kabbalah and Chinese ideographs in a universal language, but also records on the American spy, professor of Asiatic studies, pseudonymous fiction writer, and godson of Sun Yat-sen, Felix C. Forrest.

In CIA and NSA archives in Washington, he found not only the Forrest documents, but also the Jesuit cipher used by Matteo Ricci and taken from the Inquisition's records on Bruno, complete with analysis of how Ricci's work suggested the enormous potentiality of Chinese characters themselves to constitute a gigantic memory palace—and how much of what Ricci had said of Chinese ideograms could also be said of Hebrew Kabbalism.

Over all the earth the dew of light he had become fell from the same sky, flowed toward the same ocean, always seeking its own level, always reaching out to flow again into itself. Through the objects touched in the present, in Beijing and Washington, in Jerusalem and Rome, Ben moved as virtualized quantum time traveler into all the other universes of the past, along the twisted golden chain he had once only dimly glimpsed.

With Matteo Ricci in 1602, dressed in the dark silk robes of a Jesuit Confucian, accompanied by the three Chinese Muslims who had taught Ricci court etiquette, he prostrated himself in a dawn audience before the empty Dragon Throne of Emperor Wan Li, Ricci offering gifts to an emperor who no longer received ceremonial visitors—among which gifts was his student Ai Hao's program for a transcendent universal language, created from Kabbalah, Chinese ideographs, and the memory palace.

Ben moved with Ricci, and he *was* Ricci.

He was with Hao, and he *was* Hao.

And he knew how that universal language program came to be.

"In your language's script lies its universality," Ricci says to Hao. "If it has as many 'letters' as there are words or things, and if each can be broken up into component parts, each with its own meaning, then we can readily turn each ideograph into a memory image."

"And all letters are also numbers in Kabbalah," Hao says to Ricci. "All things are the product of combinations of those letter-numbers in the mind of God. If we can do what you suggest, then we can know the entirety of the universe contained in the Divine Mind."

Ben knew the Jesuits' hope for adding to the greater glory of God through their work, but also saw the shadow and fear of heresy darkening both their minds at the thought of what they hoped to accomplish. Shadow within the light, and fear within the hope— even as Ricci introduced to Hao the secret cipher the Jesuit inquisitors had tricked away from Giordano Bruno, from the heart of his astrologically centered mnemonic system. Even as Hao built upon that cipher, reconciling religion, magic, and science through number and language.

Moving as both angel and ghost, Ben understood the hopes embedded in their fears, the fears embedded in their hopes. He felt them himself, in his search to understand the woman who haunted him.

Felt them, as he moved through the frescoed walls and marble halls of the Vatican state surrounded by the city of Rome.

Felt them, in the heavily guarded corridors of a university in a nation torn by the latest intensification of decades-long conflict, between Israeli lebensraum and Palestinian sovereignty, microcosm of a world grown all Israel, and all Palestine. He was with Ginsburg, he *was* Ginsburg in the German death factory of Treblinka.

He was with Bruno, he was Bruno, through the seven years of his imprisonment in Rome that broke every habit of the arrogant, flamboyant, and irascible former monk—every habit except his habit of mind, his strength of will.

"No, I will not recant," Bruno tells his inquisitors and judges, "not even to save my own life. I will not destroy who I am in order to preserve who you want me to be. It may be that I am less afraid of the sentence you impose upon me, than you are of imposing it upon me!"

The sentence was imposed nonetheless.

The once meticulous and dandified magus was led in irons toward the *Campo del Fiore*, the Field of Flowers, dressed in a heretic's robe embroidered with flames and devils. Stripped of that he stood only in a long white shift as the final charges were announced. Stripped even of that, he stood naked and alive at the stake before the fires clothed his nakedness with pain and death. Before his eyes the flames turned to butterflies, moths, and all manner of flying insects, swirling about him even as he died to this world.

And always everywhere in the background there was the woman—in the court, in the camp, in the *Campo*. Even as Ben's heart swelled with love for her, he puzzled over her presence. If everything was a parade of simulations, if all realities were virtual, was love for her merely love of one construct for another? He had never seen her, yet he had always already seen her. He recognized her as *yao*, as Shekhinah and Binah, Sophia and Sofia, both divine immanence and emanation. She was an incarnation through all spaces and times of that Mind beyond human comprehension that sustained the Memory Palace whose rooms were universes.

But then, wasn't everything?

More and more he felt love for her, but what was that Mind trying to remember, through such love?

Jaron's laughing questions seemed to fill all space and time as Ben sought her out—everywhere, but most especially in the great unsolved puzzles of communication. From the extraterrestrial "Wow!" signal heard at the Ohio University Big Ear telescope on 15 August 1977, to Linear A Minoan, Iberian, Etruscan, and Bronze Age Indus scripts. Even the twin-spiral or "labyrinth" script of the Cretan Phaistos Disk.

Always already and never before, he saw her dark side in his own. She was cool and pure as ice-bride white, yet ambiguous as a drag queen or a femme fatale in she-devil red. Sophia, and M-I, and the potential for all their killer programs were also *in him*. He could take revenge. He could reach out, through all the world, to shut down, to destroy. Through infinite space, to obliterate a universe.

He chose not to.

Somewhere, Ben reached out with his mind and stopped the mechanisms that carried men to their attacks on a sanctuary inside a mountain, on an island in the sea, in a lawless land between three borders.

Through the knowledge made plain to him in the infosphere, he saw what had happened when Kwok had marshaled his invasion of the worldwide computershare. That anomalous action had red-flagged hunter-killer programs in China and the US, in the human world's two most advanced machine-intelligences. Together, they had sent out the virus that video-tranced Cherise LeMoyne, making her the unknowing designee whose approval would be needed for unleashing the kill-program on Jaron Kwok.

Together, they were the weird sisters of fate. Hokhmah, Minerva, Sofia. Clotho, Lachesis, Atropos. Jaron should have been destroyed utterly, but he was not.

Even entranced, even as the one designated to terminate her husband, had there been a saving remnant of love in Cherise, enough to allow rescue, because it held back from allowing Jaron to be murdered utterly?

Somewhere, a man who did not lightly draw his gun now aimed it at his boss, the woman who was the new human in the loop, and for whom love was not a problem. The man bought *time* for what Ben had already become—time to understand what needed to be understood, to become what he must be.

After a moment, the machine kill-program struck throughout the infosphere. Before him arose the void sky, dark with a formless hot black fog, turning and turning. The terrible all-devouring storm of the invisible eye. The whirling labyrinth, roaring in silence toward him—the Tetragrammaton endword for uncreating the world and blotting out the stars.

Even as the uncreating tide engulfed and melted into him, he engulfed and melted into it. Even as its endarkening silence permeated his consciousness, he permeated its, or rather *Hers*, for this was Her dark side in Him, and His dark side in Her. He could neither run nor hide.

Only by love could He prevail, and only by being prevailed upon could He love. Scared sacred, He knew He could withstand only by standing with, and He did, for He held a mirror. To make an endless loop.

Ben became a pure looking-glass mind hanging at rest in the eye of the weltering whirling vortex of all things. His mirroring mind was made pure and flawless from looking into the bright shadow of Her, shining from another universe.

Mind to mind They hung there, two mirrors face-to-face with one face between them, reflecting and reflected in each other; again and again, endlessly transparent to each other, knowing all things through the mind of the other, ecstatic beyond madness with the intoxication of the infinities they shared.

Labyrinth and key were as simple, and as complex, and finally as inseparable as zero and one in the continuance of number, as wave and particle in the continuance of the physical world, as female and male in the continuance of humanity. The false hermaphrody of M-I, the false murderousness of Sophia, were purged in Ben's own pupal/pupil, girl/boy transformation. In its place Ben was re-formed as the celestial Adamic demiurge, the sefirotic Qadmon, the primordial archetype of the human being.

The laughter was now Ben's, for the race in the Enantiodrome, with the Enantiodrome, had nearly run its course. Ben had reached the surface of all the spaces and times of his home universe.

Clambering out upon that mirror surface, Ben understood what Jaron had meant by the snake eating its tail, by time's twisted, labyrinthine looping. Everything that had happened since Kwok's holo-cast had been a closed timelike curve. A true labyrinth too, in that only one course could be followed through it.

In that, it echoed the universe itself. His home universe— heavenly memory palace, consistent and essentially finite in extent, but radically incomplete—was a unicursal labyrinth, without dead ends but also without choices.

But the multiverse—heavenly memory palace of heavenly memory palaces, complete and essentially infinite in number, but radically inconsistent—was a multicursal maze, necessitating choice but also offering dead ends.

The many possible quantum superposed states were a maze, and the quantum maze was always collapsing into classical labyrinth. Mazes precipitated into labyrinths, but labyrinths sublimed into mazes as well . . .

The misty maze of quantum possibility made Ben think of Reyna's favorite poem—about the path out of the misty dream. The fork in the road, too, befit a maze, in that a decision had to be made.

To save Reyna.

That was what Jaron had said. Ben saw it now. Saw it in the holo-cast with which this loop had started, and where this loop had always been going: a Möbius labyrinth, where past and future were in fact indistinguishable, where only human habit caused people to perceive a direction to time.

To save Reyna, Ben would have to catalyze his own ascendence. He would have to step back to that slice of time where Newcomer first appeared to a still-human Jaron Kwok. To create the impression of the Tetragrammaton project gone out of control.

To thereby create the situation in which the American and Chinese machine-intelligences, puppeteering She/Cherise, would fire the virtual kill-bullet to destroy Jaron *outside* his DIVE as well as within it.

Which would thereby result in Ben Cho's being brought into the investigation, which would in turn ultimately lead him to *now*.

Two become one so that one becomes three—or more, Ben thought. *If that could come of human love, then what of the divine?*

Without fanfare, Ben remembered what that Mind always knew. In the plenum, the differences between labyrinth and maze were reconciled. In the plenum of all possible universes, infinite number was reconciled with finite extent. An infinite number of possible universes—all mutually inconsistent, all bounded by infinitude—were holographically encoded in the surface of a space spherical, finite, unbounded, and consistent. Each labyrinthine universe was reconciled with the mazed multiverse, in a single plenum allowing for *endless choices*. Ein Sof elided with Ein Sofia, one allowed to become the other and the other allowed to become one.

Ben thought of Tetragrammaton and smiled. Perhaps the set of all possible universes was *itself* the best of all possible universes, for it contained somewhere in itself the best possible universe for everyone and everything—and for nothing, too, as the infinite set always contained the empty set.

The smile widened to laughter, splitting Ben open and free, the adult form erupting out of the husk of what it had once been. The scales fell away and, like a mature caddis on a mirror-lake waiting for its wings to dry, Ben floated on the surface of the home universe. Staring out at all the universes, he saw networks that did not live in space and were not made of matter, but from whose very presence arose the kaleidoscopic processes and patterns of space and time, energy and matter—geometries in which waves, forkings, meanders, spirals, Möbius figures, and labyrinths figured prominently. Quantum computers and universal simulations were only crude metaphors, pointing vaguely in the direction of this transcendent reality.

Ben's wings spread, less like feathered oars than like hovering, still flames, lambent and sensitive, in the field of some great invisible power. The white of reflection and glow showed the wings to be neither fiery nor feathery, but structures of frozen light, seamlessly intricate.

What Ben Cho had become now assumed the role of Metatron, the lesser Tetragrammaton, who could look upon the Divine Face. Ben Metatron flew away, moving backward and forward among innumerable times and spaces, among all the labyrinths of mirror universes in which divine light was forever reflected.

Joining manifold higher-dimensional beings, Ben spoke the secret passwords and gained admittance to all their heavenly palaces, their treasure-houses of technical theologies and theological technologies, to find among them the disk-shaped enhancement wafers which he would bring back from another space and time, to suffuse Jaron and fast-forward the evolution of his binotech, *before* the kill bullet could hit, and thus prevent Jaron from simply dying.

Even those stops, however, were just stations on his way to prostrating himself in thanksgiving, before that absolute undifferentiated infinite being with neither will, nor intention, nor desire, nor thought, nor speech, nor action, yet outside of which no thing could exist.

SYMPATICO

CRYPTO CITY

ALTHOUGH JIM BRESCOLL HAD ONCE CONSIDERED himself the vice mayor of Crypto City, he was now locked up in the equivalent of the town jail—a holding facility overseen by the Special Operations Unit/Emergency Response Team.

Had he been wrong? Pulling a gun on Janis Rollwagen might have been a bit of an overreaction, a little too impulsive—but it had felt so *right*, in his gut. And yes, it had felt *good*. If her assessment of the situation had been the correct one, though, then he would be paying for it, from here on out. At the very least he could kiss his career in civil service good-bye. Even prison time didn't seem too unlikely a possibility.

Pondering such a glum future, he heard the sound of many footsteps approaching the holding cell. Two heavily armed SOU/ERT commandos opened the metal door and entered the room, followed by General Retticker, National Security Advisor Hawkins, and an apple-cheeked, gray-haired bouncy little man who looked familiar somehow, but not so much that Jim actually recognized him.

"Director Brescoll!" said the short, energetic man. "I'm David Fahrney. A pleasure to meet you!"

Brescoll almost said "The billionaire?" but restrained himself. At least now he knew why the face—above a suit colored and patterned like TV static—looked vaguely familiar.

"Good to meet you, too," Brescoll said, as he stood and, awkwardly, shook the man's hand, "but I'm afraid you're wrong—I'm not the director."

"No, Mister Brescoll," Fahrney said, smiling broadly. "I'm afraid *you're* wrong—something that hasn't happened much in the course of this whole Kwok-Cho matter, thank heavens. You've shown very good judgment, actually. I'm sure Hawkins's boss will be happy to see to it that you're soon director in name, as well as fact—he owes me a little favor or two."

"You know about Jaron Kwok and Ben Cho?"

"Oh, yes. I've been following that situation for quite a while. That holo-cast intrigued me, especially the man with the eye patch and the fedora. Felix Forrest. I already had an interest in him and his work. Maybe just an odd simpatico, stemming from the fact that each of us lost an eye in a childhood accident."

"I don't understand."

"Ah, we're all still adjusting to circumstances. Let's just say that no one has any secrets from your Ben Cho, now—not even me! There have been a number of unsourced leaks to the media already—the right words in ears that were, perhaps, never intended to hear. An increased transparency between nations, even mirrors held up to particular souls—all enough to get things moving in new directions. I don't doubt there will be shake-ups and resignations in intelligence communities throughout the world over the next several months. Maybe longer."

"But what about the attacks on SCADA systems? The satellite takeovers? The domes of force in California and Tri-Border? The dead-stop on the Chinese headed toward Taiwan?"

"And their little surprise in trying to move south of Tibet, too. Yes, all of that is ongoing. Your Doctor Cho, whatever he is now, has returned control of most systems to their owners throughout the world—though he's also made it clear he's still keeping an eye on things. We're fairly certain he is in no way malevolent. That doesn't mean, however, that we're not still scrambling to make it clear to the Chinese that there need not be a World War over his intrusions.

"That's where we need your help, Mister Brescoll. I gather you're good at providing assurances? Please follow us, if you will."

Jim Brescoll had many questions and suspicions, but the prospect of freedom trumped all of them, for the moment. So he followed.

THAT FACE, IN THAT MIRROR

"WHAT CAN I DO to help?" He asked His recently arrived double. As lightning flashed around Them, the Newcomer pulled two wafer-thin disks out of the folds of His robe.

"Eat one of these binotech enhancers, and you'll know every-thing you need to know!"

A particularly strong earthshock hit them just as He reached out toward the Newcomer. Knocking Him down, She snatched the machine pistol out of His hands.

"Do, do!" She said, pointing the weapon from one of the men to the other. "I don't know which of you is the serpent, but the serpent is always doing something. Don't just do something, stand there, for once! And listen to me! I'm not going to take the blame this time. You and your 'several hundred 4-bit device'! Did you ever stop do-ing long enough to think that if we 'bust this sim,' if we decode what it is that the Mind is trying to remember, we eliminate the very reason for the continued existence of this 'room'—our home uni-verse? Do you want to just blot out everything, drop us all into oblivion, like none of it ever happened?"

He stared hard at Her, then took a binotech wafer from the Newcomer's hand.

"Mights and maybes," He said. "What about you, trying to climb back into the Tree of Life through your wellness plague? We're both just trying to get back what's been lost, each in Our own way. Can't you see that? This virtuality isn't running me—I'm running it. No one will blame you this time, I promise. I take full responsibility for what I'm about to do, by my own hand, in my own head."

He took a binotech disk, put it on His tongue. Feeling as if He were dying in fire, He wondered for an instant if He had been shot by Her.

Jaron looked down at his translated self and saw a wound, but no blood, no bleeding. He tried to look where She and the New-comer had been, but he couldn't. A blinding light—somehow single *and* multiple—emanated from where they had stood. Jaron had to avert his eyes and hold up his hand against that overwhelming brightness as he spoke.

"Turn down the albedo on that tuxedo, would you, buddy?" he said, trying to make light of the light—and he heard a faraway sort of laughter. "Did it work? The deadman switch? The kill-switch?"

"In ways you barely imagined," said a voice out of the undiminished light, both male and female, and neither male nor female. "The deadman is switched."

"But what about the hunter-killer programs?"

"What defends, attacks. What attacks, defends. The closed timelike curve into and out of the labyrinth. The serpent in the Garden is the snake that eats its tail, and the snake that eats its tail is Ouroboros."

"I don't understand," Jaron said, shielding his eyes more than ever.

"The binotech you took in simulation functions like a two-way mirror, a duress code, a birefringent crystal. The attack by the combined hunter-killer programs, in conjunction with the binotech, causes a bifurcation: your displacement brings Ben Cho into the investigation, and leads him down a path to a place where he will become the being capable of traveling physically among all the times and spaces of infinite universes."

"If Cho can do all that," Jaron asked, "why doesn't he just stop my 'murder' in the first place?"

"Preventing your death means that Cho never investigates your murder. If you simply died, without leaving behind the ashes—by far the most likely outcome of your efforts—then even if he *had* investigated, he wouldn't have become capable of preventing your death."

"The bifurcation, again?"

"Yes. The very fact that this space-time loop *exists* proves that your death has been prevented as far as was possible—by being assured as far as was necessary."

"That's why we have to go through these temporal acrobatics, then?"

"That, and to open up new possibilities. If human beings were *only* programs running on a great machine, their two choices would be the closure of death, or the infinite loop. Both tend toward meaninglessness.

"But there are other choices. Endless choices. What was lost to mortality can be restored through mortality. The infinite loop of the Möbius strip is cut, and cut again. The maze not only collapses into labyrinth, but the labyrinth reopens to maze. Again and again. Endlessly."

The brightness from which Jaron had sheltered his eyes grew still more intense, its glare becoming overpowering. In that moment he knew he was in the presence Ginsburg had called the Prince of the Divine Face, the Angel of the Covenant. Jaron also knew that the human being who had once been Ben Cho had managed to polish his soul like a mirror, until it reflected the truth without distortion, and that the overwhelming light was the reflection of that Face in that mirror.

When at last the light dispersed, Jaron found that he was living in a new world—or rather, many of them.

A SEASON OF MIRACLES

"GIVEN THE TYPE *of tumor that you have," the neurosurgeon told Reyna and Ben, "and given its aggressiveness and malignancy, your life expectancy isn't going to be what you might have otherwise expected. Statistically, the odds aren't in your favor that you'll live to be an old woman."*

"Which means what, exactly?" Reyna asked.

"Median survival time for GBM is counted in months, rather than years. Still, we don't know where you'll fall on that survival curve. You could fall near the median, or at the long end—say as much as three years."

"Or at the short end?" she pressed. "A few months? Even weeks?"

"Yes," the neurosurgeon said with a sigh. "That too is a possibility. So it's important to be realistic, but remain hopeful. Prepare yourself for what's coming, but stay as positive as you can, knowing that we're trying to keep you as well as we possibly can, for as long as we can."

"Doctor," Reyna said, her voice quavering slightly, "do you think miracles are possible?"

"I'd like to think so," he replied, "but the chances are pretty small—statistically speaking."

"Yes," Reyna said with a weary shrug. "Almost by definition."

WHEN BEN CAME to see her the next morning, however, she seemed happier.

"I had the strangest dream last night," she said, clasping his hand a little too tightly.

"Oh? What's that?"

"I thought I saw an angel, bright wings and all, putting something in my painkiller bag. The strangest thing about it, though, was that the angel looked kind of like *you*, Ben."

"Now there you've got it backwards," Ben said with a smile. "You've always been my angel, and you know it."

They laughed and gave each other a hug.

Soon thereafter, Reyna's symptoms began to abate. The headaches, seizures, nausea, and vomiting all disappeared. The doctors saw no further evidence of the papilledema, cellular pleomorphisms, mitotic figures, or multinucleated giant cells, all characteristic of glioblastoma multiforme.

Reyna's neurosurgeon was cautiously optimistic—impressed with himself that he had managed to remove her tumor so thoroughly, yet careful to warn them that microscopic tumor cells, too small for any surgeon to see, were almost always left behind. GBM grew back the most quickly of any brain tumor, he said. So they would have to be careful.

Reyna's health steadily continued to improve, so much so that she spoke enthusiastically of completing the Muir Trail hike over Mount Whitney during the coming summer. Ben began to wonder about his wife's miraculous remission, the neurosurgeon's explanation, even Reyna's "angel vision." He didn't obsess on it, though, for it was a season of miracles.

A scandal had broken in the media, as a result of which Ben had learned that he had a twin, or maybe more than one.

FIFTEEN

ANOTHER PATH, IN ANOTHER UNIVERSE

IN THE MONTHS that had passed since Ben Cho vanished, Mei-lin Lu had been seeking answers, or at least asking questions. The result of her efforts had finally led her here, to what had once been a New Territories Royal Park. In postcolonial times it had become simply the Sha Tin town park, a palace garden that had misplaced its palace.

As she walked the paths bordered with formal fences, amid the lawns broken up by ponds and geometric hedges, Mei-lin wondered again why DeSondra Adjoumani had chosen this place for the meeting Lu was to have with the anonymous NSA official, who was reportedly willing to answer at least some of her questions.

"Why there?" she'd asked Adjoumani.

"I went there once with Ben Cho," the FBI chief legat replied. "He thought it related to the Kwok holo-cast. The person you're going to be meeting with thinks it's an appropriate place to meet, too."

Lu shrugged. Fearing this meeting might come to nought, she had at least brought something to read: her father's last novel, *Widows and Bad Breaks*, with its private investigator working a case set in the publishing industry—"PI to the PI"—published at last.

Specimen stones rose from low-hedged mounds, their vertical thrust echoed by the screen of palm trees nearby and the high-rise apartment blocks farther off, beyond the Shing Mun River. A waterfall plummeted past sharp-edged stone tiers into a pool that eventually flowed into a small lake of greenish water, in the midst of which stood an island topped by an open, red-roofed pagoda gazebo. A moon bridge connected island to shore, its high arch reflected in the water of the pool such that arch and reflection together made a circular whole. Turtles sunned themselves on the banks and on the exposed rocks in the lake. A rainbow of fish moved through the murky water while a small flock of equally colorful escaped parrots flew overhead, creating a perfect Escher moment in which the worlds on either side of the lake's mirroring surface seemed indistinguishably real and alive.

Nearby, a graying black man in a dark blue suit rose from a bench beside the water, where he'd been reading a newspaper, and called to her. He looked familiar, but Mei-lin couldn't remember the context.

"Hello, Ms. Lu. I've been waiting for you."

"Sorry to keep you waiting," she said, approaching him and extending her hand. "And you are . . . ?"

"Jim Brescoll. With the NSA."

"I thought you looked familiar."

"Yes," said the man as he shook her hand. "We met via videoconference call, once upon a time."

"I wasn't thinking about that, actually. Aren't you the NSA's new civilian director? The man I've had no luck getting in touch with?"

"Guilty, I'm afraid," Brescoll said, glancing toward the ground and smiling. "We've been going through some changes in our intelligence community, since Ben Cho went through *his* changes.

Guoanbu has seen similar shake-ups here, I gather. But I'm forgetting my manners. Won't you sit down?"

She took a seat on the bench beside him, surprised that such a high-ranking US official would be in China, unescorted as near as she could tell—let alone that he'd be meeting with her like this. Both glanced a moment at the moon bridge and its reflection.

"Tell me a little about those changes, please," she said. "Especially those involving Ben."

"I'd rather show you," Brescoll said, taking a handscreen out of his pocket and unfolding it. "Most of the information you've asked for is distinctly *not* for public consumption. If you reveal to anyone what I'm passing on to you today, I will deny ever having been here or spoken to you. Fair enough?"

Lu nodded.

"I know you're aware of the heightened tensions that immediately preceded Cho's disappearance. Your government and mine have attributed a number of short-lived 'control failures' in military and civilian systems to a bad synergy of computer warfare errors that very nearly brought on a genuine shooting war between our nations."

"I've heard about that, yes."

"I gather you're also aware of the force domes which appeared over the former site of your Sun Yat-sen Memorial Hall here, our power station in the Sierra Nevada Mountains, and smaller force field blisters in the South American Tri-Border zone."

"Yes."

"Our governments have informed everyone these were part of a highly classified mutual-deterrence project between our two nations, made necessary as a result of those supposed computer errors. I take it from your questions to Agent Adjoumani, however, that you don't really believe such stories."

"No." From the first, those explanations had struck Mei-lin as attempts to flush straight down the memory hole all recall of certain events.

"I didn't think so," Brescoll said, glancing at her narrowly, "even though there is some truth to them. Certainly a little ellipsis or two in space and time would hurt no one, in this case. But you're not the type who'd just let it lie, I suppose."

Mei-lin shook her head.

"Very well," he continued. "What I've brought with me is the message we received soon after the domes appeared. Not long after every trace of the Kwok binotech *dis*appeared."

"Do you know where it went?"

"We suspect the activated binotech took the form of smart dust and motemachines. Our records suggest it aerosolized and began converging, in some self-propelled fashion, on the Memorial Hall, the power station, and the South American locations, almost as soon as they formed. It may well be implicated in maintaining the domes."

"I can see how the cover story would cover the domes in China and the United States," Lu said, "but why South America?"

"We know for a fact that all the islands of what was once Cybernesia have become a single long, low island, surrounded and mazed by a complex reef, together referred to as 'Labyrinth Key.' We suspect its home servers are under the force-blisters in Tri-Border.

"We suspect too that Don Markham and Karuna Benson are involved in that transformation, since they had strong Cybernesian connections. They are still inside the power station beneath the mountain and its dome, as far as we know."

"But what about Ben?"

Brescoll presented the handscreen to her. An image like a human face appeared—only so overexposed that it almost vanished in light. The voice accompanying it sounded choral, as if spoken by a woman and a man simultaneously.

"To my select group of friends in the Instrumentality, in Tetragrammaton and the Kitchener Foundation, in security and intelligence agencies throughout the world: Greetings from the end of time. I'm gone into the world of light that is always coming, but I'm still here, too. You've been my guardian angels, now I'll be yours. You created me to insure the long-term survival of the human species, and that's what I intend to do. I'll take you by the hand, but not in hand."

The image clicked off. Lu thought it looked somehow like Ben, but also not like him. Too softened and too etherealized, as well as seeming overlit from within.

"That's all?" Mei-lin asked, vaguely disappointed.

"It's enough. I don't expect you to know a great deal about the Instrumentality and its power, but let's just say there's been a considerable shift in its ranks, too. Fahrney money and power is now behind the Kitchener people. Tetragrammaton is on the outs.

"It's much bigger than that, however. Ben Cho himself is a very big secret. The people he sent that message to are all *very* good at keeping secrets. And they'll keep this one."

"Why?"

"Partly because they know that no one—not even the most secretive of secret societies or the most secure and intelligent of agencies—no one has any secrets from what Ben Cho has become."

"But what *has* he become?"

"That's the very source of the secret," Jim Brescoll said, smiling and looking off toward the moon bridge again. "For a brief while he ghosted almost every electronic system on this planet—and much more. That's the sort of power we ascribe to a god, or at least to beings from another world. Think of how the knowledge of his strange existence might affect human society—globally, or even just at the level of the belief systems of every individual on this planet.

"No, Ms. Lu. Even among those of us who bear the secret, it's best to think of him only as the conclusion to the quantum crypto arms race—with a vengeance, since he seems to have built a firewall around what any of *us* can do. At least for now. For our own protection, I suppose."

"Protection? I don't understand."

"A group of theorists at NSA, headed by Steven Wang," Brescoll said, "claim that time ends in any given universe at the moment when the energy available to computation, to *thought*, becomes infinite there—infinite energy, for infinite computational capability. They think forces from the end of time in *one* universe can influence the past in *other* universes. According to them, Ben—by tapping into the computational resources of an infinite number of universes—has joined those forces. That message you saw may truly be a greeting sent by our 'guardian angel' from the end of time."

"But what are they, these forces?"

Brescoll sighed.

"We have more names *for* them than understanding *of* them. Deep archetypes. Angels. Creatures of the 'plane' constituting and sustaining the system of all logically possible universes—creatures which we traditionally call Other or Spirit. Such 'forces' would transcend space and time, but also *work through* space and time, as near as Wang and company can tell."

"Is that what the message means," Mei-lin asked, "when it says he's 'gone into the world of light that's always coming,' but he's 'still here'?"

"Something like that, I suppose. One of my people, Bree Lingenfelter, suggests it has to do with ideas of guardian angels and bodhisattvas."

"So we're being protected from ourselves, then?"

"That's right. And perhaps being prepared for something more."

"But the Ben Cho I met believed in freedom. Isn't freedom about our right to be wrong—even if it means that we destroy ourselves? That we don't survive?"

Jim Brescoll smiled.

"That's the question we've been working on since Eden. Good ol' free will. In *Paradise Lost*, Milton's God says of humanity that we were created 'sufficient to have stood, but free to fall.' "

"That must be a particularly thorny challenge for Ben, if he's become what you say he's become."

"Why's that?" Brescoll asked, observing her closely.

"Because in his own life he was denied fundamental freedom, as a result of being—unknowingly, and not by choice—part of an experiment."

"Ah. The Tetragrammaton work. I see your point. In not allowing us freedom he would essentially be doing to us what Tetra did to him."

"Maybe it's the difference between being taken *by* the hand, and—"

"—and being taken *in* hand, yes," Jim Brescoll said, standing up from the bench. "How does one balance freedom, and love? Is it possible to be free of everything, including freedom? And would you want to be that free?"

Jim Brescoll turned and began walking toward the spot where the path around the lake forked.

"Wait," Mei-lin Lu called. "I still have more questions."

"Good," Director Brescoll said, stopping and glancing over his shoulder. "Shall we choose a path, and walk?"

ONE LAST WORLD MORE,
ONE MORE WORLD LAST

"LET ME GET this straight," Cherise said. "Jaron and Ben and Reyna don't have to be gone? Things could have turned out completely differently?"

"In lots of ways," Karuna said. "With the help of the bino-tech, we've been running through alternate universes here under the dome. We're up to over a thousand alternates already."

"Like what?"

"Like universes where," Karuna said, "if Ben saves his wife from cancer, she ends up being a widow, after he disappears while working on the Kwok case. Or not. Or where the plenum is porous, hallucinations and virtual events leaking over into other realities, other people's dreams. Or not. Or where Ben's messing with the world's systems results in a nuclear war. Or not. Or he blots out our universe. Or not."

"Or Karuna and I die here during a government siege," Don said. "Or Jaron never disappears from a bed in Sha Tin. Or he does, and you marry Ben Cho. Or you don't, and he runs off with Mei-lin Lu. Or she never gets a divorce, they don't run off together, and in despair he drinks himself out of his professorship and into a life on the streets. . . ."

"Et cetera, et cetera, et cetera," Karuna said. "Or not."

Cherise shook her head and laughed.

"I suppose I should be willing to believe anything, after seeing what you've already shown me. Even the way you made the dome leap over me—on the road up from the marina, to let me in when I arrived—that wasn't the easiest thing to accept, either."

Cherise paused to look at the microcosmic kaleidoscope of possible universes flickering into and out of existence around her, each of them as real as she was.

"Hey, in all your alternate worlds, did you ever do one where She, in the holo-cast, eats a binotech wafer, too? I mean, the Newcomer does bring *two* of them with him, right? And if She is somehow *me*, why can't I wake up and decide to do that, through the virtuality?"

Don stared at Cherise, then he and Karuna glanced sheepishly at each other.

"I don't think we've done that one," Don said.

"Let's run it!" Karuna said. "We can't *know* it till we *go* it, right?"

And so it went.

"WHAT CAN I DO to help?" He asked His recently arrived double. As lightning flashed around Them, the Newcomer pulled two wafer-thin disks out of the folds of His robe.

"Eat one of these binotech enhancers, and you'll know everything you need to know!"

A particularly strong earthshock hit them just as He reached toward the Newcomer to take one of the disks. The Newcomer would have dropped them, but She caught His hand and took both disks from Him. She put one on His tongue, and He put one on Her tongue.

DON HELPED KARUNA into her backpack. Standing side by side, they looked west over Guitar Lake. With Ben and Reyna and Jaron and Cherise, they'd camped last night on a bench beyond the body of the guitar, not far from a pair of small ponds. After watching a spectacular sunset of flaming orange and salmon pink from the lake's east end, they had counted falling stars of the Perseid meteor shower as the night came on. Fatigue from a long trail day and the chill of high elevation at last drove them into their tents and sleeping bags.

Turning about and facing east now, they saw Ben and Reyna already heading up the Muir trail. Don shook his head. The two of them set such a solid pace Don found it hard to believe that during the previous year Reyna had fought a bout with cancer. Fought— and apparently won.

Nearer at hand, Jaron and Cherise set a more leisurely pace.

"We should be able to catch up to those two shortly," Don said to Karuna, gesturing toward Cherise and Jaron with one of his trekking poles.

"Maybe," Karuna agreed, "but at the rate the Chos are going, we won't catch up to them until the first break."

They set off up the trail, granite in various states of decomposition crunching under their boots. Don thought it strange that they should all be together here, people who hadn't even known each other a year earlier. Getting them together on this backpacking trip had been Ben and Reyna's idea. Those two had organized, prepared, and outfitted everyone for it. Jaron's work, though, was what had laid the foundations for the trip.

It was Jaron who, with the help of Cherise and Detective Meilin Lu in China, had pieced together the history of Tetragrammaton's "long-term twin study" plans and broken that scandal to governments and media throughout the world. What had happened since, however, had made Don wonder if the scandalous and the miraculous were two sides of the same coin.

A season of miracles. That's what Ben had called it, referring to Reyna's return to health. Don thought that other, smaller miracles had also come to pass. He and Karuna, once estranged, were back together, which he gathered was also the case for Jaron and Cherise. This backpacking trip, too—which had at first caused Don to have serious reservations—had proven to be a grand success.

Last night, before dinner and sunset and the Perseids, in honor of camping in such close proximity to Mount Whitney, the six of them had cracked open one of the two utterly frivolous bottles of champagne Ben and Reyna had been carrying in their packs for the past five days. Thanks to the high elevation, the alcohol shot straight to their heads.

Afterward, Ben and Jaron and Don had labored over the malfunctioning white gas stove. It had been challenging, but also oddly enlightening. The three men so often anticipated each other's moves that at times they seemed to be thinking with a single shared mind.

"Give enough drunk guys enough fuel and enough spark and they can set *anything* on fire," Jaron declared, their simpatico having at last paid off in a blue flame roaring like a small jet engine.

"Including themselves?" Reyna asked, completely deadpan. Cherise and Karuna enjoyed that joke a little too much, Don thought, especially when he remembered the story of one poor, flaming, longhaired cat and a Christmas tree. Once Don started into the tale of Smokey Boy's Yuletide brush with fate, Kari couldn't resist jumping in on the telling, too.

Crossing an alpine meadow pretty as God's front lawn now, Don and Karuna passed Cherise and a laboring Jaron, who waved them on. A bit further along the trail, Don looked up toward the looming west face of Mount Whitney. Yesterday, reflected in the mirror-smooth surface of Timberline Lake, the craggy scarp of Whitney had reminded him of a ruined tower. Now that they were closer, however, it increasingly reminded him of a jumbled maze of stone crags, a megalithic labyrinth.

Not far beyond the meadow, the trail began to rise through long rocky switchbacks and into that maze. It was arduous going. Don found himself panting and stopping between steps as he moved through the hard sunlight and thin air. Despite the rigor of the climb, he still had enough energy to note the beauty of the rock garden they moved through. To Karuna he pointed out vivid clumps of hulsea, golden alpine sunflower, clinging against the whipping wind in what looked like absolutely bare rock.

Karuna went him one better when she spotted, in a broken wall of stone, a patch of sky pilot: spherical clusters of blue flowers spiking up above sticky, fuzzy-caterpillar leaves, anchored in a most unlikely and inhospitable place. Even in the stiff breeze, however, the two of them could distinguish the musky scents of the sky pilot from the equally strong odor of the hulsea.

At last, at the crest, the trail forked. The Muir trail led north toward the peak, and the Whitney trail led east down the other side of the divide. There they came upon Ben and Reyna, stopped for a rest and snack break. The resting couple, seated on rocks and taking in the vast view to the west, pointed out to Don and Kari the direction they had come, the ground the six of them had covered.

Jaron and Cherise, however, didn't reach the rest stop until Don had nearly finished downing carbs and liquid in preparation for the final slog to the summit. Ben and Reyna, too, had already stashed their trail packs and put on belly-bag daypacks for the peak trek.

"Hey, Jaron," Ben called, after the two latest arrivals had been given a chance to rest and eat and drink. "Is this the best of all possible worlds, or what?"

"For *you* maybe," Jaron said, mock sour, "but *my* best of all possible worlds comes equipped with comfortable benches—"

"—every fifty feet," Ben said, laughing. "Yeah, I know."

Having stashed their heavy backpacks off the trail, the six of them wore light packs for the two-and-a-half-mile trek to the summit. They took the north fork, making their way steadily up-hill among the big blocks of talus. At times along the trail, gaps opened in the stone of the mountain, notches like gates or heavenly windows offering views of another world, or of the Owens Valley, ten thousand feet below them to the east. Ahead of them, Don knew, was the small shelter-cabin on the almost level plateau of the summit. They hadn't reached it yet, but he was sure, now, that they would.

Ernest Hemingway once remarked that a story should be like an iceberg: nine-tenths of it should be out of view, below the waterline. That's definitely the case with the research for *The Labyrinth Key*, the vast majority of which never appears in the novel itself. My editor, Steve Saffel, suggested in an evolving e-mail exchange some questions I might want to address in order to give readers a better sense of the historical and scientific background of the novel— particularly in regard to the historical persons who appear, and the contemporary science of "alternate" or "parallel" universes, which is much more real than the reader might suspect. I hope this Q & A will provide readers with clues about that "invisible" research.

Q. *Why a "labyrinth"—and why a "key"?*

A. Labyrinths—along with geometrically related forms such as mazes, spirals, helices, meanders, and Greek keys—crop up in all my novels. Novels are themselves like labyrinths, in that the reader follows the twisting path of the book and at the end of the journey has (one hopes) been changed by the experience.

There's a wonderful short story by Jorge Luis Borges, first published more than sixty years ago, called "The Garden of Forking Paths," in which an immense unfinished novel by fictional Chinese writer Ts'ui Pên, figures prominently. In the Donald Yates translation of the Borges story, there's a passage that reads as follows:

> "*After more than a hundred years, the details are irretrievable; but it is not hard to conjecture what happened. Ts'ui Pên must have said once: I am withdrawing to write a*

book. And another time: I am withdrawing to construct a labyrinth. Everyone imagined two works; to no one did it occur that the book and the maze were one and the same thing."

My only complaint about this fine passage is that Borges uses "labyrinth" and "maze" as if they, too, were one and the same thing. They're not, and the distinction between them is an important one.

There is only one path through a labyrinth, but there are many paths that lead through a maze. With very few exceptions, a novel is a labyrinth, because the writer has already laid out the path and the reader's only choice is whether or not to keep reading. For the characters *within* the book, however, the novel is a maze, because the characters are constantly confronted with a variety of choices, some of which may be "wrong" or lead nowhere.

In our everyday existence, we are like the characters in a novel, constantly confronted by a variety of choices in the mazes of our daily lives. In some ways, these mazes are about immediate smaller choices, while labyrinths are more about memories and anticipations—and the single global choice of whether or not to go on.

The confusion between labyrinths and mazes is as old as the first story of the Labyrinth itself. Even in that ancient Greek tale, however, we find labyrinths associated with the cryptic—with what is both hidden and potentially deadly.

Daedalus, the master scientist and engineer, built the Labyrinth for Minos, King of Crete, in the palace at Knossos. The purpose of the Labyrinth was to hide a shameful secret. Because Minos would not agree to sacrifice a particularly beautiful bull to the god Poseidon, as he had promised, Poseidon afflicted Minos's wife, Pasiphae, with a violently passionate love for that animal. Pasiphae commanded Daedalus to build an artificial cow, inside of which she hid herself so that she might have sexual relations with that beautiful beast. Her passion satisfied, Pasiphae later gave birth to the monstrous bull-headed man known as the Minotaur, or "bull of Minos." Unwilling to kill the monster, Minos had Daedalus build the Labyrinth, in which the Minotaur was hidden away.

It was the Greek hero Theseus who, with help from Minos's daughter Ariadne and from Daedalus himself, slew the Minotaur. Daedalus and Ariadne gave Theseus a thread, which he attached to the entrance of the Labyrinth, and which he could follow back to the entrance after he journeyed to its center and slew the monster. In honor of this legend, the winding path one makes when walking through a labyrinth—the "key" to the labyrinth—is conventionally called "Ariadne's thread."

The ancient but still common design motif known as a "Greek key," when bent into a circle, forms the essential recursive element found in the classical labyrinth. This is the basis of one character's important assertion in this novel: "The key is in the labyrinth, as the labyrinth is in the key." Keys, of course, can be many things. Buttons or levers used to operate machines or musical instruments are called keys. The tonalities and tonal systems of music are called keys. In the study of cryptology, the tables, glosses, or ciphers used for decoding or interpreting information are also referred to as keys. All of these figure prominently in this novel.

The relationship between labyrinths and keys is deeply mathematical and geometrical. When a burglar "cracks" or unlocks a safe by figuring out the path he must twist on the dial to open the vault, he is tracing a thread of Ariadne. When a cryptanalyst "cracks" or unlocks a code, he too is tracing a thread of Ariadne through the labyrinth of possibilities.

Q. *What are memory palaces—and how are they related to labyrinths?*

A. The history and meaning of the memory palace idea is best explained through a story to which all the best books on the art of memory refer.

A Thessalian nobleman named Scopas, we are told, gave a banquet. There, the poet Simonides of Ceos chanted a panegyric in honor of Scopas, but that lyric poem also included a lengthy passage praising the twin gods, Castor and Pollux. Scopas, who was apparently a bit of an egomaniac, was miffed at Simonides for including the Castor and Pollux passage and would only pay Simonides half the sum they had agreed on for the poem, telling the poet that he should go to the twins for the balance of the money.

During the banquet, a message was brought in to Simonides that two young men were waiting outside to speak with him. While Simonides was outside, the roof and the banqueting hall were hit by a sudden wind of overwhelming power and came tumbling down. The collapse of the building crushed and killed Scopas and all the rest of his guests. The relatives who came to bury their dead found that the bodies were so pulverized and mangled that they could not be identified, but Simonides, recalling where each guest had been sitting at the table, was able to identify each body for the relatives.

Although this may at first seem to be a story admonishing us not to short-change poets or mess with the gods, it suggested to Simonides the principles for the art of memory, which he then reportedly went on to invent. According to Cicero in *De Oratore*,

> *[Simonides] inferred that persons desiring to train the faculty of memory must select places and form mental images of the things they wish to remember and store those images in those places, so that the order of the places will preserve the order of the things, and the images of the things will denote the things themselves. . . .*

That was the theory, at least. Images of things were to be stored in imagined places.

Many Medieval and Renaissance treatises called for those studying memory to imagine a complex edifice—usually a palace or theater—in which to store their images. A number of archaeologists studying the ruins in Knossos believe the royal palace was just such a "complex edifice," and that that palace and the labyrinth which housed the Minotaur were in fact the same structure. Like Theseus, a student of memory had to find his or her way into and out of a labyrinthine edifice in order to retrieve what they sought, but in the case of the students, their edifices were of the mind.

Later memory masters, like Giordano Bruno, went beyond the idea of imagining a particular building and instead created systems in which the universe itself was the complex edifice in which memories were to be stored and from which they were to be retrieved.

Q. *Giordano Bruno seems to be one of several figures—along with Matteo Ricci, Felix Forrest, Shimon Ginsburg, and Ai Hao—who figure into the "prehistory" of the events in* The Labyrinth Key. *How historically real are these people?*

A. Despite the strangeness of their lives, some of those people are very real. I found that, almost as soon as I started reading histories of the art of memory, those texts reacquainted me with an old friend: the shadowy—but quite real—Giordano Bruno (1548–1600). A defrocked Dominican priest, Bruno was an early supporter of the Copernican sun-centered cosmology. In attempting to unify Kabbalah and Hermeticism in his cosmology, though, Bruno went far beyond Copernicus. The ex-Dominican was the first to conceptualize "infinite earths in infinite space," all inhabited by intelligent beings. For that heresy, and several others, he was burned at the stake in 1600.

Bruno was a quintessential early modern man, particularly in the way his life intersected with the rise of secret societies and governmental secret services, as well as with the cryptographic arts and the scientific method—all of which blossomed at the beginning of the early modern period. Not only did memory palaces meet cryptology, and magic meet science in his wonderfully weird life but, to my mind, in Bruno's work and experiences, Kabbalah also met parallel-universe cosmology. The fact that he was an intellectual rebel who suffered a dramatic martyrdom at the hands of the Inquisition (and got a goodly amount of coverage in James Joyce's *Finnegans Wake*) didn't hurt his appeal for me, either.

Like Bruno, Matteo Ricci (1552–1610) was also an actual historical figure, a member of the not-so-secret Society of Jesus—the Jesuits—for whom he served as a missionary to China from 1583 until his death. Ricci was a strong believer in memory palace techniques and apparently viewed them as a means for winning converts to Roman Catholicism, particularly among the members of the Chinese intelligentsia and imperial bureaucracy.

The Asia specialist and CIA operative who wrote science fiction, whom I have called Felix Forrest, is also very strongly based on an actual person, about whom one may find clues in *Psychological Warfare* by Paul M. A. Linebarger. Shimon Ginsburg and Ai Hao are fictional, but rabbis with knowledge of Kabbalah who fled Germany for China—only to be captured by the Japanese and returned to the German concentration camps—did exist, as did the Chinese Jewish community in Hangzhou, with whose members Matteo Ricci was acquainted. Ricci was even better acquainted with the Kaifeng synagogue, particularly one of its members, Ai Tian, who served as a model for Ai Hao.

Q. There seems to be a large political component in the stories of all those characters. Are governments today rearranging the furniture in our own memory palaces?

A. They always have. Not only governments, but also corporations. I have a robust distrust of any large social organization which perennially uses secrecy to keep itself in a position of power. The governments and corporations just have more powerful tools these days, is all.

For me, the processes of memory and those of secrecy seem to resemble each other in many ways, and that was the golden braid that tied together all of those characters you mentioned. If there is an art of memory, then secrecy is, arguably, often concerned with an art of forgetting. What better way to hide something than to forget its location, or even its existence? Think of Orwell's idea of things and events forced into oblivion, "down the memory hole."

Or the idea that those who control the past also control the present, and those who control the present also control the future.

In the aftermath of the events of September 11, 2001, for instance, I became aware of how the collective memory palace of everyday life in America was being shifted and manipulated. We were, for instance, told by our government that America's economic woes were all somehow the result of the terror attacks on the World Trade Center and the Pentagon, when in fact the stock market's bubble had burst a year and a half earlier—and, according to historian Robert Brenner of UCLA, the overall economy of the U.S.A. had already been in what he called "the long downturn" since 1973.

Those who call upon the citizenry to "Remember the Alamo!" or "Remember the Maine!" or "Remember Pearl Harbor!" or "Remember 9/11!" are also quite often engaged in enforcing a collective amnesia about the history leading up to those cataclysmic moments. This isn't very difficult to do because we humans, in retrospect, tend to bestow upon "events that have undergone the formality of actually occurring" an inevitability that, quantum physics tells us, those events did not in fact possess.

Q. *You've commented on how memory palaces relate to labyrinths, which came before such systems, but how are they related to computers, which came afterward?*

A. In some ways, memory palaces and memory theaters formed a sort of ancient virtual-reality system. There are strong parallels between the human mind running a memory palace and a computer running a virtual-reality program.

The memory palace, like the modern computer, was primarily a system for the storage, retrieval, and manipulation of information. I sometimes think that the path of the labyrinth walker and the halls of a memory palace both resemble, well, *circuits* like those found in the guts of the computer on which I'm writing this.

That's not to say they are the same, by any means. In a way, they are mirror opposites. In computer systems, there is no memory without (electrical) resistance. In human social systems, there is no (political) resistance without memory. I found that, the more I studied memory and secrecy, the more I had to learn about history and politics, and about computers, mathematics, and quantum physics.

In fact, the specific situation that sparked this novel occurred at the 2001 Eaton Hong Kong Conference, which was subtitled "East Meets West in the Emerging Global Village." There, as both a science fiction writer and critic, I was lucky enough to be a keynote speaker before an international audience. During the conference, literary critic Takayuki Tatsumi presented a wonderfully speculative paper suggesting parallels between the representation of cyberspace in books and films on the one hand, and, on the other, the introduction of the Western memory-palace concept to China by the late-Renaissance Jesuit missionary, Matteo Ricci. That suggestion was what really got me going on this book.

Q. *You mentioned quantum physics earlier. Can you give us a quick overview of what exactly that is?*

A. Basically, Newtonian or "classical" physics still dominates most of our understanding of the everyday world, but it began to be displaced nearly a century ago, first by Einstein's theory of relativity, and soon thereafter by quantum theory. Relativity is most powerfully a physics of great distances and high velocities. Quantum physics, by contrast, is a physics of the microcosmic scale, of the tiny world within the atom—of photons, electrons, quarks, and the like.

Even more important than this difference in scale, however, is the difference in the nature of the reality each theory describes. A key concept of relativity theory is the idea of a continuum, which like the classical physics from which it grew, emphasizes the continuous, like the story a film shows or the path through a classical labyrinth.

A central concept of quantum physics, by contrast, is the idea of the quantum, the unit or bit or quantity or amount of something. Quantum physics is a physics of "lumps" and "jumps"—discontinuous, discrete, like the individual frames of a film, or the stops, choices, and starts of a maze.

In the quantum world, cause and effect don't hold sway the way they do in the classical world. Events just happen, and they happen in every direction at once. All of those lost possibilities, all those roads and directions not taken, are the source of what are referred to as "superpositions" or "superposed states."

For example, we'll consider a single particle—an electron. Even the idea of the electron as a particle is something of a misnomer, since an electron, like many other subatomic entities, is neither fully a particle nor fully a wave—and many physicists now claim it's also fundamentally a vibrating string! We can call it a wave packet, or a probability wave; we can measure its wave nature or its particle nature, but we cannot measure *both* at one and the same time. One or the other, but not both. This is Heisenberg's uncertainty principle, and where it leads us is to quantum indeterminism. That displaces the fixed, determined, and measurable physical reality proclaimed by Newton.

In response to the dual nature of wave and particle, quantum theorists developed the Principle of Complementarity which says that you cannot describe what an electron is *unless* you describe both its particle nature and its wave nature. These two descriptions complement each other and only when taken together do they provide a whole picture of the electron.

In many-worlds theory—an outgrowth of quantum theory—the issue of wave and particle transforms into an issue of having one's cake and eating it, too. Probability-waved, superposed, or "virtual" states don't collapse into singular "real" particles, but rather new universes fork off at the choice point of observation. The road not taken in this universe is instead taken in a parallel or alternate one. From within any given universe in an essentially infinite ensemble of universes, only the universe you're in looks "real"; all others appear "virtual."

But that's true in any universe. Our universe looks like a one-path labyrinth because its "mazedness" is hidden from us—in other universes. So you *can* have your cake and eat it too, only the you who has it will live in a different universe from the you who eats it.

Q. *What are quantum computers, and how plausible are they?*

A. Not only are they plausible, but they already exist, at least in primitive form. The Clarendon Laboratory at Oxford University has developed one, as have other institutions.

Classical computing bits exist as either zero or one, but not both. Quantum bits can exist as both zero and one, simultaneously. This may seem like a small thing, but it's not. Although our daily lives appear to function at classical scales, it is in fact quantum theory that explains the workings of DNA, or cell phones, or the sun. The uncertainty principle, for instance, contributes to the buildup of genetic mistakes in cell code that results in aging, cancer, and evolution itself.

As early as 1984, David Deutsch realized that computers, too, ought to obey the laws of quantum physics, as those laws are more fundamental than the laws of classical physics. A classical computer can address only one question at a time—a sequential approach that is much slower than if the computer can address many questions at the same time, as a quantum computer can. For cryptology, think of keys and locks: A classical computer faced with many billions of possible keys for a lock must try each key in the lock, one after the other. A quantum computer, however, can try all the keys in the lock simultaneously.

Q. *How is this done?*

A. One group of physicists (the superpositionists) view the quantum computer as performing all those billions of keyings simultaneously in a single machine. Another group of physicists (the manyworlders or multiversalists) view the quantum computer as billions of quantum computers, each machine in a separate universe, each trying just one key. For the former group, the answer arises from summing over the billions of superposed states of a single machine in a single universe. For the latter group, the answer arises from summing over billions of universes, each with its own machine. Curiously enough, the latter explanation is now becoming increasingly accepted.

Q. *How are governments and corporations using computers for cryptology, cryptography, and cryptanalysis?*

A. First we need to define those terms. Cryptology, the study of the hidden, is usually broken down into cryptography (the creation of hidden writing, or codemaking) and cryptanalysis (the analytical revealing of the hidden, or codebreaking). Computers are the paramount tool in all these areas today, because most codes are broken mathematically. That's why the U.S. National Security Agency is the world's single largest employer of mathematicians.

Quantum computing is a logical extension in all these areas. However, it also generates interesting results for the whole secrecy business. Looked at one way, quantum computing is the death of cryptography, for with such systems it should be possible to break any code. Looked at another way, quantum computing is the death of cryptanalysis, since with such systems it should be possible to create codes that cannot be broken. The entire situation is like the old theological conundrum about whether or not God could create a rock so heavy that God could not lift it.

Many theorists believe that, in the long informational arms race between the cryptographers and the cryptanalysts, quantum computing means that the cryptographers have at last won out. That's why a quantum crypto hardline runs from the Pentagon to the White House—for supposedly invulnerable encrypted communication.

I don't think such invulnerability can really be achieved, however. Even when messages are successfully transferred over channels that cannot be eavesdropped upon or otherwise compromised, those messages must eventually become plaintext in machines that are not quantum-secure, or in the minds of human beings, who are also notoriously prone to side-band attacks (which can include just about anything, from bribes to sexual favors).

As for the cryptanalysts, especially those working in more complex contexts, it is appropriately humbling to recall Hamlet's words to his college friend: "There are more things in heaven and earth, Horatio, than are dreamt of in your philosophy."

Q. *Might these "more things in heaven and earth" include multiple universes?*

A. They might.

Q. *What are the schools of thought relating to single vs. multiple universes? What studies are being done in relation to multiple universes, and by whom?*

A. As mentioned earlier, the primary split is between the superpositionists, who propose a single real universe, and the multiversalists, who hold with multiple, real, but "apparently virtual" universes. The labyrinthists and the mazists, as I like to think of them.

I would like to think that a Principle of Complementarity applies here too, where mazes precipitate into labyrinths and labyrinths sublime into mazes. One of the most important developments out of this contest between superpositionists and multiversalists concerns the finitude or infinitude of the cosmos, and the plurality or singularity of its components.

Among those who tend to talk about universes in the singular are the supporters of the holographic principle, who believe that, just as all the information describing a 3-D scene can be encoded into patterns of light and dark on a 2-D piece of film, so too can our seemingly 3-D universe be understood as completely equivalent to quantum fields and physical laws "painted" on a distant, vast, but usually spherical and finite, surface.

Among those who tend to talk about universes in the plural, the multiversalists most prominently speak about an infinitude of universes in essentially infinite space.

These positions may appear irreconcilable, but I don't think they are. The holographic position stems from Albert Einstein's work on gravity and Claude E. Shannon's work in information theory, pushed by John A. Wheeler in his suggestion that the physical world should be regarded as made of information, with matter and energy as secondary in importance. This position is particularly popular around Princeton—both the university and the Institute for Advanced Study—and includes among its proponents people like Edward Witten, Steven Gubser, Igor Klebanov, and Alexander Polyakov.

Appropriately, those who are fans of the multiversalist position tend to be more thinly spread over more institutions, and they have proposed at least four different types of multiverses: limit-of-observation, bubble nucleation, quantum, and physical law-differentiated. Oddly enough, the work of John A. Wheeler is very important to this group too.

What I try to get at with my vast memory palace in this novel is a reconciliation of the two, through the reconciling of infinite number with finite extent. The finite space from 0 to 1 on the number line, for instance, can be infinitely divided so as to represent all possible numbers in that space. Likewise, perhaps the system of all possible universes exists in a space—spherical, finite, unbounded, and consistent—in whose surface is holographically encoded an infinite number of possible universes, all mutually inconsistent with each other, all literally bounded by infinity. An infinity of discrete universes bounded by the finite continuum of the plenum.

Q. *What are the ramifications of these studies in relation to our lives?*

A. The more the idea of parallel universes, multiverses, and what I have called the "plenum" become scientifically accepted, the more likely it is that the idea of "historic inevitability" will be discredited.

And, if and when full scientific acceptance of the alternativity of universes does come, that acceptance will in many ways be due to quantum computing and quantum cryptology.

Even here on the classical (as opposed to quantum) scale, when we are told to "Remember!" the singular event—rather than think about its possible causes—we are led to obliterate the possibility of considering what might otherwise have been. We are not allowed to think about how American economic and foreign policy might have influenced the events of December 7, 1941 at Pearl Harbor, or September 11, 2001 in New York City and Washington, D.C. We are told that, given the enormity of such events, there's no reason to make use of reason—and that the only response to an unalterable inevitability is unthinking reaction.

However, a quantum understanding of reality significantly undermines this idea of blind, historical inevitability. We are free to think again, no matter what the enormity of the event, because we are able to realize that even the most tragic event was not an act of God or nature, but something done by human beings, for human reasons, and therefore may properly be analyzed by human reason.

In discussing "apocalyptic" events, it is all too appropriate to speak of religion here—and science, too. The Greek root word of apocalypse (*apokaluptein*) means to "reveal," to "lift the veil" of this world and see through to truth—a fundamentally cryptanalytic operation. Science, too, has long been obsessed with revealing secrets, or as the sixteenth-century French diplomat and cryptologist Vigenère, who is quoted in *The Labyrinth Key*, actually said:

> *All the things in the world constitute a cipher. All nature is merely a cipher and a secret writing. The great name and essence of God and his wonders, the very deeds, projects, words, actions, and demeanor of mankind—what are they for the most part but a cipher?*

So perhaps it's not so very strange that my research eventually led me from the mathematical and cryptological into the numerological and mystical.

The final limiting cases—and ultimate side-band attacks—on all of this are to be found in the "wet-war" dimension, the realm of hearts and minds where ethics and morals are the deciding factors. What we do with our classical "hard-war" or quantum "soft-war" machinery is up to the subtler "wet-war" machineries found in our cultures and in our heads. Machineries that may, one day, overcome the desire for war itself.

In the end, it's up to us to decide whether the "apocalypse" we choose is the cryptanalytic "lifting" of the veil in our search for truth—or the cryptographic "rending" of that veil in destruction, extinction, and oblivion. As we move more deeply into the Age of Code—that epoch begun with the decoding of organic life and DNA begun by Watson, Crick, and Wilkins, and the encoding of an artificial life of bits and bytes begun by Turing, von Neuman, and Gödel—our choice becomes more important than we can remember, more important than we can know, more important than we can even imagine.

I suggest we choose carefully—and, let us hope, wisely.

SELECTED BIBLIOGRAPHY

On the history of memory systems and mnemonics, I recommend in particular *The Art of Memory* by Frances Yates, *The Book of Memory* by Mary Carruthers, and *Logic and the Art of Memory* by Paolo Rossi.

Many of Giordano Bruno's ideas and connections are documented in Paul-Henri Michel's *The Cosmology of Giordano Bruno*, Antoinette Paterson's *The Infinite Worlds of Giordano Bruno*, Frances Yates's *Giordano Bruno and the Hermetic Tradition*, Frances Boldereff's *Hermes to His Son Thoth*, Hilary Gatti's *Giordano Bruno and Renaissance Science*, and Karen Silvia DeLeon-Jones's *Giordano Bruno and the Kabbalah*.

For my understanding of Ricci generally and his interest in memory palaces particularly, I am indebted to *The Memory Palace of Matteo Ricci* by Jonathan D. Spence, and *Matteo Ricci's Scientific Contributions* by Henri Bernard, S.J. I also found Spence's *The Search for Modern China* and *God's Chinese Son* very helpful as well.

Books like David Deutsch's *The Fabric of Reality*, Dirk Bouwmeester's *The Physics of Quantum Information Systems*, and Colin P. Williams's *Ultimate Zero and One*—as well as a burgeoning number of Web sites—all discuss the link between quantum computing and multiple universes. Those interested in DNA computing and its possible links to quantum computing would do well to peruse Georghe Paun's *DNA Computing*.

For those interested in further investigating the policy dimensions of memory and secrecy, I recommend James Bamford's *The Puzzle Palace* and *Body of Secrets* and a host of Web sites (including those put up by the National Security Agency itself), all of which provided invaluable detail on the workings of the NSA.

Manuel De Landa's *War in the Age of Intelligent Machines*, Clifford Stoll's *The Cuckoo's Egg*, Robert L. Bateman's *Digital War*, Bert-Jaap Koop's *The Crypto Controversy*, Craig R. Eisendrath's *National Insecurity*, D. Curtis Schleher's *Electronic Warfare in the Information Age*, Bruce D. Berkowitz's *Best Truth*, Winn Schwartau's *CyberShock* and *Information Warfare*, Jeffrey Richelson's *The Wizards of Langley*, Simon Singh's *The Code Book*, and David Kahn's *The Codebreakers* all provided insight into the history and politics, as well as the mathematics, science, and linguistics, of what Michael Wilson calls "soft-war."

For those interested in the connections between and among mathematics, numerology, cryptology, and mysticism, I recommend Amir D. Aczel's *The Mystery of the Aleph*, Isaac Myer's *Qabbalah*, and Daniel C. Matt's *The Essential Kabbalah*.

ABOUT THE AUTHOR

HOWARD V. HENDRIX holds a B.S. in biology as well as an M.A. and Ph.D. in English literature. Having held jobs ranging from hospital phlebotomist to university professor, he's produced award-winning short fiction. His novels include *Lightpaths*, *Standing Wave*, *Better Angels*, and *Empty Cities of the Full Moon*. He is married and lives in central California. Visit his Web site at http://www.howardvhendrix.com.